OVER EASY

OVER EASY

MICKEY BAYARD

iUniverse®

OVER EASY

This is a work of fiction. All of the characters, names, incidents, organizations, and dialogue in this novel are either the products of the author's imagination or are used fictitiously.

iUniverse books may be ordered through booksellers or by contacting:

iUniverse
1663 Liberty Drive
Bloomington, IN 47403
www.iuniverse.com
1-800-Authors (1-800-288-4677)

Author Photo Credit: Billy Fariello

ISBN: 978-1-5320-7953-5 (sc)
ISBN: 978-1-5320-7954-2 (hc)
ISBN: 978-1-5320-7956-6 (e)

Print information available on the last page.

iUniverse rev. date: 10/10/2019

DEDICATION

This book is dedicated to Jimmy Braddock…a true Cinderella Man.

ACKNOWLEDGEMENTS

Caroline, Tina, Carol, Sunny, Norman, Pete, Tim and Dave. No last names needed. And all the Condors -175th St., living and dead.

PROLOGUE

Tiptiptaptap… Raindrops on my helmet… A song in there somewhere. Like Brother Gregory's pencil on my head. "Pay attention, Mr. Burns!"

"Yes, Brother Gregory."

The runoff'll be strong down mountain. Fucking lightning. I hate lightning. Hunker down now. Cover up. Be still.

Tali gotta be gone by now. They can leave whenever they want. Probably laughing their Afghan asses off at us sitting up here drenched.

I wonder what they have for dinner after a hard day of chopping off heads in Allah's name. Missionary soup? Maybe. *Tiptiptaptap.*

Whoa, that wasn't thunder.

Incoming!

CHAPTER 1

Max Burns cleared his drifting mind of those cold, rain-swept nights in the Korengal mountains of Afghanistan. He arched his head back to catch American rain in his mouth.

Tastes like vinegar.

The intensity of the rain forced the young man to close his eyes. Had he been in church instead of standing outside a restaurant in Georgetown, one might have thought he was taking Communion.

Long way from the sweet-tasting rain of the Korengal.

He wrung his saturated Pittsburgh Pirates hat and then shook his head like a dog. He returned to staring through the restaurant window.

His well-worn army field jacket, like himself stitched up many times, was of no help that night. But the rain did not impede his quest. Ingrained army ranger tenets ran through his head.

Dismiss discomfort. No distractions.

"He is baaaack again. I'm calling the police!" Margaret said to he husband Len, inside their Georgetown restaurant.

"That field jacket is army issue. I think he's a vet," said Len.

"I don't care if he's General Patton! He's up to no good."

Len and Margaret were in their seventies. Margaret had retired from the D.C. school system five years ago. Len had given up his insurance career to enter the restaurant business. They were still very spry… and very cautious.

Len puttered around the restaurant trying not to be as defiant as Margaret.

UH OH: the assistant principal stance. Glad it's not me on the hot seat, Len thought.

After a few minutes it was obvious to Len, Margaret was going unnoticed by the young man staring through the window.

That's really going to piss her off, Len thought as he swept away at the same spot on the restaurant floor.

"**That's it!** I am calling the cops. He's scaring the customers," Margaret exclaimed.

"There are no customers, Margaret," Len said.

"**Exactly my point**!" Margaret snorted.

"I think he's kind of cute," Eva, their only granddaughter and only waitress, said flippantly as she sauntered by carrying a tray of saltshakers. "What are you going to tell the police, Grandma? There's a man looking into our restaurant window?"

Eva was twenty-four. She was five feet six with the body of a renaissance sculpture. Eva had a beautiful Spanish influence to her skin, a gift from her mother. She had black hair and dark-brown eyes, a combination that made her ancestry a guessing game.

Eva understood, and at times appreciated, her grandmother hovering over her as though she were still five years old. That was the year her parents had been killed in a car accident. She'd been raised by Len and Margaret, her father's parents, after that. Eva loved teasing Margaret. Len enjoyed their banter.

Len was not unnerved by the young man. It was Margaret who made Len nervous.

Len thought the man looked lonely - lost in his own country. The cascading rain and flashing of the neon sign made his surname and initials illegible on his fatigue jacket pocket.

"Cute, in a puppy-dog sort of way," Eva said as she scooted by Margaret.

Eva had heard many pickup lines and felt equipped to handle herself around men. But there were times when she questioned the intensity of her acerbic reactions.

The past two nights Eva purposefully did not look at the young man, at least not that her grandparents had noticed. She had stared back at him on his first visit. The window had been clear that night. He looked weathered. Eva liked weathered. It had thrown her off when he looked back at her. She was annoyed she disengaged before he did. That never happened to Eva. She was never first to disengage. He'd smiled, then continued his inspection of the premises. She made herself look busy.

Big, a three-day growth. The broken nose actually adds something.

Eva didn't have a boyfriend. School, work, and her standards made her love life nonexistent. That was okay for now. She wanted someone special… or no one. She was intrigued by the young man on the other side of the glass. She awaited his first move by the third evening.

He belongs in a men's magazine—the survival kind, not the porno kind. Maybe both.

But he's not looking at me. Maybe he's gay.

Eva watched as the young man reached into his back pocket. He took out his wallet and fumbled with it. He carefully took out a large silver coin and flipped it into the air. He caught it and turned it over onto his wrist. He smiled, apparently pleased with the outcome.

He laughed at the squishing sound of his boots as he marched in place to squeeze out excess water, a reminder they were made for sand, not rain.

"I am going to ask him to come in and have a bite to eat. If he's a homeless vet, we owe him a meal," Eva said emphatically as she headed for the door.

"Hey! You hungry or what?" Eva shouted out the door before her grandparents had a chance to respond.

He stopped his marching and looked at Eva. He wondered for

an instant if the iridescence in Eva's black hair was the result of the neon light. It was not.

"As a matter of fact, I am hungry," he said with a smile that revealed a full set of teeth, pleasing Eva. He took great care in drying off the coin and returning it to a compartment in his wallet. Eva noticed it was a silver dollar.

Sad, he's down to his last bit of change.

Corporal Max Burns's silver dollar was a special one. To celebrate Max graduating first in his class out of 130 master chef candidates in the armed forces Military Occupational Specialty School advanced program, Master Sergeant Ralph Nunez, Max's mentor and friend, brought Max home with him to Miami. The reward for Max's hard work was a home-cooked Cuban meal prepared by Nunez's own mentor in the kitchen, his *abuela,* Elsa Aleman Nunez.

After a great meal, much rum, and a few hand-rolled cigars, Nunez began to play his guitar. While Nunez played soft dulcet refrains, Max noticed an old, faded photo on a credenza: Nunez's *abuelo,* Raul Nunez. He was dressed in the combat uniform of the Cuban underground forces that were slaughtered by Fidel Castro's army during the U.S.'s aborted invasion of Cuba. His arm patch, a worm shooting a submachine gun, was squeezed into the frame below the photo.

"He was killed at the Bay of Pigs. He fought with the Exile Brigade - Operation Mongoose," Nunez said to Max as he stopped playing his guitar and watched Max Burns look with admiration at the badge and photo. Nunez picked up a music box that sat alongside the photo. He opened the box. "This coin belonged to my grandfather… I want you to have it."

"No way! I graduated second in Ranger School, not first."

"This is for the top score in chef's school… Screw Ranger School!" Nunez said, not looking for a rebuttal.

"There are specific instructions that must be followed by the owner of this coin," *Abuela* Elsa told Max. "Only use this coin when you already know the correct answer to your question - when you know in your heart what the right choice is. Then and only then may it take to the air. *Mi corazón* used it before he asked me to marry him!" The tiny lady with the big heart teared up as she scurried back to her kitchen.

"Come in! Come in before we both get washed away," Eva said.

The young man took off his cap and lowered his collar as he stepped inside the restaurant. A puddle formed around him. The original sand color of his drenched boots was now dark brown as water oozed from the seams. Margaret, seeing the mess, proceeded to take off his field jacket as though he were a fifth grader. She handed the soaked jacket and cap to Len and told him to hang them in the kitchen by the oven.

The young man had an engaging smile and a mop of hair that made him seem childlike to Eva. His body was anything but childlike. Eva tried her best to be inattentive. He turned and looked at Eva, anxious to see her up close.

"May I use the men's room?" The intensity of his look disarmed her. Eva nodded and pointed in an awkward teenage manner toward the bathroom. He sensed her imbalance as he walked between her and a chair.

He returned from the men's room with hair pushed back and dried as much as the hand dryer could render.

He was broad shouldered, further emphasized by a slim waist.... about six feet two, Eva surmised. His biceps stretched the sleeves of his wet T-shirt to their limits.

"My name is Maxwell Tecumseh Burns... Please call me Max." He held out his hand to Margaret first, the apparent matriarch.

Eva stepped in and took charge. "I'm Eva Carra. This is my grandmother, Margaret Carra, and my grandfather, Len Carra. As you can see, Maxwell Tecumseh Burns, you have your choice of tables."

Max chose a corner table in the back. Eva was not sure whether it was his presence or choice of table that made her feel anxious again.

"Does he think he's Wild Bill Hickok sitting in the corner with his back against the wall like that?" Margaret said out of the side of her mouth. Len was immediately reminded of their son, Eva's father, then dismissed the thought as quickly as it had entered. Margaret had similar thoughts and dismissed them as well, perhaps for discussion at a future time… not now. The young man was polite. This made Margaret more at ease. He sat at the table and looked around the restaurant.

It was now obvious that Max was inspecting the restaurant. He'd chosen a table that gave him a vantage point to both the kitchen doors and the dining area.

Two young couples entered the restaurant, much to the relief of the Carras. Eva seated them at the middle table.

Iowa, Max thought upon hearing the accent. *Like Corporal Hyland used to sound.*

Eva shifted into professional mode but managed to glance at Max as she came through the kitchen doors.

What is he looking for? Is he a health inspector? No way. Landlord sent him? Maybe. We are three months behind with the rent.

All the Carras were having similar thoughts.

Max ordered the special, "*zupa di pesce fra diavolo*," along with a caesar salad and a glass of house Chianti. He was tempted to add the missing *p* in *zuppa* onto the menu, but he would've had to borrow Eva's pen. He knew that was not a good move at this juncture.

"**He's paying for the meal**! I don't give a damn if he has to wash dishes," Eva muttered to herself. "The special - the most expensive item on the menu. It's my fault. I dragged his sorry ass in here. Talk about looking a gift horse in the mouth. And a caesar salad with a Chianti!" Eva arrived back to his table within minutes with the caesar salad.

Just as I thought… pre-made.

Max tasted to confirm, then pushed the dish aside. He sipped his wine and waited.

Eva steamed as she watched him.

She is gorgeous. I wonder what has her so upset.

A bell rang in the kitchen, and Eva retrieved the main course. She placed it rather gruffly in front of Max. He noticed the brusque service but saved his thoughts. The final test was upon him.

A bad specialty of the house means everything else is probably worse. If any of the contents of this dish are frozen, I am in the right place.

Max hoped for the worst.

Yup, frozen. My journey may be over.

Max sipped his wine and pondered his recent return stateside. Two weeks had passed since he had mustered out of the army in Washington, D.C... As a wounded combat veteran, Max had a room at a Veterans Administration halfway house. It was a converted brownstone in the heart of Georgetown. There was a shuttle to the Walter Reed Army Medical Center, but he walked the 4 miles most days. His papers were in, but one of his injuries had been written up as a T.B.I. (Traumatic Brain Injury). Therefore, Max, like most others treated for an I.E.D. wound, would receive the mandatory brain trauma / PTSD treatment upon reentry. The mandatory treatment entailed: Observation; Psychoanalysis, Therapy (mental & physical), Magnetic Resonance Imaging (MRI), etc... until release. It meant nothing more than free room and board to Max. He dumped the prescribed daily drugs down the toilet.

Max had spent his free time checking out Georgetown. He liked what he saw. It was an upscale area with a healthy ethnic mix, diverse demographics, colleges, government employees, well-heeled professionals, tourists. Georgetown had it all.

Logistics: first a job with an okay salary. Freedom to experiment is crucial. Find a restaurant with a decent location that is not doing well, hopefully with an owner willing to take a chance on me. I don't think that's asking too much.

Max ate one bite of the fish, mollusk and crustacean laden dish.

Pasta - overcooked but long shelf life. Sauce - from a can ... lazy. Fish - frozen. Voilà! This place has all the inadequacies I'm looking for.

Max motioned to Eva. "I'll have another glass of Chianti please. You can take these dishes away. Thank you, Eva."

Eva was more surprised than upset. "I'll wrap it up for you to take home."

"Not necessary, thank you, just another Chianti please. It's very nice, full bodied."

"I'm soooo glad it meets with your approval."

Eva took the plates into the kitchen. Max deduced, he was the reason for Eva's surly attitude. He knew he was a pain in the ass when it came to eating other people's food. He'd explain that to Eva at some point.

She can stay.

Eva was visibly pissed off when she brought the glass of Chianti. Max shrugged it off as he pondered changes needed in the restaurant.

Carpet comes up. Green paint goes. Lighting is awful. Need a full-size bar. No washer and dryer for linens, or they would've put my clothes in to dry. Be nice if the floor underneath was parquet.

Max's thoughts were interrupted by the kitchen doors bursting open. Standing in the doorway was the chef, André - according to the name emblazoned on his apron. Max pegged him at around 270 pounds and about six feet six. His hands were huge. His eyes, unusually close together, stared directly at Max.

Albanian, Max surmised by his accent as he barked orders at Eva in the kitchen.

Max knew what André was thinking. André got the gist of the universal insult for a chef: lousy food returned... and no desire to bring it home.

The Carras' worst nightmare was unfolding: André had come out of the kitchen.

"Where is this American bastard that does not like my food? Not even worthy of a bag of the dog!" André bellowed.

The door to the lion's cage had been sprung. The Carras hadn't dared to tell André about Max's lingering the past few nights for fear of André's appearance in front of human beings.

Max saw the fear in the eyes of the Carras. It usually meant trouble, not so much for Max.

André was about to approach Max, but he made an abrupt detour to the table where Eva was serving the now frozen Iowans. She was pouring a glass of water for one of the Iowans from the wrong side. Max noticed it: the Iowans did not. It might have been a feather in André's cap had he handled the situation tactfully. Instead, André grabbed Eva by the arm and practically carried her into the kitchen. The young Iowans were incredulous, but happy they were not the American bastards… who refused a bag of the dog. When Eva said, "**Stop it! You're hurting me!**" Max patted his lips clean and walked toward the kitchen. His mind locked in situational overtime: *Albanian, probably an illegal alien—it's worth a shot.*

Eva was still in André's grasp and in pain. Max hoped he didn't have to put André down. There were too many sharp edges.

Really no room for this guy to hit the floor in a tidy manner.

Max took out his wallet, where he still had his military driver's license in a fogged plastic compartment.

It'll have to do.

Max walked up to André and shoved the license in his face, just past his focal point. André's eyes, close together to begin with, began to cross. "Excuse me. I am with the Immigration and Naturalization Service field operations. We have had our eyes on you for quite some time. I will need to see your driver's license, green card, work visa, and your last year's tax return." As André stepped back, Max said, "We are doing a complete background check on all Albanians in America. You are an Albanian national, correct?" Max stood there with a wry smile as André let Eva down from her outstretched toes. Max took Eva by the hand and gently placed her behind him out of harm's way. Max noticed an exit sign over the back door, which he hoped led to an alley. Eva went out to reassure Len and Margaret that she was okay. André stammered, then said in broken English, that his green card was in his wallet in the back. Max told him to get it and meet him in the dining room for a review of his paperwork. Max walked out and stood in front of the three Carras, who were now standing side by side. They waited for Max to say something. The table of Iowans was staring at Max as well. Looking at his watch, Max counted off the passing seconds.

When Max got to ten, he looked up at the three Carras and smiled. He tilted his head and placed a hand behind his ear, feigning listening. The back door slammed shut. Max nodded, made an about-face, and proceeded back to the kitchen. He reentered the dining room seconds later holding André's apron.

After a long pause, he handed Len the apron and said, "I'm a graduate of the Culinary Institute of America as well as the army chef school. I have cooked for as many as twelve hundred soldiers at one sitting, as well as generals, and heads of state. With your permission, I would like to help you make this restaurant the finest eating establishment in Georgetown. Don't worry about tonight - I'll finish the shift for you. That's on me. Doesn't look like we are in for much of a dinner rush anyway. If you agree, you can pay me what you paid that clown, until, of course, we put this place on the map. Then, we all get rich together. Whaddya say?"

The three stood with their mouths open. The Iowans were also speechless. One of the young women at the table said in a loud voice for all to hear: "See, Tom, that's what I call being in control of a job interview!"

Eva broke the silence for the Carra family. Her screaming was accompanied by a series of quick hand claps, followed by an unusual primeval dance. After three loops around Max, Eva gave him a peck on the cheek. "See, Grandma. I told you something good was going to happen soon. Now I don't have to murder André!"

The four Iowans cheered as the production seemed to be heading toward a finale. They paid their check, hugged Eva, and tipped her well. The young woman who had made the interview comment said to Margaret, "I don't know if we will ever be back to Georgetown, but if we are, we will definitely be coming here again. This has just been the best vacation… ever!"

Len turned to Max and shook his hand. Max was still thinking about the kiss from Eva.

"Young man, I hope you can cook," Len said.

"I hope you can tend bar," Max replied.

"Tend bar? Me? Did Howdy Doody have a wooden ass?" Len called as Max went back into the kitchen. The three Carras paused. Margaret had to think about the comment for a moment, then burst into laughter. Eva also laughed, despite not having a clue as to who Howdy Doody was, or what his ass was made of. She would receive an education on Howdy Doody from Len later as they closed the restaurant. There were no additional customers. Max would have enjoyed trying out the kitchen, but he also wanted a fresh start to everything in his life at this point. The rain had stopped and the air was clear.

"I'll be here at fourteen hundred hours tomorrow. I hope you're ready for some changes," Max said as he put on his dried gear. He waved and walked away as the Carras stood and watched in silence.

The discussion was concise on the way home for the Carra family. "What do you two think?" asked Margaret.

"What've we got to lose at this point?" Eva said. "We are three months behind on the rent, no repeat business, and André is gone forever… thank God. Max is our only hope. If you ask me, someone is watching over us, so let's have a go." Eva kissed them good night, turned, and walked toward her apartment with a newfound bounce in her step.

CHAPTER 2

Max knew there was always a sense of satisfaction in being the *first on your block* to find a great NEW restaurant. His ideas were working and his cooking was really excellent. But a NEW restaurant! That was key.

After a decent night, all four sat down for a nightcap. Len, Margaret, and Eva agreed with Max's latest idea: **Close and renovate.**

Max and Len would build the bar.

Eva was in charge of paint and cheering up the place.

Margaret would make sure that money was spent prudently. Max began to feel part of a family once again. The Carras became rejuvenated just being around Max. They loved the energy and kindness. Max made them feel secure. All of Len and Margaret's trepidation about being old and vulnerable vanished around Max.

Eva was "all in" on this fresh start. They all worked harder and more efficient than ever before. The Carras were happy once again.

The renovations took six weeks. Max would not accept wages. He was excited for the opportunity to showcase his expertise and ideas. Besides, he relished the refurbishing as a learning experience. The name of the restaurant would remain: Scirocco. Max googled the definition. He liked the third definition best. *Scirocco: a swift desert wind that mysteriously appears from nowhere.*

A new sign was definitely needed. It turned out to be the biggest expense.

"The sign is on me," Max said, looking up as the sign was hoisted into place.

Margaret poked Len as she directed him to see Max's arm around Eva's waist. Margaret smiled at Len. If it was okay with Margaret, it was okay with Len. The sign seemed to solidify the partnership.

The night that the final touches were in place, the four restauranteurs walked together, until they reached the corner where Eva went left and Len and Margaret went right. Tonight, Eva would not be walking home alone. It was awkward for Max. Eva had spent most of the day calming him down, and in the end she insisted,"it was okay." Eva let her hand slide into Max's as they all said good night. Max and Eva turned away first.

"Are they looking?" Max asked.

"Of course they're looking!" Eva answered.

Max stopped and kissed her passionately. Eva managed a wave, but Len and Margaret were long gone.

The name Scirocco fit: a new menu and a mysterious new chef had appeared from nowhere.

The days before the grand opening, Max was busy handing out samples of the new menu to the local merchants and passersby. He hoped the locals would spread the word. It worked. In addition to new customers, some of the patrons under Max's brief tenure returned as well, enthusiastic about the reopening.

Within six months, the waiting time without a reservation had climbed to a half hour. The regulars, as Margaret called them, got preferential treatment, or so it seemed. Len was a natural behind the bar. He made up for his lack of swiftness with stories and fatherly advice.

"He's my old Len," Margaret whispered to Eva.

Max was full of ideas, some born in the Korengal mountains on cold winter nights when thoughts of owning a restaurant kept him occupied. One of Eva's favorite tricks involved Max studying the reservation list and deciphering the ethnicity of the patrons.

He would then surprise them with a dessert from their ancestral homelands, hoping they may have enjoyed a similar dessert in their youth. "Just like grandma used to make," one customer blurted. It was always appreciated and made people feel like they were in a home away from home.

Women liked the Scirocco - they felt comfortable at the bar and thought the restaurant was great as well. The men enjoyed the bar and were thrilled that the women liked it. Finally, they'd found a comfortable place to hang their hats.

One busy Friday evening, a stately Georgetown blue blood type gentleman entered the Scirocco. Margaret checked for a single reservation. There was none, but instinct told her to accommodate this chap. She escorted him to a double table toward the rear, justifying the poor location on the lack of a reservation. The gent nodded and sat. He fumbled about for his reading glasses to no avail. He looked annoyed until Margaret offered him one of the extra pair she carried for times like this.

He thanked her and said, "Nice touch." Eva approached the table, noticing the cautionary look from Margaret. Margaret watched Eva spend an inordinate amount of time talking without writing an order. Margaret knew when Eva was uncomfortable. Eva fidgeted.

The gent asked about preparation particulars of the various entrées. To her credit, Eva did not attempt to answer but excused herself to fetch the chef. Max came out and introduced himself. The gent merely said, "How do you do," without giving his name. They spoke for about two minutes while referring back and forth to the menu. Then Max headed back to the kitchen. Eva saw no special treatment of the courses she brought to the gent, but Max had altered the food to the gent's specific requirements without any delay in preparation.

The gent savored each morsel. Max peeked through the kitchen door. The gent was fun to watch. Either he knew what he was doing, or he was a total character.

After completing the main course, the gent asked to see the young chef once again. Max obliged.

"Young man, do you read the *Washington Post*?"

"On Sundays."

"Well, buy yourself a copy this Sunday." He paid his check with an exact 20 percent tip for Eva. He walked toward the door and stopped. He turned abruptly toward Max and said, "Page six."

The man's name turned out to be Mortimer Everett: The nationally syndicated culinary expert, universally feared as the most coldhearted restaurant critic in America. Rumor had it that Mortimer Everett had closed more restaurants than the Great Depression. He gave the Scirocco four stars. A quote from his column read, "I might have given the Scirocco five stars had I room for dessert. Perhaps next time, Scirocco. And there will be a next time. After all, I must return the reading glasses they afforded me when I so absentmindedly left mine at home… Nice touch."

Nobody had ever received four stars in the D.C. area, at least not by His Holiness Mortimer Everett.

The restaurant became *The* spot in Georgetown. The bar picked up. There was an hour wait on weekends without a reservation. Len reveled in his bartender role. He was good at it and joked, "Don't tell anyone I am one of the owners… they may stop tipping me."

Washington big shots made the Scirocco a mainstay on their dining circuit. Among the new devotees was the local Washington, D.C., television news anchor, the bright and beautiful Dana Trudeau. Her network studio was a few blocks from the Scirocco. The Scirocco was an ideal respite between her 6:00 p.m. and 11:00 p.m. telecasts and afterward for an occasional nightcap. Eva didn't like Dana Trudeau. Max wasn't sure why.

CHAPTER 3

Max's favorite customer was Edward Curlander, a former marine and a U.S. senator from New York. Max took a liking to Curlander's unassuming ways and good spirit, and he appreciated that Curlander had paid his dues serving in Desert Storm. Len liked him because he always tipped him twenty bucks.

Other politicians that came into the Scirocco carried an air of entitlement. Max chuckled whenever Curlander, after a few drinks, would berate a chicken hawk politico who had never served in the armed forces.

Max and Curlander often found themselves at the bar well after closing time discussing many topics. Many gravitated toward the problems the country faced. Max gave his perspective. Curlander would explain - while a certain idea might be good, it could never get through the political system. Max was miffed by the bottlenecks that had evolved within the political process.

"Politics will always get in the way of great ideas," Curlander would say.

If they disagreed, a debate could go on till daylight. Though never hostile, it could get intense. If Max hit on a subject with an innovative approach to fixing a problem, Curlander would say, "Explain."

Quite often Curlander took notes. If Curlander disagreed and things seemed to be in a standoff, he would say, "You're entitled to your opinion."

Many a night Max had to walk the eight blocks to Curlander's house and deliver him into the hands of his brilliant and beautiful wife, Amy. She appreciated how Max "handled" her husband. After deciding Max had no ulterior motives, Amy told him, "He may be a marine, but he can't drink worth a damn."

One of those late nights in June, while Max was walking Ed Curlander home, two bouncers came out of the nightclub down the block after finishing their shifts. They turned blindly into Ed Curlander as he and Max were walking down the street.

Ed was pretty loaded, but this incident was not his fault. Had it been five in the afternoon, the clumsy episode might have been dismissed with the tip of a hat, but closing time at a nightclub can always be eventful. Max tried to make it all go away with an apology before any martini muscles took over. Too late. One of the two reached out to grab Ed by the shoulder. Max knocked them both out with shots to their kidney and jaw before Curlander turned around. Max flagged a cab and hustled Curlander into it for the remaining three blocks to his home. Max gave the cabdriver the address and then handed him a twenty-dollar bill to avoid a conversation about the four legs sticking out from the sidewalk. As the cab took off, a half-loaded businessman came out of the club. He stopped to look at the two hulks stretched out next to each other and asked Max what happened.

Max said, "I'm not sure. I was walking home, and these two guys were giving this guy from out of town a hard time. He knocked them both out cold and got into a cab. I heard him say, 'Take me to Reagan Airport.'"

"That was no out-of-towner, pal. That was Senator Ed Curlander from New York. I'm from New York. I voted for him!"

Neither Max nor Ed had any idea that the events of this evening would be the catalyst that placed the chef and the senator on a course that would alter both their lives… and the future of their country.

CHAPTER 4

It took a day for the story to hit the media. The *Washington Post* headline read, "Curlander Bounces Bouncers!"

Dana Trudeau had met Ed and Amy Curlander at the Scirocco. She called Ed for an interview. She started out by saying that she'd also had a problem walking by the same nightclub.

Curlander called Max, sounding befuddled. "What the hell happened? What do I tell the press? Max, this is the best press I ever got."

"Tell them you apologized to the two bouncers. But they shouldn't have said those things about the Marine Corps!"

"Perfect!"

Amy didn't think it was funny. She had her hands full keeping Ed out of harms way. But help from Max was always appreciated. Most of Ed's friends were either still in the corps, dead, or as wild as he.

"Who is Max Burns?" Amy refused to let the question sit. She went for her laptop and pulled up the FBI background program available to the members of Congress.

"Ed … you should see this."

Ed peeked over Amy's shoulder. "What does it say, honey?"

"I'll give you the *Reader's Digest* version. Maxwell Tecumseh Burns III: born Washington, Pennsylvania, September 12, 1990. Heritage, paternal: Scottish and Irish. Original immigration:

Pennsylvania Colony, circa 1714. American Military lineage: 1775-Col. Desmond Mulherne; served under General George Washington in the first Continental Army; field commission: Battle of Valley Forge. European heritage- *matrilineal*: French: Marie DeGramont Duvalier, married 1712 at the Cathédrale Notre-Dame in Paris, France. Married to: Irish privateer Capt. Malcolm (The Red Raider) Mulherne, Galway, Ireland. Immigrated with wife to the British colonies in America circa 1715."

"Blah ... blah ... Hold on. Here we go ..." Amy continued, "Maternal great-great-grandfather: General William Tecumseh Sherman: Appointed by General Hiram Ulysses Grant as commander of the United States Army upon Grant's election to the presidency. Note: Subsequent to President Grant's two terms in office were rendered, General Sherman refused to run for the office of president of the United States of America, saying, 'If nominated, I will not run. If elected, I will not serve.'

"Holy shit! He's a walking definition of an army brat," Ed said.

"Hold on. Let's cut out the next three pages of sizzle and get to the steak. Maxwell Tecumseh Burns III: accepted after his junior year of high school to the United States Military Academy at West Point - appointment declined.

"IQ, registered: 146 (average of three tests) with a high of 147 and a low of 145.

"Graduated valedictorian from Washington High School, Washington, Pennsylvania, in 2007, with a 3.97 GPA. National Honor Society member for four years and also class president all four years.

"Thirty-two wrestling scholarships offered; twelve full, twenty partial. SAMPLE (United States Military Academy, Penn State University, U of Wisconsin, U of Oregon among the schools with major wresting programs). Full scholarships = DECLINED.

"Attended the Culinary Institute of America. Scholarship awarded post-thesis, entitled: 'Sensory Perception and Taste Cohesion Receptors and the Brain.' Graduated 2008. Recipient of the Culinary Institute of America's highest award: *La Papillotte,* awarded by the prestigious C.I.A. periodical."

"C'mon, honey. Get to Max's military career. I can't get him to open up about it!"

"Okay, okay. His father was the mayor of Washington, Pennsylvania, for over twenty years!" Amy read.

"Great. C'mon."

"Max joined the US Army in 2008; three year enlistment requisite for Army Culinary Program. Basic training: Fort Lewis-McChord, Washington State. Advanced infantry training: Fort Bragg, North Carolina; first in physical test results and first in mental testing, out of 9,898 candidates. Airborne training: Fort Bragg, North Carolina. Airborne qualification: Eighty-Second Airborne Division; fourth in physical test results and first in mental (1,189 candidates). Ranger School / special ops training: Fort Benning, Georgia; class 508; graduated second in class overall (due to prerequisite choice: Culinary School). Physical training results; first in mental testing, out of 329 candidates. Delta Force candidacy declined. RE- culinary specialist per terms of enlistment.

"nota bene: Undefeated US Army light heavyweight MMA champion, two years, Fort Benning, Georgia; undefeated US Army heavyweight MMA champion, two months. Fought inter-service representing the United States Army, MMA heavyweight division: TOTAL- both weight divisions: Thirty-seven fights, one defeat -September 20, 2010, to Lieutenant J. G. Gary Nicholson, Navy SEAL Team Six. Internet search: '**The fight to end all fights**.'"

"I watched that fight! It was broadcast worldwide on the Armed Forces Network. They still play it over and over. What a fight. Jeez... No wonder."

"No wonder what?" Amy asked.

"Keep going. This is great. You gotta love this guy," Ed said, enjoying every bit of Amy's detective work.

"Deployment: three combat tours, one in Iraq, two in Afghanistan. Wounded in action: Dar-I-Pech District, Korengal Valley, Kunar

Province, Afghanistan, January 27, 2012, I.E.D.; accredited with saving the remaining fourteen of the twenty-two-member platoon (eight American KIAs). Congressional record (# PA-2888767) medal recommendation synopsis: 'Single-handed responsibility verified; thirty-two EKIA (twenty-seven EKIA with .50-cal. "Ma Deuce," four EKIA with pistol, and one EKIA in hand-to-hand combat while sustaining two wounds (AK-47) to the leg and internal concussive brain injury (I.E.D.). **All** enemy combatants subsequently identified as **al-Qaeda** (non-Afghans, origins-seven different countries).

"Decorations awarded: Silver Star with Valor and Purple Heart. Medal of Honor: nomination initiated, February,4,2012. Petition Submissions: Commanding officer submission; Major General Seth Posch. In addition, petitions were submitted by all fourteen surviving members of the platoon (two succumbed to wounds, one in Landstuhl, Germany, and one to civilian suicide in Newark, New Jersey, December 24, 2013)."

"Okay. Okay. That's enough. I knew the guy had a lot of sand. Amy, not a word about this to anyone. We need this guy. Call your friend Dana at NBC. Tell her I'll give her an interview."

"Don't ***YOU*** open your big mouth after a few drinks!" Amy yelled as Ed retreated into the bathroom to shave.

Ed leaned against the sink. As the hot water ran freely, he stared into the haze of the fogging mirror. "Son…uva…bitch!"

CHAPTER 5

A few weeks later at the Scirocco, Curlander sat with Max, "What do you plan to do with your life?" He hoped Max didn't have an answer.

Max looked at Ed and said, "I want to open up my own restaurant in New York City."

"New York City! Are you kidding me? The rent and the Con Edison bills alone will eat your ass!"

After explaining, Con Edison was the utility provider for New York City. Ed went on about how Max would need at least $1 million before he could open the doors of a restaurant anywhere in New York City.

"Believe me… my dad was in the bar business in Manhattan for years. I know what I'm talking about. If the booze and drugs don't kill you, the overhead and the landlord will. Something always kicks your ass in New York City. I love it, and I hate it for what it did to my dad and our family. Hell, I grew up on the West Side of Manhattan for God's sake. I know every gin mill in New York City."

"I don't doubt that." Max said as Curlander snickered. "I am going to open a place where nobody else would think of opening a restaurant," Max said while staring into his glass of beer.

"And where might that be?"

"I have been researching a neighborhood called Washington Heights."

"Washington Heights! Did you research the Thirty-fourth

Precinct? The Three-Four in the Heights has been the busiest police precinct in the United States of America for the past twenty years. They had to divide the Heights into three precincts, it's so busy."

"Yes. I read that. But they have a great hospital—Columbia-Presbyterian Medical Center on 168th Street and Broadway—and there isn't a decent place to eat up there from 215th Street in Inwood down through Harlem to the Upper West Side. That's about a seven mile stretch in Manhattan."

Curlander had to hand it to Max. He had done his homework.

"Do you speak Spanish, my friend?"

"Some… Eva is fluent."

Curlander managed a smile and gave Max a punch on the arm at the mention of Eva being in the plan. "You devil you. She is a doll. I am happy for you, pal."

"Yeah, we have been living together in her apartment. Eva couldn't stand vets staring at her in the V.A. halfway house. She told me she wouldn't spend another night there."

"You don't reveal much, do you?"

"No reason."

Both men sat quietly on their barstools. Then, out of the blue, Curlander said, "*If*—no, *when*, I become president of the United States, I want you to be my chef at the White House. You could live there with us if you like, or you and Eva could buy a house and commute."

"Oh really, live in the White House, huh?" Max said. "From a halfway house to the White House. At least I wouldn't have to walk you home five nights a week." They both laughed as Curlander moved toward the door. Curlander insisted on walking home alone.

Off Ed Curlander went, each man contemplating future plans and feeling renewed strength infused into an already strong friendship.

Was it the beer talking? Both men asked themselves that same question on their walk home. There was never any bullshit between the two. Max put it out of his head. Senator Edward Curlander could not.

CHAPTER 6

Sixteen months after the opening of the new and improved Scirocco, a TV chef offered Margaret and Len $900,000 for the restaurant. Len and Margaret didn't own the building, but had listened to Eva and signed a fifteen-year lease. They had twelve years left on their initial lease. That long lease, the receipts, and the reputation of the restaurant was incentive enough for the buyers to lay out almost a million dollars in cash. Len and Margaret told Max they would not sell if he didn't want them to.

Hell, they're both in their seventies and always talk about retiring to Florida, Max thought.

He would never interfere with their hopes of retiring in Florida someday. The sale of the Scirocco would make his New York City ideas with Eva more of a plan than a dream. Eva was on board… all the way.

Eva loved Max and vice versa. They were good for each other, and anyone who saw them together knew it. He had been her hero from their very first meeting. After all, he had saved her from having to murder Andre' - the mad Albanian chef.

Eva was Max's first love. Oh, there had been a few high school sweethearts, but nothing compared to what he felt for Eva. No, Eva was *numera una*. He'd known she was special the first time she'd kissed him at the restaurant. That was what happened: a simple love story. When Max first asked her to come to NYC with him, she danced around the same way she had after the André incident. When she stopped, she kissed him again, took him by the hand, and walked him into their bedroom to make the decision official. Life was good.

Margaret and Len were thrilled about Max and Eva together. They had both grown to love and respect Max for many things, not the least of which was how he treated their granddaughter. Eva beamed when she looked at him. She worshipped him. Max was her first love as well. Eva had fire in her eyes and couldn't wait for their life to begin. Max also seemed to be smiling just a bit more lately. If they thought they were fooling Len and Margaret with their clandestine little love affair, they were mistaken.

Max smiled and told Len and Margaret, "You can sell the place as long as I have your permission to bring Eva to New York with me."

Eva finally agreed that Len and Margaret would be fine on their own in Florida.

Len looked at Margaret and then said to Max, "Ever since her parents died in that car accident, we've been looking out for her. It's time she found a good man to take over. Don't get me wrong—we'll miss her. But, well, you better take good care of her, or I'll have to come up there and …."

"I promise you she will be in good hands," Max said as he squeezed Len and Margaret together in a reassuring hug.

With the money from the sale of the restaurant, Len and Margaret could be on their way to Florida for a comfortable life.

They gave Eva $200,000, which was a complete surprise to her. She cried for days. They also left a hatbox with Eva with the instructions "Do not open until we leave." In it was $100,000 in hundred-dollar bills and a note: "Dear Max, thank you for being the grandson we never had. Take good care of our (your) Eva."

At first Max would not accept the money, but Eva told him, "They will be highly insulted if you attempt to give it back. Consider it a debt paid by honorable people. They want to help. Let it be."

CHAPTER 7

Eva was wary about the neighborhood known as Washington Heights. She had no prejudices against any race or religion. She had Latino blood running through her veins and spoke Spanish fluently.

Prejudice is one thing: Caution is another.

Eva was up for an adventure. Life had become exciting for her and she relished the challenges.

The Heights reminded her of San Juan, Puerto Rico, where her mother's people had come from. She had visited relatives in San Juan for her sixteenth birthday, a gift from Len and Margaret. The fast pace of San Juan was not what she'd expected as a teenager. She'd enjoyed the shops, the food, and the people. The ease with which her Spanish vocabulary returned had been a surprise to her. Her beauty had not gone unnoticed by the young men of San Juan. Eva had found herself caught up in a whirlwind of male advances that made her uncomfortable. She'd handled them very well. It had been good training for what would become a constant in her life.

"I felt as if it was a contest to be the first in my pants." Eva told Margaret on the road home from the airport. "I hope nobody won the prize." They'd both laughed.

Eva had been happy to get home and start preparing for her senior year in high school. It had been an enlightening adventure for the raven-haired sixteen year old beauty.

As long as Eva was with Max, she felt safe. Max sensed her

trepidation as they walked the streets of the Heights. They found a sublet apartment on 96th Street and Broadway. That part of Manhattan had become populated by many young people in the past thirty years. Their sublet was a one-bedroom apartment in a six story prewar building with an elevator.

Max and Eva decided that the vacant furniture store on the northwest corner of 168th Street and Broadway was the perfect size and location for their new restaurant. It had windows facing onto Broadway as well as around the corner onto 168th Street, across from Columbia Presbyterian Hospital. Eva negotiated a twelve-year lease at a more than fair rent. The ceiling, walls, and floor were intact and usable. The structural changes needed were minimal. A floor plan would have to be designed from scratch to transform the space into a restaurant. The design would be Max's job, with the work contracted out where needed on their limited budget.

"There goes the $100k before we even open the doors," Max said, smiling and hugging Eva.

Max and Eva hired some local people for as much of the overhaul work as possible. The workers were very appreciative hardworking people. Max was impressed with the craftsmanship the men and women possessed. At the mere mention of hiring a contractor, someone would always say, "I can do that," or they knew someone who could. The project took on a life of its own. Initially, the locals thought Max was *loco en la cabeza (*crazy in the head), which he might have been. After a few weeks, they knew he was, but they liked, *los gringos locos.*

The kitchen went in first. Max had seen firsthand in Iraq and Afghanistan what fire could do to the human body. To Eva, it seemed to be the only cautionary fear Max ever manifested. There was a six-story apartment house above the ground-level restaurant. That was a big concern for Max. The Ansul fire system, and all other safety requirements, would be strictly adhered to and fully functional.

After work, which was usually around midnight, Max would

often cook for any of the crew that remained late. Not only did Max enjoy the cooking and seeing the smiling faces, but he also knew word would get out that Max and Eva were good people... and Max could cook his ass off.

The first neighborhood guy Max put to work, a fellow named Carlos, warned Max about a neighborhood gang that made quite a name for itself in upper Manhattan. "They are not my people. They are Chicanos from Los Angeles. They are called the Latin Diplomats, and they are very bad *hombres*."

"Once they taste my food, they will be like putty in my hands."

"Máximo, my friend, you do not understand. There is no joke in this." Max smiled and filed it away. He knew it would not be easy in the Heights. Now there was a name to potential trouble: Latin Diplomats.

The grand opening for the restaurant, named Gringo Smyth's, was set for Saint Patrick's Day; March 17. Flyers went out to the hospital, local businesses, police officers, firefighters, and public school staff, anyone Max and Eva could get to. Part of the grand opening festivities included a free dinner for the local people and their families, who were working so hard for *los gringos locos*. The entire *vecin* (neighborhood) was excited about a new business opening up, and a restaurant at that. Eva had a surprise for Max. She hoped she could pull it off.

CHAPTER 8

It was March 3, and Max was spending eighteen hours a day trying to get things together for the opening in two weeks. Diners made critical decisions on the quality of a restaurant on an initial visit. Max wanted nothing to go wrong. Too many restaurants opened for business before they were ready. *Big mistake.*

Max glanced at his watch and shook his head. It was twelve thirty in the very early morning. There was still plenty to do, but he was exhausted. He locked up the restaurant and crossed the street to get a cab in front of the hospital.

The hair on the back of his neck went up. He knew what that meant. Either he was being followed or at the very least, being watched. His ranger instincts seemed to surface when needed.

Master Sergeant Nunez once told him, "Your ranger instincts never leave you. Get used to it and appreciate it. Remember: assess the situation before you act. Last thing you want is friendly fire, in or out. Anything can be a weapon if you know how to make it a weapon."

Max instinctively took the newspaper from his field jacket pocket. He rolled it tightly and held it fast under his armpit. He remembered Eva had asked him to bring home a draft of the menu. He did an about-face and almost walked into three young Latinos. Max looked at them and had to stifle a laugh. They looked like they'd gotten dressed in Barnum and Bailey's dressing room during a blackout. Max had to smile as he excused himself in Spanish and walked through the three young studs.

How could I forget Eva's menu for the printer tomorrow? Max thought. *I must be losing it.*

"Whoa, *chulo.* Where are you going?" one of them asked.

"I forgot something." Max answered, as though talking to an old pal.

How he could be preoccupied in situations like these was baffling even to Max, albeit after the fact. In order of importance; the menu came first. These three punks were no more of an inconvenience than mosquitos in a field tent. That would not have been the case if Eva was with him, but she wasn't.

"Hey, fucko!" the smallest Latino yelled. Max stopped, turned around, and walked back to the three macho men. This surprised them.

"You got some money, gringo?"

"Some, I'm takin' a cab in a minute…why?"

"Well, you better give that money to me. It will be safer," the smallest one chided. The other two laughed nervously as the leader slowly pulled a .38-caliber Smith & Wesson revolver out of his coat pocket. It looked heavy and huge in his hand. He was waving it like a paintbrush. The other two watched as though this was a training field trip for them. A tenth of a second had not passed when Max grabbed the gun over the top of the revolver cylinder and held it fast, the gun still pointing at Max.

Max said, "Amazing, huh? You can do this with a revolver. Go ahead. Pull the trigger." The leader tried to wrench the gun free, to no avail, and then tried to pull the trigger.

"See? It won't fire. The cylinder won't revolve while I am holding it. Thus the name: revolver. Now, you can't do that with one of these."

Max pulled out his Kimber 1911-A1 .45-caliber semi-automatic from the small of his back and jammed it in the leader's mouth, breaking his four front teeth in the process.

"This? This is not a revolver. It's semi-automatic. It has fourteen-rounds of hollow-points, topped off with a little drop of mercury. Big difference."

The two student muggers were much more nervous now than at the start of their adventure. *That is not a good thing,* Max thought.

Nervous means uncertain.

One of the two pulled out a switchblade and came at Max. Max deflected it with his elbow, but the blade put a nice gash in the leather jacket Eva had given him for Christmas. That pissed Max off. Max snapped the revolver out of the leader's hand and put it into his jacket pocket. In one motion, he took the rolled newspaper out from under his armpit and jabbed the end of it into the knife wielder's throat. He went down gagging on his blood.

"Don't worry about this," Max said, tapping the revolver with his .45. "You can pick it up at the Three-Four precinct tomorrow morning. I'm sure you know where that is."

Jeez, I got a full day tomorrow, Max thought.

I really don't need this bullshit.

Looking at the slice in his jacket, he thought, *Eva is going to have a fit.*

The other wide-eyed student involved in the Mugging 101 course stepped back. Max contorted his face and growled at him. He ran off into the night.

Definite "F" for his field-trip grade.

"I suggest you take him in there," Max said to the leader, pointing to the hospital. "I am going to get my menus and go home. I'm really tired… and now I'm irritable too." Max's demeanor changed from nonchalance to MMA mode. He stared into the leader's face. "If you cockroaches mess with me again, I will eat your liver before your eyes close! *Comprende, chula*?" Using the feminine form of *chulo* to add extra insult.

Shit! How do I explain this tear to Eva? Max thought, looking at the cut in his jacket again. He watched as the two remaining men limped away, unable to run. He went back for the menus and flagged a cab. He was glad Eva had not been present for this minor blip. He needed to instill fear, and Eva might not have understood the procedures necessary to do that. He stared out the cab window as the blocks rolled by.

Can leather be sewn?

CHAPTER 9

The Three-Four precinct was located on Broadway and 184th Street. It now occupied the entire block in a building that had formerly been a grammar school. It was the volume of crime that had made the move to the abandoned school essential.

Cops in the Three-Four were assigned there either as punishment or as a means of making detective and getting the gold shield. It was a factory, busy 24-7. There were no slow tours on any of the three eight-hour shifts in the Three-Four. Other than having the highest volume of crime in the United States, the Three-Four was different in one other respect: it actually had a revolving door. At one time or another, some of the best cops in New York City had spent time in the Three-Four, whether they liked it or not. Good cops loved it. The volume of arrests and crime in the Three-Four precinct in the '70s had necessitated the birth of a sister precinct, the Three-Three. Although the Three-Three precinct was physically closer to Gringo Smyth's than the Three-Four, the restaurant fell under the jurisdiction of the Three-Four precinct by one block. When a second precinct had proved insufficient, the Three-Zero had been created, resulting in three precincts within thirty-one blocks of each other. Every year for the last twenty-six years, one of these three precincts had been the busiest precinct in the United States, not simply within the five boroughs of New York City.

At seven forty-five in the morning, Max was standing in front of the Three-Four precinct. He watched the cops filing in and out. The 12:00 a.m.–to–8:00 a.m. shift hurried out as the 8:00 a.m.–to–4:00 p.m. shift waded in. Max knew to wait for the 8:00 a.m.–to–4:00 p.m. shift to get settled. If he began his story with the 12:00 a.m.–to–8:00 a.m. desk sergeant, he would have to start over again with the 8:00 a.m.–to–4:00 p.m. desk sergeant. It was just like the army in that regard.

At exactly 8:04 a.m., Max walked into the Three-Four and stood in front of the white line painted on the floor in front of a five-foot-high desk. A nameplate, partly out of its slot, read: "Sgt. Devon Marco." Max looked around the first floor. The omnipresent green paint, reminiscent of Max's grammar school, covered the walls and ceiling.

There must've been a big sale on this color years ago.

The detainment cages circled the perimeter. A member of the NYPD cadet program hosed down the cages after the transfer van took the night's catch to the Tombs, the netherworld holding jail for pretrial perps. Max noticed drains in the floor of the cages. They had thought of everything.

Without looking up, the desk sergeant asked in a sarcastic tone, mimicking the King's English, "And how may I be of service to you this fine day in hell, my dear tax-paying employer?" Max reached up and plopped the revolver down on top of the desk. Sergeant Marco pushed his chair back and looked at the gun, then at Max. "How the fuck did you get past the metal detector with that?"

"Must be broken," Max said.

The desk sergeant yelled over to one of the rookie patrolmen who had just turned up, "Hey, shit head! Plug the metal detector in." He turned back to Max. "Fuckin' Martinez loves screwin' with me. Leaves me a mess every morning. Where did you get this relic?" he asked Max.

"Some punks tried to mug me last night when I was coming out of my restaurant," Max said.

"Are you the crazy bastard opening up the restaurant by the hospital?" Sergeant Marco interrupted.

"That's me."

"Is that right? Hey, shit head, get the boss," Marco barked.

The boss, Captain John (Sean) Timoney, was a no-nonsense, ruddy-faced man from Dublin, Ireland. He and his younger brother, Kieran, had immigrated to America in their teens in the mid-seventies, expecting to live with their uncle. Their parents had died of cancer, as had Max's. When the two teenagers arrived in New York City, they found out their uncle had also died one month prior to their arrival. The Irish superintendent of the building let them continue the apartment lease as their uncle's last living relatives. That was the only bit of luck to befall the two teenagers that year.

They shined shoes for two years, until John turned eighteen, at which point he took the NYPD police entrance exam as a cadet and got a score of 110 percent. In later years the joke was that he probably got the extra 10 percent because he was Irish. In fact, it was his participation in the NYPD cadet program that was never needed and caused him to exceed a perfect score. He and his brother entered the ranks of the NYPD two years apart with equal marks on their tests. The Irish Christian Brothers had taught them well in Dublin. Kieran was now a first-grade detective attached to the Manhattan North Precinct in Hell's Kitchen.

Captain Timoney sized up Max, then extended his hand. "So, you're ***Himself***," Timoney said with a touch of brogue.

"Himself?" Max asked.

"Yes. Himself—the crazy bastard that is opening up a restaurant on the border of my precinct."

"Yes, sir."

"I always thought that was a great spot for a restaurant. Then I thought… How? How would anyone survive down there in no-man's-land?" Timoney turned toward the desk sergeant. "Marco! Anything I should know about out there?"

Marco held up the revolver with the empty barrel flipped open.

"Just this antique S&W service revolver. He took it off three spiders last night. Probably Latin Diplomats."

"Looks like old P.D. issue. Numbers filed off?"

"No, Captain."

"Run a make on it," Timoney ordered.

"But, boss, I'm shorthanded today." Marco started to plead.

"Run a make on it!" Timoney yelled at Marco. Then, his voice completely changed, he said to Max, "Come into my office, Mr. Burns."

Max was surprised Timoney knew his name. "Have we met before, Captain?" Max asked, knowing they had not.

"Only on paper, Mr. Burns." Timoney sat behind his very neat desk. "Pretty impressive credentials: Eighty-Second Airborne, ranger, three tours in 2 different combat zones, decorations up the wazoo, MMA champ… that should come in handy… master chef." After a long pause, Timoney looked up at Max and said, "It seems to me that you've bounced from one murder capital to another, Mr. Burns. Not cushy enough down in D.C.? So what would bring you here? Let me guess. You work for your uncle, as in Sam, correct?"

Max didn't know whether to be amused or not.

"If you are a suit, Mr. Burns, please tell me now before you get killed and I get blamed for not knowing you're a fed. Please, Mr. Burns, indulge me. What else could possibly bring you to our fine neighborhood?"

Max was a little confused for a second, then answered, "The rent, for one thing. The rent and the fact that I always wanted my own restaurant in New York City."

"Don't give me that Big Apple crap! Why would anyone want to open up a business in this section of New York City? For God's sake, even the mayor wants nothing to do with us. He wants to change the name of the neighborhood. He thinks all the bullshit will disappear if he changes the goddamn name of the neighborhood. Now there's a practical solution. Change the goddamn name of the neighborhood. These mutts'll think twice about killing one another after a name change." Timoney's frustration with politics in New York was typical for the cops that enforced the mayor's mandates. Max took it all in, rather enjoying the show.

"Don't expect my cops to be babysitting your ass. You put the target on your back, mister. I won't be responsible for some war hero getting shot in a drive-by on my watch. Do you hear me? I am stretched too thin up here. You are on the southern border of this precinct," Timoney said, as if it were bad luck for both of them for Max to be on the perimeter of his jurisdiction.

"Do you realize that one block further south and the Three-Three precinct has you? Saints preserve us. Is there no luck to be had?"

Max liked the captain. Timoney cared. That would be comforting to Eva.

Timoney respected Max in spite of the chef's surprise entrance into his world. Timoney now knew that the owner of the restaurant at the south end of his precinct was not the kind to cut and run. That meant problems for Captain John Timoney and the Three-Four. He was usually correct in his assessments.

Half talking to himself as much as Max, he said, "You've got balls all right. You'd make a good cop. But these days, why the hell anybody would want to be a cop in this shit hole is beyond me." He pulled out a form. "Listen to me," he said. "Fill this form out and get it back to me ASAP. It's a carry permit. I will sign off on it. You're going to need it for that .45 caliber you so wisely left at home this morning."

"How did you know I…."

Timoney stopped him with a stare. Max had to smile.

"Is that why you unplugged the metal detector?" Max asked, tongue in cheek.

"No. I was hoping someone would come in and shoot Sergeant Marco!" Timoney yelled, loud enough for the entire precinct to hear. To Max, he said, "You can't get through to me here, so here is my cell number. Put it in your speed dial. By the way, you should have killed those punks last night." Max thought it an odd comment for a police officer, much less a precinct CO. He attributed it to an overworked cop spouting off.

Max started to leave but turned back toward Timoney. "Opening night is Saint Paddy's Day. Why don't you bring the little woman in for dinner on the house?"

Timoney's face contorted. "I don't take anything from anyone!" Once again, he was screaming for effect, so the entire precinct could hear him.

"Okay, I didn't mean it like that," Max said, upset he might have blown a valuable ally.

"Get the fuck out of here!" Timoney yelled as he pointed to the door.

CHAPTER 10

Saint Paddy's Day in New York City was almost always windy and cold, not that the weather stifled anyone from celebrating the Irish holiday. In short, the city rocked. Unfortunately for Max and company, most of the celebrating happened downtown near the parade. The days of the Heights having an Irish celebration were long gone. Max knew that. But he'd needed a target date for opening, and he'd made one. He was most intrigued about how his brand of cooking would be received by the Latino community, which was known for its great cooking.

If I can make it here, I can make it anywhere, he thought. *New York, New York ... Haha.*

Max was nervous. Impervious to the elements, he headed north to the restaurant early on March 17. A plethora of thoughts ran nonstop and unprocessed through his mind. He felt as though being nervous inhibited a clear plan of attack. He took a few deep breaths, then decided to take a cab.

Some of the locals, Carlos in particular, had expressed an interest in working at the restaurant. Carlos had worked long hours during the construction of the restaurant, and that had not gone unnoticed by Max and Eva. Max invited Carlos to work in the kitchen.

"I'll train you to become a prep-man and eventually my second chef."

Carlos's daughter, Carmela, had worked as a waitress and was also hired. Eva would greet people at the door and be ready to help Carmela if—when—necessary. The four of them—Max, Eva, Carlos, and Carmela—would be the only ones working for the grand opening.

"Six o'clock! Ready or not!" Eva looked back at Max with her hand on the door. Max nodded. Eva unlatched the door as though she were letting loose the bulls of Pamplona. Nothing happened.

Eva yelled back, "Who did you expect, the mayor?" All four laughed, albeit nervously.

The first customer to come in a few minutes later was Captain Timoney. He was not in uniform, which threw Max for a second. He wore a fedora hat, the kind seen in many Turner Network film noirs. It suited him. He was escorting a beautiful Latina woman who looked to be about ten years his junior. Timoney introduced her by her first name only: Maria Elena. Max introduced Eva to the couple. Eva greeted Maria Elena in Spanish. The two beautiful women seemed to hit it off.

"I expect a check," Timoney said under his breath to Eva. Eva was confused, not privy to Max's prior conversation with the captain at the precinct.

"Of course. I wouldn't give it to Maria Elena." Eva smiled after she seated them and walked back to her post.

People began to trickle in. Max was surprised to see that the Latino customers were dressed in their Sunday best. Some of the men wore suits and ties. Eva said it was most likely at the insistence of their spouses or girlfriends. This was an important opening night that they wished to remember. The women were dressed as though attending a nightclub grand opening. It was a tribute and a welcome.

Timoney was surprised as well. Maria Elena told him, "If these gringos are brave enough to make a beautiful restaurant in this barrio, then my people will show respect."

Timoney replied, "We need to keep it that way." Maria Elena nodded in acknowledgment.

At eight o'clock a row of black SUVs with blue lights flashing pulled up and double-parked on 168th Street, off Broadway. The suits got out first, securing the area. The car doors seemed to open in unison while not-so-secret Secret Service agents scanned the streets and spoke into their lapel pins. Out of the first car emerged the mayor of New York City, Michael Braunreuther, and his wife, Susan. From the next car came Alexander Blair, former secretary of defense and current presidential candidate for the Democratic Party, with his wife, Marilyn. Last but not least was Blair's recently nominated vice presidential candidate, Edward Curlander, and his wife, Amy. You could hear a pin drop in the restaurant as the flashing lights streaked across the restaurant walls, a sight all too familiar to the customers, though under different circumstances. Two Secret Service agents entered first, followed by the entourage. Max came out of the kitchen wiping his hands on a dish towel, wondering why the restaurant was silent.

"Hi, Max," Amy said as she walked over and kissed him.

She was followed by Ed, who hugged him and said, "I'm not gonna kiss ya—too much at stake."

Ed introduced Max to Alexander Blair and his wife, Marilyn, followed by Mayor Braunreuther and his wife, Susan.

"Welcome to Hamilton Heights, Mr. Burns," Braunreuther said. Max took a quick look over at Timoney, who was sticking his finger in his mouth feigning gagging. "Thank you for choosing our fair city for your wonderful establishment," Braunreuther said mechanically.

"Hey, Mike, he's one of us. Cut the bullshit," Curlander yelled, conjuring up his best New Yorkese. The help laughed nervously. When the shock subsided, all present realized they were in a special place, at a special time, with special people.

All Max could muster was "How the hell?"

Eva covered her mouth as she held back tears. She had pulled it off.

Timoney looked at Maria Elena and said, "Hamilton Heights. There goes my appetite."

Max brought Captain Timoney over to introduce him to the dignitaries. Curlander insisted the local precinct captain and his lady join them at their table. Timoney hesitated, but Maria Elena sat down immediately. Max shifted the kitchen into overdrive as Eva took the orders.

The food was incredible.

"You haven't lost your touch, Max," Curlander said, wiping his face with a napkin. "Can we get a round of drinks for everyone?"

Max and Eva froze. "I don't have a liquor license yet, Ed," Max said apologetically. "I applied, but it takes about four months. I'll send over to Pop's Liquor Store for a few bottles."

Ed just stared at Braunreuther and said, "Mike! No liquor license?"

"He'll have it by the weekend," the mayor said, not looking up from his dish.

Eva sent Carlos to Pop's, and he loaded up on champagne, wine, and bottles of single-malt Scotch whisky. All the other patrons were treated like royalty as well. The mayor paraded the candidates around to all the tables. Ed said to Max and Eva, "You have any problems, you talk to Mike here. If he doesn't get things done, call me."

The politicos had pictures taken with everyone. There would be plenty of emails and photos heading south of the border on this night. Once the people out on the street realized the flashing lights were not for another drive-by, they peeked in the window to see what was going on. A few of the patrons inside seemed nervous at first. Not everyone had a green card. A signed campaign poster went up in the window.

It took a while, but even Captain Timoney began to enjoy the festivities. There were abundant cocktails, great food, and magnificent desserts, along with a real common man feel to the evening. Max made sure everyone else dining at the restaurant got good service as well. Max and Eva were pouring champagne for all the patrons in any kind of glass they could find. It was a New York City moment. Nobody was slighted. Max and Eva wanted everyone to feel special.

"Hey, Timoney, you keep a sharp eye on this place for our friend Max," Braunreuther said.

"Yes, sir, Mr. Mayor. I live to serve."

Curlander chuckled at the sarcasm, but Braunreuther knew that the sarcastic Timoney was the CO of the Three-Four because he was the best cop for the job. Timoney seemed to have a knack for keeping things under control in the Heights. Timoney didn't know it yet, but he was on the short list for deputy inspector—that is, if his sarcasm didn't blow it.

Max could not spend as much time as he would have liked at their table. His job was in the kitchen. His hopes were high and his expectations higher. Max felt they might make it in New York with hard work and a little luck.

Where's Frank Sinatra when you need him? Max chuckled to himself.

Eva was a perfect hostess. She handled things as best she could, although she hoped Max would finish in the kitchen soon. She needed his help with all the questions and conversation.

Ed and Amy loved Eva. She was beautiful but carried herself as though she didn't know it. However, she did know it, and that made her more intriguing. She was a mixture of southern European natural beauty and Spanish Caribbean fire, with big dark-brown eyes. Her olive skin tone appeared wet in certain lighting, a gift left behind in Spain by the Moors. Max loved touching her, even in passing. Not only was she beautiful, but Max also thought her to be brilliant. She had a gift for language that had gotten her a master's degree in linguistics at Georgetown University in two years. At this point she was fluent in four languages and had a working knowledge of four others.

Hmmm, a good thing for when we open franchises internationally, Max thought.

Curlander walked into the kitchen while Max was busy preparing Bananas Foster for the elderly Cuban couple at table five.

"Looks like you got it goin' on here, pal."

"I hope so. Hey, the Democratic Party vice presidential candidate! You and Amy are lookin' good yourselves. The country is in the shitter—maybe you two can dig it out," Max said while still preparing the dessert.

"I hope so," Curlander said, looking worried. "We are going to give it a try. I was hoping you would come along for the ride … but you have to do what you have to do. By the way, when are you going to make a decent woman out of Eva?"

"I have to get this place on its feet. Then we'll see. One step at a time. But let me put it this way, Mr. Vice President—my intentions are good," Max said, standing at attention and full salute.

"Your intentions are always good. That's why I need you with me. That, and those hands of yours. You know, it all came back to me about that night in Georgetown with those bouncers. You shit canned both of them, not me. You could have been quite a big shot if the papers had gotten a hold of the real story. Instead, you slid off into the night."

"Like an army ranger?" Max chided the former marine.

"Yeah, the legend of the 'Badass from the Big Apple' was born," Ed said, smiling. "Baa, Baa, Black Sheep: Badass Big Apple Black Sheep—that's what the *New York Post* calls me … Friggin' *Post*."

They hugged each other and laughed.

"Thanks to you, my friend, that night is going to help put me in the White House," Curlander said as he slapped Max on the back.

"This country could use a badass."

"You're right, Max, and I want you right there in my corner. As the lady said, it's going to be a bumpy ride."

"You can handle it."

"Yeah, I can handle it, but even a president needs a friend he can trust," Curlander said before realizing the admission of his true concern.

"Oh, you're skipping right over the vice presidency, eh?" Max laughed.

Curlander did not laugh and looked Max right in the eye. "You bet I am."

Max was a little befuddled but attributed it to the single-malt Scotch.

"Think about it, Max. You could be executive chef." They both laughed and gave each other another man hug, the kind tough guys got away with. Curlander went back to the table. Max called two of the four Secret Service agents into the kitchen for a quick meal. The other two would come in later. They were very appreciative. None of them had eaten since seven that morning.

One of the last two Secret Service agents said to Max, "You two are old pals, eh? Service?"

"No," Max said as he walked toward the men's room, letting the conversation hang. When Max returned, he was greeted with more conversation from the agent.

"Ya know, he hasn't shut up about you since I've been on his detail."

"Remember the *secret* in Secret Service," Max said. He put his finger to his lips and went, "Shhhhhhhhh."

The agent laughed and said, "Point well taken. Everything is a test, my friend … You just passed your entrance exam."

There was no introduction. Max smiled and shook the agent's hand. The agent looked out the porthole in the kitchen door and said into his lapel pin, "Fish ready to swim. Let's get the boats ready." He turned back to Max. "Here's my card, Max. Thanks for the meal. We usually don't get treated to a world-class feed like this. Give me a call if you ever need Redskins tickets."

"What makes you think I would need Redskins tickets?" Max asked, looking at the card. It gave the name Bob Cleary with a cell phone number and nothing else.

"Hey, like they say up here about the lottery, 'ya never know'!"

Max squeezed in at the politicos' table. He immediately got a "Where the hell have you been?" look from Eva. Everyone was getting ready to depart. Most of the customers had already left at this point. It was understood that the gringos might have some things to talk about, and besides, they needed to email some photos. A few remained outside, still incredulous that such a thing could happen here. No barrio tonight, a *vecin*, a neighborhood again.

Mayor Braunreuther held his wife's hand and assured Max he would receive the utmost attention while looking directly at Timoney. "And if you need anything at all, call the cell number on this card." He handed Max a card.

Max looked at Timoney, who seemed about to really throw up. Maria Elena, smiling, held his arm tightly.

Timoney said to Max, "See me at the Three-Four tomorrow morning. Your pistol permit is ready." Timoney said his goodbyes to all, politically correct in his demeanor. This was well noted by the mayor. Deportment, protocol, and loyalty—all were mandatory for even a well-connected NYPD deputy inspector.

Those still in the restaurant stood up and applauded when they started to exit.

Blair was seventy-five and, if elected, would become the oldest president by four-plus years at the time of inauguration on January 20. He and his wife were cookie-cutter politicians from Michigan. Curlander was needed to pull the northeastern states.

Amy looked stressed to Max. He gave her a big hug and handed her a bag with her favorite dessert: apple strudel. She started to cry a little as she kissed Max and Eva before being escorted into the middle vehicle.

Last out was Curlander. He and Max shared another bear hug. Everyone could see that these two were friends and that the hug was not a half-hearted political snuggle. Timoney also took note. Off the politicos went down Broadway into the New York City night.

Eva noticed that, as cold as it was, no one wore an overcoat.

"I guess politicians never stay in one place long enough to get cold," Max said when she pointed it out.

Even the women are used to the elements … and much more, Eva thought.

Max said to Eva, "Expensive night, but worth it. You can't buy this type of publicity."

Eva took forty one-hundred-dollar bills out of her pocket and fanned Max with them.

"You gave them a check?"

"Ed insisted on paying … in cash too! He said, 'It's a family thing,' and that you would understand."

Max shook his head. He did understand. Ed's family had been in the bar and restaurant business in New York City for enough years to know that you always pay. Ed knew the difficulties in getting a new restaurant on its feet.

Max put his arm around Eva.

Max saw an elderly Puerto Rican gentleman with his wife looking in the window. The elderly gentleman said, "You must be very important people." Max and Eva just chuckled and invited them inside to warm up with some hot tea and desserts.

It was two in the morning when Max and Eva locked up and started walking arm in arm toward the hospital canopy to find a cab. They were exhausted but exhilarated.

A car slowed down and cruised next to them as they walked. Max moved Eva to the inside and looked over at the vehicle and its four occupants. The car was a low-rider, typically a West Coast ride. It was a Chevy Impala SS, a 1972 vintage, painted candy-apple red. In the shotgun seat sat a big man for a Latino. At least, his arms were big. There were tats on the man's right arm and also a teardrop tat of a made man on his face. Max had him pegged for one of the West Coast Chicanos that Carlos had warned him about. Max figured he could be an Arizona desert baby and therefore a citizen. So the INS approach he'd used on André, the chef, would not fly. Citizenship wielding by these Chicanos was one way they intimidated the illegal aliens who came to the US for work. It was a sad testimonial and something Curlander and Max had talked about at the Scirocco.

"*Oye, jefe*. Very impressive tonight. So, you da new guy in *mi barrio*, eh?" the honcho said in a heavy singsong Spanish accent typical of California, not the islands. Max looked at him and kept walking. Eva pulled on his arm to keep him moving forward. The back window rolled down to reveal a kid with four gold teeth twinkling in the moonlight.

The guy riding shotgun asked the kid, "*El hombre*?"

The kid said, "*Sí*," and rolled up his window.

"You like picking on children, eh, *jefe*? I do too, hehehehe. And you are next." Max kept walking. Eva was having a difficult time steering Max straight ahead. She could feel the muscles in his right arm tense up.

"That is a very pretty *muchachita* you have there, my friend. You better take good care of her. This is a very dangerous barrio, even if you know the mayor. This is *mi barrio*, not his. You owe me $3,000 for my little brother's teeth. You have one week to bring it to me up in the projects on Dyckman Street. One week from tonight!"

Max couldn't help himself. "You got a better chance telling your elves to find your little sister's teeth on the street and glue them back together." Laughter came from the car. It stopped when the honcho glared back at the occupants.

"My name is Paco. You ask anyone about me. You ask about Paco. I don't fuck around. You have one week."

"Paco. That will be easy to write on a tombstone. That is, if you even get buried. Don't most of you get eaten by vultures in the Arizona desert?" Max snapped back.

Paco pointed his finger at Max and Eva, as though he were shooting a pistol, and said, "One week."

Max instinctively reached back for his .45, then caught himself. Paco and his boys sped off, having delivered the message.

We got through the entire night without incident. Now these goons show up.

"What was that all about?" Eva asked.

Max was deep in thought. He could see the *New York Post* headline tomorrow: "Pols Leave before Shooting Spree at Restaurant Grand Opening in Hamilton Heights; Mayor Gives Restaurant Four Stars."

"Let's get a cab. I'll fill you in. By the way, can leather be sewn?"

CHAPTER 11

Max was up early the next morning as usual. At the Three-Four, Sergeant Marco was his charming self. "Go right in. He's expecting you," Marco said blandly without looking up.

"Not a bad turnout. Now, look me in the eye and tell me you don't work for your uncle," Timoney said in greeting as he turned around.

"My uncle?" Max said.

"Your uncle as in Sam. Nobody of any consequence even drives through this neighborhood, never mind that crew stopping by for dinner," Timoney said, as though he had the goods on Max.

"I had no idea that Eva planned that. I didn't have a clue," Max babbled.

"So you're both suits, eh? Here's your permit. You probably don't even need it. It's a carry permit. You can pack twenty-four hours a day. You better." Timoney knew he didn't have to say that to Max. Timoney had a good eye for people.

"Who is Paco?" Max asked while looking at the permit.

"Shit!" Timoney said. "Where did you run into him? Jesus in heaven, I hoped he'd ignore you since you opened down low in the neighborhood. I knew things were too quiet to last. These bastards hate the cold, but you woke them outa hibernation. Tell me everything."

"It seems one of the punks that tried to mug me was this guy

Paco's kid brother. He wants three grand for his brother's dental bill," Max said, smiling.

"His brother? Louie? Pay him," Timoney said without hesitation.

"What? I am not paying anybody!"

"Pay him! It'll be the best three grand you ever spent. Paco is a killer. He kills people just to hear the groans. He thinks he's in a movie or something—a full-blown psychopath. If you want to be in business here and not have this piece of shit causing you big problems, pay him."

"I thought you might want to arrest him for attempted extortion?"

"Look, you knocked Little Louie's teeth out. Do yourself a favor and pay the dentist bill. I am trying to give you some sound advice here. Listen to me. I know what I am talking about. If you plan on being around here for the long run, you don't want to be on Paco's shit list."

"Captain Timoney, sir, I have been around bullies my whole life. I don't like them, and eventually they don't like me. If I pay this Paco, next thing you know he'll be hanging out at a window table in my restaurant every night running dope deals. Then, if he sees I'm doing fairly well, he'll want a piece of the place. I'm not giving him a fucking dime. If he wants to fight me over it, I am more than willing to oblige him, anywhere, anytime."

"Fight him? Fight him? Hahahaha. He hasn't had a fight since he was eight years old. Listen to me. He is a killer. He doesn't fight anyone. He kills people so he doesn't have to fight." After a pause Timoney asked, "How many of them at this mugging?"

"There were three of them. One went to the ER, Louie got the new smile, and the third guy ran away."

"So, that's it. It was Paco. Wanna know what happened to the third guy? Paco cut the third kid's throat and shoved a chicken leg in his ass. Then he propped the naked body up against the door to his mother's apartment and rang the bell. The kid was sixteen. Welcome to Washington Heights."

"I didn't see anything in the newspapers about it," Max said.

"The newspapers. You mean newspaper reporters and TV reporters? Hey, kid, one murder here is not news. This is a war zone. I know you know what a war zone is, my young friend. Just because you're on *terra firma* back in the good ole US of A, don't think you're not in a war zone. Pay the man!"

"Sorry, Captain. No can do. Thanks for expediting the pistol permit…I appreciate it. Say hello to Maria Elena for me." Max said as he turned to leave.

"You stay away from that bastard until I talk to him. When does he want his money?"

"Six days. He's gonna have a long wait for any money from me. I am already into Eva's savings fixing up the restaurant. As far as his brother's teeth? Let Paco chew his food for him."

"You just stay put till I get this handled." Timoney said, watching Max walk out the revolving door.

CHAPTER 12

Things were looking positive for the restaurant. The hospital sent visitors, and the locals were spreading the word about the new restaurant owned by the gringos. Eva had the photos of opening night framed and on the walls.

"Gringo Smyth's: Spanish, Irish, and American food," the sign read, with *Smyth* spelled with a *y*, so people would remember it.

"The sign is on me," Eva said with authority.

The restaurant was not open for lunch yet, but Timoney knew Max and Eva would be there working diligently to prepare for the weekend. He stopped his unmarked car on the 168th Street side of the restaurant. As he expected, Max and Eva were inside prepping the specials.

"I spoke to Paco," Timoney said to Max when Eva was out of earshot. "You got a problem—no, *we* got a problem. Little Louie told all his pals about the tough new gringo. It seems Paco doesn't take kindly to strangers sporting a rep in his barrio. He wants his money, but as a 'good neighbor' gesture, he will make it twenty-five hundred instead of three thousand."

"Thank him for the discount. I'll send along some cupcakes with the money."

"This isn't a joke, Max."

Eva noticed the change in Timoney's voice and came over. "What's up? Your little sit-down with Paco didn't come off too well, eh, Captain? I didn't think it would. Will he take a check?" Eva asked as she reached for her pocketbook.

"Eva, no!" Max said.

"Max, this is my money, and I'm making a business decision. I'm your partner, right?"

"Sure. But this mutt will never go away if he smells blood," Max said.

"He needs to save face. Captain Timoney will be good enough to tell this Paco fellow we understand the position he is in, won't you, Captain? I'm sure that will garner some consideration," Eva said, hoping Timoney would agree.

"Yes, Eva, I will."

"Who do I make the check out to, Captain?"

Timoney took off his cover and scratched his head. "Make it out to cash I guess. A check, huh? At least it buys us some time anyway. He wants the money by tomorrow midnight. I'll go over there tonight. This is a good move, Max, Eva, a good move."

Timoney took the check, put it in his shirt pocket, and left.

"Thank you, Captain," Eva said as Timoney walked toward his car.

CHAPTER 13

It was Friday night, the best night yet at Gringo Smyth's. Doctors, nurses, hospital visitors, and locals all came to partake of the wonderful food they'd heard about. Max and Eva were so busy running around all night they forgot to open the special delivery manila envelope from the State of New York. After the last person left and Miguel, the dishwasher and cleanup man, began mopping up, things became eerily quiet. Eva opened the envelope and turned the official-looking paper around to Max. It was the New York State liquor license. It had come through in less than a week. Eva danced her dance.

Miguel was smiling and said, "Eh, I just cleaned this floor!" Everyone laughed.

"The liquor will start to flow when reservations get backed up. Booze is where the money is in this business, Eva. I was thinking of asking Timoney if he could recommend someone to tend bar. Too bad the old Irish bastard already has a job. A cop might scare people away. Then again, it might be a nice touch. I know it would make you feel better," Max said as he picked her up and twirled her around.

Timoney came by Saturday at noon. He did not look happy. He came in the side door. He was not in uniform. He was nattily attired in a sport coat and slacks. Eva greeted him at the door. She commented on his sartorial splendor, but Timoney paid her little mind and shut the door behind him. Max came out from stocking the bar. Judging by the look on Timoney's face, things had not gone well with Paco. "The check didn't work. I should have known. His boys laughed when I handed it to him. He thought it was some kind of joke. I told him I wouldn't be doing this if it was a joke. Anyway, he wants cash, the full three thousand. He said his dentist doesn't take checks but maybe your funeral parlor does."

Max fumed. Timoney knew Max would be hard to control if this went sour. Timoney had thought about cashing the check himself, but that added a complication. He had to keep convincing himself that he didn't have a dog in this fight. "I would have cashed it myself, but the bank manager is the nosiest bastard in the Heights. That's all I need is him thinking I'm on the take. Paco wants cash by midnight tonight at his place or ..."

"Or what?" Max said.

"Or he will come here tonight and get it himself."

"Great!" Max said.

"That moron will scare everyone in Manhattan away from this place. Let me think. Let me think. Where is he now?" Max calmly asked Timoney.

"The Dyckman Street projects, building number three, apartment 3A. Why?"

"I am going to the bank. Eva, please get me five hundred dollars from the safe. And, Captain, I'll take that check. Thanks for your efforts." Timoney slowly handed Max the check, trying to determine Max's next move. Eva stared at Max as she handed him the $500.

"What are you going to do?" Timoney and Eva asked simultaneously.

"Finalize the transaction. Don't worry about me. I'll be fine." He handed Timoney his .45. "See?"

Max smiled and patted Timoney on the shoulder. He kissed Eva. He left on foot for their bank, three blocks north, on the way to Dyckman Street.

Max was calm. It was a pre-combat calm that he cherished. Max needed the walk to piece together a plan. It wasn't the army, where equipment he might need was on his back. Max needed to improvise for his idea of embarrassing yet another bully. He had responsibilities now—not only Eva, but also the restaurant. It was as if he had a wife and a child to care for. His MO had to change. He had been trained to react, not to feel. In the not-so-old days, he'd have gutted this dirtbag and eaten a rare roast beef sandwich afterward. The problem was Timoney. He was a cop. He would have to come after Max, even though Paco was the bane of Timoney's existence. Max was a businessman now. His life's dream was at stake. And… there was Eva, the most important part of everything.

Max had to make this theater. Everyone had to see that Paco was nothing more than a bully, gone over the edge.

Max was surprised when people welcomed him at the bank. That calmed him somewhat.

What a good citizen I must be…wait an hour folks.

Some complimented him on the great food and wished him well. After cashing the $2,500 check and exchanging a ten-dollar bill for a roll of quarters, Max started walking the thirty-two blocks up Broadway toward Dyckman Street. He made a stop at a sporting goods store and bought a cup—not a coffee cup: a hockey player's cup. He immediately slid it into his pants, much to the surprise of the saleslady. The young Dominican girl smiled at Max and asked, "Does it fit?"

Max said with a smile, "It's supposed to be tight."

He made one more stop at a hardware store for some duct tape to wrap around the roll of quarters. The gent in the hardware store also recognized Max and welcomed him to the neighborhood. Max wrapped the roll of quarters in front of the gentleman. Max paid for the tape and left the remainder of the roll on the counter.

"*Gracias, señor,*" Max said.

"*De nada. Vaya con Dios, amigo,*" the owner said, knowing the purpose of the purchase.

The area around Dyckman Street and Broadway had been an Irish neighborhood up until the late 1950s. Then came the Puerto Rican migration, followed by the Dominicans twenty years later. If you thought Puerto Ricans were hot-blooded, Dominicans made them look like Buddhists. Dominicans invented the merengue—the dance, not the pie. Both nationalities were industrious, hardworking people. Their food was as hot as their temperaments. But Paco was a Chicano. Max could not get that anomaly out of his head.

What is a Chicano doing running a gang in New York City?

At the bottom of Snake Hill, where St. Nicholas Avenue joined Dyckman Street, stood the six buildings known as the Dyckman Street Houses or simply "the projects." Max asked a couple of wannabe punks the way to building 3. They hesitated, then pointed to the building in the middle of a quadrangle.

The buildings had no courtyards. They were straight up-and-down rectangles with no fire escapes. They looked more modern than the pre–World War II buildings in northern Washington Heights where it becomes Inwood - the last piece of Manhattan before it became the Bronx. The projects had been built in the late 1940s and 1950s to accommodate veterans but had been absorbed quickly by the wave of immigrants flocking to New York City in search of a better life. There were projects in all five boroughs; perfect *de facto* housing for urban- ghetto proliferation: Multiple buildings, with underground passageways throughout that made things ideal for disappearing… day or night. The Dyckman Street projects were ranked worst of them all by citywide statistics. Sixteen murders had occurred within their perimeter in the last year alone and many of these people knew each other.

Max walked toward building #3. As he got to the steel doors, an elderly Latina woman crying hysterically pushed her way past him. She had an arm around a young girl who was bleeding from her mouth and also down her legs. The girl appeared to either be in a state of shock or possibly drugged. Max was not sure. He asked the *abuela*, "What happened?"

The old woman screamed in Spanish and then broken English when she saw Max was a gringo. "He **RAPED** her! That pig **RAPED** her! She is fourteen years old. She wants to be a nurse. He raped her!"

People hurried by, making an effort not to get involved. Some made the sign of the cross. Others shook their heads and scurried away. It became evident to Max that this was a place frozen with fear.

The little girl looked up at Max and said softly to him, "Do not go in there, *señor. El diablo* lives there." Then she passed out. Max helped them to one of the two-by-four concrete benches. He told the woman to call 911. He gave her his cell phone and started toward the building.

"Señor, polícia? *Nunca! Never*...they don't come here."

The woman looked up at Paco, arms folded on a pillow as he surveyed the Saturday morning goings-on from his third-floor window. He was smiling and paid no attention to the woman and the child. They were old news by now. Besides, he spotted Max and assumed he had come to pay his debt and, therefore, his respects... a good beginning for Paco's Saturday morning.

"Hey, *jefe*, you got my money?" Paco yelled down to Max.

Max was steaming, "I got money. Come and get it."

Max could feel logic fading - restraint was slipping away. The little girl and her grandmother sat on the bench. The girl, semi-conscious now, was shaking uncontrollably in her grandmother's arms.

Max yelled to the onlookers that peered out their windows or dared to care for the little girl and her *abuela*. "Call 911!" Nobody moved.

He realized no one visible to Paco would make the call. He turned his attention back to Paco. Clearly, Max was on his own.

"Is this what you do on a Saturday morning? You rape little girls?" Max said.

"Sometimes. **What the fuck do you care?** She your daughter, *jefe*? She tastes good." Paco said as he licked his fingers to the laughter of his minions. "You got my money, gringo?"

Max took out the money and yelled, "I got the money. But I tell you what, scumbag, here's the deal: You come and get it… right here… right now!" Max flapped the money in his hand. Phony laughter filled the air. Everyone looked up at Paco. Nobody pulled this crap on Paco.

"You a cop, *jefe*? 'Cause if you a cop, you gotta tell me. Dat's da law. I kill you anyway. Only not here, not now. I not stupid."

"I am not a cop. I'm a guy that thinks that any scumbag that rapes a little girl should get beaten to death in public." Max was pissed off but instinctively knew Paco had to feel called out… now and in public.

Paco went inside and returned with an M16 assault rifle. He waved it around for all to see. People moaned and moved back, but nobody left. Some began to come closer to Max, as though magnetized by the brave gringo. Standing up to Paco was historic. Maybe the people felt a need to be close to history. Perhaps this was what they had prayed for at night: What they had asked God to provide. They gave Max confidence. He knew he had to embarrass Paco into not using the rifle.

About thirty people within ten yards of this little get-together. That's a good thing, I think.

"You're not going to shoot me." Max pulled out his shirt and did a three-sixty turn to show the world he was unarmed.

"What? Maybe seventy-five, one hundred people watching? All it takes is one. One that doesn't think you're so tough, Paco. You think that's possible? You think no one here will nail you this time if you shoot me? If not, then pull the trigger. Or how 'bout you and me: *mano a mano,* Pacita? Just like when your father used to beat your mother. Remember that? Let's see how good you are at hitting a man instead of little girls. Did you forget how to fight with your hands, or do you need a gun? You don't have the balls to fight me right here. Look, some nice soft grass here for you to die. You know you gotta fight me. You know why? Because if you don't, these people know you're just another punk with a gun and no balls." Max said, as he walked over to a bench and sat down.

Paco knew Max was right. He could lose his grasp on the people if he didn't accept the challenge. He'd never had to take a stand in front of them before. He could see doubt in the eyes of the people that now dared to look back at him. They awaited his answer. The fact that they didn't scurry away like scared rabbits solidified his decision. Paco knew he had to kill this gringo with his bare hands.

Who the fuck is this guy? Max could see that question in Paco's eyes.

"Start your prayers, gringo!"

I got him!

Paco strutted through the front doors of the project building. He looked about six feet four and close to 275 pounds. Max was six feet two and 215 pounds.

GOOD…I like 'em big and slow.

Max saw Paco's teardrop tats up close. In Folsom, each filled-in teardrop meant one kill for gang inmates. Paco was running out of face-room.

No sweatshirt on at the window. He's hiding a weapon.

Adrenaline was running high in both men. It showed more on Paco.

Max soaked in the rush and converted it to concentration, two polar opposites fusing to help him do what he had to do… kill a man. He wondered for a second whether that process was instinctive or instilled. He'd been told in Ranger School that he was born that way; Uncle Sam just fine-tuned it. It didn't matter. He liked the feeling when justification paved the way.

Max stood up and once again showed everyone he was unarmed. He decided against the roll of quarters. He wanted no asterisk next to this beating. Max did not want the fight tricked-up, at least on his end. Max had Paco where he wanted him - the center of the arena.

The two circled around each other. Paco put up his hands and faked a quick move, then laughed to test Max's nerves. Max never blinked or moved a muscle. Paco was not going to reveal what he had under his hooded sweatshirt unless necessary.

"You come here and call me names in front of my people? Now, I must kill you in front of my people."

"Dream your wildest dream." Max said as he smiled at Paco.

The bullfighter and the bull were about to find out who would leave the *plaza de toros* alive.

Max's eyes followed Paco's every move.

"Understand one thing before you die: These people were NEVER your people. They came to America to work hard and be happy, then they run into a scumbag like the dictators they had back home. Doesn't work here, baby. Not in America. You have NO people here, *señorita*. You have nothing here except a ticket to hell, and I'm going to punch it for you. C'mon, scumbag."

Max was primed to begin.

Paco screamed and came at him.

The bull makes his charge. The matador counters with a veronica.

Paco threw a right hand that grazed Max's temple. While Paco was off balance, Max hit him with a quick left hook that landed on Paco's right cheekbone. Max wanted his beating to last as long as possible.

I must embarrass him. If I cripple him immediately, they could blame it on luck. Can't have that. The people must see that many of them could have done what I am going to do to him.

Paco was faster than Max thought he would be, or had Max gotten a tinge slower? Paco tried to grab Max.

Nice try.

Paco was getting frustrated. Max blocked a kick to the groin by crossing his arms. He half chuckled to himself about purchasing the groin cup on the way uptown.

I should let him kick me in the balls.

Max gave a quick look over to the young girl and her grandmother and almost missed grabbing Paco's leg on a kick. He lifted it up to shoulder height and kicked Paco in the balls.

Wanna buy a used cup, Paco? Only three grand.

The grandmother managed a slight smile. She knew the kick was dedicated to them. Paco doubled up but did not go down. He couldn't afford to go down. Max gave Paco a breather at this point—something he would never do in competition. But, this was a clinic.

Clinics must must have the undivided attention of the students.

After five minutes of Max peppering Paco with his hands, Paco pulled an ASP out of his belt in desperation.

df: ASP- a spring-loaded, telescopic baton. A favorite weapon of muggers. Capable of fracturing a skull with the flick of a wrist. Considered a LETHAL weapon.

Max knew both the usage and avenues of disarmament for an ASP. Max wished it was a knife so he could really show Paco up. Max disarmed him immediately and gave his right arm an audible compound fracture. Everyone winced. It was time. Max smacked Paco with a roundhouse right on the chin that broke both sides of his mandible (jaw bone). Paco went down, unconscious from the shock wave sent to his brain from the blow. Paco fell in a heap, as though all the bones in his body had disintegrated. Max slowly straddled him and kept hitting him as he held Paco's hair with his left hand. Max switched hands as though bored with the less adventurous part of his quest. Paco's face was unrecognizable at this point.

Max was in a trance. He turned Paco's limp body sideways to gain access to his kidneys, spleen, and liver in order to rupture all three. Max had passed through the magic mirror. Paco was past unconscious; he was comatose and would die if not attended to immediately. Most of those present had to look away, some left. Had one monster replaced another?

Max had lost sight of a most important fact: fear can be transferable in both victory and in defeat.

Max's arm was stopped as he was about to come down on Paco's bloodied temple for the coup de grâce. An Israeli Krav Maga kick instinctively popped into Max's mind to take the intruder's feet out from under him. Max hesitated when he saw the familiar black shoes and blue pant leg of the NYPD.

"Enough! You proved your point!" yelled Captain Timoney.

Eva stood behind Timoney with her back to the scene, her hands covering her face. She could not believe what she had witnessed. She had seen Max spar at the gym with some pretty tough professionals, but this? This was a surreal nightmare.

Could this be the man I make love to?

As Max got up and walked away, a patrolman stepped in to guard Paco's body. But nobody went near Paco: not his own gang, not any onlookers, nobody. Paco lay in a pool of his blood where he belonged. The ambulance crew waited until Timoney nodded before tending to Paco. They loaded him onto a gurney as though there was no urgency. The likes of Paco had kept EMS specialists busy for years.

The EMS driver asked his boss, "Saint Elizabeth's or Columbia-Presbyterian?"

The boss casually said, "Whichever is furthest away."

The grandmother said to Captain Timoney, "Paco raped my granddaughter!"

Another yelled, "**He killed my son**!"

Random people ran over and spat on Paco. Then the feeding frenzy started. Police had to circle around Paco's unconscious body to stop people from tearing him apart. Some Latinos ran up to his apartment and threw his things out the window. Others ran after lingering members of the Latin Diplomats and ran them out of the projects. There was no fear of weapons with the cops present, and so, like their hero, they used their fists.

Timoney asked the grandmother if she and her granddaughter were willing to testify in court. Without waiting for her answer, Timoney yelled to the people, "I know you are all pumped up now." He looked around. "We've been down this road before. Are you going to be ready to testify in court when the time comes? It's now, or someone else takes his place!" Timoney pointed to Paco.

Timoney turned to one of his cops. "Garcia, translate - word for word!" Garcia did so.

"**Yes**!" said the grandmother in English.

The granddaughter said, "**Yes**, I will testify."

"Costello! Get those two down to Columbia-Presbyterian and tell them we need a rape-kit workup. Tell Doc Harish we got Paco on this one. "Tell him: "DO NOT SCREW UP THE CHAIN OF CUSTODY WITH THE RAPE-KIT TEST. Got that?" Timoney became more of a commanding officer than a cop. Max ate it up.

"GOT IT, CHIEF!" Costello said, instinctively feeling a salute was necessary. More and more people crowded around Timoney, volunteering to testify. Timoney told a Latino sergeant to have his men take personal information and statements from everyone. "Get more Latino cops here. I want transportation for anyone and everyone that has a hard felony to talk about. Get them down to the Three-Four. Timoney looked down at Paco and said to a sergeant. "Mirandize this prick in English and Spanish...get a verbal capessh out of him... video **both** versions. No street Spanish. No guesswork! Video and clear audio. I want this airtight. Oh... I want a twenty-four-hour guard on his room."

Timoney turned to the crowd. "If you people will testify, I promise you that we will put this guy away for life. He will not be back on the streets of Washington Heights... unless **you** let him back. Let's hope the death penalty gets voted back into this state. Translate, Garcia! Get 'em while they're hot, Marco. **C'mon, move**!"

Timoney felt like a cop again. He liked the feeling.

Timoney told his driver, "I'll take the car."

The driver asked, looking at Max, "What about this guy? You want him for assault?"

"Shut up, you moron, and try to think like a cop for once in your life! Help out with the complaints," Timoney ordered. He turned to Max and asked, "You all right?"

"Is he dead?" Max asked, wiping his face on a towel an Emergency Medical Service attendant threw him. Try as he might, Max never could recall the particulars of a fight once it was over.

"Could be." Timoney said matter-of-factly.

Eva was staring at Max with a hand over her open mouth.

"Eva, are you okay?" Timoney asked.

"I…I don't know. I need to talk to you when we get back to the restaurant. Please?" Eva asked Timoney.

"Sure thing." Timoney said, as he held the rear car door open, gesturing for Max and Eva to get in.

Eva could not hug Max. She didn't say a word as she stared out the window back to Gringo Smyth's.

Max insisted they go through the back door to the restaurant. The staff was already busy getting things prepped for Saturday night's bill-of-fare. If they knew what had happened, they didn't let on.

Max went straight into the bathroom to cleanup. He barked out orders from there.

"Carlos, did the veal shanks come in?"

"Sí, señor Max."

"Well, let's get them prepped and going."

"Already on it, boss."

Max's orders were short and to the point. His hands were swollen and bleeding, his T-shirt soaked with blood. Max went straight into the men's room. He cleaned off a bite mark on his arm with Clorox and a paper towel. Other than some bruised ribs and a welt under his left eye, Max was okay. His hands, however, remained closed. Max filled the sink with ice and added water to make it colder than cold. He buried both hands in the sink and continued with his orders to the staff. Max knew the worst part of the day was not over. The worst part of the day would be talking to Eva.

It seemed a walk in the park, taking down one of the most feared gang leaders in Manhattan since the Five Points days of the Civil War, Timoney thought.

"Scary." Timoney said aloud, not knowing Eva heard him.

"He enjoyed it." Eva said, looking at Max but talking to Timoney. Timoney was thinking the same thing.

Max didn't hoped his morning visit to the projects could get lost somehow....disappear into the ozone layer.

It's over! Let it go.

He avoided eye contact, especially with Eva. He stayed in the kitchen all night, jamming his hands into the ice to stop the swelling and involuntary closing. He made himself busy to avoid the inevitable: **The talk**.

Eva kept busy as well. At least there were no repercussions at the restaurant. Not yet anyway. Eva couldn't help having mini-conversations with herself. She would ask herself a question, then answer it. She stared at the menu readers looking in the window. She didn't engage them as she normally did. She wasn't sure if they were checking out the restaurant or curious to see the owners. In short - she was scared.

Welcome to the Heights.

CHAPTER 14

After the last customers were out the door, Max came out of the kitchen and grabbed a beer from the cooler. He tried to hide the effort it took to bend down and sit. Eva knew he was hurting.

"How 'bout a beer, honey?" Max said, trying to get a feel for his next battle.

"Sure, slugger."

This is not going to be fun. Max surmised.

"So, Paco doesn't take cash or checks?" Eva asked in an effort to begin.

"Eva, Part of me went there with the intention of paying the bastard. But a little girl came out of the building with her grandmother and...."

"I know. I saw them."

"You were there for that?"

"We got there before you did. Timoney and I were across the street. I was scared to death. Timoney had a SWAT team on the roof across the street for God's sake! He was going to shoot Paco if he aimed his rifle at you." Eva said, trembling.

"I screwed up. That would have solved the problem in a heartbeat. Well, as Shakespeare said, 'All's well that ends well.'"

"Timoney doesn't think it's over. He said something about needing a quick arraignment for Paco... this week if possible. He asked me if you still had Mayor Braunreuther's phone number handy."

"Why?"

"We may need to call in a favor. The more time that passes before a trial, the more chance of someone getting to the people willing to testify. The mayor can get this on the court calendar immediately. That's what Timoney said."

They both sat and said nothing. Max played with his beer bottle. Eva watched him.

"Did you enjoy it?" she asked.

"Enjoy what?" Max knew damn well what, but he found himself in a conundrum: the answer to Eva's question was yes, and Max was not a liar. *How do I explain the truth?*

"Did you *enjoy* beating Paco like that?"

"Wait till everyone has gone," Max said to Eva. He kept his mouth shut except to slug on his bottle of beer, his mind working overtime.

When the last *buenas noches* was uttered and only Max and Eva were left, Max put a bottle of beer on the table for Eva. He looked into her beautiful dark eyes and said, "I will never lie to you … ever. What I am going to tell you, I have not told to anyone. I never had anyone I trusted enough to explain my actions and thoughts to, not even a priest. But I am going to tell you… because I love you and you have a right to know if we are going to spend the rest of our lives together.

"YES! Yes, Idid enjoy beating Paco today, and I would've killed him.

"There is a great sense of satisfaction inside me when a bully receives his fare dues. Today was one of those days."

Max struggled to put his feet up on a chair. He rubbed the back of his right hand up and down the cold bottle of beer.

"The first time I ever heard the word *bully*, I was ten years old. My father and I were watching a documentary on President Theodore Roosevelt. Roosevelt would wave his fist and yell 'Bully!'

to the crowd. It meant something good then. Dad was a big fan of Teddy Roosevelt. Me? I was an Abraham Lincoln disciple. We'd have debates about which president served the country better. Everything was a lesson in our house. My mother would shake her head. If she wanted to end one of our debates, she would mention a new recipe, and off I'd run to the kitchen to observe."

Eva knew she was in for a long night but she wasn't letting him off the hook.

"The second time I heard *bully* used was when I was fourteen and a girl in my eighth-grade class had the guts to call out the class bully to his face. His name was Dante, Dante Liguori. For the longest time I couldn't blot him out of my brain, and now I almost forgot his name. It was Dante's third attempt at the eighth grade. He must have been close to seventeen years old.

"Dante was born in Sicily and came here with his parents when he was twelve years old. His parents only spoke Italian at home. Imagine, Honey, four years in America and not having a good handle on the English language." Max paused as though he actually felt sorry for Dante at some point in the past.

"Sorry. It's been a while since I conjured up this crap. Anyway, Dante dealt with his inadequacies and embarrassments by bullying everyone at St. Mary's Elementary School. The fact that he shaved every morning and was fully grown into his six-foot frame made him even more menacing to the kids and probably added to his embarrassment. The mandatory choir practices were especially tough for him, standing taller than everyone... And I don't think being named Dante helped much either. I actually felt sorry for him until...."

Max was clearly uncomfortable as he began the second part of his story.

"My best friend was not another wrestling pal or football jock. No, Tommy Hennelly was a little guy, but what a mind. I could listen to him for hours. He was brilliant, an incessant reader. He preferred the fantasies that books provided over the dread of his daily life. He read books for excitement and used the internet to research. Tommy was the kid in class that knew the answers to every question before the teacher asked them. But Tommy never raised his hand to answer any questions. He stuttered. His stuttering was so bad that even the Christian Brothers knew not to call on him. They graded him solely on his written work and perfect test results. The fact that Dante sat directly behind Hennelly in homeroom was a disaster of mammoth proportions for Hennelly. Hennelly prayed for graduation day to come so he could move on to high school. Hennelly's big nightmare: Dante Liguori would finally graduate and sit behind him through four years of high school. Tommy was a very funny guy. It was odd that he seldom stuttered when he and I were together. That made me feel good." Eva ran her fingers across his bruised knuckles.

That's a good sign.

"This sounds like a two-beer story." Eva grabbed two more beers and opened them behind the bar. She took a deep breath and went back to the table.

"I was the second biggest kid at St. Mary's. There were thirty-eight kids in my class about half were girls. I had been wrestling since the third grade. I was good at it too. My dad would show me holds and moves he learned from his wrestling days at Pitt. Working on the farm made me strong. Maybe that was the reason Dante never messed with me. I don't know. Maybe I was the nearest thing to a real threat for Dante, the bully. I knew our time would come. The closest we came to blows was at recess one day in the school cafeteria at the beginning of our…my last year. I had grown some that summer. I'd been lifting weights to prepare for the high school wrestling tryouts. At the end of the prior school year, we'd been assigned a project about our pets at home. Each student had to bring in an experiment and show their results after the summer. Tommy's experiment had to do with raising a baby hamster on a special diet of greens. He had the cute little fellow in a shoebox, and kids had gathered around to see it. I will always remember the smile on Tommy's face as he enjoyed the positive attention. Dante leaned in and smacked the bottom of the box, sending the hamster flying upward out into the air. If it had fallen onto the marble floor of the auditorium, it would have meant the end for Mr. Hamster. I reached in and snatched it as it came down."

"You didn't squish him, did you?" Eva asked.

"No. But here's the part you'll like: Mary Duggan kissed me."

"The plot thickens." Eva quipped.

"Dante had a crush on Mary Duggan… just what I needed. Mary, of course, wanted nothing to do with Dante. The applause and cheers faded when everyone saw Dante's reaction. Dante and I stared at each other, knowing the time had come for a visit to the park.

"When Brother Gregory came by to see what was causing the commotion. I knew that any altercation on school property meant automatic expulsion. I got lost in the crowd. Naturally, this meant more to me than it did to Dante, so I made myself scarce. The crowd dissipated. There was an ongoing buzz about whether this would get settled in the park later that day.

"It never happened. It would have been up to Dante to make the challenge. He didn't. I looked at this as a sign of weakness in the mighty Dante and filed it away." Max took a long slug on his beer.

"What did occur after the hamster incident was a concerted effort on Dante's part to harass Tommy Hennelly more than usual. Tommy didn't tell me about the increase in pressure. I was not in all of Tommy's classes that Dante was, so I was not privy to much of the bullying firsthand. The harassment didn't occur when I was around. Then, things changed. It was wrestling season, and I was going to school early and getting home late most school days. I noticed Tommy withdrawing from some of his favorite activities, in and out of school. Then, he started missing classes. He was losing weight. He became quiet, even with me. Our rides together on the school bus became infrequent, then nonexistent. I would call him on the phone and ask him if he was too sick to come to school or if it was something else. He wouldn't say, and his parents had no clue. Jesus, I should have pressed the point. I should've made him tell me what was wrong. I still think about it often. Maybe Tommy didn't want to see me get hurt by Dante."

Max looked up at Eva. He hoped she had heard enough, but her eyes told him to go on.

"It was February 12. I remember 'cause it was Lincoln's birthday and we were off from school. The wind was howling well into the night. Huh, some nights all I hear is that wind. The sound, the intensity, exactly the same as that night. It is still so clear to me.

"Those were the dog days in western Pennsylvania, but graduation was only ninety-eight days away. Hennelly and the rest of us could get through less than a hundred days."

Max put his head in his hands and looked at the floor. He did not want Eva to see the unwelcome tears forming in his eyes.

"Next morning, my dad told me that Tommy Hennelly had committed suicide the previous night. Tommy had placed his father's twelve-gauge double-barrel shotgun in his mouth and somehow was able to pull both triggers simultaneously. I screamed. My father held me so I couldn't run away. My tears stopped hours later in bed, as an odd feeling came over me… a peaceful feeling. Then, the epiphany, no equivocation, total clarity: Dante killed my friend and I'd be justified in killing Dante. I had no idea at that time, but I had stumbled upon my own interpretation of the Soldier's Creed. Maybe it was genetic, a family thing. I didn't know. I didn't care. But it's a tenet that has stayed with me. I don't seem to have control over it. I rarely remember details, but I never regret my actions. So there must be something right buried in it."

Eva was in a place she had never been before. She was in love with a man who had no boundaries: A man who could kill, and justify his actions.

What the hell am I hearing?

Max could see Eva's anxiety building. He held her hand. "Bear with me, Eva."

"Believe me, I'm not going anywhere." Eva was trying to hide the quixotic thoughts racing through her mind.

Max held her trembling hands and continued: "I remained calm. I showed no emotion at the closed-coffin wake… or the funeral mass. All the parents and students from St. Mary's attended, including the Liguori family.

"I sat in the church pew and tried to put myself inside Tommy's head that night.

Why would he rather die than go to school another day? Was it that bad? Apparently so. How did I not see that?

"I made another decision that day: I would sit at Tommy Hennelly's desk for homeroom every day. I didn't ask permission; I simply moved in. Nobody questioned the move or my motive. It didn't go unnoticed, especially by Dante.

"It took about two weeks after Hennelly's internment for Dante to revert back to his old ways. Not even causing the death of another human being could change his ways. That was the deciding factor for me. All I could do… was wait."

"It was between a teacher change when Dante chose his next victim: a chubby, happy-go-lucky kid named Sawyer, that never bothered a soul. We were in the classroom, waiting for the teacher to show up, and Dante demanded a candy bar that was sticking out of the kid's lunch bag. I don't think I said anything. I don't remember. I never seem to remember. I stood up slowly and grabbed a fistful of Dante's hair. I pulled him out of his desk seat and into the aisle. I held his head at belt level, rendering him immobile and facing hell… where I planned to send him. He whined and squealed like a suckling pig. I kneed him in the face as I pushed his head downward to add damage. Again and again. Again and again. Dante's nose slammed flat against a broken left cheekbone. The sound of bone and cartilage smashing, changing shape, relocating, meant nothing to me."

A small price to pay.

"Blood was everywhere, all over the blackboard in the rear of the classroom, the green walls, the tan shades. Nobody stepped back to avoid the splattering blood. It was as though they welcomed this bloody baptism. They were all in. We had five minutes between periods that meant one and a half minutes left. Ninety seconds is a long time when your face is being rearranged. No one pulled me away. To the contrary, all the kids, boys and girls, felt vicarious pleasure with each kick.

"I felt they were probably thinking… *Lucky Max, he must feel this on a much grander scale. Good ole Max!* AND how right they were.

"I kept it up until the upper-body weight of Dante's torso was too much for either arm to hold. I let him slump to the floor in his blood. I sat down; we all sat down, and awaited my fate." When the bell rang and Mr. Wesley, the music teacher, entered the room, he didn't notice Dante Liguori lying in the back of the middle aisle until Dante's name went unanswered for roll call. The students instinctively sat at their desks at the bell and buried themselves in the first available book they could pull out. My mind was blank. I stared ahead… I had no regrets. I thought Dante was dead. It didn't matter if he was. If he was dead, all well and good. If he wasn't, I hoped he understood the reason for the beating. When Mr. Wesley took off his reading glasses and asked, 'What happened here?' the chubby kid, Sawyer, who was in danger of losing his candy bar, broke the silence.

'He fell!'

"Others chimed in." 'Yes, he fell!'

"Even the most timid chimed in. 'We think he was drinking because …'

"He smelled funny, and he fell down."

"Off his desk."

"He was trying to grab the crucifix from the wall."

"He was cursing at Jesus!"

"That's right! We all heard it."

"He said things about Jesus being gay!"

"They all came to my rescue. Whoever threw in the 'Jesus is gay' thing realized the attention that a Christian Brothers' grammar school would give to this matter. After the ambulance came and took Dante Liguori away, Mr. Wesley said, rather matter-of-factly, to the principal, Brother Gregory… 'He fell.'"

"I'll never forget Brother Gregory saying, 'Pity! Class dismissed for the day.' I thought I saw a smile on his lips.'"

"According to Pennsylvania law, sixteen is the legal age to quit school. And so, Dante disappeared. And me? I was chosen class valedictorian. I dedicated my speech to my best friend: Tommy Hennelly. My speech was entitled: The Bravest Person I Have Ever Known. That…was how my last year in grammar school went."

Max looked up at Eva. "You asked me if I enjoyed what I did today. My answer is… YES, to see a smile on that little girl's face. She was Tommy Hennelly today."

"That's it! That's all I have to say about it. That's all I know about it."

Max looked into her eyes for a hint of understanding. He saw none.

"Are you still my girl?" he asked.

"You're goddamn right I am!" Eva said with a smile.

"You're a great broad, Eva," Max said and kissed her.

"I love you, Maxwell Burns."

"I love you too, Eva Carra."

CHAPTER 15

Timoney stopped in for brunch late Sunday morning. He was alone.

"Where's Maria Elena today, Captain?" Eva asked.

"I'm on my own. I need to see Max, but I'll have some of those eggs Benedict, if you please. I'll see him on his break." Timoney seemed abrupt.

"I'll tell him you're here. Relax. Let me get you a Bloody Mary or a mimosa," Eva said as she finished writing the order.

"Eva, I don't drink alcohol," Timoney said as he placed his napkin on his lap.

"Oh. Sorry."

"No need to be sorry. I drank my quota a long time ago. I rather enjoy a clear head at all times. A cop is a cop 24-7… especially in the Heights. I'll have a club soda with a wedge of lime, and please, call me John when I'm out of uniform. It helps me to relax. Besides, you two are friends as well as, dare I say, clients?"

Timoney finished his meal and read the *New York Times* until things slowed down. He made sure the remaining clientele were not locals. Eva and Max joined him at his table.

"How was brunch, Captain? I mean John," Eva said. She instructed Max, "When Captain Timoney is out of uniform, call him John."

"I'd appreciate that. In uniform, Captain Timoney, please. I don't want anyone to think I am being biased toward you two. Keeps things aboveboard. Capeesh?"

"10-4, John. Isn't that a Bible passage: John 10:4?" Max's attempted joke garnered a blank look.

"Listen to me," Timoney said, leaning over. "The remaining Latin Diplomats are on the move out of the Heights. As a matter of fact, my sources tell me, they were happy to be rid of Paco. It seems he wasn't very nice to them either. But Little Louie is out and about trying to conjure up some respect. He's not having much success. That's good and bad."

"How is it bad?" Eva asked.

"Well, the little bastard has lost his rabbi. I am afraid he might try something out of the box to get attention."

"He's Jewish?" Eva said.

"I'll explain later," Max said.

"Try what?" Max asked Timoney.

"I'm not sure. I know he's a sneak and looking to make his own rep. The only way he will be able to do that is if he pulls off something big. Remember, he's a foot too short, scared, and a moron. All of the above spell trouble. I need to keep my witnesses on ice. That's a big concern. You two need to keep things... business as usual. The Latino community needs to see that the *americanos* are not afraid. That's important! These people come here from wherever, and nobody gives a damn if they live or die, only that they vote. That hasn't changed in a hundred fifty years. But, if they see you two give a damn about being here in the Heights and will not be pushed around, that will inspire them. It will let them know there is a real America underneath all the bullshit, even in the *barrio*! You said it yourself: change a *barrio* into a *vecin:* a ghetto into a neighborhood. It may sound corny, but you two are what these people hoped Americans would be like—not taking crap from anybody and giving a damn about the little people," Timoney said, with a hint of Irish immigrant pride shining through.

"Maybe you should run for president yourself, John." Eva said.

"I can't... I wasn't born here. You of all people should know the rules!"

Touché! Eva thought.

"I love this country. It needs a good kick in the ass once in a while, but she's mine all the same. Anyway, keep your eyes open and keep me posted on **anything** out of the ordinary. You keep that .45 close. You should teach Eva to shoot." Timoney said.

"My drill sergeant told me, 'Never teach your woman to shoot a gun or play golf. It will be your downfall,' " Max said. "Don't worry, John. I won't let her out of my sight," Max said, giving Eva a hug.

"Since she is a co-owner, I can get her a pistol permit as well."

"Bring Maria Elena next time," Max said.

Timoney was putting on his coat and said, "Not when there's business."

Max and Eva both thought his last comment odd. Timoney didn't think it necessary at this point to tell them Maria Elena was Paco and Louie's mother or that she was nowhere to be found.

"By the way, John, do you know a good bartender who is looking for work?" Eva asked.

"I'm Irish! Everyone I know is a bartender. Let me check with my brother, Kieran. He still enjoys a patient pint now and again. Maybe some of the retired lads are looking for a job behind the stick. It might be a good idea to have a former cop behind the bar. Let me work on it."

CHAPTER 16

Tuesday morning rolled around a bit too soon for the two owners of Gringo Smyth's. Having only one night off a week was a physically and mentally difficult part of the restaurant business. Max and Eva were light-years away from being able to hire a manager. They both knew they would need to do that eventually if they planned to have any life outside of Gringo Smyth's.

Max was doing some ordering. Eva was on the computer. There was a knock on the office door of the restaurant. Max slid back the peephole. There was a well-dressed, good-looking Latino gent standing outside in a suit and tie. Max thought he was a salesman who dared to venture up into the Heights. If that was the case, he deserved an audience.

"Mr. Burns? Detective Kieran Timoney sent me. My name is Antonio Pasqua Yeltzakov, NYPD detective, first grade, retired. And now, bartender to the stars," the good-looking fellow said with aplomb.

Max let him in. He looked too young to be retired.

"My friends call me Tony Easter. I know, I know. I look too young to be retired. I am out on three-quarters disability. Took one in the throat in the South Bronx, workin' the Four-Four." He pointed to a small, round hole next to his Adam's apple, then turned to show them the exit scar, three times the size. "That's why my voice is raspy. Chicks seem to like it. I speak English, Spanish, and Russian."

"Russian?" Max and Eva said simultaneously.

"My father was a Russian army officer who decided to stay in Cuba rather than freeze his ass off in Minsk. My mother was Cuban. They were great dancers. Can I see the bar?"

"Sure." Max said as they proceeded into the main dining room.

Easter inspected meticulously as he moved behind the bar. "Needs some work. I'll get it set up properly. Good… partition between the bar and the dining area. When do you want me to start?"

Max looked at Eva. She winked in approval. "How 'bout tonight?" Max said.

"Time?" Easter asked.

"Well, we open for dinner at six," Eva said, smiling.

"Fine. I'll be here at four to set up. I get fifty dollars a shift. Five nights is fine, but I'm outa here by midnight. Okay with you two?"

"Well, we need someone six nights," Eva said.

"Six shifts makes for a grouchy bartender."

"You're right," Eva said. "We are slow enough on Sundays, and Mondays we're closed. Five shifts it is."

"Later," Easter said. He kissed Eva's hand, then shook Max's. He then made an about-face and out the door he went.

Max and Eva had a satisfactory laugh. They felt they had added another faithful asset into their ranks.

Eva said, "This is getting crazier and crazier."

"I have a feeling we are in for a Nantucket sleigh ride, my dear."

"What in God's name is a Nantucket sleigh ride?" Eva asked, holding his arm.

"You ever see prints of whalers in their skiffs being pulled through the sea by harpooned whales?"

"I think so," Eva said.

"That, my dear, is a Nantucket sleigh ride. Those whalers never knew what their fate was to be!" Max said as they watched Tony Easter saunter down the block like a rock star.

CHAPTER 17

The surviving victims, witnesses, and other plaintiffs for the State of New York, Southern District, case against, Francisco "Paco" Caamano, were growing in number. Timoney was surprised and encouraged, "the more the merrier." Timoney was lucky if he had one witness in past tries at Paco. If this time, some started falling by the wayside, as in prior attempts, Paco would still get convicted. Timoney had been to that movie before, but this time the numbers were growing, not shrinking. The community had seen how Max stood up to Paco. Nobody had ever dared do that; not for Latinos, and no *gringo*! It was the talk of the *vecin.* People were now proud to be associated with the case. "If the gringos care, we must care."

The district attorney convinced the judge to keep Paco in jail until the trial. A timely arraignment was accomplished without the help of the mayor. Max did not have to call in a favor. Timoney was happy about that. Timoney knew there was a price for everything in New York City. It was good to have the mayor owe you a favor. The newspapers and TV reporters were slow to cover Paco's arrest. Timoney said, "Too many false starts. Neither the fight, nor the name of the restaurant was mentioned in the papers. Max thought that odd, but cherished the restaurant being under the radar for this type of bad-press. The Latino community understood Max's wish for anonymity. Carlos put the word out: do not mention Gringo

Smyth's. Like it or not, Max and Eva were now an integral part of the Latino community.

Paco faced six murder charges, twenty-three attempted murder charges, five rape charges, forty-one extortion charges, twenty-six assault charges, and twenty-one grand larceny charges. When Paco's apartment was searched, the police found over a kilo of cocaine and fifty-six pounds of marijuana. If only a few of the charges stuck, Paco was going away for a very long time.

Little Louie was running around trying to find someone that was still afraid of him. Carlos told Max one of the *mamasitas* had hit Louie over the head with her umbrella last week and chased him out of her store. Louie wasn't staying at Paco's apartment. Nobody knew where he was living. Nobody cared. He wasn't in the Heights; that was all that mattered. There was a sighting of Little Louie driving by the restaurant in his tricked-out Hyundai. Louie had become a joke… Timoney and Tony Easter weren't laughing.

CHAPTER 18

Assistant District Attorney Angelo Morano was the prosecutor assigned to the case for the Department of Justice, Southern District, State of New York. His parents were Cuban exiles, and he was a good friend of Tony Easter. They were from the same neighborhood, both members of the Purdy Street Boys: A gang from the Parkchester section of the Bronx. "That was back in the days when gangs were put together for survival not crime," Easter had told Max, educating him on the difference, one night after a few beers at the bar.

Morano had been a cop for exactly twenty years, putting in his papers on the exact day marking his twentieth year of service with the NYPD. He'd made it to sergeant and could have gone right up the line with the department, but he refused to kiss ass. He didn't have to. During his last seven years on the job, he went to St. John's University School of Law at night. After passing the bar, he made his way up through the ranks of the Bronx DA's office. "Morano knew the streets," Easter explained. Right before retiring, Manhattan DA Robert Morgenstern had Morano transferred to the Manhattan DA's office. There were no Ivy Leaguers on Morgenstern's assistant DA crew. He recognized the city needed homegrown talent. "Get me lawyers that grew up on the streets of New York City, and I'll get you convictions! I told five different mayors that same thing," Morgenstern reiterated at his retirement dinner. He was looking right at Anthony Morano when he said it.

Morano knew the streets all right, and he knew who the scumbags were. More important, cops liked him. That was key. He was one of their own. But Morano would need all the shrewdness he could muster on this case, because Paco had lawyered up big time. Sixty-eight-year-old Lazlo Weinstein, five-foot-four lawyer to the mob, appeared at the arraignment like a bad penny, ponytail and all.

Morano was not afraid of Weinstein. Win or lose, Morano always learned something from their scraps in court. But Morano and Timoney were perplexed. They'd expected a storefront *abogado.* Who was paying the freight for this two-grand-an-hour attorney for a mutt like Paco? Weinstein was way out of Paco's league. Something was up: Paco had a rabbi.

The arraignment was completed with no hassles four days after the arrest. The trial was set for six weeks out on June1, at 10:00 a.m. There would be no bail available for Francisco "Paco" Caamano. He was considered a flight risk.

Weinstein shot a wry smile over at Morano. He knew this case had been pushed forward on the court calendar. No bail was a foregone conclusion. Weinstein did not say a word. Win or lose, the press would put his name on page 3 of the New York newspapers. That was all Weinstein seemed to care about these days. But if he did get Paco off, his career would hit an all-time high, resulting in an all-time low, for the city of New York. Morano had seen Weinstein's complacent attitude many times. Most observers of his technique never knew whether he did or didn't give a damn. He was that big, and whoever hired him dared not cross him for fear of needing his services in the future. Morano, however, would not be lulled to sleep by Weinstein's complacency. That being said, Morano was clearly uneasy at Weinstein even being on this case. His very presence meant there were unknown variables, something no lawyer relished.

CHAPTER 19

The winter wind and snow ceased whirling through the caverns of the Manhattan skyscrapers. April's rain had run its course. People in New York City looked straight ahead as they walked. It was "face season," Tony Easter called it—no more looking down at your shoes while heading for the subway stations.

The hospital staff directed visitors to the nice place across the street for food and drink, and things edged forward in a positive direction for Gringo Smyth's. An occasional reporter would stop by. They couldn't get much out of anyone. Besides, who would relinquish entry to a good restaurant just to get a story?

Maria Elena was on Eva's mind whenever she saw Captain Timoney. Eva was usually good at steering clear of other people's lives. However, she was aching to just mention Maria Elena's name. Eva liked her and could use a friend outside of the restaurant staff. Timoney, in his inimitable way, made it evident to Eva that Maria Elena's whereabouts were Maria Elena's business.

Timoney would drop by a few times a week to keep Max up to date on things. Finally, when the captain was leaving the restaurant one afternoon, Eva blurted out, "Say hello to Maria Elena for us!" Max shot her a look.

Timoney turned around slowly as he put on his coat. "You won't see her for a while. She went back home to Mexico for a visit." He buttoned his jacket and left. That was that. Timoney hoped the topic of Paco and Louie's mother would never have to come up again.

Max looked at Eva and said, "Say hello for us?"

Timoney checked in with witnesses on a rotating basis by phone or in person as he perused the neighborhood. He requested Kieran's detective squad be assigned to the case, and the request was granted immediately. John Timoney was thrilled to have his brother, the only person he trusted implicitly, involved in the biggest case of his life. None of the bigwigs, especially Commissioner Radcliff, wanted to take the fall if the case went south again.

"Give him whatever he wants on this one. Let the Irishman live or die with it," Radcliff told his chief of detectives.

First-grade detective Kieran Timoney was based out of the Manhattan North Precinct located on Fifty-Sixth Street between Ninth and Tenth Avenues, close to the northern border of the western Manhattan neighborhood known as Hell's Kitchen.

Hell's Kitchen had quieted down over the years, in large part thanks to Kieran Timoney's squad of detectives and plainclothes street-crime units, known as the Kitchen Sink Squad. There was a need for decent apartments for performing artists based in Manhattan. If the theaters and concert halls were to be graced with the best talent in the world, that talent would need places to live. Most of the Westies, the gang that controlled the Kitchen, were now dead, doing time, or so deep into booze and smack they didn't know where they lived anymore. The Kitchen was now back in the hands of the police, much to the appreciation of the Disney corporation and Broadway theater operators in general. "A Clean House for the Mouse," read the sign in the bathroom of the Manhattan North Precinct, referencing Walt Disney's Mickey Mouse.

Kieran's job was more public relations and reassurance than investigation. Kieran had his brother's back, and so did Kieran's squad of detectives. Everyone on the job knew the brothers were rising stars. Cops instinctively knew whom they should hitch their wagons to.

Everything was moving along nicely. Everyone was talking. It had become the thing to do. The witness list was actually growing, and many written statements had been taken. Latino pride had resurfaced in all five boroughs. Some witnesses were military, currently deployed to Iraq and Afghanistan. Thanks to some help from Ed Curlander, that would not present a problem. But most were local. There were some gang members in holding pens on Rikers Island who were anxious to make plea bargains in exchange for their testimony. The DA's office expected Weinstein to eat them alive, and, as such, they would only be called as a last resort.

It boiled down to this: thirty-seven witnesses were solid, sixty-four more were questionable, and six had to be subpoenaed. The charges were still growing. Max was amazed at how this pile of garbage from LA had such control here in New York City. That piece of the puzzle was still missing. Latino residents in Washington Heights had their own little *revolución* going on. "It's all good," Carlos said over a beer with Max.

CHAPTER 20

Max and Eva were home in their apartment on a Monday night off. They spent most Mondays watching some TV or reading. A big night out was a movie. The doorbell rang. Max and Eva looked at each other rather than at the door. Max walked to the door and looked through the peephole. It was Mr. Woods, the superintendent for their apartment building. Max opened the door and invited Woods in. He was a big black man who had done service in Vietnam, according to the faded tattoo on his right arm: *Ia Drang Valley: Nov. 11–14, 1965; 7th Air Cavalry—**Garryowen Forever***.

When Max and Eva first took the apartment, he'd had no place to stow his gear. Woods had offered to let Max use a storage room in the basement. The building was a pre-WWII type that took up one-quarter of a square city block. It had many nooks and crannies within its basement walls. Woods seemed a little embarrassed about why he was calling on Max and Eva. "Mr. Burns, there is an awful smell coming out of the storage room where your gear is stowed. I think maybe an animal got in there and died or sumpthin'. Would you check it out please? These building inspectors are a pain in my ass."

Max said, "I'll go down there right now. I'm very sorry. I don't know what it could be. Let me get my flashlight and go down with you."

"Well, Mr. Burns, I'll ride down in the elevator with ya, but I'm watching Oprah with my wife. God forbid I should miss Oprah with my wife. If you'd just check it out for me, I'd appreciate it."

"Sure thing, Mr. Woods." Max reached in his pocket and gave Woods a fifty-dollar bill.

"Thank you, Mr. Burns. I knew you'd understand. You can use that room as long as you like. Feel free to put your own lock on the door—after that smell is taken care of."

The quick acceptance of the fifty bucks told Max he was now renting a storeroom. Max would be unofficially charged for the room, an agreement that would buy him complete privacy.

"I'll be back in a few minutes, honey," Max said as he and Woods headed to the elevator.

When they reached the basement, Max and Woods went in separate directions.

"Good night now, Mr. Burns."

"Good night, Mr. Woods. I'll get things taken care of down here."

Max could smell the pungent odor immediately as he turned the corner. *What the hell can that be*?

Max opened the door. He had to cover his nose and mouth with his sleeve. After kicking a few of his things around on the floor, he looked under his assault pack. There were three half-rotten dead rats in it and four others within a few feet. Max found a shovel by an old coal bin. He shoveled them up and brought them around to the incinerator furnace that had been converted for boiler use. Max opened the furnace door and threw the rat carcasses in. He went back to the storeroom and found some vintage aftershave in another rucksack. He sprinkled it liberally around the room. It seemed to work. At least it was better than when he'd walked in.

What the hell killed these bastards? New York City rats eat rat poison for dessert, Max thought as he picked up his army assault pack and shined the flashlight in. He had to rub his eyes to make sure he was not seeing things. Some tiny, half-eaten Korengal mushroom spores had grown out of the remnant dirt left in the bag.

Last supper for those rats.

Max shook his head after a few moments.

Wow! This sure takes me back to the Korengal. I wonder how Ghazi Haider is doing.

Max let his mind drift to that day in the Korengal when he met Ghazi Haider.

CHAPTER 21

A day off in hell... Max thought as he stretched out on his bunk. Today would be a good day to find the mushrooms he had spotted days earlier in the Korengal Valley. He didn't have to be back at base camp to start dinner until 1600 hours. It was summer: fighting season.

Be careful.

It was humid and damp underneath the green canopy below the tree line, an ideal place for mushrooms.

The Korengal mountains were a few klics north of the main forward operating base (FOB) perimeter and were unsecured by American forces. The mountains and valleys of the Korengal were considered no-man's-land. The terrain was too mountainous to be defined by a linear DMZ. There were no straight lines in this war.

The mushrooms Max had spotted were unlike any he had ever seen before. They were worth the risk. He had marked the spot on his GPS. He wasn't supposed to be out here on his own. The fact that he was a great chef gave him some room to maneuver with regard to indigenous foods and market runs, but this was a stretch. Max knew the Taliban were big on kidnapping.

They're gonna need a shitload of 'em.

Max would never be taken alive.

This part of the Korengal was on the far side of the Pech River in an idyllic forest, so out of place in this godforsaken land. Max's GPS took him to the exact point he had referenced.

There they stood, having grown larger and more plentiful in a matter of a few days. The mushroom coloration was a mixture of green, then brown, with the umbra caps of the mushrooms changing to a gold color. Upon further inspection each had a perfectly round black spot at the top - middle crown, an eye staring back at anyone who dared pluck a mushroom from its home. The stems were green and juicy to the touch. Max cut the first one and brought it to his nose. Max's olfactory acuteness was vital to creating *chef d'oeuvre.* He thought this mushroom to be very similar in smell to freshly cut white truffle.

Wouldn't that be something! Max thought.

He admired their beauty as a gardener would a flower.

Odd that nobody harvests these fungi. Perhaps the war has placed gourmet cooking on a back burner in the Korengal.

Max was traveling light in order to move fast and carry back as much fungi as possible. His weapon—a Kimber 191, A1- .45-caliber semiautomatic pistol, with fourteen rounds hot and three additional clips, was holstered on his right side. He used his ranger-issue knife to neatly cut the stalks as low to the ground as possible. His phone was his only means of communication with base camp. His assistant, Corporal Caroleena, was at the ready back at camp. Caroleena had begged him not to go on this trek, but to no avail.

A particularly large mushroom caught his full attention. As Max bent over to harvest it, he was taken completely by surprise when a tall Afghan stepped quietly out from behind a tree and stood over Max. The man was dressed in a white *Khet partag* outer robe and a *Karakul* hat - garments worn by tribal leaders or men of importance. It was not easy to sneak up on Max, or so Max thought. This fellow had appeared without alerting any of Max's senses: sight, sound, or scent. Max knew he was vulnerable and stood up cautiously.

The man greeted Max in Dari with the Muslim salutation: "May Allah smile upon your endeavors." Max started to move his right hand toward his sidearm. He stopped when he realized the man was unarmed, save a decorative *Janbiya,* a curved dagger sheathed in his waistband. The Afghan seemed to be alone. He placed his right hand on his heart and showed his left palm in a biblical-like gesture to express that he harbored no ill will. Max folded his knife and put it in his pocket to reciprocate. Max answered in Dari. This impressed the mullah who thought:

He has been in-country for a lengthy period of time and has taken pains to learn the language of the people.

The mullah introduced himself as Ghazi Haider, a *Tajik* tribal leader from this region. Max knew that local allegiances fluctuated daily in the Korengal. Ghazi Haider knew Max would be aware of this. *He seems astute.* Ghazi thought.

"Would you rather I speak in English?" Ghazi asked in perfect English.

English! *This is an educated man. A leader. A leader of what?* Max thought.

"As you wish," Max said in Dari, hoping Ghazi would choose English, since the mullah's English was better than Max's Dari. Max wanted the conversation to be perfectly clear to both parties.

Ghazi Haider would be a religious man as a tribal leader. In the Korengal that usually meant Taliban. Devotion to the Taliban cause was never as steadfast as devotion to the Muslim faith itself. The Taliban were a homegrown nuisance.

"Do you care to walk?"

"Depends where we walk," Max said.

"Then you choose the way."

Max began walking back toward the direction of camp.

Ghazi asked, "What are you doing here?"

"I'm picking mushrooms."

"I see that. You are very far from your home?"

"Ah, yes. Well, me? I am a chef. That's why I am here." Max stumbled through his answer.

"So, You are a chef! And you will use these mushrooms to feed the soldiers of your country… who are now in my country?"

"Yes, after I do some experimenting. I look for exotic foods wherever I go and...."

"I see. Research is a good thing. Judging by the philosophy of your government, you have been to many exotic places, yes?"

"It is true. I have been sent many places by my government. And you? Have you been to many places?"

"No need. These mountains and valleys are my home... Afghanistan is my country. I have not yet seen all of it. Maybe someday, Allah willing, when Afghanistan is free. Perhaps I will be able to walk wherever I wish. I dare not leave now. Once again there are intruders."

"Americans?" Max said, trying to cut to the chase. Max felt no danger and did not feel the mullah had ulterior motives, other than perhaps hearing Max's point of view.

"Americans, yes. It seems your turn to be here. Although your motives are vague to me. There are misguided people on both sides of that river. Time will bear this out. We have a saying here in Afghanistan: **'You have the watches... we have the time.'"**

Max conversed as freely as he could while avoiding delicate information. Surprisingly, none was sought. The conversation was philosophical and existential, historical and contemporary, spiritual while circumventing a name for God. It was the best day Max had spent in-country. Max welcomed the opportunity to think about something other than the ingredients for his next batch of soup. This man—this teacher—was simple in his logic yet aware of the complexities of his life in the Korengal.

If there is ever peace in Afghanistan Ghazi Haider would be a great leader of his people.

The conversation was invigorating and enlightening for both men as the hours flew by. The mullah was very interested in the United States and its people. He asked about the farm Max grew up on and spoke of the harsh inadequacies in his country's soil. They spoke easily about anything and everything that came to mind. Max asked about Afghan food and recipes. The mullah laughed at this.

Ghazi said, "If there is food, it goes into a kettle. The kettle goes on the fire. A wife calls me when it is time to eat." There were times they laughed heartily, a good sign.

At one point, the two men rested on a rock that jutted out over the beautiful Korengal Valley below. Max noticed a medallion around Ghazi's neck. It looked to be a peregrine falcon sitting on a rock in the middle of a semicircle. Max thought it might be some sort of tribal or family crest. It was very old and worn thin.

This man is no poppy farmer.

It was a wonderful day. Max hoped his newfound friend felt the same way. Each had absorbed much about the other's way of life. The sun began to pass behind a mountain peak. Max peeked at his watch. It was 1520 hours. Max needed to be back in camp by 1600 hours to prep for dinner, or questions might be asked. It was time to start moving toward base. He told Ghazi that he would like to cook for him one day.

"I would like that very much. But I doubt whether your generals would approve of me eating in your, how do you say… mess hall?" Both laughed.

Max said, "I will cook in your home if you would permit it."

"Then you would be insulting my wives," Ghazi said as he started to walk away. He came back and shook Max's hand. Max could feel sincerity coming through the calloused hand of this newfound friend. Ghazi walked away again but took only a few steps before turning around. He walked contemplatively back toward Max once again. A stern look had come to his face.

Ghazi held out his hands and simply said, "Your bag." Max slowly handed him his assault pack with the mushrooms inside. Max instinctively became guarded at the tone of this request. Max had been trained to know when a balance of power shifted.

Ghazi said, "You would feed these mushrooms to your countrymen and your generals?"

"Yes! Why?"

"And to yourself as well?" Ghazi asked.

"I must try them first."

Max was guarded but calm. He did not feel a sense of urgency, but he recognized the change in Ghazi's demeanor. He did not want to cast mistrust onto the day, but he was guarded. Ghazi looked at Max for a few seconds longer, as though contemplating a decision. Then he dumped the mushrooms over the side of the mountain and handed the empty pack back to Max. Max was stunned but more curious than upset.

Ghazi said, "Walk with me." They walked to a snare, where a rabbit was caught, frantically trying to escape. Max thought that the snare might have been Ghazi's initial reason for being on the mountain. Ghazi slowly removed his knife from its sheath. He cut a mushroom from the ground. He then gouged out the black spot from the middle of the mushroom cap, carefully leaving it on the tip of his dagger. Max's mind was racing. Ghazi took the rabbit out of the snare by its nape and proceeded to open its mouth. He placed the black spot into the rabbit's mouth and held its jaw closed. The mullah closed his eyes and seemed to be praying as he gently stroked the rabbit's back. He placed the creature on the ground and washed his hands vigorously with water from his water-skin pouch.

"Your computers do not have all the answers when it comes to the mysteries of Afghanistan, my friend. You must be very careful with the many facets of the Korengal mushroom."

Max looked quizzically at Ghazi, then down at the rabbit. The rabbit gently snuggled up to the mullah's feet. It curled against his ankles as though about to sleep. It took ten seconds to die. Max slowly bent over and picked up the dead rabbit. He checked for vital signs—there were none. Ghazi Haider walked away down the mountain path as Max stood mesmerized by the dead rabbit in his hands.

A stunned Max shouted down toward the path, "if you don't want us here, why didn't you let me feed this poison to my men?"

From out of sight, Ghazi's voice reverberated through the valley. ***"THERE IS NO HONOR IN THAT!"*** The words resounded as the echo bounced loudly from mountain to mountain above.

There is no honor in that ... There is no honor in that ... There is no honor in that ... There is no honor in that.

Those words became a mantra for Max Burns. They evolved into the salient point of a philosophy Max would carry with him forever. No longer merely words, but a code of honor: validation truth, sincerity, trust, brotherhood, deeds, and life itself, all inclusive in a mantra of validation. ***Honor*** was his pathway. There was something else in the message. There was clarity with regard to past actions.

Everything can be justified if honor is at the helm.

CHAPTER 22

The next time Max saw Ghazi Haider's face, it was on a computer at the FOB headquarters. The C.I.A. info available stated: Ghazi Haider- leader of the opposing Taliban forces for the northern sector of Afghanistan and possibly for the entire country. As Max did his internet research on the C.I.A. platform, he became engrossed in Ghazi Haider's biography. It portrayed an almost mythical figure. The C.I.A. did not know whether he was dead or alive. According to the US Army Profiling, Ghazi Haider was number 5 on the most-wanted list, behind Osama bin Laden, yet the report clearly stated he was not to be confused with al-Qaeda, since he had fought **against** al-Qaeda successfully. Ghazi had fought alongside the US's C.I.A. advisory forces against the Russians in 1989 and subsequently against the Taliban. He was second in command to his cousin Ahmad Shah Massoud, the "Lion of Panjshir" and leader of the Northern Alliance army. The Northern Alliance was considered the fiercest Afghan mujahideen force opposing the Russians, Taliban, and Osama bin Laden's al-Qaeda. The Russians feared Ghazi Haider; "The Ghost," as much as they did Massoud.

Hell, these two were the brain trust for the forces that kicked the Russians out of Afghanistan! Evidently, Ghazi is a brilliant tactician, taught well by Massoud, loved by his men, and respected by his enemies. Ahmad Shah Massoud was killed by Osama bin Laden operatives posing as journalists on September 9, 2001, two days before the World Trade

Center attack. Ghazi Haider then became de facto leader of all Afghan mujahideen fighting against al-Qaeda and the Taliban.

Now, he's Taliban fighting al-Qaeda? Doesn't make sense.

Ghazi wouldn't have me responsible for killing American soldiers.

Hmmm. He fought with Massoud. I wonder what turned him. Christ, Massoud was nominated for the Nobel Peace Prize in 2002. And Ghazi was family. What turned him? Or has he flipped at all? Maybe he just wants everybody the fuck out of his country? I would too.

CHAPTER 23

Max sat on his old footlocker in the New York City basement storeroom, mesmerized by the half dozen mushroom spores that had fought their way back to life. He thought about something that Ghazi Haider had said about the many facets of the Korengal mushroom: "Fungi know to remain dormant until conditions are right for rejuvenation."

Summer is almost here in New York. This cellar seems as natural a habitat as possible here.

Max thought as he looked around, noting that no outside light was available.

He stared at the surviving spores as though they were freshly hatched chicks. He looked around the storage room and saw an old fifty-gallon aquarium. *Perfect!* There were a few dead potted plants on the floor near the back wall. Max pulled out the dead stems and dumped the dirt in the aquarium along with the remnants of the Afghan soil. He kneaded both soils together and smoothed the surface out as though making his bed in boot camp. Then, he gently took the mushroom spores from the assault pack and transplanted them into the aquarium. There was an old sump sink that could be used for dampening. *They don't need much. The damn things started growing on their own down here.*

He put the aquarium on a shelf and covered it with a soaked piece of plywood for a cover, securing it with one of his ten-pound barbell plates. He didn't want any more rodents causing a ruckus. There was an old rocking chair that someone had left behind. It was beat up but functional. Leaving the 30-watt bulb on, Max plopped down in the chair and admired his rescue efforts.

It's as if they want to be left alone.

Max understood.

His cell phone rang.

"Are you okay? What's going on down there?" Eva asked.

"I'll be right up." In the elevator he decided not to tell Eva about the mushrooms.

No sense getting into it with her now. Maybe after I figure out what to do with them. They smell so much like truffle.

In the weeks to come Max went down to the basement to check on "the children" once a day.

My, how you've grown.

He harvested the mushrooms when they grew to the approximate size of a golf ball. He'd brought home some surgical gloves he used at the restaurant, and wearing the gloves, he cut out the black spot in the middle of each one, careful not to leave any remnants. The black centers went into a film container marked with an *X*. He wasn't sure why he saved them. *Hey, maybe I'll need to kill some rats sometime.* He then slid the doughnut-shaped mushroom caps onto a straightened metal clothes hanger, leaving the metal hook at the bottom. The last step in the process was to hang the mushrooms behind the basement furnace to dry. It took at least twenty-four hours to dry out the mushrooms in the sauna-like conditions near the furnace.

The mushrooms grew heartily in their bleak improvised environment. Max decided to experiment. He put some of the mushrooms on peanut butter, then put the concoction on pieces of cardboard ripped from boxes. He left the mixture on the floor in the middle of the storage room.

There seemed to be no fatalities among the rodents that came to dine, but whenever Max reintroduced a black center, a rat never got more than five feet from its last supper. It was just as Ghazi Haider had demonstrated that day in the Korengal. It was the black spot that was the lethal component. But Max had to be absolutely positive it was only the center that was lethal. It was a huge leap of faith to presume that the farther away from the mushroom's black center, the less lethal the meat of the mushroom would be.

Max did some research on Eva's laptop. There were more than ten thousand known varieties of mushrooms. Of those, 1 percent were known to be lethal, and 4 percent could make you sick. Three known types were hallucinogenic.

None of these photos of the bad guys look anything like my mushrooms.

Max researched further. There were many dangerous edible foods and oddly enough some parts of poisonous foods were considered delicacies. They were avoided by the general populations of the native habitat yet sold as delicacies on black markets elsewhere in the world.

That's why they're expensive, Max ole boy!

The lionfish came up as a partially edible food with lethal parts. The article went on to say that the extrication of the edible sections of a lionfish had to be done by a very savvy chef. The edible portion of this fish was a delicacy in the Far East and sought after by connoisseurs the world over.

Lionfish were prolific, having few predators within their domain; the food chain virtually stopped with them. As a result, they were killing off various species of coral dwellers and subsequently the coral, in all oceans except the Arctic and Antarctic. There was a bounty on them in Florida and Bermuda.

It is good to be king! Max thought.

He looked at his collection of mushrooms.

The smell and texture of these mushrooms is so truffle-like. Mine aren't even close to the size or coloration of the poisonous species shown, yet the center is lethal. But if the outermost parts are similar to the taste of the white truffle, I could be onto something. White truffle from Europe is traded like a commodity on black markets all over the world. Last *time I looked, white truffle was going for $2,000 an ounce, depending on availability and quality.*

It was not the money as much as the magical taste of the elusive white truffle that inspired Max to press on with his research.

Rich folks in Europe hide white truffle with their jewelry. Once you taste any food group—eggs, for instance—with just a minute sprinkling of white truffle, you are hooked. The white truffle is a luxury even for connoisseurs of fine food. Habit forming in its own right.

Max shaved the mushrooms starting from the perimeter. He brought down a coffee bean grinder to methodically grind up the mushrooms. He labeled them by concentric section. The sections were determined by variation in color and proximity to the center. The approach was rudimentary but systemic enough for Max: The center was M#10X, followed by M#9, M#8, and so on, all the way down to M#1. He put them into old film canisters he found in the storeroom. He wasn't sure whether all these classifications were necessary, but better to have too many than too few. Max was flying by the seat of his pants, but the exhilaration he felt was undeniable. He'd been intrigued from the very onset of his discovery of the enigmatic mushrooms and how instrumental they were to his meeting with Ghazi Haider. It was part of a puzzle that propelled him back to that day in the Korengal when an Afghan mullah—military commander of enemy forces—had befriended him.

He chose not to kill his enemy in a dishonorable way. I wonder how I would've handled such an opportunity.

Max didn't keep secrets from Eva, but this was too weird to get her involved. There were mysteries to be uncovered. If he could discover a wonderful new taste, he could write his own ticket in the culinary world. No, he would not let Eva or anyone else in on his little secret just yet, not until he'd tested and confirmed all side effects of the mushroom. There was one thing Max did know for certain: at some point in time he would have to partake of each classification, except of course… M#10X.

CHAPTER 24

Max walked the sixty blocks to work on this beautiful May morning. He wanted to make a stop at Rodrigo's Pet Shop on 131st and Amsterdam. He had walked by the shop a few times. The lapdog puppies were frolicking in the front window as usual.

Max brought some pieces of mushroom with him. He thought an opportunity might arise for testing some of the mushroom caps. He checked out a glass tank containing three white rats as he meandered toward the rear of the store. He noticed an open door leading to a large back room.

Carlos had told him that Rodrigo's Pet Shop was famous for its backroom entertainment—dogfighting and cockfighting. There was a round, dirt-filled pit, approximately eight feet in diameter, in the middle of the back room, which was twice the size of the actual pet store.

Evidently the money is made back here… Sick! Max thought.

"It's round so they can't run into a corner," a voice with a Spanish accent said. Max nodded, turning to look at the man who had appeared.

"Can I help you, my friend? My name is Rodrigo. I am the owner of the shop," the man said as he shut the door and locked it.

"I was thinking about a pup for my girlfriend," Max said, caught off guard.

"The 'let's start a family,' dogs are in the front window."

Before Max took the hint and moved back into the shop, a particularly majestic-looking male dog took exception to Max talking with Rodrigo. The dog was in a heavy duty cage similar to the type used to transport zoo animals. Max asked Rodrigo about the nasty attitude of the muscular canine.

"He has a date tonight, and he knows it. He doesn't get fed until he wins," Rodrigo said matter-of-factly.

"What if he loses?"

"He won't need a meal. And I get to eat his steak. But he doesn't lose. He's a champion."

Rodrigo was called to the front to answer questions about parakeets. Max walked over to the dog's cage. The dog stopped barking and looked deep into Max's eyes. Max had seen that look before in MMA cages during pre-fight instructions, that time when you looked for an edge: fear, nerves, impatience, insanity… any edge you could glean from the seven second face-off.

An index card on the cage read: "Alapaha Blue Blood American Bulldog. Name: Tango." Another index card on the cage read in English and Spanish, "DANGEROUS / PELIGROSO!"

The dog was handsome in a contemptuous, almost conceited way, like a thoroughbred horse awaiting a starting gate to open. He had fire in his eyes. Max envisioned him standing in the ring thinking:

Let's get this over with. I'm hungry.

Tango was trained to kill. Max could relate. He felt a strong connection with this dog.

"This might ease your pain tonight champ." Max tossed half the mushroom into the cage. Tango didn't stop to investigate something that passed for food. He snapped it up in one bite and stared at Max as if to say, "More!"

Phew! Nasty.

Max wandered around the store for a few more minutes. He stopped to check out the white rats. He tossed in the remainder of the M#3 section for a crude clinical test. The three sniffed the mushroom, then nibbled away. It took longer to eat than Max thought, so off he went. He would stop by tomorrow and check on Tango and the rats. Hopefully, Tango would not feel much pain in the arena tonight and would remember Max as a benefactor tomorrow.

Max had a mile or so to go before getting to the restaurant. He bought a *New York Post* newspaper. It was a fine day for walking and reading the paper.

To hell with April in Paris. New York City in May is the place to be.

Life was getting more interesting by the hour. He read that the jury had finally been picked for Paco's trial. Max had heard from Timoney that Weinstein had been dragging out the juror selection as a stall tactic. It hadn't worked. The judge was Phineas Mandegaard, a tough but fair judge with twenty-three years on the bench. He took no bull from either side. Morano was happy with Mandegaard presiding.

Baseball season was in its third week. Max wondered how a Pittsburgh Pirates fan like himself would be accepted in New York City.

I'll hang up Dad's picture alongside Roberto Clemente behind the bar. That should stir up some conversation.

CHAPTER 25

The Democratic Party presidential primaries votes had been closer than anyone expected. Both sides of the aisle were still bickering endlessly in the Senate and the House. Clearly, the system was broken and in dire need of repair. The previous twenty years had confounded the most astute analysts of the U.S. political system. One thing was certain: The early announcement of Ed Curlander as a VP running mate was a good strategic move for Blair. It definitely drove the promised Blair/Curlander ticket forward to victory.

However, Alexander Blair had made a few political gaffs on the campaign trail, and a lame attempt to cover up a heart condition, had caused grumblings about Blair's ability to fulfill a presidential tenure…or two. His (their) numbers were heading in a southerly direction. Did the Democrats have the leeway or the guts to shift gears? They did not.

Ed's enthusiasm for VP slot may have been a bit hasty. Blair hoped for that…shrewd move. Max thought.

He remembered how Curlander had alluded to the presidency at Gringos. Politics was not Max's cup of tea, but Max had skin in the game, this time.

Max's thoughts were focused on the mushrooms the last six blocks to the restaurant. He needed to understand everything about them. He thought about Ghazi carefully cutting out the middle of the mushroom.

The concentric circles of lighter shades moving outward, like ripples on water. What surprises does each circle hold? Ahhhh, the aroma… so similar to the white truffle. What are you hiding within your circles?

He hoped his high school biology classes would help with regard to his pet shop experiments. Rodents, specifically rats, possessed organs, brain patterns, metabolism, and so on that were very similar to those of the human body.

This is why rats and mice are used in clinical laboratory experiments. I thought it was because nobody liked them.

CHAPTER 26

Eva was in the back office working on the computer when Max got to the restaurant. She abruptly switched it off and swiveled around in her chair.

"Things are looking okay. By my calculations, we should be out of debt and making a profit in seven years, ten months, and three days—that is, if we stay open every day, including the holidays, twenty-four hours a day." They both laughed. Max handed her a rose he'd bought from a street vendor, and Eva kissed him on the cheek.

"I thought you were coming in later today," Max said.

"I needed to catch up on some things," Eva answered whimsically.

"I am thinking of putting up my heavy bag in the basement to get my ass back in shape," Max said.

"Good idea…and stop sampling the new desserts you've been working on."

"More to love, baby," Max said as he gave Eva a big hug and kiss.

"That does it! The bag goes up tomorrow."

Eva asked. "Do you think Mr. Woods will mind?"

"I'm giving him fifty dollars a month for the use of that storage room. That should keep him happy. It's twelve by eighteen feet. Do you think fifty dollars is enough?" Max asked.

"It's fifty dollars too much as far as I am concerned."

"Well, considering a storage unit would be two hundred seventy-five a month …."

"Okay, fifty dollars for a gym and storage area is a good deal. Maybe I can get it written off as a business expense on our taxes. By the way, I got an extension on both our taxes until July. It will be worth it to get things sorted out. Your cash from my grandparents is unusual since you're not a relative. Mine is workable. Oh, hell, I'll get it figured out. Did I tell you? Len and Margaret want to come up and visit."

"It would be great to see them, but delay them until the trial is over. No sense having them worry."

Eva nodded her approval. Max's phone rang. It was the DA's office. He listened a moment and then said, "Sure thing. When? Fine." Max hung up. He looked over at the bar, where Tony Easter was setting up, and said, "Old friend of yours is coming by, Tony—Angelo Morano."

"Ammo, eh! Haven't seen him in a while. Good man, Ammo," Easter said as he continued stocking the bar.

"Ammo?" Eva looked quizzically at Easter.

"Yeah, for Angelo - Morano. It's a neighborhood thing."

Twenty minutes later there was a knock on the front door, and Tony let Ammo in. They hugged like long-lost brothers. Max and Eva liked that. Ammo and Easter talked for a minute or so. Then Morano looked toward Max. Easter introduced them all. No hugs. Max and Eva weren't from the old neighborhood.

"How 'bout a beer?" Max asked.

"No thanks," Ammo said. "I'll be as brief as possible. We need to discuss some important points that I know are going to pop up during the trial. Paco's lawyer, Lazlo Weinstein, is a shark! I already have three witnesses looking for NYPD protection. I know his people are out and about with a fistful of fifties. I can feel it."

Morano paused for a second and pulled up a chair. "Sit! We gotta talk." Morano's voice and demeanor changed. He reverted back to being a cop as he questioned Max.

"You ever been arrested, Max?"

"No."

"Use drugs?"

"No."

"Ever kill anybody?"

Max hesitated and said, "I served three tours: Iraq and Afghanistan." Morano and Max paused and looked at Eva. It was obvious to Morano that Max and Eva had never discussed this topic before.

"I see that. Silver Star, Purple Hearts. Good stuff!" Ammo said. Morano headed in another direction. "Why did you go up to the Dyckman Street projects on the Saturday morning in question?"

"I went to pay Paco."

"Be more specific!"

"I went to pay Paco for his brother's dental bill."

"That's right! You didn't go there to beat the shit out of him. That is important. Then what?"

"I saw this young girl and her grandmother coming out of building # 3. The girl was bleeding and crying."

"What else?"

"Her grandmother was holding her up. The grandmother was screaming that Paco had just raped her granddaughter."

"Then what?"

"Then, I guess I flipped out and told the scumbag to come down."

"Stop right there! You didn't flip out! Why did you call him down?"

"So I could beat the shit out of him, for Chrissake!"

"No! You called him down to pay him. Correct?"

"Correct!"

"Then he took a swing at you, and you had to defend yourself, right?"

"He did swing first."

"You're goddamn right he did!"

Max realized that Morano's job was to get Paco sent away for life. Max digested it all and regained his composure. He understood he needed to be on the same side of the street as Morano or get chewed up on the witness stand.

"Yes, I wanted to pay him, and he tried to hit me."

"He did hit you, right?"

"Right!" Max said.

"Okay!" Morano said as he patted Max's tense shoulder.

Easter stepped in. "You got it, Max. Welcome to New York City, my man. Morano knew Max was in good hands with Easter and Timoney babysitting, he eased up. He'll be fine, Ammo. I'll fill him in about the way things are."

"Listen to me, Ammo said. Weinstein will try to discredit you. The other witnesses will be watchin' like a hawk. If you crack, they'll all run for the hills… along with our case. If you don't want that scumbag eating your food for free every day, pay attention to me, Tony, and Timoney and nobody else. You are leading this parade. And by God, you are going to take it all the way up Broadway and on to Attica."

Morano got up. He shook Max's hand and looked at Eva. "How're you doin'?"

"Just ducky," Eva said, not fully grasping Morano's good intentions.

Morano smiled at Easter and said to Eva, "You better be ducky! I'm not sure if Weinstein will call you, but you need to get with the program too. Capeesh?"

He looked at Tony, who nodded at him and said, "She's cool." Eva shot Tony a look.

"Good. Then we all understand each other," Morano said. He hugged Tony again and said, "Keep me posted. And keep your eyes open for the little prick. Any sightings?"

Easter pulled a notebook from his back pocket. "Three. Blue Honda, New York plate CV4576, overdue for inspection, in case you need to pull him over for cause. I got dates and times right here, no video." He flapped the notebook shut. Tony Easter had their back. Eva felt a little more secure.

Morano left. It was time to prep for the dinner seating. Eva seemed more relaxed as she moved about. Max knew she was more worried than she let on.

Quite a gal, my Eva.

That night, after Eva fell asleep, Max went downstairs for a quick check on "the children." He also wanted to hoist the chains over the rafter to support his heavy bag. The children were showing improvement in their new home. Max got the heavy bag secured and ready for action. He sat and thought about random things… and nothing at all. He was very much at peace in his man cave. He went back upstairs, snuggled in close to Eva, and fell asleep.

CHAPTER 27

Max was anxious to stop at the pet shop. He didn't know what to expect as he walked over to the tank that was home to the three white rats. There they were; all three alive and kicking. They looked fine to Max. They seemed more relaxed than yesterday. Max asked Rodrigo if they were the same rats from the day before.

"Yeah," Rodrigo said, scratching his head.

"What's the matter with 'em?" Max asked, anxious for input.

"A bad day all around. None of my rats ever got along so nice with each other. Mice? Yes. Rats? Never like this. Very strange. It's all good. I can charge more for them." Rodrigo seemed to be in a bad mood. Max observed the rats for a while. They weren't dead. That was a good thing.

They seem…comfortable.

Max knew the results of this little experiment were not a scientific certainty by any stretch, but he liked what he saw.

The only known fact established in the Korengal and reinforced with my experiments here is that the black spots on these mushrooms are lethal. An argument could be made that the concentric circles extending toward the rim might have varying degrees of potency and perhaps other qualities. It's ***taste*** *I'm interested in! The black spot is the core, and all other parts seem relative to that core with exponential qualities. It's a premise that needs to be proven. Next step? Human consumption.*

It was time to check on the dog. Max walked toward the back

room. There was no Tango, only his empty cage. The room looked like a crime scene. The pit was bloodied and unkempt. Chairs looked like they had been thrown around. Max went to the front and asked Rodrigo how his gladiator had fared the previous night.

Rodrigo sneered and said, "That mutt cost me ten grand last night!"

"What happened?"

"**He wouldn't fight!** The piece of shit wouldn't fight. He was the champion of all five boroughs for eight months. He could have taken that dog on three legs. Instead, I had to put a .22 in his brain to finish him off. He stood there and let a fucking lapdog eat him alive. I mean it! The other dog ate him alive… and he acted like he didn't give a damn! He just stood there like a statue and got torn apart. The other dog even backed off a few times. I don't think he understood what was happening. I didn't, I never saw that. Never! Not from a champion like Tango." Rodrigo said, shaking his head.

Max felt sick to his stomach. It had to be the mushroom. *What else could it have been? What a major fuckup! That poor dog. I better stop playing God until I know what I'm dealing with. Poor bastard.* Max was pissed at himself for basically killing Tango.

"Maybe you should shut down, Rodrigo. Maybe the gods are trying to tell you something."

Not paying attention to Max, Rodrigo said, "Now I got a pregnant bitch with his pups in Louisiana that I am going to be stuck with. I'm the laughingstock of the pits."

"Really?"

"Yeah, really!" Rodrigo said.

"What are you going to do about the pups?" Max asked.

"I had people bidding on them up until last night! I can't sell them for the pits now." Rodrigo said, disgusted. "I got some time before I get they're here. I'm going to put them in the window and hope they sell before they're not so cute anymore. If nobody buys them, I drown 'em. Useless. Fucking useless. I could have gotten five grand a pup… dog or bitch."

"When is the bitch due?"

"Next week or so. They send them north about six weeks after whelping.

Why? You want one?" Rodrigo asked, thinking he might have a sucker.

"Maybe."

"I give you one cheap, real cheap," Rodrigo said, trying to hustle an immediate sale.

"How 'bout I make you a nice meal in trade for a pup?" Max said.

"Depends on the meal. Better be a great meal to get a pup."

"You like mushrooms with your rice and beans, Rodrigo?" Max asked.

"They're okay, I guess," Rodrigo said.

"Good. You'll enjoy this meal. It'll change your whole outlook," Max said as he walked out in disgust. The rats were good news. The dog? He felt terrible about Tango. Max's resolve intensified. He was more determined than ever to find out everything possible about these mushrooms. As he walked north, he flashed back to his mother reading, *Alice's Adventures in Wonderland,* to him. Like Alice as she approached the cake marked: "Eat Me." Max was becoming, "***curiouser*** and ***curiouser.***"

CHAPTER 28

Brunch was busy into the early afternoon. People tended to eat their main meal early on Sunday in Manhattan. There was football, the *Sunday New York Times*, Central Park, whatever a nice day with no work might bring. There was no Sunday dinner served at Gringo Smyth's, so Max, Eva, and the staff were usually out of the restaurant by mid-afternoon. Monday the restaurant was closed. Tuesday started Max and Eva's workweek at the restaurant.

Max pondered the day off. *Eva will sleep in on Monday morning unless something needs her attention. Tonight after a workout on the heavy bag, maybe I'll try a mushroom taste test.*

Sunday was a special night for Max and Eva. This cab ride home was accompanied by a feeling of accomplishment for the week. They were ahead of schedule on their financial projections and bills were getting paid. The purveyors liked doing business with "the pros" at Gringo Smyth's. That meant better cuts of meat and the freshest fish and vegetables available, which was so important to a quality restaurant. Of course, there were a few minor bumps in the road—an upcoming murder trial for one. Other than that, all was right with the world. On their day and a half off, they would kick back, make love, and lounge around in whatever was comfortable. For Eva, that was often one of Max's T-shirts. He might wear his sweatpants from his MMA days, the ones with a US Army Ranger insignia on the right thigh. He was proud of those worn-out sweats. They reminded him of his training for the inter-service championship fight. It had been the toughest fight of his life. He'd lost but had not been beaten. That was how everyone who had seen the fight described his valiant effort.

It was time to get back into shape. The heavy bag was the answer. He'd also start running again after this damn trial was concluded.

Eva fell asleep after making love with Max. He checked to see if she was sleeping with that certain smile on her face. Max admired how Eva could fall asleep within seconds—a gift not possible for combat vets. He slipped out of bed and dressed for a workout. Of course, there would not be much of a workout after making love with Eva, but fifteen minutes on the heavy bag wouldn't make him a liar out of him.

Max looked at his watch: 12:15 a.m. An uninhibited elevator moved slowly but surely to the basement. Max stopped at the furnace to take down the dried mushrooms. He stared at the dried crop.

The shavings had begun to outgrow the film canisters, so when Max had time, he had begun to transfer the contents to some Mason jars. His taxonomy remained the same: Outside edge of the mushroom was M#1, the next ring was M#2, and so on to the deadly M#10X. He decided to taste dried granules rather than the fresh edge of an uncured mushroom. Tasting granules would also be a test of shelf-life expectancy and quality control. If the mushrooms were to be used as a garnish, or in lieu of the expensive white truffle, shelf life needed to be established. Ideally, in a perfect world, Max hoped the intensity of the dangerous qualities would abate, leaving the truffle-like taste and no side effects.

Max unlocked the storage room, flicked on the light, and stood in the doorway for a moment. He sat in the rocking chair to ruminate on how to begin. Logically, Max should start at the beginning. The M#1 Mason jar looked him dead in the eye from the end of the shelf.

Max reviewed his objectives: survive, taste, analyze intensity, monitor aftereffects. Off came the top of the M#1 Mason jar. The color was a mocha cream, the lightest coloration of all.

He wet the tip of his pinky and touched it to the tiny granules. He examined the granules for a moment, then placed the sample on his tongue.

Pungent yet similar to white truffle.

Max could not help but think about the variety of recipes that could be enhanced with the mushroom. Immediately, eggs came to mind, along with fresh vegetables, gravies, and soups. Again he wet his pinky and tasted.

Strong. Needs an additive. Overpowering if too much is used. A pinch is all that is needed. Max was thrilled with the outcome. He sat back in the rocker and took it all in. His mind became calm. He closed his eyes. His mind drifted toward the events in his life that led to his coming to New York City: the farm and his family in Pennsylvania, the Korengal, Eva, the Scirocco, Len and Margaret, Paco, and now, his basement laboratory.

If only Mr. Swenson could see me now, he thought, remembering his high school science teacher.

Max was content. He felt good. He fell into a peaceful sleep in the rocker.

Max never dreamed at all before his deployments. Tonight, he fell into a deep sleep in the rocker. That in itself was unusual for any combat vet. This was a pleasant sleep. He had read once about dreams manifesting themselves in black and white. Evidently, Max's subconscious would have none of that. The dream started as gray, but then Max's subconscious request for color was granted and infused bright colors diffused into his dream, as though he had touched down in the land of Oz.

As though sitting in a movie theater, he could observe, but also direct his dream. He time-tripped back to his hometown of Washington, Pennsylvania and walked with his father as he had as a young boy. People he knew said hello. Men tipped their hats and shook the mayor's hand. Friends stopped to talk to both of them. Friendly lips moved without sound. His father would smile, then take Max's hand and continue on their way. Streets turned to fields. Fields became forest. Farther along, they stood at the base of a mountain.

"Are we going over this mountain, father?" Max asked.

Mr. Burns said to his son, "If this is the right way, we will. You must do everything in your power to do what is right. What is right may not always be the easiest path. Nevertheless, that path must be followed, even in a dream."

"But I don't dream, father," Max said, looking up into his father's eyes.

"You do now, my son," Mr. Burns said. "Remember—it is most important to know when you are dreaming and when you are NOT."

Max's cell phone rang. He awoke in a sweat. A quick look at his watch told him it was 5:15 a.m.

"Max, where are you?" Eva asked.

"Yeah! Honey, I'm down in the basement. I fell asleep in the rocking chair."

"What rocking chair?"

"I'll be right up." Max threw water on his face and went upstairs. The lumbering elevator seemed to take ten minutes to get up to the fourth floor. Eva was at the door.

"Are you okay?" she asked.

"Yeah, I dozed off," Max said.

"You still look exhausted. That must've been some workout. I thought I had taken care of your evening exercise," Eva said, smiling. "Jeez, you're soaked. Take a nice hot bath."

"Bath?" Max said. "Men don't take baths."

"I'll run you a nice hot bath with some Epsom salts. You probably overextended yourself on your first workout. You'll be sore in a few hours if you don't listen to me."

"Okay. No bubbles."

"Lie down until it's ready, Superman." As she ran the water, she said, "I love these old bathtubs. Even you can fit in them."

When the bath was ready, Max took his sweats off. They were soaked all right. Max was not tired, however, he felt… rested.

"Are you trying to poach me?" Max asked as he eased himself into the water.

"Get in, you big baby. Real tough guy. Just soak. I'm afraid you might be catching something. This'll boil it out of you," Eva said, shaking her head at his reaction to the hot water.

Max eventually stretched out. Eva put a rolled-up towel behind his head. He couldn't remember ever falling asleep quite so quickly as he had in the basement. Pulling guard duty in the army had taught him how to prevent dozing off. Some guys resorted to a touch of Tabasco sauce on the rims of their eyelids. Max never had to do that. There were usually warning signs if you started to nod off, none of which had kicked in down in the basement.

These mushrooms need more thought. If they're to be used in recipes, maybe they need to be cut like a drug. Qualitative and quantitative control would take experimentation. There was so much to learn. He also needed to further define the proportion of potency to taste categories.

How far can I go for a great taste? Am I getting too far into the forest… where it all began?

The bath felt great. He could feel the heat right through to his bones.

CHAPTER 29

The trial was upon them. In three days the next major event in the Big Apple would converge at the courthouse in Lower Manhattan. Francisco "Paco" Caamano's story and picture had gone viral. This was no rural, justice of the peace adventure in Pennsylvania. This was national news. Some reporters found out about the restaurant. The good news? The reporters only showed up during the day, and Max rarely came out of the kitchen while prepping for dinner. Eva stayed in the back office. Max sent Carlos out to answer questions in his "worst" broken English. Sometimes attention petered out - sometimes not. Once, while Timoney was in the restaurant office talking to Max and Eva, a *New York Post* reporter knocked on the door for at least ten minutes before giving up.

Eva was getting jumpy. She tried not to let it show. Timoney came in for dinner the night before the trial. He asked Eva to sit with him when she had a chance. When things slowed down at the door, Eva brought over a carafe of tap water for the both of them and sat down. Timoney sipped the water. "Ahhhh! Finest drinking water east of the Rockies. Too bad! Do you know that the State of New York, with the blessing of the federal government, has sold the rights to *frack* for natural gas all around the Croton Reservoir? That's where this beautiful water comes from. The last bit of God's gift to the sinners of New York City, the very staple to all life on this planet, and those greedy bastards would rather suck oil than drink water." Timoney turned his glass in his hand as he spoke. "There are a hundred sixty-four chemicals used in *fracking* for natural gas; thirteen are lethal. Helluva way to die—poison. I wonder who they'll blame when people die from drinking water."

"Jeez!" Eva said, staring at the contents of her glass.

John changed the subject abruptly. "Eva! Big doin's tomorrow. The circus is about to play the big time. There's going to be a lot of press and other things going on, good and bad, about everyone: You, me, Max. Hell, anything the lawyers and tabloids can conjure up. Be strong. It's all theater. Be yourself. Stick to what Morano and Tony Easter tell you. I don't think you'll be called. If you are, those beautiful brown eyes will get'em, as soon as you're sworn in. The city is fed up with these punks. I consider this the most important case I've ever been involved with and I have been in the middle of some beauts. Max is going to need your support. If he thinks this is too much for you, he may back off without knowing it. We can't let that happen. We need Max to keep his foot on the gas. We're too close to putting this bastard away for life. Remember what Morano said about this whole case collapsing; it starts from the top, not the bottom. You and Max are at the top of this pyramid. You're the magic ingredients we never had before… Americans fighting alongside Latinos to keep the city safe."

Eva looked around at Carmela, Carlos, and Tony Easter. Tony nodded at Eva as he cleaned a wineglass.

"10-4, Captain, er, John." She got up and gave him a kiss on the cheek, then saluted him. Timoney knew she'd come through. Max, on the other hand, was another story. His involvement was complex. Timoney asked Eva if he could sit with Max for a few minutes.

"Your turn!" Eva said to Max in the kitchen. "Timoney needs to give you his pep talk." She came out and told John that Max would be five minutes or so. Timoney nodded and deferred to his warmed apple strudel.

"How was dinner, John?" Max asked when he had a chance to come out.

"Excellent, my boy. You ready for tomorrow?"

"I guess so. Never been through anything like this before."

"I know. The first one is nerve wrenching. You're the best thing and the worst thing we have going for us on this case. Just remember what Morano told you and keep your cool. Weinstein needs an angle, and you're it. He is up against it with our witnesses. The only angle Morano can think of is you."

"Me?" Max said.

"You! You, losing your temper on the stand. He wants the jury to believe that you provoked this fight—one bully claiming territory from another—king-of-the-hill bullshit. If you crack, then he can go from there to undermine charges and witnesses, one by one like dominoes, and the walls come tumblin' down."

"But he didn't commit a crime against me! I'm just the guy that got him here."

"We know that. But we need to establish that there was no plan, no subversion or coercion involved with the authorities, as far as the fight goes. Spontaneity! That's the key."

Timoney sat back, waiting for a reaction from Max. Max leaned forward and whispered to Timoney, "Would you like another strudel?"

"Don't mind if I do."

CHAPTER 30

The courtroom looked as Eva had imagined a court room would. She and Max were seated in the first row of the courtroom behind ADA Morano. Morano leaned back over the rail toward Max and whispered, "Count to ten then turn around and smile!"

"Smile at who?" Max asked.

"Just smile."

Max turned around. There they sat—the faces of the Dyckman Street projects. They all smiled back at Max. Some waved: some threw kisses. Max acknowledged them with a thumbs-up.

"They've been waiting for you two for hours." Timoney said.

A court officer entered from the judge's chamber and placed papers on the towering bench. Then he said in a booming voice: "All rise. The court of the Southern District of the State of New York will come to order. The Honorable Phineas T. Mandegaard presiding."

"Be seated." the judge said matter-of-factly. It was just another day at work for Judge Mandegaard.

Eva wondered if they hired the court officer because of his booming voice. "Jeez, honey. It's like on *Judge Judy.*" Eva said as she held Max's arm.

After establishing all parties were present and accounted for, Weinstein immediately started things off by asking for a postponement. His request was denied. Weinstein didn't look surprised. Paco tried to look nonchalant but came across as arrogant.

Eva said a prayer to herself… Max thought about not fucking up. This was day one.

Max and Eva gave Carlos more day-to-day responsibilities because of the trial. There were delays of all kinds: excused jurors; summer vacations; Mandegaard's asthma; a witness fainting, etc...

It was mid-June before Max took the stand. He was last in a long parade of witnesses that Weinstein tried to discredit. Weinstein was more successful than expected. Morano had a pretty good idea of who would not sustain Weinstein's scrutiny. There were also peace loving, hardworking Latinos that brought to light the reasons for the existence of the American jurisprudence system as far as Mandegaard and Morano were concerned. Morano walked the older witnesses from their seats to the witness stand. Max saw Morano issue a wry smile to Weinstein when he escorted *Señora* Valdez, grandmother to the raped fourteen-year-old girl, to the witness stand. Morano's consideration did not go unnoticed by the jury of six men and six women, five of them Latinos. Weinstein would soon find out that his Latino overload of the jury would backfire. The tactic of arguing a prejudicial arrest would not float with the list of charges Paco had accumulated. In short, Latinos were fed up with being victims of other Latinos.

Max was anxious to get things over with—he had a restaurant to run. He was finally called to the stand by Morano. Morano went into some background about Max's army service and his commendations. Max was visibly embarrassed. Morano loved Max's reserved, almost shy demeanor with regard to his service record.

That bodes well with any jury… especially in the Latino community.

The armed forces had been a popular road to becoming an American citizen for years. More than 20 percent of the US troops that fought in Iraq and Afghanistan were of Latino decent.

"Why did you come to Washington Heights to open your restaurant?" Morano asked.

Max answered, "I wanted to open a restaurant where people

from the hospital and the neighborhood could enjoy good food. Most restaurants in the Heights serve breakfast and lunch and then close for the day. Columbia-Presbyterian Hospital is world-class. Patients and visitors come there from all over the world. People need a place to go to forget their problems for an hour or so."

Then it was Weinstein's turn. Timoney sat up straight in the gallery. Morano tried to be as casual as possible as Weinstein approached Max.

"Mr. Burns! Good morning. Thank you for your service to this country. **Have you killed many people?"** Weinstein jumped right in, hoping to throw Max off kilter.

Max hesitated for a beat. **"People?"**

Weinstein turned around toward the jury. "Yes… **people**."

"If you consider enemy combatants bent on destroying the United States of America as people, yes, sir, I have."

Weinstein was visibly pissed. Morano was smiling inside, as was Timoney. Neither of the two had coached Max on this issue. Max had surgically taken the human factor out of the question. Eva felt it came from the Max's self-imbued logic, discussed after the Paco thrashing. Max knew it was the balance beam all surviving combat soldiers walked to maintain sanity. Eva wondered how many times this very same question surfaced within Max. A tear came to her eye. They were entering a place she dared not venture into with Max. They were digging deep. Eva was not sure she wanted to be there when things began to surface.

"Enemy combatants! No women or children?" Weinstein asked, trying to bait him.

"No, sir, not unless they ate my cooking." Everyone laughed.

The judge lowered the gavel. "Answer the questions, Mr. Burns!" The last thing Max wanted to do was turn the judge against him.

"I don't understand, Mr. Burns. Your cooking?"

"Yes, sir. I was a chef in the army in both Iraq and Afghanistan—three tours in-country."

Max always blurted out his number of tours in deployed combat zones. There was no vanity involved. It was something every combat vet did without hesitation. It established this fact: Max knew all his jobs, and he did them well. The jurors did not feel tours in combat zones were matter-of-fact accomplishments.

"It says in my background report you were awarded a Silver Star with Valor and a Purple Heart. And, that you single-handedly killed thirty-two men—one with a knife, another with your bare hands. Is that true, Mr. Burns?"

"So they say." Max mumbled.

"Speak up, Mr. Burns!" Weinstein snapped.

"I don't know how… or how many."

"Why not, Mr. Burns? You don't keep track of your body count? **It's 32, Mr. Burns!**"

There was a long pause. Max looked out at Eva, trying to stop her tears. Now, it was out there for the world to know. Like many combat veterans coming home, he was facing the sleeping-dog syndrome. No combat veteran purposely dug up their own junk. It could start a litany of questions that frequently had no correct answers. Weinstein needed to find Max's buried junk and see if it could turn the table on Max Burns. Max took a deep breath and said, "I don't know… because I never asked."

"You never asked? Why not?" Weinstein was as close to Max's face as the witness box would permit.

"No need." Max answered. There was silence in the courtroom.

Weinstein broke the silence, tacking in a new direction. "Do you miss it?"

"Miss what?" Max collected himself.

"Do you miss killing people, Mr. Burns? Did you enjoy killing people?"

Eva was afraid of the answer. She immediately flashed back to their conversation at the restaurant after the Paco beating, when he'd told her about his pal Tommy Hennelly. She prayed Max's answer was one they could live with and the case could survive with.

This was it. Timoney was biting on his fist. Morano twirled a pencil in his fingers, accidentally snapping it under the pressure.

"Well, Mr. Burns? Yes or no?" Weinstein insisted.

After a long pause, Max turned slowly and asked the judge if he could address the court before answering the question, wanting to do so more for Eva's sake than the jury's.

The judge said, "First, answer the question. Then I'll allow a brief statement. I think that's fair." Mandegaard glanced at Weinstein, then stared at Morano. Weinstein welcomed additional exposition with anticipation.

Morano was beside himself. He looked at Timoney. "What the fuck is he doing?"

Timoney shook his head.

"No!" Max said.

"No, what, Mr. Burns?" the judge asked.

"No, Your Honor, I don't miss the killing."

"Mr. Burns, before you continue with your statement, you may speak with counsel first if you wish."

Mandegaard was dangerously steering Max toward a suggested consultation with Morano. Morano was knocked off guard by Mandegaard's direction. Morano froze in his chair, fearing a mistrial.

"That won't be necessary, your Honor," Max said.

Then Mandegaard asked Weinstein, "Do you have a problem with any direct discourse to the court, Mr. Weinstein?"

"No, Your Honor. Even though I find this proceeding highly unusual, I concur." Weinstein liked the odds of Max screwing himself, so he let Morano and Mandegaard off the hook forevermore by agreeing to it.

"Proceed, Mr. Burns," Mandegaard said, as he stared again at Morano, letting him know everyone had lost their chance to stop Max in his tracks.

Max faced the courtroom, not the jury, as he spoke. "There is a basic military premise that all combatants live by: an enemy ceases to be a person when he's trying to kill you, your brothers, or your sisters. When America was attacked on 9/11, I watched on TV as the planes flew into the two World Trade Center towers. Then, not far from where I lived in Pennsylvania, some brave American civilians gave up their lives to take control of the plane they were in, rather than let enemy insurgents crash it into our nation's Capitol Building… or wherever the enemy was headed. I considered it a privilege to be of age to do something about that. I didn't personally know anyone who died in the 9/11 attacks. I didn't need to. My country was now at war, and al-Qaeda terrorists were gaining strength - surfacing around the world."

Max paused. He wasn't sure where to go from here. It was obvious to everyone in the courtroom that this wasn't a prepared statement. Max gathered himself and continued:

"Four years ago on a January morning in Afghanistan, things did get personal when eight of my brothers were killed instantly by an I.E.D... Two more died later on. One died in the hospital in Landstuhl, Germany. Another blew his brains out in the attic of his parents' home in Newark, New Jersey… Christmas Day a few years back. I was lucky enough to be sitting on a fifty-pound sack of potatoes, with a sack of apples below my feet. Our MRAP - that's a troop carrier with a fifty-caliber machine gun—was blown straight up into the air. All I remember is looking out of the windshield and seeing clouds. It was like a silent film of being on a horse that reared up in slow motion."

Max paused again and looked down for the rest of his talk.

"I was in the best shape of anyone in my platoon because of those potatoes and apples. Huh, I am a chef, you see, but I'm also an army ranger. So, I did what I had to do. The vehicle slammed straight down on what was left of the undercarriage. I climbed out the hole in the cab roof to the machine gun— a Ma Deuce, 50 caliber.

"You find it hard to believe that I don't know how many enemy combatants I killed? I DON'T WANT TO KNOW! WHY? If you know, you come home with numbers in your head. Then you compare numbers: number of enemy killed; number of friends killed. Warriors cannot dwell on numbers. And...**THEY SHOULD NEVER BE ASKED ABOUT... NUMBERS**. That's a bad question to ask ANY combat veteran, Mister Weinstein.

"There was something I did enjoy that day. What I did enjoy, Mr. Weinstein, was finding out that some of my brothers and sisters were still alive and would make it home. Unfortunately, many didn't. And there are no numbers for those that come...And sadly, home is harder than war for many who did make it...home."

Max fought to stop from remembering specifics about that day.

"You asked me how many I killed. *I killed every fuckin' one of them.*"

You could hear sobbing from some, sighs from others, and not much else. The judge turned to Weinstein and asked in a stern voice, "Any further questions, counselor?"

Weinstein was barely audible. "No. That'll be all... Your Honor."

"Mr. Morano, closing argument?"

For the first time in all his legal forays, Morano was floored by an unsolicited statement from a witness. Max had unwittingly taken a huge chance, but hit a home run. Morano had a twenty-five-minute closing argument prepared, based upon what he'd thought Weinstein's argument would be: that Max had gone to the projects to kill Paco.

Morano knew that after Weinstein regrouped, he would bring that up in his closing argument. Morano took a leap of faith and decided not to mention anything about the fight. Oddly enough, it had only been briefly touched upon with the rape section of the case.

Morano thought: *You can't figure these things out beforehand. All you can do is prepare.*

Morano began, "ladies and gentlemen of the jury, thank you for your service. *'Thank you for your service.'* Isn't that a beautiful phrase? I try to use it every time I see a service man or woman in uniform—at airports, in the street, in restaurants, anywhere. But let's forget about any military involvement in this civilian case. There is none, really. A witness happens to be a war hero. That sells lots of newspapers, but what we are really here for today is justice—justice for the families of murder victims, for rape victims, for the beaten, the crippled, those who cry out from the grave. They beg to see if the justice Americans brag about really does exist. The world is watching us, saying, 'Let's see the justice you preach about in America. Is your justice for the rich only? Does it exist for everyone… citizen or not? Show us.'"

Morano paused as he walked over to the jury.

"What about this fourteen-year-old girl, Consuela Jardines, who had to sit here through weeks of facing the man that raped her. Are you going to let him out onto the streets to laugh in her face and have the opportunity to rape her again?" Morano's voice changed. **"This is your city! I don't care where you come from. Take it back!"**

Morano walked over and stood in front of the table where Paco and Weinstein were seated.

"Here he is. Not much of a threat now, are you, Mr. Caamano? I think prison might show what type of man he really is: a bully who thought he could beat the system through fear and intimidation. You have heard the testimony of the witnesses, victims, and their loved ones. How did we finally get here, you ask? Citizens of New York City got us here today.

Morano moved about as though in his living room. He wanted to demonstrate that he owned the courtroom, and that ***all people*** had the right to American jurisprudence, including the Pacos. It worked. Morano was pumped up and on his game.

He'll make a great DA one day, Timoney thought.

"In the eight years since Mr. Caamano took up residence in New York City, nobody has stood up to him. Nobody! He has made a mockery of our judicial system. Now it's your turn to stand up, just as Mr. Burns did. A fellow citizen of this great city has lit the flame - you must fan those flames. He showed the world that this devil is not indestructible but merely another coward, finally caught and beaten down to size by someone who dared to risk his own life to help a fourteen-year-old girl he didn't know. You have him! He is right here and you know in your hearts that he is guilty beyond all reasonable doubt. ***Carpe diem*** is an ancient Latin phrase that means, *seize the day*. That is what **you** must do today.

After a short pause Morano walked away from the jury box toward his seat and said to Judge Mandegaard, "The City of New York rests its case, your Honor."

Morano sat, exhausted mentally and physically.

"Mr. Weinstein, closing argument for the defense?" Mandegaard seemed almost cheerful.

Weinstein stayed seated for what seemed a very long time. Finally, he slapped his hands down on the desk, got up slowly, walked over to the jury box, and rested his arms on the railing. He looked at the jury without saying a word. Then he turned toward Judge Mandegaard and asked, "Your Honor, may I approach the bench?"

Morano stifled a **"Yes!"** He shot a quick look at Timoney. Both of them knew what this meant: a plea bargain. Timoney gave a thumbs-up, not in victory, but to signal Morano not to give up too much.

"Mr. Morano, Mr. Weinstein... in my chambers." Judge Mandegaard slammed the gavel down. "There will be a twenty-minute recess. This court will resume at exactly 2:35 p.m." He stood, his robe sweeping from behind the bench. "Let's go, gentlemen."

Weinstein started talking to Mandegaard before the door had even opened to the judge's enclave. Morano blurted out as they entered, "Don't let him give you that; 'poor Jewish kid from Queens getting a scholarship to Fordham Law, bullshit! And 'how kind the Jesuits were to give a poor little Jew from Maspeth a full ride at a Catholic law school.' A reliable source told me his application stated he was half Algonquin and half Ashkenazi."

"Are you going to share how your great-grandmother made chicken soup for Sitting Bull, Chief Weinstein?" Mandegaard asked. He and Morano chuckled while the judge poured himself three fingers of twenty-five-year-old Scotch whisky out of a crystal decanter.

"Whaddya lookin' for, Weinstein?" Morano asked.

"Guilty: Manslaughter on the two mutts from the rival gang. Those are your only eyewitnesses on actual stabbings and shootings." Weinstein said.

"Six witnesses," Morano said. "First degree aggravated sexual assault and kidnapping on a minor: guilty on all counts." Weinstein nodded in agreement, and Morano asked, "Time?"

"We'll take twenty years. Down in Huntsville, Texas, where initial charges are outstanding took place, this way it's Texas with incarceration costs and…."

"Whoa! Texas can have the bastard, but twenty years? Out in fourteen? You must be dreaming, Weinstein. Let's not forget you're fucked on this one." Morano said.

"He's right, ya' know." Mandegaard said as he sipped his Scotch.

"Murder one: Three counts. Rape gotta be in there. That little girl is scarred for life," Morano said to the judge. Weinstein started to say something. Morano interrupted. "This powwow is over. Let's get back to work." Morano started for the chamber door.

"Hold it!" Weinstein paused. "Three counts of murder one; first degree aggravated sexual assault of a minor; kidnapping, and we drop the rest of the crap."

"Time?" Weinstein asked, knowing he was defeated.

"**Life**! The only thing you get is the great state of Texas paying his rent. Plenty of Native Americans in Texas. Maybe you can get a tax write-off when you visit Paco, and see how your tribe is doing, Lazlo!" Morano put his hand on the doorknob when Weinstein failed to answer.

A big sigh came out of Weinstein. He looked up once at Morano, but before he could say anything, Morano was shaking his head and said, "*No mas!* Not on this one."

The judge was swirling the bottom of his perfectly timed whisky and said, "I'd take it if I were you, Weinstein. I hear Huntsville is darling in the summer. And they can't hang him since we already tried and sentenced him.

"Why Huntsville, may I ask?" Mandegaard asked.

"He wants to be close to home. His roots are in Mexico. His mother is there now. What the hell do I know? I do what I'm told. I'm gettin' too old for this shit!" Weinstein said as he walked out the chamber door.

Morano asked Mandegaard, "Do you buy the mommy bit?"

Mandegaard thought for a second and said, "I really don't care. He killed a cop in Texas. They might hang him anyway. New York State is well rid of him. Only a mother could love that mutt anyway."

"I'll take one of those if you don't mind."

They toasted, and Mandegaard said, "good job, Ammo."

"Thanks, Colonel."

"Quite a young man you got out there. I wish I had more like him under my command!"

"Fuckin' 'A', Colonel." They toasted again and finished off their drinks.

There was a knock on the door. "Come in," Mandegaard said.

Weinstein stood in the doorway. "Texas? Definitely Huntsville?"

Mandegaard finished his Scotch. "Sure…. Home to Mommy and fresh *frijoles*. DEFINITELY, Huntsville. You get the papers ready and notify the authorities in Texas, Mr. Morano."

The three walked back into the courtroom. It had been fifteen minutes. Nobody had given up their seat.

"All rise! Hear ye, hear ye. This court is now back in session," the court officer shouted. Eva loved that part.

Mandegaard spoke directly to the jury. "Ladies and gentlemen of the jury; in an age where people tend to shirk their duties to both their country and their community, I wish to thank all of you for your service to the great City of New York and the judicial system of the Southern District of the State of New York.

There has been a guilty plea entered in chambers. The defense has entered a plea of guilty to the following charges: three counts of murder in the first degree; one count of first degree, aggravated sexual assault of a minor; one count of kidnapping of a minor. Determination of sentence has already been agreed upon by the state and counsel for the defense."

Mandegaard put on his glasses. "I will now read the sentence heretofore agreed upon... The defendant will rise. Mr. Francisco Aguilar 'Paco' Caamano, you are hereby remanded to the City of New York Department of Correction facility at Rikers Island, until such time that you are transferred to the Texas State Penitentiary at Huntsville, Texas to begin serving a life sentence without parole."

Mandegaard smiled at the jury and said, "And to this jury, I wish to once more thank you for your service. You are hereby dismissed. This court is now adjourned." Mandegaard slammed the gavel down for the last time in this case. He got up and left for the confines of his chamber and the comfort of another glass of twenty-five-year-old Scotch.

Everyone cheered and hugged each other as Paco was escorted out in handcuffs.

Everyone wanted to kiss Max and Eva... a Latino thing. Every conceivable dialect of Spanish was going a mile a minute. Even Eva had problems piecing together the nonstop Cuban, South American, Mexican, Puerto Rican, and Dominican dialects being spewed. Max was humble. Eva was her gracious self. Max caught a glimpse of Louie leaving the courtroom, staring at Max. Max blew him a kiss. When he looked back for Louie, he was gone.

At least Paco came at me one on one. Louie is a foot too short and a sneak. You don't know where they are until they are on top of you.

Max wanted to avoid the press and go straight to the restaurant. The reporters were too busy with Consuela and her grandmother to notice Max and Eva getting into a squad car with Timoney.

Max could now entertain other things. It was back to business for him and Eva. It was late afternoon, Carlos should be prepping for the evening menu. Max wanted to make sure everything was going according to his instructions. Max was proud of Carlos and his daughter, Carmela. All they'd needed was a shot—someone willing to give them a chance.

"How about a little club soda and lime up at Gringo Smyth's, Captain?"

"Maybe later. I just wanted to tell you… I consider you both friends. You did a great service for this community today. These people will never forget you." He changed the subject abruptly and told his driver to avoid the press and get on an uptown avenue. "Hit the siren." They looked out the rear window and saw Consuela Jardines and her *abuela* talking to the press. They would have to watch the rest on the eleven o'clock news.

CHAPTER 31

When they got out of the squad car on Broadway, the street in front of the restaurant was packed with people. They cheered, sang, and danced. They surrounded Max and Eva. Max saw Carlos and Carmela inside in panic. They had locked the doors and stared out the window as though under siege, which they were. Tony Easter was inside laughing his ass off. Max looked at Eva and decided to open the doors of the restaurant.

What the hell!

"Hey, Tony, first one's on the house!" Eva yelled. Tony's laughter almost turned to tears as the crowd came barging in the door. Max and Eva hugged and kissed each other. For the first time they felt like they belonged in the Heights.

"It doesn't look like there will be any dinner served tonight," Eva said.

"No… no it doesn't." Max said as he held Eva tightly to his side.

"These people deserve a celebration and Gringo Smyth's is just the place to do it." Eva said.

It would also give the bar a good kick start. Tony Easter was moving as fast as he could. Max started to go back behind the bar to help, but Tony said, "Stay where you are. I'll catch up. I'll only be tripping over you!"

Max watched, and after the initial rush, Tony had it all under control. Max said to Eva, "Maybe he thought I wanted half his tip cup." They laughed and turned on the CD player. Max was a Jeff Beck fan. That was what played at first, but it didn't last long. Jeff Beck was soon replaced by salsa: *muy picante* (very hot)"! Strangers helped move the tables and chairs back to the walls.

"Man, can these people dance," Max said to Eva.

With that, a big *mamasita* grabbed Max and pulled him out onto the newly commissioned dance floor. Eva laughed. Max surprised her. He was a good dancer. He kept dancing just to keep Eva laughing. Then Eva joined in, her Latina roots coming through on the dance floor to the applause of one and all. Her *bunny hop* had been completely abandoned with the advent of the *salsa* blasting.

Timoney stopped in after finishing some paperwork. As soon as he walked in, he got pulled into the dance vortex. Eva said to Max later on, "Did you see Timoney? He was dancing like he was trying to keep warm on winter night."

It was a New York night. Gringo Smyth's finally closed at four in the morning. The only people still there were Timoney, Max, Eva, Tony Easter, Carlos, and Carmela.

Tony came over to Eva and said, "Here's the register tape. Best night yet. Put this somewhere safe." Eva looked at the tape. He had rung up over $3,000 on booze.

Tony said to Max, "You oughta think about opening a Latino disco around here, my brother!"

Timoney piped in, "No you don't! Maybe down in the Three-Three Precinct, but not in the Three-Four! You keep your big ideas to yourself, Easter." They laughed, all except Carlos, who had to clean up. Carmela said she would help. Max gave them each $200 extra. That didn't go unnoticed by Timoney and Easter. The two winked at each other: a *good people* wink.

CHAPTER 32

Saturday morning looked like the start of a beautiful day, if it weren't for the hangovers. Max and Eva had the luxury of sleeping until nine o'clock. It was sixty-seven degrees and sunny. Max went for his first run since Georgetown to rid his body of any remnants of the night before.

He ran twice around the upper loop in Central Park: eight and a half miles. His cruising pace averaged out to seven-minute miles, much slower than he expected.

Not exactly Ranger School worthy but okay for a civilian.

The mushrooms came to mind as he cooled down and walked past the trees in Central Park. He wanted to try out some of the outside edge - M#1, in a recipe. He was satisfied with his taste tests. He knew they were truffle-like. It was not the palatable experience he worried about. He was still in the dark on safety factors and his improvised theory on the gradation of a mushroom. He decided to create a recipe for the evening setting, using a dash of M#1, and try the first one on himself.

It was time to head home for a quick heavy bag workout and to check on the children. That would loosen him up for what he hoped to be the Saturday night rush at Gringo Smyth's.

A Saturday night rush. Man, things are moving along.

Tony Easter had been keeping the bar running smoothly. Quite often there would be a cop or two at the bar. Max knew Tony was taking care of the boys. That was okay with Max and Eva. Eva felt good about having cops around, and they always behaved themselves. They knew Gringo Smyth's was Timoney's hangout. There was frequently talk at the bar of a deputy inspector promotion coming up for Timoney. The Paco case was a big one for the city and the department. It put Timoney high on the A-list for promotion.

Tony always rang good numbers on the register. Eva did percentages on liquor sales, and the ratios tallied up well. Eva would oftentimes go to the restaurant early. She and Max usually went uptown separately but came home together. Eva was implementing all kinds of innovative computer software for the bar and restaurant. She had inventory control down to the last beer bottle and asparagus spear. Max loved it… and her.

Max walked out of the park at Ninety-Sixth Street and home to the apartment. The elevator wasn't responding, so he searched around for the alleyway entrance to the basement. He went through the back alley and out the other side of the huge apartment building that stretched to the next block. He had walked too far and right past the door to the basement. He finally found the correct door. He tried the knob. It was locked. He banged on it pretty hard. The door opened. Woods, the superintendent, stood there with a sawed-off shotgun cocked and hot.

"Whoa! Hold on, Mr. Woods! I … I got lost. And the elevator …."

"Get in here, you crazy motherfucker! I coulda blown your white ass all over the mother fuckin' alley! What is the matter with you, man? You need a key? Here, take this key. This key fits all the access doors in this building. I'm inside tryin' to gather enough courage to bang my old lady, and you come breakin' down the goddamn door. You scared the shit out of me! Not to mention my old lady. She is probably shoppin' for some motherfuckin' jewelry by now."

"HAROLD! WHERE THE FUCK ARE YOU?"

Ahhh, the little woman. Max thought.

After apologizing to Woods, Max went into his storage room / gym / rainforest. He checked on the children first.

Fine little growth spurt you kids are going through.

Max hit the heavy bag for a solid half hour. He thought about Paco while hitting the bag.

Gotta shake the Paco thing.

Paco was the last person he had fought that he didn't like. In competition he had respect for his opponents. The Paco fight had been for real, and he wondered why he hadn't been able to shut off the compulsion to beat Paco to death. It didn't scare him, but he felt something had been left unfinished. He tried to shrug it off, chalking it up to his military experience. It was discomforting.

Max gathered some aged M#1 for the trial meal experiment. He was focused and in good spirits. He decided on a *duck special* for the evening. He wasn't sure how duck would fly with the clientele if all went well. He chuckled to himself at the pun and was relaxed and confident about a mushroom recipe. If all went well with his meal, he would add enough mushroom for thirteen specials.

If the duck doesn't fly, I'll make an appetizer of some sort for tomorrow evening.

Max would not produce a trite *à l'orange* dish. He found it much too sweet. Instead, he made a brown sauce with a port wine base. Instinctively, he felt the port would be a good partner for the "Duck M#1." He had no plans to add his secret ingredient to any of the customers until his own taste test was complete.

Max prepped his dish. It looked wonderful and smelled out of this world! Carlos watched Max's every move. Carlos was trying his best to absorb everything Max showed him and some things Max did not. Carlos had finally found something he loved to do. Max asked Carlos, "Are you enjoying your role as a student chef?"

Carlos said, "It beats boosting cars, *amigo*." They both laughed. Carlos's creative juices were stirring, and his enthusiasm to prepare fine food was apparent. His daughter, Carmela, was thrilled with the change she saw in her father. Carmela had all the attributes of a good waitress: pretty, smart, honest, and bubbly. She was four years younger than Eva. The two women had become close. Carmela was taking morning courses at Hunter College. She'd switched her major to restaurant and hotel management after witnessing the restaurant business firsthand. Her tips were getting better as the restaurant gained momentum. She was making more than her father on busy nights. She dared not tell him, for fear of extra cash rekindling his old heroin habit.

Max sent Carlos for some innocuous spice from the back of the spice cabinet. As Carlos was busy retrieving it, Max sprinkled a small amount of M#1 into the port wine sauce and whisked away until it disappeared. He chuckled once again at the M#1 designation he used. His mind drifted as he rhythmically whisked.

Max recalled Sergeant Nunez going off about the M14 rifle compared to the old M1: *"The M1 Garand rifle was a trustworthy gas-operated rifle used by the US military in World War II and Korea and initially used at the inception of the Vietnam War. It was heavy and had small clips. That's what killed it. But … it functioned well. It was replaced by the M14: a piece of junk that jammed when overheated, and it overheated when combat became intense. It made the manufacturer billions. Nobody talked about it back home, but the M14 seemed the cause of more American soldier KIAs in Nam than direct hits by the, obsolete but irrepressible AK-47, used by the National Liberation Front and the North Vietnamese Army. The M14 was a disgrace that was covered up by both politicians and the military brass. They finally got it right with the M16. The M14 was written off as another snafu in Southeast Asia by everyone, except the American soldiers that lived to curse the weapon."*

"Here ya go, boss."

"Thanks, Carlos."

Carlos stood next to Max and watched as he always did with a new recipe. This was one time Max wished school was not in session.

"Make sure the other ducks are prepped and ready for the oven."

"You got it, boss." Carlos obediently headed for the prep table.

Now, let's see what we've got here.

Max tasted his new creation. It was foreign to his palate, so it took a bit longer to assimilate.

Nice. Not quite the white truffle pretender I hoped for… similar, yet unique. Perhaps I put too much in. It did take over the port wine somewhat. It's potent all right and does need some fine-tuning. Quantitative Apportionment 101: you can always add more.

Max was relieved that small amounts seemed best to enhance future creations.

All I have to do is live through the testing.

He went out to the bar for a glass of club soda to clear his palate for another taste. When he came back to his dish, he saw Carlos eating away. Max stood there looking at Carlos, then at the half-eaten plate.

"This is *unbeleeeevable, amigo.* Your best yet! You must show me before I eat your whole meal!" Max conjured up a chuckle.

No accounting for different taste.

He didn't know whether to laugh or call an ambulance.

The Saturday-night seating was a success. There were ninety-six covers (meals) this evening in the forty two seat restaurant. The duck sold out, except for one last order. Max could not take his eyes off Carlos the entire night. He saw no obvious change in Carlos. Max knew about Carlos's heroin addiction. Carlos himself had told Max that he was seven years clean. It made Max more nervous than usual. As far as Max's own self-awareness, he felt nothing different to speak of. Everything was going… nicely.

Eva asked to be fed. "Can I have some of the duck dish Carlos has been raving about?"

"We have one left," Carlos said. "You gotta save me a taste, *mi* Evita."

"*Absolutamente,* Carlito, my chef extraordinaire." Eva gave him a kiss on the forehead.

"You betta kiss *El Máximo,* Evita, or he gonna think you got somethin' goin' on with meeee," Carlos said, smiling.

Eva went up and kissed her hero. "Best night ever on the floor, not including the bar receipts, *Máximo*!"

Max was happy but still nervous. He and Carlos both seemed fine.

But this is Eva we're talking about here!

"Sure, uh, right!" Max said, preoccupied by what his next move would be.

A small taste should be okay.

It seemed like everybody was watching. Carlos was particularly interested, wanting to know exactly how the meal was prepared.

How the hell am I going to get the M#1 into the sauce? Carlos would certainly notice a difference in taste.

Then he remembered the port wine from the bar. "Let me go out to the bar and get some of the good port wine for my lady." Max said as he bowed.

Max went out to the bar. Tony Easter was sitting at a table counting his tips after ringing out.

"We had a good night at the bar, boss. The receipts are in the cigar box with the printout." Tony said as he kept on counting, turning bills to face each other.

"Good job, Tony," Max said.

Max grabbed a wineglass and poured some port into it. He turned his back to Tony and took a touch of M#1. He rubbed his thumb and forefinger together to get a small amount into the port.

What the hell is *the correct amount? I'm a chef, not a chemist.*

Although of late, he wasn't sure. He was swirling the glass as he approached the kitchen. This made Carlos and Eva a bit curious.

"What concoction have you got there, honey?" Eva asked.

"Just the port… port wine doesn't get much call around here. It needs to breathe a little before I sauce it up," Max said, looking into the glass. Nobody ever doubted the master. He made all his sauces from scratch.

Eva loved how Max moved as he prepared a dish. It was free-flowing, bordering on artistic. Max was always immersed in his creations. Several comparisons came to mind: *Jackson Pollock painting, Leonard Bernstein conducting while turning pages, Gene Kelly in, An American in Paris… I love my old movies. Oh well.*

"Go out to the dining room and eat like a human being. I'll bring it right out. What would you like to drink?" Max answered his own question. "Have club soda. I want you to guess at the essence of this dish."

Eva thought Max looked a little nervous as he brought the dish out. She dismissed it as enthusiasm. She started in on a small piece of duck first. She wasn't sure whether she had ever eaten duck before.

They're so cute.

If Max prepared it, the dish would be like nothing she could envision anyway. First bite: Eva savored for a few seconds and said nothing. Second bite: Carlos, Carmela, Tony, and Max all watched Eva for a reaction. She cleared her throat, took a sip of club soda, then ate another bite. She cleared her throat again. Then, without saying a word or looking up, she patted her lips and got up. She walked around the table and put her arms around Max's neck. She looked him in the eye and said, "My dear, simply put… this is a masterpiece." She kissed him.

"No. **You** are the masterpiece." Max said as he kissed her back.

Eva cut a piece for Carlos, who was on board with the masterpiece comment. "You gotta teach me this one, boss!" Carlos said while chewing voraciously.

"Don't talk with your mouth full, Carlos," Max said as everyone laughed.

Eva gave the rest of the meal to Carmela. Eva was tired and wanted to put the receipts in the safe. She went to check on the bar receipts. "Nice job tonight, Tony. I hope they're taking care of you with good tips?"

"Don't worry about me, Eva. We are building a nice, steady crowd. The bar is getting more regulars from the hospital and the neighborhood," Tony said, still counting his tip money. "Nice people… respectful."

They left Carlos to do his cleanup work. Eva told Max in the cab that she thought the duck dish should be a part of the regular menu. Trying to get her off the duck topic, Max said he could use the same ingredients for many different recipes, duck was one of many possibilities.

"What was that distinct taste that came through? It was just delightful. I tried to place it and still can't quite put my finger on it. Neither could Carlos."

"You liked it, eh? That's great. There will be more. It can be very fattening, though!" Max thought that might get her off the trail.

"Really? Fattening?"

She looked at him as he started laughing. She attempted a futile punch on his arm.

"Let's get home, gang," Max said.

The elevator was functional. Max and Eva were feeling great for getting through hard one of their busiest nights.

Max took a shower. Eva decided on a bath after Max was through. She wanted this nice feeling of euphoria to last. And, besides, a bath would be a nice prelude. As Max exited the bathroom, she touched his cheek as she slid by him and said, "don't fall asleep."

Max hadn't planned on falling asleep. He was feeling pretty mellow himself and hadn't been able to stop thinking about making love to Eva since she'd kissed him after the meal.

M#1? Nice touch. <u>Nota bene:</u> research notes.

Max lay in bed waiting for Eva.

What the hell is she doing in there? He decided to peek.

Eva was immersed in the tub, her arms hanging loosely over the sides of the four-legged porcelain monster that claimed half the bathroom. Her eyes were closed, and her head lay back on a towel.

"Is that my favorite pool boy?" Eva asked as she opened her eyes with a smile, sending a sexy look his way.

"It is, madam. May I dry you?" Max reached for a bath towel.

"You may."

Eva slowly arose from the water. The clinging white bubbles began racing down toward her feet.

Venus lives.

The rinse water from the sponge beaded on her bronze skin before continuing its effortless glide. She stood in front of Max and touched his cheek as she turned her back to him and raised her arms. Max began patting her dry, mesmerized by the drops of beaded water running, then stopping, then running again, rounding the curves of her perfectly chiseled body. He took his time. When he got to Eva's long legs, he dropped to his knees. He gently ran the towel down each leg as though removing marble-dust from a newly completed sculpture. He turned her around and looked up at her face. She touched his cheek once again and smiled. He caressed her buttocks in both hands, as she tightened in anticipation. He looked up between her firm breasts and erect nipples. She was looking upward, her long, wet, iridescent hair hanging wildly.

His un-rushed kisses to her navel and thighs were welcomed. The bath oil made his lips and cheeks glide to where life began. He kissed gently until she bowed her legs to allow his lips and tongue to make their way. He guided her backward so that she leaned on the side of the four-legged porcelain stallion she had emerged from. It was the perfect height… when she arched her feet. She ran her fingers through his hair and held on to make sure he couldn't leave… too early.

My beautiful goddess.

He lost himself in her faultlessness, until after her feet scraped along the tiled floor. She took a moment, then looked down into his eyes and smiled. She offered her hand as she stood. They kissed deeply. Silently, she took him into the bedroom… It was his turn.

CHAPTER 33

Sunday brunch required an early morning setup. Max and Eva had not gotten much sleep. That was fine on this particular Sunday morn, both smiling throughout their chores.

Max was excited about testing the M#1 on some egg courses.

It must be subtle. Americans are picky about their eggs, not like Latinos. Latinos love to screw around with their eggs in the morning. A spritz of M#1 in the hollandaise sauce. A little more than a spritz in the huevos rancheros.

Carlos was off on Sundays, so Max had a free hand.

"People are lovin' the brunch, Max." Carmela said. Max had to ration the M#1 for the large brunch special: bouillabaisse. He smiled at the amazing aroma the M#1 unveiled. He asked Eva to taste the bouillabaisse. She loved it, and it sold out quickly.

By four thirty the restaurant was cleaned and locked, not to be opened again until Tuesday morning. On Sunday nights, Max and Eva brought the weekly receipts home with them and called for a cab in lieu of walking to the hospital canopy. Eva felt safer doing that even though daylight had not faded. It also gave them a chance to sit and have a beer or two if they wished. Max's cell phone rang as they sat at the window table. It was Timoney. Max put the phone on speaker.

"Hey, Max, are you and Eva still at the restaurant?" Timoney asked.

"Yeah. Everything okay?" Max asked.

"That depends. What are you two doing tomorrow morning?"

Monday was their only day off. Eva rolled her eyes at the thought of Max getting roped into something. Max caught her look in time to weigh things. "Whatcha got?" he asked.

"Well, I thought you might want to be my guests down at city hall for the swearing in of the newest deputy inspector to the NYPD," Timoney said.

Eva screamed and jumped up to do her victory dance. Max said, "Do you hear that? If I didn't know better, I would think something was going on between you two. What time and where? And congratulations, **Inspector Timoney**."

"City hall: 10:00 a.m. sharp. The ceremony begins at 10:30," Timoney said.

"We will be there. Well deserved, my man. See you tomorrow."

Timoney ended with "I'll be the good lookin' one in the blue uniform with all the medals, ha-ha. Sleep tight, you two!"

Max and Eva were thrilled for Timoney. He was a good friend that deserved the promotion.

It's about time they got something right around this city. Max thought.

Their taxi arrived. The cab shot down Broadway unimpeded late on a Sunday afternoon.

Eva looked at Max. "I wonder who'll replace him in the Three-Four."

"I was thinking the same thing."

Max would ask Timoney about his replacement at an appropriate time. Eva snuggled close and rested her head on his shoulder. Nothing further was said. They settled into their own thoughts. Both were happy… and sad.

Perhaps the engagement ring will cheer her up. Only a few more payments left before Christmas.

Max wondered how he should go about proposing.

Nobody ever called me Romeo Burns. I'll ask Curlander. No! Amy. NO! I'll ask Tony Easter.

Max's thoughts went back to the restaurant. His objective was to keep the restaurant going full bore. He hoped to try a lunch trade at some point if the workload was bearable. He would definitely need more staff for that. Eva fell asleep on his shoulder.

The next morning, Max was up at six forty-five and out the door by seven. He ran a quick four laps around the reservoir in Central Park and was home by eight thirty. Eva was still in bed when he got home. Max had to tickle her to get her up. She hated that, but it worked when they were pressed for time. Usually the mere threat of a tickle got Eva moving. This morning it took the real thing. Max didn't own a suit. He'd never had to wear one. Senior prom had been a rented baby-blue tuxedo, the Culinary Institute had provided his *chef whites*, and his army uniforms were still in his closet. He did own a corduroy sport coat and jeans… his civilian dress uniform.

Max was checking the weather on TV when Eva came out of the bedroom. He stood there speechless. She glowed and looked absolutely beautiful. She made a simple outfit elegant: a white blazer, a dark blouse, and a skirt that was just short enough. Max was always a sucker for a beautiful set of legs, and Eva had them. She looked like she'd walked off the cover of a magazine, sunglasses and all. He'd never been more proud that she was his woman.

A few more months until ring time.

"Ready?" she asked. Max stared as she walked by him in her high-heeled shoes. He gathered in her scent as she passed. A thought ran through his head: Max hoped he had never taken her for granted with all work and no play.

She's never complained… not once.

He wanted to take her back into the bedroom and make love to her. Eva tickled **him** this time, and he jumped. "How do you like it? C'mon, lover boy. But hold that thought for later."

For some reason both Max and Eva had thought the ceremony would involve only Timoney. Not the case. There were eighty-two promotions on the agenda for the ceremony. Mayor Braunreuther would be a busy man today. The ceremony started with speeches followed by promotions: twenty-four sergeants; eighteen lieutenants; nine captains; twenty four detectives in all the grades; two deputy inspectors; and two chief inspectors. Then there were the medals and commendations. It was a full day of pomp and ceremony. That was all right with Max and Eva. Today was for Deputy Inspector Sean (John) Timoney. Nothing else mattered.

Eva knew she looked great. And, she knew how to walk in high heels. Her speech and mannerisms seemed to adjust accordingly. She knew how to work it. Max followed behind Eva with a smile on his face, and everyone could see why. He loved that she was his girl. Everyone in attendance, men and women, could not take their eyes off this dark-eyed beauty. She looked like a movie star. Everyone involved in the ceremony had their families in the audience—including soon-to-be ex-captain John Timoney. All the Timoney family members in the United States were present: John Timoney and his brother Kieran. Kieran was on the stage receiving a medal for his team's cleanup of Hell's Kitchen, recently renamed, "The Theatre District" by His Honor Mayor Braunreuther, master of urban geographical name changes. Everyone cheered louder for their respective honoree. Eva cheered loudest of them all when Timoney's time came for his promotion. Eva's outburst allowed the men to gaze at her, at least for a few seconds, without catching heat from their wives.

Mayor Braunreuther pontificated about how crime was down in the city. "Commissioner Radcliff has integrated such masterful innovations, blah, blah, blah."

The rank and file checked their watches and held their boredom at bay as they listened to the inevitable bullshit part of the day. They pondered the important things - promotions meant more pay and favorable shifts.

After the ceremony, both Kieran and John came down from the stage and worked their way over to Max and Eva. Eva gave Kieran a hug and a congratulatory kiss on the cheek. John got the whole nine yards with a full-blown kiss on the lips, replete with a smacking noise at the end. She then held on to his arm as though he were her father. Deputy Inspector Timoney was the envy of the room. Mayor Braunreuther came over to greet Eva and Max. Timoney had not briefed him on their attendance, but Braunreuther, ever the politician, knew whose hand to shake in a crowd. The fact that presidential candidates had come to Washington Heights… rather Hamilton Heights, to visit these two folks should never be overlooked. Besides, being next to Eva was better than kissing cops' wives.

Maybe Max and Eva will tell their politico friends what a great mayor I am? Never miss an opportunity.

"How's the restaurant going?" Braunreuther asked Max and Eva.

"Good," Eva said. Braunreuther grabbed Eva's hand and said, "I hope this guy isn't overworking you, my dear." He took an extra few moments to drink in Eva's beauty. She was on the verge of embarrassment when Braunreuther asked, "What do you think of your friend Ed Curlander's move to run for president as an independent candidate?"

"Really?" Max said as he and Eva looked incredulously at each other.

"He announced it last night at a press conference in L.A… First he got rid of Alexander Blair and then the entire Democratic Party," the mayor said, looking back and forth at the two of them. Braunreuther found it difficult to believe they didn't know about Curlander's proclamation.

Eva had never been politically involved. Neither had Max really, they voted, that was the extent of their politics. Ed dropping his Democratic Party affiliation—that was a shock to both of them. Max digested it, smiled and thought:

Ballsy move. Timing is right. The country is fed up with a system that shuts itself down for party hubris.

Max said to Braunreuther, "Good for him. People are getting sick of politicians wallowing in self-serving agendas. It's all about reelection, job security and padding their pockets." John Timoney coughed to stifle a laugh. Braunreuther looked at Max. He hesitated then chickened out altogether, realizing it could only be to his detriment to reveal his point of view to someone so close to a presidential candidate.

While Eva was charming the entire NYPD, Max decided to sneak off to call Ed Curlander. It would be a slight not to call him after such a big play. Max walked down the hallway and stood gazing at a lifelike painting of former New York mayor, Jimmy Walker, known to New Yorkers of his time as "Beau James," because of his sartorial splendor. Max stared at the painting as the phone rang.

Might be time to buy a suit.

Max got Curlander on the phone. He'd thought he might get away with leaving a message. Curlander was happy to hear from his pal.

"Where the hell are you? It sounds like you're in a cathedral," Curlander said.

"I'm at city hall with Eva."

"You got married without telling us?"

"No. We're at the NYPD promotion ceremony. Our friend John Timoney was made a deputy inspector by that putz Braunreuther. So what's new on your end?" Max asked, very matter of fact

"You know what's new! I am running for president of the United States of America. That dilapidated Alexander Blair was dragging me down like a weighted chain. I couldn't get him to quit the race. Most Democrats are scared shit of what he knows about them, so they were afraid to dump him. **Screw them all!** This country is so fragmented I figure it's time to sweep the pieces into a tapestry that can work. Maybe I can stop the bullshit and unfreeze the entire political system. Anyway, I am paying a lot of people good money to figure this crap out… I still want you with me, brother!"

Max was knocked off guard by the statement. He was relieved when Curlander did not wait for a response.

"Hold on. Someone wants to say hello."

"Max? It's Amy. How are you? How is Eva? I miss you guys terribly."

"How are you, sweetie? We miss you too. Hold on. I am going to get Eva. She is talking to Mayor Braunreuther. She could use a break."

"**You're kidding me!** Not you guys with these boring politicians. You two were my only hope. Oh my God, poor Eva. Put her on."

Max moved hastily back down the hall as he talked to Amy. Eva was still talking to the mayor and Timoney.

"Excuse me, Mr. Mayor… John. I have Amy Curlander on the phone for Eva."

Braunreuther's eyes lit up. He was glad he'd held his tongue.

Max handed Eva the phone. "Amy?" It was time for Eva's mysterious folk dance. She left Mayor Braunreuther standing there, wondering if she was in the throes of epilepsy.

Deputy Inspector Timoney introduced Max to his new boss: First Chief Inspector Joseph Doheney. Doheney was about six feet four or so and still in good shape. He had a strong grip that both men seemed to appreciate.

"I heard about you, Max. It's a pleasure to meet you. I wish we had more citizens like you in this city."

"Just trying to make a living, inspector."

"Yeah, well, ya' got balls, son." He looked around the room and called over his shoulder, "Hey, Dunne, come here for a second." Peter Dunne, a newly appointed captain, came over immediately. He was a good looking man of about forty. Max thought he looked rather young to be a captain. Doing the math in his head, he would have put Dunne on the job for almost twenty years. That was retirement age for most, but these guys were born to lead. They loved "*the job*." Actually, it was their fellow officers they loved.

"Captain Peter Dunne, this is Max Burns," Doheney said.

"Glad to meet you, captain. Congratulations," Max said as they shook hands.

"Captain Dunne will be the new CO up at the Three-Four. I thought you two should get acquainted sooner rather than later."

"Good to finally meet you, Mr. Burns. Deputy Inspector Timoney has filled me in on most things. I'll be available if you need me. I grew up in the Heights. I know the cast of characters and every back alley on all fifty-five blocks from river to river. Here is my cell phone number. Use it. I mean that."

Max was relieved. He couldn't wait to introduce Eva, if he could ever get her off the phone. Eva handed the phone back to Max after speaking briefly to Ed Curlander.

Max made a quick introduction and then excused himself, which was fine with Captain Dunne. Dunne was at ease talking to women. But Eva was no ordinary woman, and she could tell Dunne seemed very attentive. Eva played with Dunne for a few seconds. Then she cut it off in time for him to realize that the dress blue uniform wasn't working this time.

"Max, wish me luck," Curlander told him. "I want to see you soon. When I get up to NYC, we'll get together. I miss kicking your ass at 3:00 a.m. By the way, I have been keeping tabs on that Paco weasel. To tell you the truth, I was confused about Huntsville being the only stipulation. An FBI contact told me it's 'cause his mother, Maria Elena Rodriguez Caamano, just bought a house near Huntsville, 'to be close to her little boy.' Seems the old man bought it for her. So put it all to bed now, pal. I need you on my side when the shit goes down here in D.C. … even if you're not a marine. Seriously, whenever you want … you gotta place here with me. You know that, right?" Ed brought the point up one more time, hoping it might stick one of these days.

"I am a friggin' chef!"

"Then you'll be my chef, you thickheaded grunt! But you gotta bring Eva with you. If not, you can wallow in that hellhole they call Washington Heights… or whatever Braunreuther is calling it."

"I'm not going anywhere without her, pal."

"Finally getting smart. Call me soon. Keep me posted."

"You too. Adios," Max said.

"And good luck to you and Eva, Max. We're all going to need it!"

"Ed, like they say up here in NYC about the lottery, 'you gotta be in it to win it!' I'll be watching," Max said.

Maria Elena… Paco and Louie's mother? Common Latina name. But Timoney said he had an in with Paco. Eva will love this.

Eva was talking with Kieran Timoney. Kieran assured her that Captain Dunne had been briefed. Since Deputy Inspector Timoney was now in charge of the entire borough with the Manhattan Street Crime Division, he would still be involved. Kieran himself was a first-grade detective and boss for the Manhattan North sector: Marble Hill south through Hell's Kitchen to Thirty-Eighth Street, and east and west from the East River to the Hudson River.

Eva was relieved to hear all this. She didn't like to talk about her fears and trepidations to Max. Her silence was her way of showing that she was strong too.

Max came back to Kieran and Eva. The conversation abruptly changed. "You two are coming up to the Audubon Ballroom for the festivities later on, right?" Kieran said.

"First we're hearing about it. Sure." Max looked at Eva.

"You go… I'm going to do some work at the restaurant since we'll both be in the neighborhood. I'll grab a cab now. I can meet you later."

"Eva, come on, honey."

"No, I insist. You boys run along and play. It'll make my week easier getting some things done today. Call me when you are ready to leave the party and pick me up in front of the restaurant."

"It's our only day off, Eva! The restaurant'll be there. We can go in early tomorrow… I'll help you. C'mon, baby." Max pleaded.

"**You**, helping **me** with the books? That's what I'm trying to avoid." Eva chuckled, then touched Max's cheek, kissing his lips tenderly for all to see.

Kieran said, "I promised every cop here, I'd get you there, Eva. Gonna be a lot of disappointed men in blue uniforms today."

"Oooooh… And I just love a man in uniform. Please, I enjoy the peace and quiet without anybody asking me about saltshakers. I'm going to lock myself in the back office and be as quiet as a church mouse. You boys have some fun. Call me a few minutes before you're leaving the Audubon Ballroom. I love you." Eva kissed Max on the lips once again and made an about-face as she waved goodbye.

Eat your hearts out. Max thought.

Eva walked through the giant doors, held open by the white-gloved hands of two uniformed sergeants. She looked like royalty passing through the portals of city hall.

Beau James… keep your eyes to yourself.

She seemed to walk in slow motion. All eyes were on Eva. At this point every cop in the room could have had his pocket picked.

Max just smiled and said, "be careful… I love you!"

Eva blew him a kiss. Then, without turning around, she waved goodbye to one and all… as she walked her walk.

CHAPTER 34

The Audubon Ballroom was located on 165th Street and Broadway in Washington Heights. It was just south of Columbia-Presbyterian Hospital and three and a half blocks from Gringo Smyth's. The restaurant's proximity to the ballroom made Max feel better about Eva taking a cab there.

Max always marveled at the architecture of the Audubon Ballroom when he walked past. Loyal followers of Malcolm X considered the Audubon Ballroom sacrosanct. It was the site of his assassination on February 21, 1965. It had been slated to be razed by the city and a research center for Columbia University constructed in its place. Muslims applied pressure, and a settlement had been reached that resulted in saving two-thirds of the ballroom to establish a museum dedicated to Malcolm X and his teachings. The only stipulation was that the city could use the ballroom for events.

Today, the stage where Malcolm X had been murdered would be utilized by cops roasting cops, a cementing process within the blue code. It was akin to the military in that respect. Max could relate. Hopefully, all comments, shenanigans, and ball busting would be forgotten in the days to come. Nevertheless, some things were never forgotten.

Most of the brass left early. Max could see why, as this rite of passage was the most entertaining thing he had ever encountered.

There were imitations of everyone, from past presidents of the United States to top cops. Nothing was sacred today. One at a time, cops with their beer muscles pumped up got onto the stage to perform their *shtick*. Acts that were a bust got booed off the stage immediately. Others, even though Max was not privy to specifics, were absolutely hysterical to him. Nobody escaped the comedy routines of their brothers and sisters in blue. Often as not, the person being roasted was forced to stay and suffer the indignities. Some acts were a complete surprise to the wives and families, but all were embraced as good fun. It was a day to celebrate and rely on designated drivers. When one of the newly appointed sergeants was introduced to the audience as presidential candidate Ed Curlander, the entire place went wild with applause and cheering. Max was taken aback by this. At first he thought it would be for the quality of the mimicking about to ensue. When Max asked Kieran if that were the case, Kieran said, "no way! Cops all over the US are getting on board with your buddy Curlander. Our NYPD unions are ready to endorse him...PBA and all officer unions. He better not be another bullshit artist." Max was happy to hear that and would pass it on. He would pay attention to the contents of Ed's speeches more closely. It would be an important endorsement and great timing.

Deputy Inspector John Timoney stayed while those more vulnerable left. This said volumes to Max. *Timoney can take the heat... or is he too tough to be screwed with?* Everyone knew John did not drink alcohol and therefore, would remember everything said, and who said it. He was the high school principal standing in the hallway at recess.

Max was standing alone toward the back of the ballroom, thinking it was about time for an exit. Then, an all-too-familiar sound shattered his thoughts and shook his body. Simultaneously, the ground shook. Everyone in the hall froze at the sound of the explosion. Instinctively, Max knew it was a bomb. The ballroom became silent and still for a full second. Captain Dunne ran to John Timoney and whispered in his ear. Max watched their brief conversation. Then Dunne got on his cell phone and ran out the door. Timoney looked around the room. Kieran ran to his brother as cops began ushering their loved ones out the side doors. Both Timoneys looked around the room until their eyes locked on Max. Max felt the hair on his neck go up and ran toward them.

When he got in front of them, John said, ***"We think it's the restaurant!"***

Max dropped his beer and ran full bore out onto the street. He ran north into the white smoke that was now billowing down Broadway. The pungent smell of C-4 explosive was too familiar. ***BOMB! Not gas!***

The closer he got, the more the residue filled his nostrils with an instantaneous message to his brain.

"Eva! Eva!" Max screamed as he ran up Broadway. He could see the source of the white smoke rushing out from what used to be the front windows of Gringo Smyth's. The flames were fighting for an exit from their confinement and lapped all the way up to the fourth-floor windows of the apartment building. FDNY Engine 93, Ladder 45, Battalion 13, from the 181st Street firehouse pulled up as Max arrived. Bomb squad members present at the ballroom ceremonies had jumped in their cars and got to the scene at the same time as Max.

"***It's HOT! No one inside***" Battalion Chief Dave Delaney yelled to his firefighters, who were well aware of the state of the fire, but this fire merited an official command with the growing attention of civilians and cops. The pump trucks immediately began pasting the open flames that came out onto Broadway and lapped straight up, blackening the red brick walls.

"EVA! " Max screamed. He ran at the fire looking for a way in. It was futile but he had to try. He ran to the battalion chief. "Did you see her? Did she get out?" Max screamed. The chief stared but said nothing. There was nothing he could say. He had heard these same queries many times before. He had learned not to say anything at this juncture, yet the answer was always the same, when a spontaneous explosion was the cause of a fire.

Max grabbed the chief's shoulders and screamed in his face, "Did she get out? Did you see her come out?" A captain and two firefighters grabbed Max to pull him away from the chief. Instinctively, Max prepared to defend himself. At this point, both Timoneys appeared and stepped in. John explained Max's aggressiveness to the battalion chief. The two men were of equal rank with mutual respect for each other, but the FDNY had full jurisdiction here. It was not an unfamiliar situation for firefighters: firefighters inherently knew when to stand down. Max began running from bystander to bystander, some looked familiar to him. "Did you see Eva come out?" Their heads slowly dropped to their chests in silence. Nobody had seen anyone come out. Nobody could have gotten out. Max looked up as flames licked the sides of the building up to the roof.

Max screamed, ***"EVAAAAA!"*** He staggered backward against an EMT truck on Broadway and slid down to the blacktop. Broadway was blocked in both directions by the four - alarmer. There were more cops than firefighters at the scene doing what they could, which amounted to traffic and crowd control. It was evident to all, and now to Max, that nobody survived this horrendous blast and the resulting inferno.

Eventually, there were no more "maybes" to cling to. If Eva was inside the restaurant, she was gone. Max stayed there until the site was eventually just a smoldering black hole.

It was a *hot fire*. A *hot fire* after a blast was either arson, highly inflammable contents, or gas related. In this case arson seemed a certainty. The blast source had yet to be confirmed. The fire marshal, also a combat veteran, also knew from three blocks away what caused this fire. After a cursory examination, he confirmed to the battalion chief and to the Timoneys that a crime scene should be established. "C-4 plastic explosive, probably an amateur, not familiar with the size of the charge needed," he said.

Doctors ran from the hospital to see what they could do.

There were few tenants at home on the first three floors above the restaurant. Monday was a workday for most. It was not supposed to be a workday for Eva.

Tony Easter arrived and went around the barricade. He saw both Kieran and John. A quick conversation ensued, and Kieran nodded toward Max. Tony ran over to him. Even Tony was lost for words and just hugged Max's limp body.

"I'll get the little bastard for this!" Tony yelled as he ran to his car.

Max was confused at first and then digested what Tony had said. *"I'll get the little bastard for this!" Get who? Who? Little Louie!*

Max ran to John and Kieran. "Little Louie. Little Louie did this. Paco put him up to it! Tony is going to get him right now," Max said, expecting that John would condone Tony's actions, but the deputy inspector didn't look happy. John had already sent two cop cars up to the projects to pick up Louie. He gave the orders as soon as he'd heard it was the restaurant. Tony Easter was a new wrinkle.

All Easter can do is screw things up! Timoney thought.

"Don't let Easter near Louie!" Timoney told Captain Dunne.

"Yes, sir."

"Get going. If Easter fucks this case up, I'll have your ass as well as his. You tell him, I'll put him in jail for obstruction. You tell Easter I said that! Capeesh?" Timoney screamed at Dunne.

"Yes, sir." Dunne saluted. He probably shouldn't have, but he did. Dunne pulled on the arm of a rather large sergeant, and both men jumped into an unblocked squad car.

Tony Easter was roaming the projects screaming at everyone to tell him where Louie was hiding. By the time Dunne pulled up, Easter had already broken down the door to Paco's apartment. Dunne grabbed Easter and told him what Timoney had said. Easter, knowing that Timoney was not to be trifled with, calmed down.

Easter drove back down to the site of the blast. He saw Max being restrained as a body bag was taken from a hole in the back wall of the restaurant. The bag was half the size of a human body. Max lost his breath. He had seen this before. Only remnants of a body had been found.

"EVAAAAA!" Max screamed an ungodly final scream as he looked up toward the heavens. He had to be restrained again, a difficult job that was turning uglier. Deputy Inspector Timoney once again stepped in. Max pleaded to see her one last time.

Timoney turned Max away from the body and stared into his eyes. "Remember her as the beautiful woman she was, not like this. It's what she would want."

Max was weak and could not fathom the magnitude of the loss. He wandered aimlessly at the scene. It was surreal.

This can't happen here.... in America.

The irony of living through an I.E.D. in Afghanistan overtook him. He shook his head in disbelief.

My head... my head hurts so bad.

Max cradled his head in his hands and wept as he moved side to side.

Little Louie was not living at the apartment in the Dyckman projects. He was hunkered down in the Bronx with some friends who were growing tired of the current situation.

Louie walked into the Three-Four Precinct the day after the blast. He asked to see Captain Timoney but was met by Captain Dunne.

"Yo...you wanna see me?" Louie said with a smile on his face that Dunne wanted to smack.

Under scrutiny, Louie's alibi held up. It seemed that, at the time of the blast, Louie had been at George Washington High School on 192nd Street and Audubon Avenue, thirty blocks uptown from Gringo Smyth's. Louie had been there all morning and afternoon enrolling in a New York City sponsored computer class. He had signed all the enrollment documents, proving he was there all day. He had a list of people that could verify his presence; some were teachers. Nobody told this to Max. Timoney vowed to make Louie's life miserable until he found out the specifics about who had bombed the restaurant. This was a murder case. They would need the cooperation of the FDNY fire marshal's office, as well as Kieran's detectives and street snitches, to hang this one on Louie.

Louie had taken out an order of protection (OP) against Max after Paco's trial. When Timoney told Max about the OP, Max gave a wry smile.

Planned it all along… the fuckin' weasel.

Timoney was crushed. He had grown very fond of Max and Eva: rebels like the Irish immigrants who had ventured into New York Harbor in the mid-nineteenth century. Timoney knew he had to use any and all resources to stay as close as possible to Max. Eva's murder devastated Timoney. He felt as though he had lost the daughter he never had. Timoney was a tough guy on the outside, where he thought it mattered most.

"I never felt like taking a drink more than I do now!" he said to his AA sponsor from his new office at One Police Plaza. He prayed he wouldn't. But he had to tell his sponsor how he felt.

Ed Curlander blamed Braunreuther for being gutless with regard to his neglect of the Heights. Curlander needed to yell at someone and Braunreuther fit the bill. Curlander wanted the Department of Homeland Security to step in since a bomb had been used. The FDNY commissioner asked Braunreuther to get the suits to beg off. Curlander's intentions were good, but the feds would only get in the way. **"Useless!"** Timoney said to Captain Dunne and Max with regard to the feds getting involved.

Braunreuther was a savvy politico. He knew better than to make a call that would piss Curlander off. In true pass-the-buck form, he designated the job to newly appointed Deputy Inspector John Timoney. Timoney called Ed Curlander immediately to thank him for his help and support. "However, sir, with regard to the current investigation," Timoney said, "things would be best handled locally by the NYPD and FDNY people. Being a New York City person, sir,

I know you understand." Curlander knew when to back off if things were in good hands. He felt confident in this son of Ireland turned NYC street cop, even though he had only met him the one time at Gringo Smyth's. Curlander hung up the phone after acquiescing to Timoney, but not before ending the conversation with a demand for results. Timoney knew a man in Ed Curlander's position had to finish the conversation with at least some semblance of victory. Curlander admired Timoney for having the balls to ask him to back off, since Braunreuther did not. Curlander filed it away.

The mayor told the police commissioner that this was to be Timoney's case soon after that phone call. Braunreuther half hoped Timoney would not be successful. He disliked Timoney's momentum. And if this dead end case came up empty, Timoney would be holding the bag.

Captain Dunne was a bit put out.

The Three-Four is my precinct!

He came around after recognizing he was in a different arena now. Dunne was a quick study and realized, THIS arena could benefit him if he played it straight with Timoney, *et al.*

Timoney was finally able to get through to Max by phone after two days of calls, messages, and texts. Max did not sound like the person Timoney had come to know. His throat was raw. His mind wandered. He was obviously deeply depressed.

After a few minutes of forcing the conversation, Timoney said, "Look, Max, we need to have the next of kin make the decision on Eva's remains."

"My God, Len and Margaret. They don't even know!"

"Yes they do. I called them. They flew up this morning. They know everything. They brought Eva's dental records for identification purposes. They want to see you."

"Where are they?"

"They're with me now. We are at McGonnel's Funeral Home, across the street from Incarnation Church on 175th Street and St. Nicholas Avenue. Where are you?"

"I'm at… the restaurant."

"I thought so. Stay there. I'll send a car down to get you."

Max paced back and forth on the corner of 165th Street and Broadway. He breathed in deeply to smell the last remnants of the malodor.

He dreaded going to the funeral parlor. He was glad there hadn't been any funeral parlors in Afghanistan and Iraq.

Hindus in India do it right. They light the funeral pyre at dawn. By dusk, the ashes are ready to be spread over a body of water. How ironical… Eva has already gone through that.

It seemed like forever for Max's eyes to adjust to the bleak lighting as he walked from the street into the funeral parlor. The funeral parlor was a throwback to the 1950s and could have doubled as a palm reader's lair. The funeral parlor was empty, save Timoney, Len, Margaret, and the undertaker, a Mr. Robert McGonnel. Max's thoughts of what a funeral director would look like were confirmed, complete with a cold weak handshake and a barely audible voice.

Max did not know what to expect from Len and Margaret.

Will these people… these wonderful grandparents that raised their five-year-old orphaned granddaughter hate me? They have every right to!

He made up his mind that, however they treated him, he would just stand there and take it for as long as needed.

Max was shaking as Margaret slowly turned and looked into his eyes. He could say nothing. His mouth moved, but nothing came out. Margaret was calm. She looked like an angel. Max stared at Margaret, then at Len. Len looked lost.

Time seemed to gear down to a different tempo for this surreal world. He saw Timoney sitting on a bench staring down as he moved his hat round and round to occupy his hands.

Then, Margaret smiled and walked over to Max. She hugged him tightly. Len came over and stood next to them. Max put his arms around both of them and cried. He rarely cried, but he was learning how. It was an ironic reversal of guardianship: Margaret and Len holding the big man from collapsing. These wonderful people whom he'd grown to love were the only family he had left in the world. They had every right to hate him… and yet, they did not.

All Max managed to stammer was, "the only thing you asked me to do was take care of her."

Margaret stroked his hair gently as Max said over and over, "I'm so sorry… I wish it was me."

The sunlight blinded them as they exited McGonnel's Funeral Home. They waited a moment to gather themselves and crossed St. Nicholas Avenue. The gray spires of the Church of the Incarnation towered in front of them. Without saying a word to each other, they all went in. They sat in the back pew and held hands. Nothing was said, each deep in his or her own thoughts. There were no tears from Len or Margaret. Max guessed they had shed their share of tears at home and wanted to be strong for him. Timoney had told them as much as he felt they should know, including that Max had not eaten or slept since the tragedy. And, that he had been seen at the restaurant site at all hours, trying to peer inside the cracks of plywood that covered the windows. Friends, employees, doctors, hospital workers, customers, and neighbors had been calling the Three-Four Precinct to tell Captain Dunne about - *"The gringo that searches for the ghost."*

Margaret spoke first. "Come here, my boy. She loved you very much. You need to get hold of yourself. She would not want to see you like this."

"I know. I know. I can't help it. I miss…" Max could not finish a thought. His battered mind ran away in choppy half sentences. "I was a chef in the army. I didn't want to see people die. I wanted… smiles. Eva smiled… I love her so much. I wish it happened to me. If there was a way …."

"There is no way! It is what it is. The hardest thing in the world is to lose someone you love. Len and I lost her mother and father twenty-three years ago. We thought it was the end of the world. I couldn't get Len to stop drinking. I couldn't stop crying. Then one day, I looked at Eva as she sat there on the floor playing with a doll. She looked up at me and said: *'Don't cry, Grandma. You should never cry over anything that can't cry over you.'* **This...** out of the mouth of a five-year-old girl who had lost her mother and father. And you know something? From that point on, I knew everything was going to be all right. I walked over to Len and took the bottle of vodka off the table and said to him, **'No more. It's over... Eva said everything is okay now.'** He looked up and nodded. From that point to this day, Len never touched another drop of alcohol, and I never cried again. Eva will always be with us when we need her, and she will be with you when you need her," Margaret said, patting Max's hand. Len just sat in the pew, nodding.

"Come. We need to talk to Mr. McGonnel," Margaret said.

Max now understood where Eva had gotten her sand. He felt he had just breathed a lungful of pure oxygen.

The three walked back into the funeral parlor. Margaret had ordered the cremation when they had first arrived. At some point in time they would spread Eva's remains into the Atlantic Ocean. She told Mr. McGonnel she wished to take Eva back to Florida with them today. She asked whether that were possible on short notice. She also asked whether that would present a problem as far as airport security was concerned. It was a question only Margaret would have thought to ask. McGonnel looked over at Inspector Timoney. Timoney gave a nod. McGonnel said that ALL arrangements were moving along and would be ready... soon.

Margaret said to Max, "I ...we, would like to see...where."

He gave one last glance over at Timoney, who nodded once again in agreement.

Max, Margaret, and Len slowly walked the eight blocks to the site of the restaurant. They only stayed a few minutes and then took a cab back to the funeral parlor. McGonnel tried handing the urn to Len. Margaret stepped in and took it. They had a plane to catch. When there was a pause in conversation, Max kissed them both, then hailed a cab. Margaret rolled down the window before the cab pulled away from the curb. Max stared at the urn on the seat between Len and Margaret. Both put a hand on top of the urn to steady their granddaughter from falling… as they had done so many times before. Margaret handed Max a piece of paper with their address and phone number in Florida as though he did not have their contact info already. He kissed Margaret again and told her he loved her. He went around to the other window and shook Len's hand and kissed him on the forehead. Len said nothing but managed a smile. He seemed very far away. Max took one last look at the urn. He could not grasp that the contents of this jar contained the remnants of the woman he loved … the woman he would never see or hear laugh again.

The three Carras left for JFK airport.

In the taxi Margaret turned to Len as he stared out the window. "Len… you didn't tell him, did you? **Don't you ever tell him!"** Len slowly shook his head, as though he eventually did comprehend what Margaret was demanding of him.

Max walked slowly toward his apartment. He was numb. He was empty. There was no feedback from his brain. Maybe that was a good thing. His phone was off. He didn't know how long it had been off, because he couldn't remember when he'd powered it down. He turned it back on and listened to an old voice mail from Eva. He was halfway back to the apartment when his phone rang. It was Ed Curlander. "Max! How ya doin'? I've been calling you every ten minutes!"

"My phone was off."

"We're coming up! What can we do?"

"Nothing. There won't be any funeral. She's gone. Len and Margaret took her … home. Don't come up. Don't put yourself in the middle of this crap, not now. It's gonna get ugly," Max said.

"Whaddya mean, ugly? It's already ugly! Don't do anything

stupid. Hear me? Come down here. Take a break and come stay with us," Ed said.

"I don't know. I need to check with Timoney tomorrow morning to see where the investigation is going. He tells me there'll be problems finding the actual torch. I don't care if they do or not. I know who did this and why. I'll finish it this time." Max was off on a tangent that scared Curlander.

"Listen to me. Forget this revenge bullshit! I'll have this taken care of. You just work on getting yourself together."

"No. No. This is my fight. I made the mess; I'll clean it up."

"Amy wants to talk to you." Before Max could say no, Ed put her on the phone.

"Max. Oh, my Max ..." Amy was crying uncontrollably. "Please come down here and stay with us ... please."

"Not now. I can't right now! I love you both. Eva loved you too."

Curlander got back on the phone. Max was in a fog and did not absorb any of Curlander's conversation. He let Ed talk as he walked toward the apartment. He was in no rush to get there. There was nobody to come home to. There would be only reminders of what used to be and what might have been.

Max stopped in front of Rodrigo's Pet Shop. He hadn't been there in a while. He stared at the pups playing in the window as Curlander's voice chattered away. There was one pup off on its own, one roughneck of a pup that the others wouldn't play with. It looked different than the rest, majestic even as a pup. As Max walked in, Curlander's voice became audible again. "Look, you need a friend right about now ..."

"Is that Tango's?" Max asked Rodrigo. "It sure looks like him."

"*Sí*, that's Tango's pup. Only one in the litter that lived!" Rodrigo said. "The breeder told me it fought its way to daylight. *Heeeheee.* What a mess!"

"Huh! Tough guy, eh? Has it gotten its shots?"

"Yesterday."

"How much for it?" Max asked.

"We know what happened to you. I am sorry for your troubles, my friend. You take the damn dog. You owe me a meal, remember?"

Max stared at Rodrigo. It unnerved Rodrigo for a second. He knew Max was a bad motherfucker and not in a good state of mind. That was a fact known to the entire Latino community in Nueva York.

"Get me a leash and all the stuff I need."

"That, you gotta pay for, jefe."

"Don't call me jefe!" Max snapped. He wasn't sure where that reaction came from. Then he remembered: Paco and Little Louie called him jefe. It was $175 by the time he got out of Rodrigo's Pet Shop with a bed, toys, bones, bowls, and a new best friend.

Curlander was still talking. Max interrupted. "Ya know that friend you said I needed? I just found 'em. Ed, I'll be okay … I need to work on things." Max held his new best friend up over his head to see whether the pup was male or female. *Lincoln is your name. Sounds better than Mary Todd.* Max managed a smile.

"Call me tomorrow," a frustrated Curlander said and hung up.

Max proceeded to let the six-week-old pup walk with him for exactly one block. Every person on the street stopped to play with Lincoln. Max knew he would never get home at this pace. He finally hailed a cab for the remainder of the trip. Then it was home for the two young warriors.

CHAPTER 35

Lincoln helped. Max didn't need to explain things to Linc. They needed each other. Linc took Max away from the pain and the nagging question, Did she suffer?

Max wondered what Eva would've thought about Lincoln Burns. "Eva would have loved you, pal. Wouldn't you, honey?" Max said out loud, looking to the heavens. Sometimes Max cried as he sat and petted Linc. Sometimes he cried for a long time. But it seemed okay to cry with Linc. When Max was at his saddest, Linc always seemed to do something to console him or make him laugh. It was as if Linc knew it was his job to pull this guy out of the depths of depression, so they both could start a new life.

Lincoln Burns was a rip. He ate everything he could possibly get his teeth into. Max was at home day and night now. He kept an eye on the dog and employed advice from training videos to make sure he chewed on his toys and nothing else. Max only left the house to walk Linc and buy food for him. Max was losing weight but not from running. He had stopped running. He had no desire to do anything, much less eat. He was relying on health food drinks and vitamins and minerals that were easy to swallow. Liquids went down easier than solids. He was in survival mode… by choice this time.

Max knew he needed to start working out, though his body actually exposed hidden muscle. This was a good time to tune up. He had lost the *restaurant weight*.

The restaurant, Max thought.

The building had not been condemned, but Max had heard that the keystone beam had gotten so hot it had become twisted. Eva had taken out the proper insurance. Max tried reading through the various coverages to keep his mind active. Criminal acts were not covered, making the general liability insurance null and void; Max was also not liable for damages to the building. A separate policy for business interruption...and another for contents seemed viable... It was all too much. Max swept the policies into the desk draw, never to be seen by him again. Weeks went by, and Max began receiving checks from the insurance company. He found that amusing since he had never put in a claim.

That's my Eva.

The heavy bag had always been Max's go-to workout. Now, it became an outlet. Max got back on it with the same intensity that he'd mustered for MMA training. He was hitting it so hard he needed duct tape around the bag to hold in the guts. He took Linc down to his makeshift gym while he worked out. Linc loved exploring amongst the contents of the storeroom. One night Max had to pull everything to the middle of the room to find him.

Nights passed excruciatingly slow. Max hated going to bed. Sleep was elusive and some nights never came at all. Sometimes in the middle of the night, he would go down to the storeroom and visit the children. There were nights when he was tempted to eat an entire mushroom to sleep, once and for all, with Eva. He thought it ironic that he had the means to produce a sleep deeper than anyone could know yet... unattainable for him. Or was it?

Maybe just a tad more toward the middle than the edge.

Weeks passed. Linc was getting strong. He was smart too. One day after a strenuous workout Max sat in the rocking chair. He was up to forty-five minutes on the heavy bag and weighed in at 196 pounds. That had been his light-heavyweight fighting weight in the army. He wondered if he'd be able to fall sleep after the long workout. He looked matter-of-factly at the Mason jar marked M#4.

It seemed to stare back at him. Many jars were already doubled up. The larger-numbered jars had less in them, since they were closer to the center with less to harvest. The deadly M#10X was still in film canisters, which were now six deep.

"Here goes nothin', Linc." Max wet his forefinger and put it in the M#4 jar. As he touched his finger to his tongue, the jolt went instantly to a taste sensory somewhere in his brain. Nothing ever tasted horrid or rancid to Max. Everything edible had its own properties, and taste was simply the byproduct of its properties. He thought there might be a difference in taste as he ventured toward the middle of the mushroom. The taste of the M#4 was definitely stronger than the M#1.

The only reason to use a higher number for culinary purposes would be for a differential in taste quality. I'll need proof of safety and the aftereffects as well.

Max sat in the rocker with Linc on his lap. He closed his eyes in an attempt to garner some peace and contemplate the lingering taste. Would there be mind-altering effects? He didn't know, and he didn't care. Any change would be welcome. Hopefully, the perpetual merry-go-round in his head would at least slow to a tolerable pace.

Linc fell asleep as Max stroked his back. Both man and beast felt calm. Soon Max drifted, hoping to weave his longing for Eva into a pleasant dream. He saw her walking in the clothes she'd worn on her last day.

Why are you walking so slowly, Eva? he asked, as he watched her leave city hall once again. *Why aren't you talking to me? Everyone is looking at you... Can I touch your face? Cops all over. This is the safest place on earth. Look, Eva, over there, over there! It's André, the chef. He's a policeman now. Inspector Timoney needs to see his green card... Please don't kill him, Eva. I'll protect you! I'll have Timoney give him a ticket for not being a chef... Wait! Don't leave. Rats! There are rats in the streets. I can't protect you out there, Eva. Why are you waving? You can't leave... Linc ... Linc ... Go get Eva! Tell her there are rats everywhere...* ***Eva!***

Max awoke. He was soaked from perspiration and tears. Linc was on the floor looking up at Max. Max shook his head to clear the cobwebs. He looked at the clock on the table. It was 7:35 in the morning. Max smiled at Linc. He had been in the chair for almost six hours.

"Let's go upstairs."

Linc was good for Max. Training Linc became an obsession. It took Max's mind off everything else. Max was training himself as well.

Max decided to employ some ranger interrogation-impedance training to stifle the horror that Eva's murder imposed on his every waking thought. He tried not to think about Little Louie as yet; it made him obsess about the many ways to kill him. Max had to gear down and reconnect to the world to be functional. He did not like having his thought patterns random and scattered. He found himself starting things and not finishing them… multi-tasking. Sometimes he would forget what he had started. Reading became a chore, not a pleasure anymore. He did not like who he had become.

Linc was alive and commanded attention. He was Max's reason to live.

Max was running low on cash. He'd always asked Eva for cash when he ran short. It was Eva who had run the show. He missed her more than he could bear. An article by some expert in the grieving field advised confronting the loss and grieving, letting things flow out according to one's natural capacity.

Go fuck yourself, he thought. *Confront what?*

The question consumed him. His opponent was intangible. If it were tangible, he would have put an end to it at any cost.

Max went to the bank and pulled out the unused debit card Eva had gotten him. He asked a bank official how to activate the card to get cash and how to deposit the insurance check for $150,000. Max got the gist and went to the cash machine to try his luck. There was already $168,000 in the account, which was a joint personal account Eva had created for them. The business account was a joint venture as well. Evidently everything could be put into one pot. He closed the business account, which had $1,200 in it. He felt a tear coming on and rubbed it away before it could start another melancholic journey to hell.

“C’mon, Linc,” he said as he put $500 in his pocket. “Let’s go to the park.”

CHAPTER 36

Manhattan was starting to cool down as summer came to a close. September was a good time to be in the city. Central Park was great for Max's head and Linc's socialization. Max's research had emphasized the importance of socializing fighting breeds with other dogs while young. Max did not want Linc to revert to innate behavioral instincts. Linc was now six months old. He was a roughneck pup. That was okay. Max had been around dogs his entire boyhood in Washington, Pennsylvania, and he had been fond of the bomb-sniffing dogs in Iraq and Afghanistan. He thought it odd that the army made you pay to ship your bomb dog home after a tour in-country. It was common practice for the dogs to be set loose when they got older or lost a master. Some of the guys put their loyal canines down rather than leave them to be tortured or eaten. That practice would have been put to better use for some officers Max had come across.

If only Eva had a bomb dog! The thought momentarily popped into his head. His loud whistle brought Linc running.

It was difficult for Max to think about the explosion without shaking. There was a part of his brain that tried to force the explosion into to a vivid reenactment of what Eva must have experienced. He recalled what he had gone through when his vehicle hit the I.E.D. in Afghanistan; minor league compared to this. He fought that impulse at all costs.

Time to move … Go anywhere … Get moving.

"C'mon, boy. Let's head home." As he was walking out of the park, he heard his name called and turned around. Carlos was walking toward him.

Carlos hugged Max and asked, "How are you, *amigo*? It is good to see you. Can I walk with you?"

"Sure, Carlos. I miss you, my friend." He was glad to see Carlos.

"And who is this guy?"

"This is my friend Lincoln."

"Ahhh, this is good. Everyone in the neighborhood is asking about you. The people love you in the Heights. Everyone is praying for you."

"I miss them too, Carlo. How is Carmela?"

"She graduates next Sunday. She just finished her last semester at summer school. She is going to work at a hotel on Long Island," Carlos said, sticking his chest out. He was proud of Carmela. He was also worried about Max.

"How about you, Carlos? Where are you working these days?" Max asked.

"Ahhhh, I am cooking at a bodega up on Dyckman Street."

Max got a chill at the very mention of Dyckman Street.

"I work weekends there. It's not like Gringo Smyth's. No … mostly sandwiches and breakfast on the weekends. I make *huevos rancheros* for that weasel Louie, every Sunday morning. He got kicked out of the place in the Bronx and is back in Paco's apartment. I spit in his food. I would piss in it if he wouldn't taste it… *Bastardo!*"

Max almost hyperventilated at the mention of Louie. Immediately, Max started piecing together a possible connection to Louie without breaking the Order of Protection.

Ahhh, Carlos mi amigo. Maybe something a bit more tasty than that… for his huevos rancheros.

They walked uptown through Harlem toward the Heights. Carlos was talking a mile a minute when Max stopped him and asked, "So, Carlos, when is Carmela's graduation?"

"Next Sunday. I can't go… I have to work. I need the money. She understands."

"Well, if they let me do your shift at the bodega, I'll work it for you and you can go to the graduation ceremony. You really should be there."

"You would do that for me, Máximo?"

"I sure would, Carlito. You were always there for me, my friend. You warned me early on. I should have listened to you. I'd like to get back into a kitchen again - it's been too long. You'd be doing me a favor too."

"I will ask Juan and Esperanza if this is okay to do. Juan is my friend since we are babies in Puerto Rico. I think he will say yes, but it is Esperanza who says the last word. Let me call him."

Carlos called Juan on his cell phone. After a few seconds, he hung up and said, smiling, "Okay. As long as you stay out of Esperanza's way! I told him you are the best!"

"Carlos, don't tell anyone, okay?"

"*Comprendo…* I got you covered, Máximo." Carlos wrote down the address and the phone number of the bodega. "You must come by on Friday night to take a look at their setup. This is what Juan asks of me. I meet you there at 8:00 p.m. Imagine, Carlos showing Máximo what to do in a kitchen. Well, not so much a kitchen. You will see, hahahaha."

They were on 132nd Street and Lennox Avenue. Carlos had to meet Carmela. Max took a hundred dollars out of his pocket and said, "Please give this to Carmela for graduation. Tell her… tell her that both of us, Eva and I, are… would be… very proud of her."

Carlos looked at Max and said, "*Sí, señor Max and señorita Eva. Gracias.*"

"Good luck to you and Carmela as well, my friend. See you Friday night," Max said as he waved goodbye.

Max filled his lungs with fresh air to re-inflate himself. "**Are you kidding me!**"

Now calm down. I have no plan... no plan at all. I want to see what it's like being... close. That's all. Louie doesn't come into the bodega. He gets his food delivered.

So how the hell am I going to kill him and get away with it? Max felt giddy.

He wished Louie was Paco's size so he could beat him to death in some alley.

No. Louie is a sneaky little bastard.

Max found himself walking a little faster than usual. Linc was doing a quickstep with an occasional trot to keep up... a rush to nowhere. Walking with purpose felt good. What that purpose was, he didn't know. What he did know was that before you got close to the enemy, you needed to have a plan. "Nothing wrong with having a plan, Linc."

Max stopped off at the butcher shop around the corner from his apartment. He got some chopped sirloin for Linc and a twenty-four-ounce porterhouse for himself. He made one more stop at the Korean produce market for fresh spinach, garlic, and sweet potatoes. Max was hungry for the first time in four months and seven days. Something whet his appetite.

Max broiled up a fine old-fashioned steak dinner for himself. Linc finished his dish of chopped meat and fresh vegetables in about ten seconds. Then he stared at Max munching on the steak bone. Max had to give it to him.

Max was anxious to get to the storeroom. He wasn't sure why until he got there. As he hit the heavy bag, a face appeared. It was Paco's face and not Louie's. Max wasn't sure why Paco turned up; he was not in charge of such things. He just went with it - fifty-six minutes nonstop plastering Paco's face and body. If the bag were human the torrent would have killed it. Not many heavyweights in the pro ranks could do more than a half hour straight with the intensity Max gave to it. Linc had taken to sitting on the rocker while Max worked out. He was getting big and less curious about the surroundings of the storage room. Besides, Max had told him to sit and stay.

When Max finished, he took off his wraps and changed places with Linc. This was the most restful evening he'd had since before… that day. He picked up Linc and put him on his lap. Max was deep in thought without help from the children. Clear thoughts seemed to filter through his brain. Clear thoughts, not necessarily good thoughts:

If I get a shot, do I take it? If opportunity knocks, should I take advantage? I don't know, Linc. I don't know. Eva would tell me, he's not worth it. And he's not! The little scumbag. I wish he was bigger. He's like a mosquito in a field tent. I wish Louie was in jail and Paco was out. I could kill Paco with my bare hands. I should have killed him when I had the chance. Timoney said Louie's alibi checked out. That means someone with juice hired a torch to fill the contract. Louie doesn't have the money, the balls, or the know-how to use C-4. The bomb was probably obtained by the same person that paid for Paco's lawyer. I wonder if Angelo Morano was curious enough about Weinstein to do homework on that. I'll call Timoney in the morning and nose around a little.

It was time for Linc's last walk of the day.

"Well, big fella, I didn't answer my own question, did I? What AM I doing? We'll find out Sunday morning. Hell, that's in three days. I guess I don't have a plan…yet."

Keep me safe, baby.

"You would've loved her, Linc. She would've spoiled you rotten. Wanna go out!"

CHAPTER 37

Max was up at seven in the morning, refreshed after a solid sleep. It was hard to imagine what the day would bring. He told himself he would not force anything. He likened this day to taking the point on patrol. He needed to be focused at all times. Today was slightly different. If he did have an opportunity to encounter the enemy, would he take him out? That depended on the objective of the mission. Max was now a civilian, not a soldier. Different rules were in play. Not written rules, back-home instinctive rules. Max did know one thing. There was a neat and simple way to kill Louie: M#10X and *huevos rancheros*. An intensive police investigation might implicate him. If the police were thorough, they would find out that Max cooked Louie's breakfast that Sunday morning and that Louie ended up dead shortly after.

Coincidence? That's a stretch. How the hell would I get past that minor detail? I have friends on the NYPD? I'm the only one who attempted to clean up this neighborhood? That won't mean squat if they like me for the murder. Even cops get locked up for killing scumbags these days. There would be nowhere to hide stateside. I could become a contractor and go back to Afghanistan. Hell, I'd be doing the city a favor.

At ten after eight, Max called Timoney and asked if he had ever checked with Angelo Morano about the Paco-Weinstein hookup.

Timoney said, "Way ahead of you, kid. Weinstein told Morano

that a beautiful Latina woman came into his office with a suitcase containing two hundred fifty grand and plopped it on his desk. She left a note that read, 'Client: Francisco Paco Caamano - Get him off or get him to Huntsville!' He started to talk to the woman, but she turned around without saying a word and left. He looked for her at the trial, but she never showed."

Max bet the woman was Paco and Louie's mother, Maria Elena. He still hadn't let on to anyone that he knew about her being Paco's *mamasita*. Max filed the new information away. He hoped that Maria-Elena would never become a bargaining chip but, good to know if things got messy.

CHAPTER 38

Max went about his day. He and Linc made a visit to the park for a run. He'd made a long leash that fastened around his waist for such runs. It was good to be running again. Thanks to Linc, Max had a reason to run. Linc was good for about four miles so the upper loop was perfect.

Not bad for a pup.

Linc was enjoying the daily exercise and was starting to physically fill out. He was making friends and socializing on Dog Hill, a section of Central Park utilized for off-leash frolicking in the early morning. Max watched while Linc interacted with the other dogs. His play was aggressive but not mean-spirited. There were a few older dogs that ruled Dog Hill. A bullmastiff put Linc in his place a few times by simply holding him down. There was also an Alaskan malamute with an attitude that took no puppy crap. Linc took a wide berth around the Alaskan beauty with grey wolf genetics. Linc's instincts were good. He caught on to the alpha-dog concept without excessive aggression. Of course, he was only seven months old, but Max was happy with his attitude so far.

The day flew by. It was soon time for an early dinner.

Mom called it suppertime, Linc… Big doin's tonight! Max fed Linc and left him to his toys.

Max took the elevator down to the storage room. He sat in the chair with his head back for ten minutes or so. He closed his eyes and rocked. He stopped abruptly and grabbed a film canister of M#10X to take with him. *Just for feel,* he told himself. Max wanted the tactile sensation of having the poison on his person. It was a dry run for the dry run in a way. He needed to be familiar with any possible awkwardness.

No surprises come Sunday.

Off he went on the walk uptown. Max marveled at all the lights accentuating the beautiful George Washington Bridge as he traversed 179th Street at Broadway. The George Washington Bridge, known as the GW, linked the island of Manhattan to the state of New Jersey at the two highest points in Manhattan over the Hudson River. The GW eased the daily commute of New Jersey residents crossing into Manhattan and alleviated the traffic in the two tunnels and on the crowded PATH trains that also serviced Manhattan. But the G.W. Bridge brought more to the party than that. It was also a convenient meeting place on the New York side for drug buyers and sellers. There were teenagers heading back to their homes in the New Jersey suburbs with their fresh stashes, and dealers heading south to distribute their wares in bulk. Drug sales and usage, along with the accompanying crimes, had forced the city to add another police precinct in Washington Heights. Thus, the Three-Three Precinct had been established on 165th Street and Edgecombe Avenue in an attempt to stem the violence in the southern sector of the Heights. The addition had only served to catapult the Three-Four and the Three-Three to the positions of number one and number two busiest police precincts in the United States of America… perhaps the world.

Hell… these people have never been to Fallujah.

CHAPTER 39

The bodega was spotless. It was more of a grocery store than a deli. The dry goods were in the front. The register was on the back-side shelf, away from the counter.

Smart move. Nobody can reach in and grab the money while the clerk is facing the other way.

When Max walked in, Juan was at the register and greeted him. Juan was excited to meet the man who had brought Paco down. Max had hoped Juan wouldn't associate him with his dismantling of Paco, but that was too much to hope for, especially since the bodega was two blocks west of the Dyckman Street projects.

Max introduced himself, and Juan said, "I am honored that you come to my bodega, *señor* Max. Please, come."

When Max saw the kitchen in the back, he understood how the money was made. There was Carlos and a big Latina woman. Both were cooking chicken and rice—*arroz con pollo*—for the final dinner rush. Max was surprised to see a Pakistani kid working for them. He looked to be about fifteen years old. He was systematically packing a delivery box mounted on the front of a trike, almost ready for his last few deliveries of the evening. Max noted that the names and addresses were noted on the round white cardboard tops covering aluminum containers. The kid had the orders arranged in sequence of delivery. This was clearly not his first day on the job. He had his system squared away.

"Ahh, Máximo, *que pasa, amigo*?"

"All good, Carlos," Max said, choosing to respond in English. Although he had come to learn Spanish fairly well, he didn't want to make any mistakes caused by slang cooking terminology. Clarity was of the essence. "And who is this beautiful *señorita* you are helping out today?" Max asked, taking a shot that she would be friendly.

"This is Esperanza. She is the wife of my friend Juan." Carlos said carefully.

Esperanza was all business. She wiped her hands on her apron and shook Max's hand with the grip of a lumberjack. "Can you cook? I hear you can. But are you fast?" she asked with authority.

"I fed two hundred thirty army grunts three times a day in forty-five minutes," Max said.

"Grunties? Hmmmm, we shall see…Grunties, eh!" Esperanza said.

"You will be working with Esperanza on Sunday," Carlos said with a nervous smile. Max was not sure he was ready for this… Esperanza picked up on it.

"What? You no like working with a woman?" Esperanza asked, ready to bite Max's head off.

Max stumbled for an answer. "No… it's fine! There's not much room for two people, that's all…."

"You think I am too big?" Esperanza said with her hands on her hips. "More to love, baby," she said, giving a little Latina salsa move and a huge laugh. She'd proved her point and Max backed off: This kitchen was hers.

"You be here at 7:00 a.m. sharp. Wear comfortable shoes… This concrete floor is a bitch and so am I." Everyone laughed, albeit half-heartedly. Esperanza was sharp.

I gotta gain her confidence.

Max looked at the grill temperature, the morning menu, where the eggs would be, and what needed prepping. The cooking area was set up to be functional, not pretty. It was an efficient use of space in Max's opinion. He'd taken a six-month course at the Culinary

Institute on how to set up a kitchen workplace; it had suggested a minimum of three times this space.

This is a kitchen in a closet.

Esperanza pointed to some items with her spatula. "All that is prepped Saturday night at home. Don't you worry about the specialty items. All you gotta do is add the eggs and beat 'em. Now ***you*** beat it! I am busy. I will see you here at seven on *Domingo*. Don't be late!" Esperanza said, scooting him out.

Max smiled and said he would be there without fail. He told Carlos to enjoy the graduation. Carlos told him, "My Carmela cried when I gave her the gift." Esperanza heard this. Esperanza heard everything.

Killing Louie won't be easy.

Max stepped outside the bodega. Rashti, the Pakistani delivery boy, had returned for one last delivery run.

Latinos hired a Pakistani boy to deliver the food…interesting.

Max surmised that Latino kids had too many friends, and friends meant obligations, thus this Pakistani kid. Max watched Rashti work. He was quick and efficient. He had the exact money ready so Juan could ring up each order. He was smart enough to keep any cash tips in his jockey shorts. He had a credit card attachment on his phone, which he'd insisted upon implementing after numerous robberies in the "old days." Rashti had gotten sick of being robbed, so he came up with a solution: He refused to deliver food to the parents of his muggers. The young wannabe gang members had gotten the message loud and clear at home: **"Don't fuck with my eggs!"** Juan and Esperanza had backed him on his ministrike. Oddly enough, it was at this point in time that Rashti's tips doubled. Rashti and his delivery bike now had free reign over the streets. Cars stopped for him, people said hello, and some tipped him when he wasn't working. Nobody messed with Rashti.

Max greeted Rashti in Urdu. Rashti gave Max a quick double take and answered in Punjabi as he parked the delivery bike. Rashti could have answered in either language. He chose Punjabi to show

Max that he was not some street rat from Karachi. Max smiled and nodded to Rashti apologetically for his assumption.

"Are you from around Islamabad?" Max asked, making a guess based on Rashti's accent.

Rashti was amazed at Max's accuracy. He lived five klicks north of Islamabad. Rashti was all smiles now and feeling somewhat comfortable with Max. He had finally found an American that understood something about the outside world. Rashti's dream was to get an American education and become a foreign diplomat. He had not seen his country since he was six years old, but his father and mother never ceased to remind him of the wonders and beauty of their native land.

I like this kid… I can't get him in trouble.

"You are him, aren't you?" Rashti said while packing the wagon. "I know you are… **him**. I thought you would be bigger. It is good you are **him**. It is also good that I know you." Rashti put out his hand in friendship and shook Max's hand vigorously.

Max smiled. He didn't dare tell Rashti to keep quiet about him working at the bodega this Sunday. He figured Rashti probably didn't have too many people to tell anyway.

Max carefully observed the final packing of the delivery bike as he talked to Rashti. The names, addresses, and contents were printed clearly and packed **LIFO: last in, first out**. Max picked up the marker to see whether it was the permanent-ink variety. It was.

No problems in the rain.

Max took a cab home, hoping for a silent cabdriver. Max had his own method of avoiding the mundane conversations of monotonous cabdrivers: Look out the window and shut up. When he didn't answer the first questions, the cabbie usually looked in the rearview mirror to check him out. The driver would see Max wasn't paying attention and usually leave him alone. For thirty blocks Max was able to think.

The odds of pulling this off were not in his favor. Esperanza would be on top of his every move. He would have to gain her confidence through efficiency.

He smiled as he envisioned Esperanza and Juan in bed. All he could picture was a scene out of a 1950s pornographic cartoon—130 pounds of Juan in his black socks sticking out from under 250 pounds of Esperanza… as though she'd fallen from the ceiling on top of him. He forced that last visual out of his head.

At least he has someone.

Many questions had been answered by the visit to the bodega. It looked to Max like the daily operational procedures were fixed. He could assume those procedures held true for the breakfast meal on Sunday.

No reason for deviation.

Esperanza was the obstacle that needed to be dealt with. He would have to keep moving with the hands of a magician. She had to be distracted at some point. If the opportunity did not arise, Max would never get another chance. Louie always ordered *huevos rancheros, picante*, according to Carlos. Max remembered what he had told Eva after the Paco fight. "Maybe revenge is a dish best served hot!" THIS dish would be served *picante*!

If I get the shot Sunday, I'm taking it.

Once the plot overtook the debate, things were in-play.

Max tipped the cabdriver five dollars on the eight-dollar fare for his inattentiveness.

When he opened the apartment door he was greeted warmly by his four legged pal.

"C'mon, you lunatic." Max and Linc went for their last walk of the day. Linc was trained but still a pup. No recent accidents, mainly because Max had established a regimen and Linc loved being outdoors. This walk was not as long as usual but appreciated.

After the walk, Max grabbed his freshly laundered hand wraps and took Linc with him to the storeroom. Heavy bag time, then on to the rocker for some R&R.

It'll be sleight of hand with Esperanza next to me.

Max would be the second short order chef. Therefore, Esperanza would be doing the brunt of the work. Max was anxious to show Esperanza he could boogie right along with her. But it always took time to get acclimated to a workstation. Sprinkling the M#10X would not be practical. There would not be time. The M#10X would have to go into the eggs in one piece. There was no telling at what point that opportunity might arise, so there was nothing to practice. Max looked over at the aquarium. There were a half dozen mushrooms ready for harvest. He moved out from under Linc and left him sleeping on the rocker. Max picked the latest harvest and took them to the furnace to dry out.

These should be ready by tomorrow night, Max thought. He washed his hands in the sump sink. He poked Linc to follow him and locked the storage room. He thought he would have a restless night trying to sleep, but he was asleep in a matter of minutes.

Strange thing: peace.

CHAPTER 40

Although Max's designation in the army was chef, that did not preclude him from combat assignment. He was primarily a ranger. This was especially true in the Korengal, where incoming ordnance was a daily occurrence and threat of base camps being overrun was always a possibility. It had never happened to Max's main HQ, but the men in the makeshift HESCO outposts had been knee-deep in crap all the time. These guys and gals had to eat too! Max had spent weeks in various forward operating bases (FOBs). Every day had brought something new. There had been times he was on a perimeter or a rally point in an apron with a different type of weapon each time.

This current situation needed stealth. This Louie thing was more special ops than field operations. Max was assassinating an enemy. All rangers were trained in special ops. There was always specific fine-tuning, since each job was different.

My training never included poison. That's an Agency specialty.

Max often looked back on his last cooking assignment at the Korengal FOB camp. The CO had come into the mess tent kitchen after dinner one night. He'd ordered everyone out but Max.

"I know you're a short-timer, Burns… if your luck holds up. Friday, zero six hundred hours, your ass will be on a C-10 out of this godforsaken shit hole. You'll be stateside by next week. God knows I'll miss ya'. I put on ten pounds in fuckin' Afghanistan because of your cookin'.

But you have one more assignment. Don't ask me particulars, 'cause I haven't got a fucking clue myself. You'll prepare dinner for twenty-four guests tomorrow at nineteen hundred hours sharp in the *officers' mess.* Here's the menu. Everything you need will be flown in tomorrow at approximately zero eight hundred hours. Make this happen. The mess hall crew will prepare the room and wait tables for our guests. The staff will leave camp shortly after serving the final course. You're in charge. Don't fuck it up! Oh yeah, see me before you leave Friday morning. I need that leg-of-lamb recipe you promised me. Good luck, Burns. Well done, soldier!" The CO then initiated an abnormal gesture: he saluted an enlisted man. Max sharply returned the salute.

When the major was out of the mess area, Max looked at the menu: lobster bisque, caesar salad, lemon sherbet, prime rib, roasted potatoes, creamed spinach, Bananas Foster.

Hmmmm, no wine. Probably Muslim hotshots and American politicians; so they can say they were in-country.

Not the case. The dinner guests were twenty-four badass Navy SEALs, with no rank or names evident on their fatigues. These guys were hardcore, definitely an elite team put together for a specific mission. Max had come across SEALs in Iraq. They had been called in to replenish some army Delta units in Ramadi that were getting torn up pretty bad. He'd always admired their sand and their ability.

When they were all finally seated, Max noticed the guy at the head of the table staring at him. The man jerked his head back a bit when final recognition clicked in.

"I'll be goddamned!" the SEAL muttered as he stood up. Max didn't realize it yet, but this guy was the Navy SEAL that had beaten him in the final round for the U.S. Military Service Medal for the MMA heavyweight championship: **"The fight to end all fights."**

This badass was now sitting down at Max's improvised dining room with Max about to serve him a six-course dinner.

Max knew something big was up if they'd brought these pros into the Korengal. Max hadn't asked - he had nobody to ask. There were twenty-four SEALs in all: two troops, comprising four teams.

Two of the teams are probably backup. These guys don't usually work in more than two teams at a time. They don't need to.

The heavyweight champ stood up and said, "Listen up, you maggots! See this army ranger here?"

"Ooooooh," they all said at once at the mere mention of *army ranger*. Max couldn't hold his badass look for more than a few seconds. He laughed and shook his head at these guys acting in unison.

"Hey! He cooked this fuckin' food!" the champ said.

"Hoooooyah!" the others replied in unison.

Max still didn't recognize the SEAL in charge.

How the hell does this guy know I'm a ranger?

"Listen up! This army ranger here?" the SEAL said again.

"Ooooooooooh," the others said once again in unison.

"This is the motherfucker that I told you guys asked me about... on many an occasion. Remember the ranger I fought in the finals of the all-services MMA championship?" The honcho SEAL asked.

"Hoooooyah!"

"Well, this is the motherfucker right here!"

Max got it: Lieutenant Commander, Gary "Nick" Nicholson, undefeated heavyweight champion in MMA competition for three years across all services.

"One more minute in the ring with this guy, and I might not be here today," Nicholson said, patting Max on the shoulder. "**And**... he was a light heavyweight they bumped up to fight me. All those army heavyweights knew better." The cocky grin that followed made Max think of smelling salts for some odd reason. It wasn't that the other heavyweights in the army division had wanted to move Max up in class for this bout; that decision had been made by the army brass. It seemed Max had trained with, and beaten, every army heavyweight in the division fairly easily. Max was the army's only hope against Nicholson. It almost worked... almost.

"I come to find out after the fight, he broke my jaw in two places and cracked three of my ribs ... this motherfucker right here!" Nicholson said, physically shaking Max.

"Booooooo."

"And I still kicked his ass. That's how fucking bad I am!" Nicholson screamed at the top of his lungs.

"Hoooooyah!" they all yelled, then laughed their asses off.

Max said, "I wish I knew I broke your jaw before my lights went out!"

Nicholson and Max hugged so hard they almost went through each other. Both had great respect for each other.

It's good to see him again.

A hoooyah went along with the hug, followed by laughter. As Max met each SEAL and shook their hands, only first names or nicknames were given. That was protocol when a big job was brewing. Max could tell by their eyes that they were wired in.

The army's Special Forces training takes you to the very edge of your sanity with the hope you can make it back. SEAL training? You are not expected to come back.

Max remembered hitting Nicholson as hard as he'd ever hit anybody. After taking the hit, Nicholson smiled at Max and said, **"Dream your wildest dream."** Max never forgot that line that. It was the only time he lost concentration in a fight. A split second later, Max was unconscious. It was a lesson he would never let happen again.

So, that punch broke his jaw, eh! Odd. I never felt it... or heard it.

Then Max said to everyone, "And then he cleaned my clock with a kick... or so they tell me."

"Hoooooooooyah!" There was applause and whistling.

Now Max understood why there was no liquor on the menu. Their job was imminent.

Max came out of the kitchen after the desserts were served. The men stood up and cheered for him. He dismissed the waiters and sat with the men through the Bananas Foster and Cuban cigars. There were seconds and thirds in some cases. One SEAL said to another who was downing a third dessert, "How the hell are you going to get over that wall, Croke?" Immediately, silence fell upon the room. They all turned and looked at the SEAL who had blurted out the statement.

"Hey, Mugsy… you gotta big mouth!" one of them said. Mugsy got the message.

Max hung out until about midnight. He and Nicholson talked for hours.

"How the hell did a ranger end up a chef?" Nicholson asked.

"Why does everyone ask me that? I guess I am a better cook than a ranger."

"I doubt that!" Nicholson laughed. Then he got serious. "Say a prayer for us, Max. We'll be headin' stateside one way or another in forty-eight hours."

"Copy that… I'm heading stateside myself on Friday," Max said. "I'm glad I got to do this job for you guys before hightailing it… seems a fitting send-off."

"For both of us, Max. And for one other motherfucker!"

Nicholson stood up at attention and gave Max a salute. This was the second time in two days an officer had initiated a salute to him. It was a highly regarded honor, usually reserved for KIAs. Max took it all in and swelled with pride on both occasions. But this time? This was more than special. The only man who had ever put him on his ass was now saluting him. It was… honorable.

Max snapped to attention and returned the salute. "Aye, aye, Commander," he said, using the proper naval retort. He made an about-face and marched off so Nicholson could never say, he'd seen a tear in a ranger's eye.

The next night Osama bin Laden was dead in Abbottabad, Pakistan, a forty-five-minute helo ride from a base camp in Jalalabad. Subsequent to this operation, the US pulled all fighting forces out of the Korengal Valley. The army moved all supporting troops from the Korengal to Helmand Province in southwest Afghanistan, where 90 percent of the world's raw heroin is grown… the sale of which supported the bad guys.

CHAPTER 41

Max's morning run was longer than planned. Sometimes he was capable of running for hours, falling into a runner's zone. Linc was still too young for real distance running. Linc needed water, so they walked over to one of the Central Park water fountains that had a lower spout for dogs. Max looked at all the beautiful women jogging on this beautiful October day.

God, I miss Eva.

Max loved how she'd made love to him. Her skin was unforgettable: the color, the smoothness … Max was certain - the likes of Eva were never to be found again.

Max and Linc had run the lower loop in Central Park. That left them at Fifty-Ninth Street at the southeastern entrance of Central Park. Linc was exhausted. Max sat on a park bench. Linc lay next to the bench on the cool grass. Not even the pigeons bothered Linc at this point. Max looked up at the brass statue on the corner that rose up to about forty feet. It was a civil war general on his horse. Max walked closer after securing Linc's leash to the bench. Lo and behold, there stood a statue of General William Tecumseh Sherman, mounted majestically on his horse. The statue was magnificent. It looked as though it were new, thanks to an embarrassed Donald Trump, who had paid to have the statue cleaned up and redone. Trump happened to own the Plaza Hotel across the street at the time. This statue was too close to The Plaza to be a hangout for

New York City's pigeon population for Trump's liking. Evidently, the pigeons had gotten the Trump memo, because the statue now gleamed in the Central Park sunlight.

Max stood staring up at the bronze likeness. An elderly gentleman nearby looked up at the statue and smugly said, "He must have died from his wounds when the war was over… one hoof up in the air."

"No sir. He died on my great-great-gramma's front porch in New York. That's old Sam he's up on… Sam was sixteen hands high at the shoulder and could run like a deer. No sir… consumption and pneumonia killed Bill Sherman. He died peacefully, though. He lived a few blocks from here, actually."

Max went back over to Linc, who was growling at a teenager.

Hmmm. A street kid looking for a new pet to bring back to fight in the hood.

"Can I help you?" Max said.

"Hey, it's all good, my brotha… I wanted to pet him." The kid sauntered off with his ass hanging out of his pants.

Max looked at Linc. "Sorry, fella. You're gettin' to be a tough guy, eh? I like that!"

Max passed by the elderly gent once more and said, "He liked a jar of whiskey now and again."

The gent watched Max walk away.

Another screwball and his dog in Manhattan, the gent thought.

Little did the gent realize, Max Burns was one of the last living relatives of the general whose likeness was cast in bronze on the corner of Fifth Avenue and Central Park South.

CHAPTER 42

Indian summer was a treat for New Yorkers. It had seemed as though there were only two seasons to be reckoned with - winter to summer. Not true this year.

Max walked by a newspaper stand and picked up a *New York Post* and a pack of gum. The headline read: "Dems and GOP in Trouble; Curlander May Be the Answer!"

Our boy is doing well. Max hit Curlander's number on his speed dial.

Curlander picked up and said, "Is this my chef executive?"

"How the hell are ya?" Max asked, avoiding an answer.

"Don't you read the papers? They're shittin' in their pants right now. How're you doing? That is the question for today."

"I am okay… I am at peace."

If only that were true. If the shit hit the fan tomorrow, maybe Curlander could get me a cell with a window. Curlander's a good friend, who happens to be running for president of the United States. Damn nice of him to be worrying about me at a time like this.

"Yeah, I'm pretty good. I got my little canine companion here. His name is Abraham Lincoln Burns."

"I remember when you got him. You were in tough shape then, *amigo*. Hey! Now I don't have to get a presidential dog, I can use yours." Curlander was always thinking.

"Why not? He's a purebred Alapaha Blue Blood American

bulldog. His mommy and daddy were from Louisiana. That oughta help you with the Deep South vote!"

"All you high rollers go for the purebreds," Curlander said. They both laughed. "The world has been asking me for a name for this independent party of mine. How 'bout the American Bulldog Party?"

"Hmmmm," Max said. "It'll match that mug of yours on posters!"

"Very funny. Listen, I am going to be at my senate office in Manhattan for the election results. Make sure you get your ass down there on election night. I'll get them to send you a few passes. How many do you need?" There was a pause. Curlander knew he'd screwed up.

Max let him off the hook. "Can I bring the dog?"

"You better… Does he bite?"

"No, but he hasn't met any politicians yet. Get me two passes," Max said

"You got it… Check your mail. I'll get you to Washington one way or another, pal. So long, Max."

"Adios, Ed. Best to Amy."

"Jesus," Max said as he read the paper. "I think he's going to do it, Linc old boy. I think he's gonna be the next president. How would you like to take a dump on the White House lawn? If I wind up in jail, Linc, that's where you're goin', big fella… the White House. You have won the doggy lottery, my friend."

CHAPTER 43

Max left Linc sleeping upstairs. He went down to the basement and stopped at the furnace to check on the mushrooms from the night before. The mushrooms had not spent a full twenty-four hours drying out. Max purposely wanted to curtail the drying process. He had kept the black middle intact for the special occasion. He did not want the black spots completely dried out and hard… not today. His timing was right. The black spots in all six mushrooms had a putty-like consistency, changing shape easily when rolled between Max's thumb and forefinger. They could be mashed, or broke apart easily.

Perfect consistency every way.

This was exactly what Max wanted: various consistency meant various possibilities for deploying the deadly sphere. He would not have time to sprinkle the M#10X in Louie's meal, not with Esperanza hovering over it.

Max wasn't sure what Esperanza thought about the Paco incident. In that northern part of the Heights and also in Inwood, it was still a topic of conversation. Max figured that both she and Juan knew everything about him. It was well known that Carlos had worked at Gringo Smyth's for Max Burns, hero of the Dyckman Street projects. Of course they knew who Max was. What Max hoped they didn't know was; that he knew Louie's breakfast was delivered from the M&E Bodega every Sunday morning. Hopefully

Carlos hadn't opened his mouth about telling Max. It was too late to do anything about that now.

Keep it simple.

If Juan or Esperanza thought that Max knew about Louie, they would not let Max work in the bodega. Juan and Esperanza had too much to lose. Max was not positive which meal would be Louie's order of *huevos rancheros, picante.* Max had to be sure. If he was not absolutely positive, it would be an abort.

There were five black spots. Max rolled each one separately in his fingers into 5 little round balls, each the size of a pea. No need to test again for the crumble effect. The sixth crumbled spot would remain in his pocket as a possible alternative.

Perfect.

Max wrapped each black pea in separate gum wrappers he'd saved. On the way up to the bodega, he would remove each one from their wrapper. He would also have a canister of M#10X powder just in case.

That was it! Everything else would have to be luck and sleight of hand. Whatever presented itself tomorrow morning would determine the outcome.

Max's phone rang about eight o'clock that evening. It was Margaret. This was the first time he had spoken to her since the cab ride. Max felt terrible he had not been in communication with her and Len.

"Hi, Margaret, how are you two? Everything okay?" He worried about their health.

Margaret seemed to be talking in circles. Max asked about Len.

"Well... his mind isn't what it used to be... very forgetful lately. That's one of the things I was calling about, Max."

"Is he okay? Are you both okay?" Max was getting nervous. He needed tomorrow to go smoothly. It would be difficult enough to sleep tonight. Now something was up with Margaret and Len.

What the hell is she trying to say?

"Oh, he's okay. He's strong as an ox. It's his mind that is ... well, not so sharp anymore, Max. He has a bit of what the doctors call... dementia."

"Dementia?"

"Yes. It's no fun getting old."

"Dementia. That's memory loss and things like that? I am so sorry. I'll come down there as soon as I can," Max stammered.

"No, no, Max, it's okay... I wanted to ask you something about when we were up in New York. I know you spoke to Len for a little bit. Did he say anything to you that was strange or out of the ordinary?"

It was clear Margaret was fishing for something.

"Like what?"

"Well, he just rambles about nonsense sometimes....

"Not that I can think of," Max said.

Ok, good...we'll talk soon, Max. We love you," Margaret said, hanging up rather abruptly.

Max stared into his phone, not having had a chance to even say goodbye.

He paced the floor of the apartment. Linc seemed to know something was up and looked at Max, following his every move. Max felt there had to be something else wrong besides Len's dementia.

Max took Linc down to the storage room. He rocked with Linc in his lap. He rocked and nodded. He did not partake of any of the mushrooms. He set an alarm on the old Big Ben clock he had found in the storeroom in case he fell asleep. He did. The alarm blasted at 4:00 a.m. He would not be late for work today!

Max headed upstairs for a quick shower, fed Linc and took him for a walk. Then he grabbed a cab uptown.

Max was a half hour early. He couldn't stop fondling the M#10X canister and rolling the six individual black spheres. He put one sphere into his right pants pocket and two in his top left shirt pocket. The remaining 3 spheres were in his back right-side pocket. He would be working on Esperanza's right side. Max wanted her to be the one to cook Louie's breakfast. He did not want to have anything directly to do with it. If and when things went before a jury at least then, Esperanza could swear Max had nothing to do with Louie's meal preparation. This was Max's gig. He would take the fall if Juan and Esperanza got jammed up. That would be the honorable thing to do.

Max thought back to that day in the Korengal Valley when he'd met Ghazi Haider. Would he think this was an honorable thing to do to the murderer of his family? Haider hadn't let Max use the mushrooms on his men.

This is different. This is not war! This is the final step in the eradication of a disease.

Max stood in front of the M&E Bodega. It was not yet daybreak.

"Buenos días!" It was Juan and Esperanza. Max was daydreaming and didn't recognize them at first. He thought that he had better start paying better attention to what was going on around him. Max was good at hiding any signs of inner turmoil. It was all part of a ranger's way and a mandatory skill for a prizefighter's survival.

"Let's go, Máximo," Juan said.

Esperanza squeezed Max's cheek and said, "I see you are handsome in the morning as well."

Max smiled and said, "You're pretty good lookin' anytime, *señorita* Esperanza."

"*Señora por favor…* I'm a married woman. My husband will have to beat you up." Esperanza laughed so hard that her boobs took on a life of their own.

Inside they went; Juan to the front, Max and Esperanza back to the grill. She turned the grill on to maximum heat. It would stay like that for the next six hours. She tossed Max a full-size apron.

"No thanks, Esperanza. I don't need…" "You'll need it! Put it on!" Esperanza ordered. "The oil and eggs will burn you and ruin your clothes. This grill will be on high for six hours; eggs cook in six seconds."

Jesus! My pockets covered? Max put the apron on loosely so he could get to his pockets. *Doable … Shirt pocket is tricky … Scratch the left shirt pocket, too close to her line of sight.*

Esperanza and Max hauled out egg-carton squares that held four dozen eggs each. The egg cartons were stacked up on the shelves to the right and left of the grill, giving each of them their own workstation. The bacon had been cooked lightly the night before and would be finished off on the back of the grill. Esperanza used a brick to clean the grill when the oil blackened under the intense heat. She nodded over to Max to do the same. He'd thought the brick on his shelf was used to flatten grilled cheese sandwiches. Max dug in and pushed away.

That's where she got those forearms.

Then it began. The phone rang nonstop on all four lines. The phone lines were Juan's job. He was good at it too. About every twentieth call or so, Max could hear Juan switch to English. There were still some gringos left in the Heights and Inwood. Max didn't have time to think. Esperanza shot clothes pinned orders down the wire in front of both of them. Esperanza increased the volume as Max became more proficient at turning out the food. Esperanza didn't miss a thing. She didn't overwhelm Max, but she didn't baby him either. Max loved the action.

Esperanza told him, "Juan writes the names on the order tickets and on the white tops of the carryout containers. Put the order into an aluminum plate and put the order ticket on top with the correct name. Rashti will tape it on. Don't mess it up, gringo! You pay if you mess it up!" Max was reminded of his CO's similar order with regard to the SEAL dinner.

Esperanza is the CO of the M&E Bodega and Juan's life as well!

It was quite the system. Rashti showed up at exactly 7:00 a.m.; it was his job to place the plates in their proper delivery sequence, which was totally up to his discretion. They were all done and ready to roll after Rashti taped them and placed them in the trike delivery box.

Max and Esperanza cracked eggs like the experts they were, one in each hand. Esperanza checked Max to see how much work he could absorb. He looked over at her periodically, and she would pull some stunt with an egg that he had never seen before. Some made him laugh aloud. He almost forgot his mission he was having such a good time. He noticed that a moment before Rashti put the tops in place, the plates had to slide by Max in threes.

Then he saw it: *Louie Caamano—Dyckman Bldg #3, 3A ... Confirmation!*

Esperanza was on it. Max looked over. The ticket indicated an order of *huevos rancheros, picante.*

Further verification... sufficient confirmation.

Esperanza looked at the ticket on the line. Then she started spooning salsa onto the three eggs. Max knew it was time to act. He reached into his right back pants pocket for an auxiliary sphere. He squeezed it flat between his thumb and forefinger. Max held it tight enough that it would not crumble into anything else except the intended target. When Esperanza looked at the shelf to her left and reached for the hot sauce with her right hand, Max tossed the deadly putty in the center of the salsa. He hit the multi-colored salsa dead-on. It sunk. If he had hit the yellow eggs, there might have been a problem. He hoped the dark coloration would go unnoticed when mixed into the the multicolored salsa and eggs. Esperanza continued beating and added two quick shots of hot sauce to the eggs. Max was now off-beat... but caught up.

Bon appétit, Louie.

Rashti filled coffee orders, packed the bike, and took off with the first orders. He would take five more loads. Breakfast cooking went on until 11:30 a.m. sharp, at which point Esperanza said, "Finito!" Max felt as though the final bell rung after a ten rounder.

He did some math in his head to keep his mind from playing games. He figured they had done about 170 breakfasts.

That's good business for a bodega on a Sunday morning. It's a good day for me too! Not so good for you, Louie.

It was a little past noon by the time they'd cleaned the grill and the residue from the busy morning.

Esperanza turned to Max and said, "**I saw you!**"

"What?" Max said, forcing a smile.

"I watched you! You thought you could do it, eh?" Esperanza said with a snicker.

"Do what, Esperanza?" Max's heart was pounding out of his chest.

Could she have seen me?

"You thought you could out cook Esperanza, eh?"

Max took a deep breath and bowed to her as if she were royalty. "Nobody beats the queen at her game… not even the king."

"King? My Latina ass!" She laughed, banging her bum with her hand. Max laughed too… a laugh of relief.

"You did good, gringo. I think you got some Latino blood flowing through that pale ass of yours," Esperanza said, pinching his cheek.

Max laughed as he took off his apron. He excused himself to wash up in the bathroom. He took the remnants of the mushrooms out of his pockets and flushed them down the toilet along with the M#10X granules. He washed himself as though he were about to perform surgery.

When he came out, Juan handed him fifty dollars for the shift. Max took it to avoid suspicion.

Esperanza tapped the pocket with the money and said to Max, "Don't loose that, gringo. Important stuff in that pocket."

If she only knew what was in there a minute ago.

"**Very important,**" Max said.

He kissed Esperanza on the cheek and shook Juan's hand as he left. As he started walking down Broadway, Esperanza shouted from the doorway, "You got a job here anytime you want, *gringo*… Anytime!"

"*Gracias*!" Max yelled back as he waved.

He walked south toward home. He would grab a cab in a

few more blocks, but for now the fresh air felt good in his lungs. He found himself almost running while random thoughts raced through his head.

Maybe the deed is done… maybe not. An obsession with Louie will not become my life's work. Louie is a bad guy… not fit to live. I've done my best with the cards I've been dealt…I'm done.

Max could feel Eva's presence, ordering him to cease and desist:

"Enough! It's finished now. You have much to do, Max. Forget revenge and live your life… I don't ask for revenge - I ask to watch you grow."

Max heard Eva's voice as if she was walking beside him holding his arm.

"Okay, baby…okay," as he nodded in agreement.

CHAPTER 44

"**Taxi.**" Max shouted. He climbed into a cab and grunted his destination.

"Where are you from?" the cabbie asked to no avail.

Washington Heights, then Harlem went speeding by like vintage 8 mm film with splashes of sunlight.

Linc was happy that his master had come home. Linc was getting used to having Max around 24-7. Max gave the apartment a quick check to see if Linc had chewed anything other than designated goodies. He thought Linc was past that stage, but a long day alone could cost Max a shoe or two.

Max walked Linc to Rodrigo's Pet Shop. Rodrigo was open seven days a week but closed early on Fridays to prep the pit-room for the dogfights. When they got there, Max shortened up the leash and walked in. Linc was wagging his tail so hard it hurt Max's leg. It was as if Linc recognized his original home. Linc was good with the animals… even the cats. This place had been the origin of his socialization with other animals. Max hoped that this initial life lesson would hold up into adulthood.

Rodrigo came over. "You got him in good shape, *amigo*… he looks stronger than his father at this age. You wanna see what he can do in the ring in a few months?"

Max looked at Rodrigo and said, "This dog will never see the inside of a ring. I owe you a meal … What do you like to eat?"

"Oh shit, I almost forgot."

"I don't make shit, but for you I could make an exception."

"You don't like me much, eh gringo. I can tell… that's okay. You like the animals. That is the important thing. I do too! I also like nice pork chops… and whatever else you are good at making."

"How about some nice mushrooms with your pork chops?" Max said, smiling.

"Yeah, okay… and yellow rice. You gotta make me rice and beans too, eh?"

"You got it," Max said. "I'll come by tomorrow afternoon."

"Okay, gringo… tomorrow I wait for your lunch. You sure you don't wanna pit that dog?"

Max smiled as he walked out. He wouldn't kill Rodrigo. No. It was too soon to be knocking off every scumbag in Manhattan. There weren't enough mushrooms in the world for that. He would make Rodrigo a little something to remember Tango, Max, and Linc by. Max still felt guilty about Tango. There was a certain amount of justification that needed to be applied.

He and Linc stopped at the supermarket. Max stocked up on food and provisions. The butcher gave Max some bones for Linc. That would pass the time of day at home and keep his teeth in good condition. As soon as he got home, Max put two pork chops in a marinade he whipped up and then put them into the fridge for the next day. He went down to the storage room with Linc for a heavy bag workout. He put in forty five minutes without a break.

Not bad for the amount of sleep I had last night.

He took a Mason jar of M#7 upstairs with him. He used more than an experimental amount. It was as though the cap had come off a pepper shaker.

This ought to be fun to watch, eh, Linc? We'll fix the bastard who killed your father. We'll get all the bad guys that mess with us, right, boy? Nobody screws with us.

Max made himself some oatmeal and coffee. He couldn't look at another egg. Linc had some chopped meat and vegetables mixed in with a little olive oil for his coat. Max was fending off any invasion of thought. He turned on the TV. That was something he hadn't done since he and Eva snuggled up on Monday nights. It was the beginning week of football season, not that he cared. The Washington Redskins were playing the New York Giants in D.C...

Max was dozing off when he heard a familiar voice. Ed Curlander was the halftime guest. When he walked out to the end zone for the interview, the crowd cheered wildly for him. Max sat up and took notice. Curlander had been doing well in the polls. Max thought that Ed's independent party might merely be a spoiler for one of the two major parties. For a crowd to cheer a politician anywhere in America during a football game was rare; to be a Giant fan and have it happen in D.C. was unheard of. Curlander was good. He was better than good...he was human. He talked about having played linebacker at Boston College and also on the Marine Corps team. He answered the questions without dodging them, and spoke without it sounding like a campaign speech. Max liked what he was seeing and hearing from Ed. The election was two weeks away.

Who the hell am I going to bring to the election-night shindig? Maybe Timoney would like to go ... Jeez, Timoney. How can I look Timoney in the eye? No, not Timoney. Maybe Angelo Morano or Tony Easter? Cops and DAs. Don't I know anybody else in this town except law enforcement people? Maybe I won't bring anybody. I don't even know if I want to go. Hell, I could be on Rikers Island by then. A chill went up his spine. *Eva, don't let that happen, baby. I did what the justice system failed to do. Technicalities...* ***Don't train me to kill and expect me to forget how.***

Max flashed back to a conversation he'd had with Timoney after Timoney had questioned Louie: "We can't arrest him, Max. We know he had something to do with it, but he has an airtight alibi. For God's sake, he was in a high school auditorium with two hundred people. He dressed like a bullfighter to get noticed. It worked! Everyone places him there. Our hands are tied, Max. Don't worry—one of these days he will get his. This is a tough town but fair… he'll get his."

Max returned his attention to the TV. Ed had just told the country on national television that he was calling his party the **American Bulldog Party,** and that his mascot was an Alapaha Blue Blood American bulldog from Louisiana named Abraham Lincoln Burns. Max ***had*** to show up at Curlander's campaign headquarters now! The TV broadcaster didn't know what to say. He laughed, shook Curlander's hand, then handed things back up to the booth.

Wait until all those snobs at the American Kennel Club start flipping pages in their doggy dictionaries to find out what kind of dog you are, Linc.

Ed's was the kind of politics the American people hadn't seen since Teddy Roosevelt, and they were eating it up.

My dad would be ecstatic.

Curlander did not stand on ceremony. He shot from the hip and Americans loved it. He could very well be the next president. The current two-term Democratic president was done, and it was a three-man race. Votes would be spread pretty thin with three candidates going at it. Max felt pretty good about Curlander's chances of beating Alexander Blair, the Democrat. Max wasn't sure how Texas Republicans always seemed to crop up, but here was another one.

Must be oil money.

His name was Clarence Houghton; a former governor of Texas like the rest of the herd. He was famous for electrifying the fences on the Texas side of the border with Mexico.

Curlander stepped down from the stage with a simple wave and a "*Semper fi.*"

Brilliant! He let every veteran in America know he was a former marine that understood their problems. He's the guy. You could be on the new fifty-cent stamp, Linc. ***You*** *will definitely be at the campaign center.*

The Washington Redskins got beaten by the NY Giants. This

was of no consequence to Max, but it brought back what the Secret Service agent had said to him at Gringo Smyth's: "If you come to D.C., I'll see that you get a couple of Redskins' tickets." That seemed so long ago in a land very far away.

Huh, Redskins' tickets. Why would he offer me Redskins' tickets? Like… that's incentive to go to Washington and work for Ed Curlander… two Redskins tickets?

Max thought about the White House kitchen. He wondered what it was like.

Probably pretty well equipped. What about the layout?

"C'mon, Linc. Let's get some fresh air." Max had to keep moving. The partners went for a walk on this brisk Sunday night. A chill in the air spoke of an early winter.

How did things get so complicated? I need a job… I need to simplify and get back to basics. What do you think about that White House lawn now, pal?

Max drifted into thoughts of Eva.

You would have loved her, Linc. You would have protected her… better than I did.

For a day on which he had hopefully committed murder, Max Burns slept very well. He knew this was the calm before the storm. He lay in bed wondering when and how he would hear about the demise of one Louis Caamano. Would it be in the newspapers? Perhaps Kieran Timoney would knock on his door… apologize, then arrest him?

"Sorry max…You have the right to remain silent… Put your hands behind your back… Thank you. How is Linc doing? You'll have to let us take him to the White House for you… You're going to Rikers Island."

"Well, Linc, if they want me, they can come and get me. That weasel needed to die. Maybe I'll run into his brother in prison. I'd love to kill him right in front of all his tattooed pals in Huntsville. Then I could die in peace. At least his mommy will be close by. Ya' know, pal, Timoney told me he had Paco's ear and could fix things.

Maria Elena had to be his rabbi to her little boy, Paco. I wonder if she was anything more than that to Timoney... Glad he picked our side in that fight. I hope I can repay him someday.

The next morning Max awoke around eight. He had a meal to make for his pal Rodrigo. When Max and Linc returned from their walk, the first thing Max did was pull out the plastic bag from the refrigerator containing the pork chops and special M#7 marinade. It smelled wonderful.

First: rice and beans. He had put the black beans in water before going to bed. It was time to boil them. Then came the rice. Rice was important to a Latino. The trick to good rice was to *never* remove the top of the pot to check on the rice. Sticky, hard, mushy, dry, or any combination thereof was a sure sign a chef was a rookie. The pork was allowed to be a disaster. After all, in many poor Latin American countries, meat was always questionable, but the rice must be perfect and the beans must be... beans.

"You mustn't overcook the rice or the beans, Linc ..." Max said out loud as he cooked away. "Remember that in your travels, my friend."

The meal to be ready around noontime according to plan. Max broiled the pork chops slowly. They came out black and crusty around the edges of the fatty perimeter. The marinade was fully absorbed. *Perfecto!* Linc and Max grabbed a cab to Rodrigo's.

It's fitting Linc is here to witness this debt being paid.

The cabdriver said, "Hey, man, where did you get that chow? It smells good. I gotta stop for lunch right after I drop you off. Man, you got me goin' now."

Max felt like talking on this particular cab ride. After all, the subject was food. "A special recipe I made: Pork chops with rice and beans... with mushroom marinade to liven things up."

"Listen, man, I'm Dominican. My momma made pork chops with rice and beans and it never smelled this good... *Lo siento*, I'm sorry, *madre mio*." He said blessing himself looking up.

"Special recipe... **Pork Chops Rodrigo**."

Max and Linc got out in front of the pet shop. Linc loved the place.

I guess Rodrigo is kinder with the, "For Sale" residents. Max figured Linc would remember mistreatment if there had been any and show a different reaction. Max loved animals more than people in most cases. He reckoned it was because most animals couldn't defend themselves against humans.

Linc, stay happy and healthy... you're the lucky one.

Max walked up to Rodrigo and tapped him on the shoulder. "Hey, you crazy bastard," Max said. "Here's the meal I promised you... We're even."

"Ahhh, gringo, aren't you going to eat with me?" Rodrigo asked.

"That wasn't the deal. Here ya' go... Enjoy it."

"It smells wonderful, *amigo*. Thank you," Rodrigo said, sniffing at the bag.

"I'll stop back to see if you enjoyed it. Eat slowly ... Enjoy every morsel."

"*Hasta luego*," Rodrigo said. "*Gracias, hombre!*"

Max could not help but smile as he walked. He was like a school kid who had just put a snake in someone's locker!

What's so funny? I might be killing the bastard. Two murders in two days ... Will the NYPD put the two murders together? I hope this M#7 isn't lethal. I only want to wound the bastard ... I can see the New York Post*:* ***"Serial Killer on the Loose!"***

CHAPTER 45

Max and Link wandered back to Rodrigo's Pet Shop at around three thirty. The front door was wide open. Canaries, parakeets, and larger birds were flying all around the store. Many had found the opened door to freedom. Max looked down the middle aisle between the fish tanks and the snake section. There stood Rodrigo in his jockey shorts, which happened to be long overdue for a wash. His arms were outstretched and looking straight up into the air as though waiting to ascend into heaven. Every cage was open. Everything from monkeys to ferrets had taken over the store. The fish were the only species not free at this point. Their bug-eyed herky jerky movements seemed to say, "**What about us?**"

The inmates were running the asylum.

The animals had a choice: the streets of Harlem or the insanity of the store. Most choose Harlem to go forth and multiply. It became evident quite soon that the animals were much happier with their emancipation than their new neighbors. Locals screamed at the sight of strange creatures never seen before.

There was a little girl about ten years of age in the store. She was dressed in the tartan uniform of a private school. She was trembling as she stared at Rodrigo.

"Are you okay?" Max asked.

She struggled with her words. "He… he told me, I must help him build an ark! What… what's an **ark**?"

"It's a boat. Don't worry... the forecast is sunny and mild for the rest of the week. What is your favorite animal here?" Max asked as he patted her head as she looked around.

"Well, it was the ring-necked dove that I visit after school every day," she said, whimpering uncontrollably.

"Since all these animals have been emancipated...freed, I think it's all right to take the bird home with you for safekeeping. Noah here seems to have lost control of the passenger manifest," Max said, ducking under the birds zooming overhead.

"I would... but the chimpanzee pulled its head off!" The girl started screaming and ran out the door in tears.

"Let's go, Linc... Our work here is done. Rodrigo can explain his need for an ark to the folks at Bellevue."

Max and Linc hoped into a cab at the front of the store. The cabdriver immediately asked, "What the hell is going on in that place? I almost ran over a goddamn monkey coming down the block." Max and Linc stared out the window as exotic animals investigated their new urban habitat.

Just when Harlem residents thought they had seen it all!

CHAPTER 46

It was another brisk morning. Winter seemed on schedule. Max and Linc arrived home after their daily morning run in Central Park. Max saw a text message from John Timoney on his cell phone. It said, "**Call me ASAP when you get this message. Insp T.**"

"This is it! Jeez, Linc, it said Inspector Timoney… not John Timoney. That means business. He said to call him immediately. Okay, I need to call him back… Breathe… Okay, here goes."

"Hello, John? Max. Everything okay? The text sounded urgent!" Max said.

He thought he sounded pretty good.

"Where are you now, Max?" Timoney asked abruptly.

"I'm at the apartment… I just finished a run with…."

Timoney interrupted. "Come up to the Three-Four immediately. We need to talk."

"I'll be up there within the hour."

"Tell the desk sergeant you're here to see Captain Dunne, **not me**. Got it?"

"There were no goodbyes, Linc. I have to see Captain Dunne, not Inspector Timoney. This is it. The shit has hit the fan. I can't take you, pal… too much going on. If they don't let me come back to get you, I'll call Ed Curlander… He'll have someone come for you." Max was rambling to Linc.

The revolving doors of the Three-Four awaited him.

Max showered and took a cab. When the cabdriver said, "Beautiful day," that meant; staring-out-the-window time, for Max.

No sense rehearsing anything. I'll need to improvise. Nerves will account for a certain amount of anxiety... Whatever they tell me, I'll react as though it's news to me. If they insinuate my involvement, I'll handle that with a blank look and then ask my two friends, jokingly of course, if Weinstein is available. Then... weigh their reactions. Short answers... I can't bullshit these two!

He got out in front of the Three-Four. As he paid, the cabdriver said, "I knew you were a cop." Max smiled and walked in. He was about to speak to Sgt. Marco when the sergeant just pointed with his pen toward Captain Dunne's office. Max knocked on the opaque glass door that now read, "Captain Peter Dunne." When he got into the office, Max put out his hand and made sure he kept eye contact with both of them. Both men were in uniform. Timoney now wore the white shirt and black tie of a deputy inspector.

Timoney let Dunne handle the entire show. It was evident that this was Dunne's precinct now. "Have a seat, Mr. Burns."

Very officious. Max thought.

Timoney was looking out the window, which faced a back alley wall about twenty feet away. The *"talkative-cabdriver defense"* was in play for Timoney.

"Mr. Burns." Dunne said.

"Call me Max, please."

"Max," Dunne said, "Louis Caamano was found dead in his apartment this morning at 10:41 a.m., by his girlfriend."

Max was silent but sat up in the chair. Then he looked up at Dunne and said, "Pity." That was all Max said, just... pity. It came to him without forethought. It was what Brother Gregory had said to the class at St. Mary's after Max had severely beaten Dante Liguori. Max felt in control.

Dunne looked over at Timoney. Timoney turned his head to look over at Max. Then he said, "It's over, Max!"

"IT'S OVER?"

Max decided to sit there until he found out from Timoney exactly what the definition of, "over" happened to be.

Then Timoney said to Max, "You can put it to rest now. The little bastard, God rest his immortal soul, overdosed on a speedball."

Max looked quizzically at Timoney and then at Dunne. "A speedball?"

"A mixture of heroin and cocaine. An old favorite of his according to his girlfriend. She hadn't seen him since late Saturday night. They had a little spat over at the Inwood Lounge. He went home and shot up. She thought he had quit using. Not according to the medical examiner's report. There wasn't much in him. It must have been shitty horse," Dunne said without remorse.

"See, Max, there is justice in New York City. It's over, my friend. Try to move on now. Happened a little sooner than later, eh?" Timoney piped in.

"Not really." Max let the reply slip out of his mouth without thinking. "Gentlemen, I appreciate you telling me about this in person. It makes it… final. Thank you both for everything." Max shook their hands for the second time in about two minutes. He couldn't wait to get the hell out of there.

Timoney said, "Take a little vacation, Max. Get out of New York City for a while. It'll be good for you."

"John, I've got two invitations to be at Curlander's party headquarters this Tuesday night. Why don't you come with me? I'm not sure what to expect, but what the hell, it's a free meal and a few drinks… well, a free meal anyway."

"Sure, that should be quite an experience. Be good to spend some time with the next president of the United States… I'll meet you in front of his HQ. I have a meeting at One Police Plaza that afternoon. I'll go home and change into a suit."

"A suit? I don't own a suit," Max said.

"You don't need one," Timoney said. "I don't want to be in uniform. 'All politics is local,' as Tip O'Neill said. The New York

City is no different. My bosses would kiss some real ass to be at this. It's a big deal, ya know!"

"I can get more invitations," Max said. "You can give a few to the boys downtown."

"Screw them! How's six o'clock out front?" Timoney asked.

"Done. Call me on the cell. I might be inside… He wants me to bring the dog!"

"Who?" Timoney said.

"Ed Curlander. See you then."

Max walked a block before laughing out loud. He knew he shouldn't get cocky, but he couldn't help it.

Speedball, Max thought, *good name for a racehorse.*

Max walked down past his old restaurant to see what was going on. He stood in front of the boarded-up corner that had once housed his dreams. Plywood and graffiti now marked the site of Eva's murder.

I shouldn't have dragged her to New York. Who do I think I am, Superman? Most guys take the woman they love to some suburb… I brought the love of my life to hell.

A black Lincoln town car pulled into the bus stop. A short, balding man in his seventies got out. "Mr. Burns? I'm Abe Liebowitz. I am—was—your landlord." Eva had dealt with him, so Max did not know who he was. They shook hands. "I recognize you from the newspapers," Liebowitz explained. The two of them looked at the remnants of the restaurant. "Good food, I heard… I am very sorry for your loss. She was a very nice lady, sharp too! She squeezed an extra two years out of me on the lease. Nobody gets twelve years on a lease from Abe Liebowitz. Doesn't matter now, does it?" Liebowitz said.

Neither could take his eyes off the building. "Do you want to rebuild? I would help. You were the best tenant I ever had here. You never saw my face coming around looking for money, did you? Believe me—I, too, wish this never happened."

"I am done, Mr. Liebowitz. My whole life was destroyed in there. If Eva was here, maybe."

"Just a thought. This is a good neighborhood, Mr. Burns. I grew up on 175th Street and Broadway. The movie theater there was once the Loew's 175th Street Theatre. It was the most beautiful theater in Manhattan, even more striking than Radio City Music Hall… smaller, but more beautiful. Then it became the church of the Reverend Mike. He pulls up every Sunday in a Rolls-Royce at 9:00 a.m. … He leaves at noon with bags of cash… not coins!" Liebowitz shook his index finger and his head to emphasize that the church was all cash. "The reverend is the king of the silent collection. They throw the money at him. I should have such a job. Where do you get a job like that? I have to chase people for money. And I provide a roof over their heads, water and heat for their bodies. People chase him to give him money. I don't understand. It is what it is."

Liebowitz took a deep breath and looked around. "I love this neighborhood. I own sixteen buildings here. My father was a shoemaker on 173rd Street for fifty-two years. Now, I own sixteen buildings. I rent apartments to kids in college mostly. Even the Dominicans are moving to the suburbs. God bless them. They are wonderful people… hot-tempered, but wonderful.

"Kids starting out today can't afford downtown prices, so they come to Washington Heights. They aren't afraid. They take the subways… they make a life. You see, Mr. Burns, life is a struggle to both eat and have a place to sleep. I provided the place to sleep. You provided the food. It is very basic. But, you must know how to hunt or you starve or freeze. You, you are a hunter. A good hunter always knows more about the animal than the animal knows about the hunter. Just the words of an old Jew from Washington Heights… not Hamilton Heights. If you ever come back, here is my card."

Liebowitz handed Max his card, walked a few steps, and turned back around. After a pause, Liebowitz asked, "Was she your wife?"

Max stammered but managed to say, "no… not yet… I mean… soon… No."

Liebowitz said, "Wonderful woman ... beautiful woman... smart... very smart. Good luck, Mr. Burns." Liebowitz got back in the town car and disappeared down Broadway.

Max started walking. He was gratified that Liebowitz had such respect for Eva.

Can you be in love with someone who is dead? Or is that what is called longing?

He didn't know the answer. It didn't matter. He didn't know what *longing* even meant, but he could feel it.

Maybe Timoney is right. I should get the hell out of New York City for a while... maybe after the election.

Max voted early. Curlander's party affiliation was listed as the American Bulldog Party. Max laughed and thought about what his grandfather's Irish brother had said when he'd visited America for the first time: **"Great country this!"**

Ed's running mate was a gent by the name of Jeremy Tubbs.

If Ed picked him, he's good enough for me. Why anyone would want to become the president of the United States is beyond my comprehension. Nobody likes the president. Once you get out of the eighth grade, you begin to dislike whoever is president. By the time you are halfway through high school, you probably hate the president. I wonder why that is? Did George Washington go through all of this bullshit? Hell, Washington didn't have a political party. Lucky you, Georgie.

Max thought about what he'd wear that night.

I'm not going to buy a suit! The last time he'd worn a suit had been for his First Communion, and that suit had had short pants. Sure, he had his dress blues from the army, but that wasn't a suit. Even with his dress blues, Max had sometimes needed to ask his pals to help him with his tie. Eventually, he'd gotten too much bullshit over asking them for help, and he'd bought clip-ons instead. The clip-ons were safer anyway.

They oughta be standard issue.

He thought back to when he had gotten into a fight in Bangkok. It was in some Thai bar after a photo shoot for the army MMA team.

A Muay Thai kick boxer was there for PR reasons. He was a bit upset about all the attention Max was garnering after the MMA title fight. After a few drinks, the Thai boxer decided to challenge Max. Max tried to avoid the whole mess, but the Thai boxer pushed him too far. Max and his pals had a few drinks in them as well and figured what the hell! Max's buddies were ragging on him. The Thai boxer was about five feet seven and maybe 145 pounds. Max's teammates cleared the floor of tables. This little guy was like a pinwheel that had flown off its stick. Max saw nothing but feet flying. The beers didn't contribute to Max's acuity. Within five seconds, Max found himself lying across a table, staring up at a slow-moving ceiling fan. Then the gods smiled on Max. The Thai boxer tried to pull Max up by his tie to finish the job. The clip-on tie came off. For a split second, the Thai boxer stood there looking at the tie in his hand. It was a split second too long. Max hit him with a shot that bounced him off the bar rail and knocked him out cold. **"So much for Thais and tie ties in Thailand,"** Max said later, after many more beers with the boys that evening. He'd won $300 on that one.

Max wondered: *Does this $300 ruin my amateur status?*

The fight had certainly ruined his clip-on-tie.

Max gave Linc a bath after his walk. It was his first bath and perhaps his last. The entire bathroom was dripping wet. Linc couldn't wait to get out of the tub. He shook himself dry and covered every inch of the apartment, including the ceiling.

Max still had the corduroy sport coat Eva had bought him.

Eva never did see the cut in the leather jacket she gave me for Christmas, he thought.

He had his jeans, his ten-year-old loafers, and a nice button-down shirt to go with the jacket.

This is as fancy as it's going to get.

Max and Linc got to election headquarters at about five forty-five. Pandemonium was the only word for it, even though the polls in New York wouldn't close until nine. This was no place for a dog, although it did resemble a zoo. Max planned on waiting out front for Timoney but when he and Linc approached the HQ door, that option ceased. The security guard at the front asked for Max's invitation. Max showed him.

Max nodded toward Linc and said, "he doesn't have one."

The guard said, "he doesn't need one." Then the guard yelled to everyone inside, **"He's here!"**

With that, the place went crazy.

Who's here? Max looked behind to see.

He didn't see anyone behind him. Everyone ran toward the door, yelling and fussing over… Lincoln. "Here, boy… Oooooh, he's so cute!" There were all sorts of oohs and aahs. Max hoped the Curlanders were inside. Cameras flashed and people took pictures on their phones. Max and Linc were swept into the melee as though they were rock stars. They were practically carried into the back room where Ed and Amy Curlander were holding court with assorted VIP guests, including Mayor Braunreuther and the governor of New York, Carl Paharik. Max was somewhat surprised. Both of these gentlemen would be in big trouble with their respective parties if Curlander didn't get elected. They'd both endorsed Ed. Braunreuther was a Democrat, and the Paharik was a Republican. If Curlander didn't get in, that could mean a political end for both of them. They had played their hand.

Amy saw Max come through the door and waved over to him. She looked in Max's eyes as only a woman could to see whether he was truly okay. She pulled Max to the side prior to taking him over to Ed and got her little speech off her chest. She told him how much she loved Eva and how he needed to go on with his life. Max appreciated Amy handling this on the side to get it over with. He loved Amy and hated tears. Amy hugged him once more and let him go. She looked down at Linc and scratched his ears. "So this is the official mascot of the American Bulldog Party, eh?" she said. Max had thought Curlander was jesting when he'd said he would make Linc the mascot of the party. Max was learning that Curlander always meant what he said.

Ed shook Max's hand then pulled him over for a hug. Linc let out a growl, and Curlander backed off. He laughed and said, "I like that! Protect and defend. Yeah, I do like that … we'll use that!" Then Curlander put his hand down, and Linc licked it. Curlander said, "You better lick it, pal, if you want a seat on Air Force One." All within earshot laughed.

Max's phone rang. Timoney was outside. Max told Ed he had to go get Timoney. Ed called two security guys. Max didn't know whether they were Secret Service or not at this point, but they were definitely former marines. Curlander told them to escort Timoney directly to the VIP room. Timoney showed the security guys his ID and his off-duty nine millimeter Glock. Curlander gave the okay for Timoney to remain armed with a nod of approval. Max reintroduced Timoney to Curlander.

Timoney said, "Good evening, Senator."

"Good evening, inspector." Max was taken aback that Curlander knew about Timoney's promotion.

Then Braunreuther appeared. "Good evening, inspector." Braunreuther looked a little perturbed that Timoney had been granted access to the VIP room. Timoney was definitely uncomfortable. He was thinking,

I knew I shouldn't have come.

Then Curlander said to Timoney, "The first thing I asked Braunreuther was, if you ever got appointed deputy inspector. I try to remember everything important, inspector, especially friends of friends." He put his hand on Max's shoulder and shook him. Max was embarrassed. Curlander had been drinking a bit. He was not drunk, but this was not a good night for cocktails. Max knew how Curlander reacted to every stage of his alcohol consumption. Max had told him once, "You drink like a sailor, not a senator." Curlander didn't liked that very much but he knew it was true. So did Amy. Max didn't care whether Curlander liked it or not. Max was devoid of the *kiss-ass chip* that everyone else in the room possessed to varying degrees. It was a big part of why Ed and Amy liked him.

Mayor Braunreuther said hello to Max. He then said, "I am sorry for your loss." Max nodded. Timoney was trying to look non-political. It was important to Timoney that Braunreuther know, he was there as a guest, and had no political aspirations. If Braunreuther smelled a whiff of competition, he could ruin Timoney's career in the NYPD. He wasn't going to suck up to the mayor, but he wasn't going to show him up either. Max and Timoney were the only two people there that weren't starry-eyed over the politicos, athletes, actors, and billionaires milling around the VIP room.

Some of the most powerful people in the world were flocking to Ed Curlander's side. You could feel the blood-letting of the old political ways. Ed Curlander's third party move was more like a coup than a shrewd political move.

Max was way out of his element, unlike his dog, who acted like this shindig was for him. Max was called onto the stage with Ed and Amy to officially introduce Abraham Lincoln Burns to the world. Max left Timoney in the midst of the crowd. He knew how uncomfortable Timoney was hobnobbing with these phonies. Max felt the same way. When he looked for Timoney, the inspector toasted him with a bottle of water and smiled. Oddly, at this very point, Max wondered whether Timoney had any inkling about Max's participation in Little Louie's demise.

Did drugs have anything to do with Louie's death? Was I lucky there were drugs in his system?

After a round of newspaper photographs and a Q&A period, Max looked around in the crowd for Timoney. He was nowhere to be found. Max understood and smiled. We are alike in many ways: the Irishman and the soldier.

Curlander introduced Max to his VP candidate, Jeremy Tubbs. Tubbs was the jovial type with an eternal smile and factory-made teeth. He was short in stature and wide in girth. He reminded Max more of a used car salesman than a vice presidential candidate from

Wisconsin. Wisconsin, Minnesota, Michigan, Illinois, and Iowa were on the fence with regard to an independent third party and were vital to success. They would need to win them all. It had been Tubbs's job to get that herd into the corral. Ed whispered to Max, "Tubbs is the best political debater in the country."

Tubbs said to Max, "So you're **the** chef, eh?"

"Yes, sir, I am **a** chef," Max said as he glanced up at Linc on top of a table on the stage. Max swore Linc was posing. Everyone wanted their picture with Lincoln Burns, official mascot of the American Bulldog Party.

"Well, I hope you can help me out with a healthy diet, son. I sure could use it. I never thought I'd live this long in the first place. I'm a long way from selling used cars back in Oconomowoc, Wisconsin."

Max smiled and said, "I think I may have bought a car or two from you somewhere along the line, Mr. Tubbs. And… yes, I can get you on a healthy diet. I'll email a cholesterol-free diet to Ed. Both of you should get on it."

"Hell no! email it to me. Once we get elected, he won't give a damn what happens to my fat ass!" They both laughed. "Thank you, son. I hope I'm in office longer than the cars I sold. I leave my fate in your good hands. Thank you again for your patience indulging an old man." Tubbs gave Max his card. Max liked him. He was a natural salesman. Ed would need him when it was time to tangle with the Senate and Congress.

So this guy is Ed's LBJ.

Amy found Max. She grabbed his arm and led him away to a cooler of bottled water. Max grabbed one for each of them.

"Max, we miss you like crazy. You need to join us," Amy said and then paused as if she were going to cry. It was rare for Amy Curlander to let her guard down. "I need you too… we both need you. I hope he doesn't get elected. Don't ever tell him I said that… please. I don't feel good about any of it."

"Amy… **he** is going to be the next president and **you** are going to be the First Lady. You've got a right to be nervous. I bet there has never been one First Lady that didn't say the same thing you are telling me right now." Max paused a bit. "Is he drinking a lot?"

Amy hesitated for a second but then realized it was okay to answer. This was Max asking. "When he's out and about… not at home … He tells me he has to… that it's part of the game. How do you tell a marine—hell, **the president**—he's not good at something? I know he's a good man and everybody loves him but … he's a lousy drinker!"

"I'll talk to him… not sure what good it will do but I **will** talk to him."

"You don't understand how much he needs a friend that's not afraid to tell him what he needs to hear. Come with us Max, please," Amy begged. "It will be a good four years."

"I'd say eight. I went to the Culinary Institute, not Harvard! I know on what side of the plate your fork goes, but I'll be damned about, which side of the aisle is which, on Capitol Hill!"

"What you know, Max, these people will never know."

"Amy, listen to me. When Eva died, I don't know, I got lost. I have no dreams, no future plans. I am flat right now. I don't know where I'll wind up. I need to get out of this funk before I make any decisions. I never thought I would have to deal with death again, not on this level. Last time I was gutted like this I lost eight good friends within minutes in Afghanistan.

"You did the right thing… that's all you need to know!" Amy said.

"It's not that easy, Amy…."

"I'm not asking you to be out on the front lines. He needs you behind the scenes. Not just him… the United States of America needs you!"

"Nice try, Amy… you should have been an army recruiter!" They both laughed and hugged each other. Amy realized how corny she must have sounded.

Ed came over and said, "Hey, you, that's my FLOTUS you're hugging, soldier… you comin' along for the ride with us?" Max patted Ed on the stomach. "Maybe… you're starting to look like him." Max nodded toward Tubbs. "Is Tubbs his real name?" Max asked.

Amy and Ed laughed so hard that people turned to see what was so funny. Curlander decided to file that joke away for another time.

Max looked on stage for Linc, who had hogged enough attention on national TV to convert all the dog lovers in the red **and** blue states. Max was about to get Linc when a young woman about seventeen years old came up to Curlander and whispered something in his ear. The information put a big smile on his face. Ed winked at Amy and yelled over to Tubbs, "Jeremy! TV time." Ed waved at Tubbs to check the TV for results that were beginning to trickle in from the West and Midwest.

Max was not going to sit in front of a TV all night and have Linc underfoot in the crowd. Max could wait for the outcome. He gave Amy a kiss on the cheek and a hug good night.

Max said, "Tell him good night and good luck. I will never be too far away if either of you need me… I promise."

"I am going to hold you to that," Amy said and kissed him again on the cheek.

"First time I ever kissed a FLOTUS."

"You still haven't. So you have to stay very close if you want that to come true. We love you, Max. You are always welcome at our home… and bring your dog when you are both White House-broken." Amy waved and walked back to where Ed was pontificating.

Max gathered up Linc, who was more than happy to see him. "Goodbye, Linc," people gushed. "We love you, Linc … Be a good boy, Linc."

You'd think he was Rin Tin Tin, Max thought.

Then he realized he didn't know who Rin Tin Tin was himself. His dad used to mention Rin Tin Tin every time he saw a dog do something stupid or brilliant.

I'll google it.

Max saw Timoney standing outside the headquarters. The

deputy inspector had been up in the front room with the volunteers the entire time. Max said, "phew ... there is some intense Americana going on in there, John."

"You haven't seen anything yet. This? This is the fluff."

"You can have it," Max said.

"You got a ticket to ride, as the Beatles said. If he wants you bad enough, he'll get you. Maybe it's not such a bad idea to hitch your wagon to his for a few years. You're young enough. Then you can open a chain of restaurants with the presidential seal on the doors... maybe get a TV show!"

"I like my freedom too much. I can't get into all this bullshit."

"Maybe it's time you had some structure... like in the army. This is the chance of a lifetime, Max. Most people would kill for this opportunity."

Max was taken aback by the word **kill** coming forth from Timoney in any context. Max took the opportunity to bend down and put the leash on Linc, so he didn't have to look Timoney in the eye. "Yeah, I know," he said. "My head is on backward right now, John. All I know is I have to get it straightened out before my next move. I'm always jumping at things. I'm coming around but I need to chill for a while longer."

"I get it. I'm proud of you. You could be on Rikers Island right now for doing something stupid to that little bastard... but you held fast. I know it took a lot for you to backoff. The smart money was on you losing your cool and strangling the little prick. But you didn't. You're the kind of friend that man in there needs." Timoney paused as he looked around the street. "I'm going home. Need a lift? I got the company car," Timoney said, nodding toward a chauffeur-driven black Lincoln parked in the bus stop.

"Pretty fancy-schmancy, as Mr. Liebowitz would say," Max chided.

"Ahhh, so you met Liebowitz, eh?"

Max said, "You know Mr. Liebowitz?"

"I had a phone line dedicated to him in the Three-Four precinct house. He belongs to Pete Dunne now. Good night, Max and good night, Lincoln....thanks for the invite, Max. Keep vigilant and in touch, my friend."

Timoney patted Linc on the head and then Max on the shoulder. That was about as much affection as anyone ever got from this *son of Erin's Isle*, Deputy Inspector John Timoney. The driver, a NYPD sergeant, opened the rear door for his boss.

Max was visibly shaken as Timoney sped away in the car.

Can't help being nervous around such a good cop?

The East Side of Manhattan was buzzing after the polls closed throughout the state of New York. As expected, Curlander and Tubbs took New York by a wide margin. The bars were now open and doing a booming business. Max and Linc looked in vacant store windows as they walked north on Third Avenue. The commercial rentals down in this part of Manhattan were twenty times the cost of what Max and Eva paid uptown. It was also twenty times safer.

Max thought about what Timoney had said about Louie.

Maybe Louie did die from an overdose. Either that or the lethal properties in the mushrooms went undetected. If that's the case—if an autopsy by top-notch medical examiners couldn't detect the mushrooms—that means the mushrooms are undetectable. Do I have to kill someone else to find out? I hope not.

Nothing got past Timoney. Sure, Louie was dead. That was the most important thing to Max. Timoney wouldn't cover for anybody. Max liked that about him. He knew he had played with fire.

Thank God it's over.

Linc was beat. Max hailed a taxi for the rest of the trip home. Linc fell asleep with the movement of the cab. Max stared out the window as the cabbie's questions fell on deaf ears.

CHAPTER 47

Max put Linc upstairs on the rug where he liked to sleep and then went downstairs to check on things. The Mason jars were filling up after all the months of harvesting. Max wasn't exactly sure why he was saving all ten different categories. He had a pretty good idea of what could be used for cooking and what could not. Should there be more experimentation after things settled down? Should he throw everything into the furnace? He decided to wait.

He sat in the rocking chair and thought about Eva… walking away and waving that day in City Hall… always in slow motion. He fell asleep.

Max awoke early next morning to the sound of Woods's broom as he swept the basement floor. Max came out before Woods saw the lock was off the door. Woods jumped.

"Max! You scared the shit out of me!"

"Sorry. I fell asleep again last night." Max was up to date on the storage room stipend but gave Woods two more months rent just to keep him happy.

"Why thank you, Max. I do appreciate it."

"Want me to sweep up in there?" Woods asked.

"Sure thing. Give it a good sweep." Max stood behind the fish tank. He wanted Woods to see there was nothing odd going on in his storage room. Woods nonchalantly checked it all out and was satisfied that he would not be involved in anything problematic. Max thought Woods might have had some run-ins with the law. He had one **tat**, *a clock with no hands,* that was a giveaway. If so, it would explain a few things: Woods obsession with keeping things legit; Woods submitting to such close scrutiny by Mrs. Woods; Woods lack of interest in talking about the army…or the past.

"I hope you don't hear me on the heavy bag."

"Not at all."

Max decided it was a good time to explain his crazy hours in the storeroom. "I fall asleep reading sometimes after a good workout. It's so peaceful… can't hear a sound."

"Yeah. It **is** kinda peaceful down here. Nobody botherin' ya'." Woods started to walk away and said to Max, "Hope President Curlander likes black folk." Woods walked away, sweeping as he went.

Max was confused, then stunned before completely digesting Woods's remark.

"Jeez, he did it! The sonuvabitch did it!" Max ran up the stairs to the apartment. He turned on the TV. There was Curlander hugging Amy. Then they showed clips of earlier in the night of Linc as the official mascot of the American Bulldog Party, the party of the president-elect of the United States.

"His name is Lincoln Burns, Linc to his friends," President-Elect Curlander said to the TV audience.

"Look at yourself, Linc," Max said, pointing at the TV. Linc wanted to go out. Max hitched him up, and off they went to the park. Max grabbed a *New York Post* on the way. The headline read, ***"The Marines Have Landed!"***

"Well, I'll be damned. You take a pretty good picture, Linc."

CHAPTER 48

When they got to Central Park, Max fastened the leash to a bench so he could read the paper with both hands. There were six different photos of Linc in the *New York Post.*

Max noticed people looking at him. They were discussing whether the dog tied to the bench was indeed, ***the*** Lincoln Burns.

"Excuse me, young man," said an elderly woman walking a well-coiffed standard poodle. "Is that the president's dog?"

"No, ma'am, that's my dog. He happens to be a friend of the president-elect."

"Well, isn't he the new mascot of the American Bulldog Party?" she asked.

"Yes he is, ma'am. His name is Lincoln Burns, and he is the mascot of the American Bulldog Party."

"He doesn't look like a purebred. Does he have papers?"

"No, ma'am. These are all the papers he needs right here in my hands." He held up his copy of the *New York Post.* This story tells you exactly who and what breed he happens to be."

Max had not thought about Linc's AKC papers. He made a mental note to ask Rodrigo about it.

"But does he have pedigree papers? Is he registered with the AKC?" she asked.

"Madam, he's lucky to be alive," Max said, trying not to be rude.

"Good day to you, ma'am." Max folded his paper, untied Linc from the bench, and walked away smiling for the first time in a long while.

As he walked out of the park, he noticed others looking and talking as he passed by with Linc. Linc seemed to be walking a little differently. His head was a bit cocked to one side as he cantered down the path with his… attendant.

Just what I need. A famous dog to attract the attention of everyone in New York City.

By the time he got home with Linc, Max was exhausted himself. Everyone wanted pictures with Linc. There was one little girl who wanted his autograph. "After he finishes obedience school," Max said. At least things eased up when they'd gotten to their own neighborhood.

This is not good!

The last thing in the world Max coveted was attention.

"Linc, ole boy, I may have to paint you a different color," Max said. "How 'bout pink?"

That evening, as Max and Linc tried to take it easy and chill out after a long couple of days, the phone rang. It was Ed Curlander.

"You didn't believe me! I told you! I told you… you thickheaded grunt." Max could tell that Ed had a few drinks in him.

"Yeah, you told me… congratulations, my man. You did exactly what you said you were going to do… **Mr. President."**

"Thanks, pal. I couldn't have done it without you."

"What are you talking about? I had nothing…."

"You had everything to do with it. Not only when you took care of those bouncers in Georgetown, but all those late nights together. I remember everything we talked about: Afghanistan; WashPa; General Sherman; peace; food; Abu Ghraib; Ghazi Haider; women… all of it. None of it bullshit… and believe me, I know bullshit. People suckin' up and kissin' ass. NOT YOU!"

"How do you know? Maybe I did bullshit you. You marines have no common sense about anything."

"Well… it sounded good anyway." Both laughed.

"Come and work for me! It'll be more than cooking… I promise you. I need somebody who's got my back," Ed said. "Look what happened to Abe Lincoln when he surrounded himself with enemies. His cabinet hated his guts. Some people still think there was a conspiracy in his cabinet to assassinate him. Come down and help me. I am scared shitless!"

"Ed, I love you like a brother. Let's see what happens in the near future. Hell, you don't take the throne until January 20th. I still have a few demons I need to exorcise. You don't want some psycho down there in the White House, do you? One should be enough!" Max said, only half joking.

"Maybe two psychos are better than one. D.C. is filled with lunatics… most of them voted me in." Ed said, getting a little sloppy at this point. It was only 7:35 p.m.

"Is Amy there?" Max asked.

"Yeah, she wants to talk to you."

Once Ed had handed over the phone, Max asked, "Amy, how are you holding up?"

"I'm okay. My heart is going a mile a minute. I am not handling this too well."

"You'll be fine. Take a yoga class…amazing…really."

"What?"

"A yoga class. Find a good instructor and start taking yoga. It will help with breathing and relaxation. Take my word for it."

"Ohhhhh, get your ass down here!"

"I will see you soon. I promise," Max said. "Goodbye. I love you both. Yoga… bye." Max hung up.

Max didn't know when or where he would see the president and the First Lady. He was not anxious to see them at this point. He had remnants of his own matters to sort out.

Max was blending himself a health food drink and searing some chopped sirloin for Linc when the phone rang again. Max let it ring until the voice message started: "Hi, this message is for Max Burns…

This is Dana Trudeau, with the NBC News affiliate in Washington, D.C. We… we met in Georgetown a while back… at the Scirocco Restaurant. I was wondering if…."

Max picked up the phone and tried not to sound overly anxious. "Hello, this is Max Burns. What can I do for you, Ms. Trudeau?"

"Oh, so I have the right Max Burns. Do you know there are twenty-three people with the name Maxwell Burnses in Manhattan alone?"

"Imagine that," Max said awkwardly.

"Yes, well. Do you remember me, Max?"

"Of course…**d.b.c.**!" Max said.

"Excuse me."

"Your favorite dessert: **d.b.c.** - **d**eath **b**y **c**hocolate."

"You nailed it! First time I've ever been remembered for having a sweet tooth," she said, with a bit of sexual innuendo. "You've got a good memory." She had hoped he would remember her for other reasons.

"Well, you can ask any bartender about an old customer, and he'll be able to tell you his drink before he will remember his…or her name. Same with a good chef.

What can I do for you?"

"I want to do a story about you."

There was silence. After a long pause that had Dana Trudeau on edge.

"Don't you mean, you'd like to do a story about my dog?"

"An interview actually… and yes, with him as well… both of you. You two have captured the hearts of America, Max."

"Ms. Trudeau…." Max started, but she interrupted him.

"Uh-oh, Ms. Trudeau is it? This conversation is sliding backward into formality. In my business, that's never a good sign."

"Dana. Nothing formal intended." Max paused for a long moment before deciding to speak about recent events. Indeed, Dana was a journalist, but she was also a woman. He decided to open up for the first time. "I lost my girlfriend a few months back. She was blown to pieces in our restaurant by bad people I pushed into a corner. And, to tell you the truth, I'm feeling a little cornered myself. I don't think this is a good time for an interview."

"Max, I knew all that. I'm… I'm sorry. I thought perhaps enough time had passed. I'm sorry," Dana said, partially trying to rescue the attempt at an exclusive interview, and partly because she'd hit a nerve on a guy that was more sensitive than she expected.

"Believe me, Dana, I have nothing entertaining to say to a television audience. But I tell you what, when I do, you will get an exclusive interview with Abraham Lincoln Burns and Maxwell Tecumseh Burns, and that is a promise. How does that sound?"

There was silence on Dana's end for a few seconds. Then she said, "I don't usually get turned down."

"I bet you don't. But you're not getting turned down, you're getting moved to the front of the queue. And I always keep my word."

"I guess there's nothing I can do except take a rain check… She must have been quite a woman."

"Pardon me?" Max hadn't quite heard her last comment.

"Just thinking out loud. I do understand and I will respect your privacy and decision. Backing off is dangerous in my business. Rest assured, I'm going to hold you to your promise."

"I gave you my word, Dana. I'll even make you dinner."

"You're on! As long as the dessert is…."

"**d**eath **b**y **c**hocolate."

"You now have my cell number on your phone. Talk soon, I hope," Dana said.

"*Adios,*" he said.

"*Hasta luego,*" she replied.

Max hung up. He paused to gather himself. He looked at Linc and said, "let's eat."

Linc devoured his meal in his usual manner. Max sat on the couch and drank his health food concoction. He thought back to his days in Georgetown and savored those times in the Scirocco restaurant. His new life began there. Life was almost easy. It was what he needed after coming home from the dregs of the earth on the other side of the world.

Eva didn't like Dana Trudeau.

Max wondered why. He came to a simple conclusion: Beautiful women don't like other beautiful women.

Dana was beautiful. Eva was gorgeous in her own sultry way. Eva never needed makeup. Dana was always dressed to the nines and made up by professional makeup artists. It wasn't Dana's fault that she looked like a movie star every time she came into the Scirocco. Her studio was a few blocks away.

Eva probably thought herself haggard looking from working all night. Trudeau usually arrived around eleven forty-five, after her final newscast. That had to be it. Eva was on defense, and Dana was on offense. Women hate an uneven playing field.

Despite Dana being a local celebrity in D.C., Max had never detected an attitude that would put her into a "nose in the air" category.

Her job is to get interviews. She wouldn't get very far being a bitch about it... maybe she would. Too late. I made a promise. Not the end of the world.

Max looked up in the air and said aloud, "Forgive me, Eva. It's just an interview."

CHAPTER 49

Thanksgiving was days away when Max got a call from President-Elect Edward Curlander. Ed invited him to spend Thanksgiving Day with them at their home in upstate New York. Max said he would on one condition: that he be allowed to do the cooking. Amy grabbed the phone after Ed had consulted with her about Max's request. "Max, it's Amy, sweetie. How are you?"

"Good, Amy." He was lying, and she knew it.

"I want you here as a guest. You don't need to be cooking here on…."

Max interrupted her. "Amy, have we ever sat down and eaten a meal together?"

"Sure. At the restaurant we…."

Max interrupted again. "No, Amy. I cooked, you ate. I sat down while you were finishing your meal. I'm a huge pain in the ass when eating other people's food. I'd ruin the meal by criticizing everything. Think of it as therapy. Besides… I need the practice."

"Okay, but you have to make two desserts for everyone: apple strudel and death by chocolate."

"You got it. Where is home here in New York?"

"Pearl River. We will have a driver pick you up. Email me what you'll need, and it will all be here when you get to the house. There will be twelve people, including you. We are scheduled to sit down and eat at 4:00 p.m."

"Tell the driver to pick me up at 6:00 a.m. Is your email address the same?" Max asked.

"That's the only thing that is the same. Oh, and bring Lincoln. Do you want to speak to Ed?" Amy asked. Amy was actually thrilled that Max would be cooking. It took a lot of pressure off her and her new housekeeper, Mrs. Prendergast.

"No thanks, he's all yours. See you Thursday morning." Max hung up the phone and started thinking about the menu. He was finally enthusiastic about something. His culinary juices were stirring again.

Max was not bitter about the months off. He'd spent quality time with Linc and trained him to respond to hand commands. He was back on the heavy bag and starting to run again. A job right away would not have worked. He would have had the same problem as every single person in New York City who owned a dog: Who took care of the dog during the workday? Ten hours at home for a pup was a big reason why dog pounds were full. It was something he needed to keep in mind when—or if—a job opportunity did arise. His money was holding up…thanks to Eva.

Over the next three days, Max went back and forth with Amy and Mrs. Prendergast by email and phone. Ed had told Max during one of their late-night conversations at the Scirocco that he had to get rid of Elisa, his housekeeper of twelve years because she was an illegal alien. He hated to do it but he would have gotten crucified early on in his political career had that been unearthed. He told Max that his stand on immigration took on a whole new meaning when he had to let Elisa go. He'd given her $20,000 and sent her back to Mexico, a rich woman by Mexican standards. Ed had promised to bring her back one of these days. Now they had Mrs. Prendergast: a stern woman right out of central casting. Initially, she was in a tizzy about not preparing the first Thanksgiving Day meal for her new employer. Max told her she could help and thus learn how he prepared the meal for the following year. She wasn't crazy about hearing that. Max didn't care; he didn't think she'd be around next year anyway. Max had her go to the market at least six different times. Needless to say, she did not start her new career off as a big fan of Max Burns.

At six in the morning on November 23, Linc and Max stepped into a chauffeured black Cadillac Escalade and took off for Pearl River, New York. Max had his bag of treats and tricks with him. He'd brought samples of M#1, M#2, and M#3. No sense running short.

Ed and Amy Curlander lived in the house Ed's dad and mom had purchased back in 1971. When Ed's parents first bought the house, Pearl River, New York, had been a bedroom community comprised of mostly NYC cops and firemen. Pearl River had been considered "**the country**" back then. Now, it was suburbia. Ed's father, Charlie Curlander, had owned a bar on the Upper East Side of Manhattan in the heydays of the 1970s. In those days, the Upper East Side had been comprised of young professionals in need of good watering holes. In 1968, Charlie bought Murphy's Bar and Grill on Seventy-Seventh Street and Second Avenue. It was a beer-and-ball joint when Charlie bought the saloon. It had been a speakeasy during Prohibition. Charlie put down $27,000 of his poker winnings accumulated during his tours in Vietnam. Thus, The Mad Hatter of Second Avenue was born.

The place was a gold mine and the hottest singles bar in Manhattan. Sooner or later, every celebrity who enjoyed a cold beer and good late-night bar food ventured through the doors of *the Hatter.* Joe Namath lived around the corner and was inspired by the *Hatter* to buy his own bar: Bachelors III.

Charlie Curlander was craftier than most bar owners and managed to save every dime he could glean. He learned early on he would have to stop drinking alcohol if he were to keep both the bar and his marriage intact. Charlie dedicated himself to the Alcoholics Anonymous program in 1972 and was active until the day he died.

He milked the bar with barely any improvements for twenty-six years and sold the business and the property for $3.6 million…big money in 1985. He'd died of pancreatic cancer in 1996. Ed's mom had died a year later of breast cancer. Ed and Max would always have that in common. That parallel universe had been revealed back at the Scirocco around two o'clock one morning.

The car pulled into the Curlanders' driveway after a lengthy Thanksgiving Day drive up the beautiful, foliage-laden Palisades Parkway. The Secret Service agent had to use the siren and blue lights only once on a congested George Washington Bridge.

The house was an unassuming Victorian like most others in the neighborhood. It had a wraparound porch like Max's farmhouse in WashPa. That brought back fond memories immediately. Max noticed there was no name on the mailbox, simply a number.

It was zero- seven forty-five. Everyone was asleep except for two Secret Service agents and the indomitable Mrs. Prendergast, who was standing on the porch. A Secret Service agent greeted Max with an outstretched hand. Max recognized him. Max had prepared a meal for him on opening night of Gringo Smyth's.

"Bob Cleary, Mr. Burns. Good to see you again."

"Good to see you too, Cleary. Still taking care of my man, I see. You're gonna have your hands full."

"I already do."

Max let it slide.

Cleary was making friends with Linc as Max put his hand out to Mrs. Prendergast.

"Mrs. Prendergast, I presume?" Max said. "I just want to thank you for putting up with me barking orders at you, and all those emails to Amy… uh, Mrs. Curlander. Let's make this a Thanksgiving to remember." Max smiled and kissed Mrs. Prendergast on the forehead before he realized he probably shouldn't have. He excused himself and headed toward a door he thought led to the kitchen. It was a broom-closet. Mrs. Prendergast snickered and pointed toward a different door. Max nodded at her and stepped into the massive kitchen. His eyes opened wide at the sight of a Viking 2300 stove and a restaurant-grade tunnel dishwasher. The kitchen was set up to accommodate large groups for dinners and entertainment. It was a masterpiece.

I couldn't have designed it better myself.

Max started making breakfast for Mrs. Prendergast and for Ed and Amy, who were still sleeping. Max included Cleary in the invitation for breakfast. It was not protocol to eat with the protectees, but Cleary was also a former marine - Cleary was family.

"Eggs Benedict all around?" Max nodded toward Cleary and Mrs. Prendergast.

Both nodded back as Max proceeded to whip the hollandaise sauce. He took his french press coffee maker out of his bag and prepared coffee for everyone. Mrs. Prendergast located a bed tray. Up Max went to the master bedroom with the Eggs Benedict, coffee, and fresh-squeezed orange juice. Mrs. Prendergast accompanied him and knocked on the door for him.

"Come in!" Ed growled in a raspy voice that bespoke of a rock star hangover.

"Are you decent?" Max asked.

"What the hell do you care?" Ed asked. Mrs. Prendergast opened the door, revealing Ed alone in his disheveled bed.

"No First Lady?" At which, Mrs. Prendergast immediately turned on her heels and retreated a short way down the hall, leaving Max to handle the results of his question on his own.

"She's in **her** room. Honey, it's Max," Ed shouted as he banged on the wall behind his bed.

Amy appeared at the connecting door in a beautiful silk robe over her pajamas. She looked embarrassed about coming from a separate bedroom. She simply said, "he snores when he drinks." She ran over to Max and put the tray to the bed. She gave him a hug and a kiss.

"Well, you better get in bed with him right now before your breakfast gets cold and this scenario leaks to the press."

"Haven't you people ever heard of a microwave oven?" Ed grumbled, moving over to let his wife get into the bed with him.

"...Don't believe in them," Max said. He placed the two-person tray on their laps and said, "Enjoy... I'll be downstairs if you need me."

Mrs. Prendergast stepped forward from the hallway and said, "Ring once if you need anything, madam."

Prendergast was right out of a Dickens novel. Max was starting to like her, she seemed the loyal type, and that was a trait he admired.

Max realized he had forgotten about Linc. He looked out the window and saw Cleary in the backyard throwing a tennis ball to Linc. To Max's surprise Linc was retrieving the ball and giving it to Cleary as opposed to gnawing it to death. It made no sense to disturb them. Cleary seemed like a good guy. He liked dogs.

Max was back in a real kitchen once again. He rubbed his hands together and then washed them before he put on his rubber gloves. Max decided to start with the stuffing while the coast was clear. He had a mix pre-made for corn bread that was the basis for his stuffing recipe. Among the other ingredients were shiitake mushrooms. There would also be a dash of M#1 to put a Max Burns signature on the meal.

Mrs. Prendergast came in to help. Max put her to work. She was helpful and recognized immediately that Max was a pro. She watched every move he made. Max felt it. He moved faster than usual, showing off and keeping Mrs. Prendergast on her toes. She did well. Max was appreciative of her not getting in the way or crowding him with assumed authority.

By one o'clock the guests started showing up. Ed and Amy hustled about with last minute details and greeted folks at the door. Cleary was familiar with everyone, but stood at the door making sure they were... who they were.

Amy's mother looked to be in her late seventies but seemed quite spry. Amy's younger sister, Lyn; her husband, Roy; and their son and daughter, Chris and Mary Claire, were all smiles. The nine-year-old Mary Claire fell in love with Linc immediately. She kept Linc busy while Agent Cleary inspected the perimeter once again. There were two other agents outside that Max had not been told about. Cleary was always included in the meals, the other two agents were not. Remembering how he fed ALL the agents at Gringo Smyth's, Max made up two dishes for the agents. They would have to eat this Thanksgiving dinner in a van. Ed's older brother, Larry; his wife, Judith; and their sons, Mark and Colin. seemed in good spirits. The boys looked to be around Max's age. Both were good-looking Wall Street types… a bit too stuffy for Max's liking. It was obvious to Max that neither had done military service.

There was a beautiful mahogany bar in the library and another full bar in the basement. Everyone headed for the library bar. There was one more guest still to come.

The doorbell rang at 2:10 p.m., and Dana Trudeau came through the door looking like Miss California. Max was off to the side in his apron.

Jeez!

He wondered what **she** was doing there. He knew Dana had joined Amy and Ed for dinner a few nights at the Scirocco. Amy introduced Dana, Mrs. Prendergast and Max to everyone at the library bar.

"Well, hello there, Max," Dana said. "Is Max still okay?"

"If d-b-c Dana is still okay," Max said.

"As long as you didn't forget how to make it."

"I never forget how to make it."

Dana showed a slight smile for the double entendre. "How are you doing and how is Lincoln Burns doing?"

"See for yourself. He's out there with Agent Cleary."

She peeked out the window and said, "Cleary will keep him busy. He's part hound himself."

Good ole Cleary… He' s probably be all over her with his dashing secret service approach. Can't blame him?

Dana Trudeau was a D.C. player, and she knew the ropes.

That's *why she's here.*

In Washington, D.C., nothing was purely social. There were always multiple reasons for being invited to an affair and as many reasons to accept or decline. The A-list was a game of chess played with real people. Right now Ed Curlander was the white king. That was how it worked in the nation's capital. But it was always important to keep in mind, if a pawn made it to the other side of the board, he could become an ass-kickin' queen.

It was two thirty in the afternoon, and Ed was behind the library bar holding court.

Charlie Curlander recognized the fact that he was not able to drink liquor. Might his son realize the same? Max was not sure.

Max peeked out of the kitchen at intervals, checking on Curlander to see what kind of shape he was in. He seemed to be okay for now. Max knew, if Ed kept a steady pace going with the Scotch, the entire meal could become a disaster. Amy was on edge and calculating Ed's transition schedule as well.

Max decided he was not going to let anyone or anything spoil the Thanksgiving meal. He walked into the middle of the group. Curlander was going on about some political hack who had bad mouthed him during the campaign. Max said to everyone in general but with Curlander in mind, "Pardon me, ladies and gentlemen, I have a request. This particular Thanksgiving meal is made up of many different spices and tastes from all over the world."

"Yummy," said Dana Trudeau.

"I am going to ask that you hold off on the hard liquor until after dessert. It will only ruin your taste buds, and I don't think you'll want to miss what I have in store for you. So, indulge me, and please be seated." When he'd finished his statement, he took Ed Curlander's rocks glass out of the president-elect's hand and gulped it himself.

He put the glass on the bar, patted Ed on the back, and walked into the kitchen. You could hear a pin drop.

Cleary had watched from the kitchen. He slapped Max on the back and said, "You've got balls, my man! You got brass fuckin' balls!" Cleary was careful not to laugh out loud. Mrs. Prendergast came into the kitchen after passing out hors d'oeuvres. Max's move had solidified that he had Ed's back and Amy's as well. Mrs. Prendergast continued to smile and went about preparing the plates for Max's handiwork. Mrs. Prendergast had hired two waitresses from a local service. They arrived on time at three fifteen. The girls had been vetted by Cleary weeks earlier. They did not know who they'd be serving prior to entering the house. Both were about eighteen years old and nervous. Max calmed them down and prepped them. Max would leave the table between courses and coach them for each course and the presentation. Ed, as head of the household, would carve the turkey, as was the tradition all over the land.

Max sat in the first corner seat at the far end of the table near Amy. Curlander was at the head of the table directly facing Amy. She could see every move he made without being obvious. Curlander was still pissed at Max for taking his drink away. Ed didn't know what to do next… so he said grace. When grace was finished, he looked at Max. Max gave him a thumbs-up and began making small talk around the table.

Needless to say, Amy was thrilled by how Max had handled the Scotch incident. Right across from Max sat Dana Trudeau. Max tried not to be as distracted by her as the two Ed's nephews. She had much less makeup on than Max remembered.

She looks better without makeup.

The two lads were chatting her up as though it was a competition, which it undoubtedly was. They had as much chance as Cleary did with her. In between being unimpressed by their remarks, Dana said to Max, "You still have the touch. Very impressive, chef Burns!"

"Thank you, Dana. The best is yet to come."

"I hope so," Dana whispered without looking up. Max caught

it. The two lads caught it too but, nevertheless, remained relentless. If Dana had said that to one of them, it would have meant victory. But it was said to the chef, the hero, the apparent favorite of the president-elect and his First Lady. Dana had admired the friendship between Max and Ed Curlander in the Scirocco days. Ed and Max had been the last men standing on many a night. Dana had always wanted to stay and delve into those conversations. She knew she could have held her own. She always choose to let the boys play.

When the turkey was carried through the kitchen door, it was preceded by the most tantalizing aroma. Max nodded to Mrs. Prendergast to bring the turkey to Curlander for carving. Upon its arrival, Curlander stood up and said, "I would be honored if my good friend Max Burns would do this bird justice by properly carving it. I'd only butcher the damn thing." Mrs. Prendergast brought the bird down to Max for carving.

Ed said, "I would like to propose a toast. To my wonderful wife, the next First Lady of the United States of America, Amy Curlander. I fully realize I am nothing without you; not a man, not a husband, and certainly not a president, without you by my side."

"Here, here!" came from one and all as everyone drank a sip of the wine Max had suggested.

Ed continued, "One more toast, please. Allow me to indulge myself. After all, 'I am the president,'" he said in a Richard Nixon imitation that was quite good. This brought a chuckle and applause from everyone: To everyone here, I want you to know that you have my pledge to make this country we love a better country, a fair country, a country that not only Americans will be proud of but that the entire world will come to admire once again."

"Here, here!" everyone said again.

"Last toast, I promise: To my good friend Max Burns. We have Max to thank, not only for this wonderful Thanksgiving Day meal, but also for his past and, hopefully, future service to this great country of ours. I toast you, Max. Even a president needs a good friend… someone who is not afraid to take a cocktail out of his commander-in-chief's hand and tell him to sit down and eat his vegetables!"

There was a pregnant pause. Then Max stood up. "Okay, chief. I'll carve the turkey. I don't think the citizens of the United States intended to vote for a nine-fingered president.

Ed said, "Can I give the finger to the Speaker of the House?" All the adults laughed. Amy got up and clapped her hands.

Max carved the turkey. That in itself was a clinic. When Max uncovered the stuffing, the aroma stopped everyone in their tracks. Max had made copious amounts of stuffing. He would be glad he did. The touch of M#1 in the stuffing was doing its job. The gravy had also been treated with M#1. The meal brought silence to the table. The only thing to be heard was "Please pass this… or that," and the rattling of silverware.

No conversation- the ultimate compliment.

Max took it all in.

Max fixed a dish for Linc. Linc was exhausted from playing but always attentive to his master's food.

When Max came back and sat down, Dana said to him, "This doesn't count, you know."

"What doesn't count?"

"This doesn't count as the dinner you promised me, when I interview you… **This** is not the dinner."

"No, **this** is not the dinner, because **this** is not the interview. **This** is Thanksgiving," Max said in a controlling manner she was not used to hearing… but liked.

"Good. Do you think you'll be ready soon?"

"Pass the squash please," Max said. "That's right. You did say you were used to getting your own way, didn't you?"

"Ah, you remembered." Dana said as she reached for the squash dish.

"I don't miss much. I am just a regular guy from WashPa… and what part of Pennsylvania are you from, Dana?"

"Very good. You caught my Harrisburg twang, *did ya*!" she said in the colloquial accent.

"*Ah, ya*," Max said, mimicking right back.

"Harrisburg High School, class of 2007, and then Penn State, class of 2011."

"I went to Jefferson High in WashPa. Graduated in 2006. Then I went to the Culinary Institute in Saratoga Springs, New York. I got out in 2008. Then, Iraq and Afghanistan. Now I'm sitting here at the table with the next president of the United States, the next First Lady, and a beautiful news reporter who wants to interview my dog. **Great country this!**"

Amy was listening to the banter. Max surmised the two women were closer than he realized. When Dana excused herself to go to the ladies' room, Amy whispered to Max some insight on why she had become so friendly with Dana:

"Dana arranged to conduct an interview with me early in the campaign when I was uncertain of Ed's decision to run. I had a complete meltdown when Dana asked a question about… Ed's reputation as a drinker. I couldn't stop bawling, Max. Dana shut the entire interview down. She told her producer that Amy had gotten sick and canceled the interview. I heard her tell the cameraman that if he told the producer anything about what happened, he'd be in West Virginia covering 4-H club fairs!" Amy said. "She didn't have to do that, Max. She could have been the next Oprah with me on national TV slobbering like some teenager whose prom date didn't show up. And, I seriously doubt Ed would have been elected. That's how bad it was. She has never said a word about it since, not to anyone, and you know how D.C. is with secrets," Amy said in a low but forceful tone. "She's solid."

Max was glad to hear that. He respected Amy's opinion.

When Dana came back, Max asked, "Are you ready?"

"Depends," Dana said. Amy and Dana chuckled at the comeback. "What did you have in mind?"

"Death by chocolate… for starters," Max said.

He excused himself and told the waitresses to begin serving the desserts.

At most Thanksgiving dinners, the desserts were usually merely picked at or taken home. Max had prepared fourteen death by chocolates and fourteen apple strudels. There would be extra for people to take home and enough for the gents in the van.

When Max brought out Amy's apple strudel and Dana's death by chocolate, Dana asked Max, "Did you know I was coming?"

Max said, "Coming? But you haven't even tasted it yet."

Amy and Dana broke out in laughter. The rest of the table asked, "What's so funny?"

Max said. "You'll have to ask the First Lady."

Max watched Dana eat her death by chocolate. She purposely ate slowly, her tongue knowingly finding chocolate on her lips. She put on a sensory display that stopped the meal. The two nephews had no chance of losing the napkins from their laps. Max could not help but smile and failed in an effort not to look. Max knew she was doing this to torture the nephews. She was a tease and a damn good one. Amy knew there was a secondary target.

Women always know what other women are up to. Men don't have that gift.

After dinner, the library bar reopened. With a full stomach, Ed would have plenty in his belly to absorb a few Scotch whiskies or whatever. He was holding court once again. He had a permission slip. He was among family and about to become the next president of the United States.

Max got Linc leashed up to take him for a stroll. He grabbed a plastic bag from the kitchen and headed for the front door.

"Want some company?" Dana asked.

"Sure. Better lose the heels."

"I have my running shoes with me. I'll be right down," Dana said as she walked slowly up the stairs.

"She's a runner." Max said quietly to the dog.

When Dana came down, she was wearing a beret pulled down

over her blond hair, a pair of jeans, a flannel shirt, a ski vest, and her running shoes. Max took note of the fact that the shoes had some hard miles on them. She looked great. Max noticed she was the same height as Eva.

"C'mon, Linc, old boy. Dana Trudeau is about to give you the once-over."

Dana scratched Linc behind his ears. "They all love this."

"Seems that way… He likes you."

Cleary opened the door slowly with a wry smile on his face.

"Thank you, Bob. How was your dinner? Did the men like theirs?" Max asked.

"You're an artist. They thank you as well. And remember… I have season tickets to the Redskins if you ever need one… or two." Cleary chanced a quick look at Dana's breasts.

It was a clear evening with a nearly full moon rising in the sky and no wind to disturb the fallen leaves. Max had Linc walking on his left side and instinctively bowed his right arm to accept Dana's left arm.

Dana thought, *That was instinctive. They don't make guys like this anymore, not in D.C. anyway.*

She liked what she was seeing and feeling.

Comfortable. Like an old flannel shirt.

That was the word she was looking for.

It had been a while since she'd felt so at ease or inquisitive about a guy. They even walked in step.

"So, Dana Trudeau, what would you like to know?"

"Spare me the poetry, Max Burns."

They both chuckled at the rhyme.

"How are you doing, really?" she asked.

The waxing moon shone bright and fluttered shadows from the tree branches. Max watched puffs of cold air bellowing from Linc's mouth. He looked at Dana. Her beautiful lips admitted a soft version of visible breath that seemed gentle. He decided on an answer that he would not have given to anyone else.

"Well, I'm getting a little tired of people dying around me. That's for sure."

"I can relate to that to some extent. I'm sick of the news being so damn depressing." Dana caught herself. "I'm sorry, Max. I didn't mean to say my life is anything compared to what you've been through. I read the transcript of the Caamano trial. I'm proud of you.and relieved..."

"Relieved? About what?"

"Relieved that you finished what you started."

"You think so?"

"You're damn right I do. Anyone who knew your story would say the same thing."

"Is that what your interview is about, telling my story?" Max became a little concerned.

"Only if you want it to be. I'll only go as far as you want me to go. That's a promise."

Max wanted to marinate on his volunteering to be interviewed.

"What about you? Tell me about Dana Trudeau. What makes her tick?"

"Well, I'm pretty structured."

Max interjected, "I think you're structured pretty well myself."

"Thanks, big fella. You're put together fairly well yourself," she retorted.

"Sorry. Can't seem to let those slide."

"What do you want to know about me, Max?"

"You have a boyfriend?"

"Not at the present time."

"Why not?"

"Dreams, work, etcetera. I have things I want to do. Relationships suck when you have to give up things you know you want to do. It might work if two people have similar goals."

There was a lull in the conversation. Both parties digested the other's comments and thought about goals.

Dana knew about Eva and the bombing. She instinctively redirected the conversation. "Lincoln Burns is probably the most famous dog in America right now. How do you think his benefactor, Max Burns, is going to avoid the limelight?"

"Linc deserves the attention. He's an all-American story: Ghetto to the White House. 'Some are born great, some achieve greatness, and some have greatness thrust upon 'em': Shakespeare, *Twelfth Night; Malvolio* reading a letter… I think."

"Hmmm, I thought that was Churchill. Are you showing off, Max Burns?" Dana said with a wry smile.

"Is it working?"

"Not sure yet. Keep going."

"That's all I got."

"I thought so."

They both laughed. Dana held fast to Max with both arms as they walked.

"All right. Quick toss-up questions - short answers only," Dana blurted out.

"Government?"

"Mortal sins."

"Organized religion?"

"Venial sins."

"God?"

"We are his toys."

"Interesting. You'll need to elaborate at some point," Dana quipped.

"You asked for short answers. Your turn," Max snapped back.

"Hell?"

"A dictator."

"Revenge?"

"Sweet."

"Justice?"

"Universal."

"First Amendment?"

"Essential - See previous answer for, Hell."

"Not bad. I can tell you were a journalism major."

"And you're the chef."

"That I am."

They walked in silence for a while. The quiet caught up to Max. He fell into that awkward moment when you think you must say something.

"How would you clean up the mess on this little planet of ours if you were God?" Max blurted.

"If I were God? Hmmm, if I were God, I would quite simply part the clouds and appear to the entire population of the planet. After the inhabitants of this planet digested the fact that God is a woman, I would say, 'Those of you that believe in one God, congratulations, good guess!' After the cheers settled down, I would say, 'I have a question: If you all believed in one God, why did my name become so important to you?' Now the fun part. I would bring the clouds back together and watch the men walk home behind their wives, kissing their asses all the way! Then? I'd go get my nails done."

Max laughed and held her hands together as he breathed hot air on them to warm them up.

Who the hell is this guy?

Then Max held her hand in his jacket pocket.

They had walked about a mile without even realizing it.

"Some heavy philosophical crap for a first date," Max said.

"Oh, this is a date, is it?" Dana said, smiling.

"Feels like it." Max was honest.

"Does, doesn't it?" Dana said.

The remainder of the walk back to the house was lighter after a few laughs at the expense of the Curlander nephews. The walk relit a candle for Max that had been extinguished long enough.

When Max and Dana arrived back at the house, Amy was playing show tunes on the piano and singing along with Ed and the guests. It was quite a scene. Cleary sang, more or less, alongside Mrs. Prendergast.

After the Curlander Chorale systematically destroyed every song Rodgers and Hammerstein had ever written, everyone settled down by the large stone fireplace in the library. One by one, guests started their trek home. Max wondered what Dana's plans were. Max did a Google search on his phone.

The last shuttle flights from LaGuardia and JFK were at midnight. She'll need to leave soon.

Ed, Amy, Max, Dana, and Cleary were the last people around the fireplace at about ten thirty. The turkey and the rest of the food had done in Cleary, who was now half-asleep. Max looked at Cleary, Ed, Amy, and finally Dana.

"Okay, pilgrims," Max said, "it's time for my dog and me to head back to Plymouth Rock."

Ed said, "You're not going anywhere! Hell, do you think Cleary is Batman? Isn't that right, Cleary?"

Cleary nodded and said, "Yes, sir. Whatever you say, colonel."

Amy chimed in, "I'd love some eggs Benedict in the morning. We have plenty of room. Cleary can drop you off tomorrow on the way to JFK with Dana."

Max said, "I don't think…."

"Do you have something more important going on than accepting an overnight invitation from your president?" Dana said as she twirled some Napoleon brandy around in a snifter.

Of course, Max did not. He looked over at Linc, who was out cold in front of the fireplace. Setup or not, Max knew he would be an idiot to stop the momentum.

"Okay. But I am only doing this for your sake, Cleary," Max said with a sly smile.

"The sacrifices we make for our country…." Cleary mumbled with an envious look on his face. The rebuff was a little out of place for a Secret Service agent, but Cleary was part of the team. Curlander gave him a wide berth in which to maneuver. Cleary knew how to keep his mouth shut. He had earned the additional latitude.

"Great!" Amy said. "You have the second room on the right as you walk down the hallway, Max. Dana, would you kindly show Max… in a bit? It's directly across from your room."

Dana just stared into her glass and circled her finger around the rim, making a ringing noise.

God may be a woman after all. Max thought.

Ed said to Max, "I have a closet full of things you can wear tomorrow, even some presidential underwear if you are looking for a souvenir." Amy laughed after she smacked him on the arm. Amy shot a coy smile at Dana as if to say:

My job here is done.

Dana was smart enough not to look back.

Ed and Amy announced they were retiring, and Cleary soon followed. Max put a few big logs on the fire which meant to one and all, he'd be up a while. Linc was still curled up next to the fireplace, but keeping Linc warm was not Max's primary goal… he wanted to keep the conversation going. The white shag rug in front of the fireplace was as inviting as a cloud passing in front of the sun on a hot summer day. Max walked back over to Dana and put her brandy on the bar. Then he put out his hand. She clutched it, feeling the strength of his arm as he helped her up. They walked over to the shag rug. Dana pushed off her running shoes. Max kicked off his loafers.

Max said, "Would you look at this mutt? I hope he doesn't get a big head now that he's famous."

They sat close to each other on the shag rug, their backs up against the couch.

After a few moments of peaceful silence watching the fire, Max said, "This is a first for me."

Thinking that maybe he was presuming too much at this point, Dana asked, "What is?"

"Having dinner with the president of the United States and an after-dinner drink with God."

They both smiled. Max initiated the kiss after Dana touched his cheek. Then Max gently pressed his lips onto her long, beautiful neck and lingered there until it was time to find out, how each other kissed. Finally, Dana stood up and put her left hand out. "C'mon," she said as she nodded toward the stairs. He walked behind her and watched her beautiful syncopating derriere as she walked with him in tow.

She had no bra under the flannel shirt she let drop to the floor in his room. She unbuttoned his starched blue button-down shirt and ran her hands gently over his massive chest. When she looked up at his face, he pulled her closer, clutching her cheeks with his hands. Then he moved his hands slowly down to her breasts. He circled her nipples with his fingers until they reached to be kissed.

Dana could feel him. She unbuttoned his jeans and let them drop to the floor. Her jeans needed his help. As he kissed her, he slid her jeans the rest of the way to the floor with his foot. Her thong underwear made no indentations on her perfect athletic body. Max attempted to remove the tiny thong. That was when the thong curled up into its defensive posture.

The damn thing is alive!

The resulting problem was solved instantly by Dana. His boxer shorts presented no such problem.

He picked her up and placed her on the brass bed. There was no rush. Both wanted to look, touch, explore, admire, and kiss.

How is he capable of such gentleness? Dana wondered.

She moved his hand between her legs and pressed on it. His fingers found their way as silk and wetness guided him. Dana reciprocated, her fingers finding him. All the time they kept kissing, giving more than taking from each other, each kiss filled with more feeling than the last.

Then, as though she could not wait any longer, she guided him in her with a look that said, now. Max moved slowly until she was full. As he moved in and out, he watched her surrender to it all. She grabbed tightly to the covers on both sides of the bed, her hands forming fists. She pulled the covers closer, then let go. She clung to his back as though her life were in jeopardy. Max withdrew slowly outside of her, and then, with reassuring presence, he went as far inside as he could, over and over again. They made love for a long time, facing each other all the while. It was their first time, and they wanted to kiss.

"With me … please … **Now!"** Dana said, struggling with the volume of her intensity.

Max kissed her again and moved with forceful intention to meet with her. She pushed her face into a pillow to suppress a primal scream. He responded to her with an explosion of physical helplessness that he'd thought he would never feel again.

He gently moved a tuft of hair that partially covered her eyes and kissed her gently. Dana turned over, wide-eyed, smiling as she stared at nothing. They spooned and fell asleep.

CHAPTER 50

When Max woke the next morning, he looked at his watch—eight o'clock—and then for Dana, but the bed was empty next to him. He wondered briefly whether the previous night had been a dream.

Damn mushrooms.

But it hadn't been a dream. He rolled onto his back, put his hands behind his head, took a deep breath, and let it out slowly.

Oh … my … God!

He felt relaxed. He refused to put a label on his best Thanksgiving ever.

Great day. Perfect night.

Max wished he had brought his running gear. It was a gorgeous day for a run. He jumped into the shower. He grabbed an old flannel shirt that seemed to fit and went downstairs to see what he could see. Dana's door was open when he walked by. He knocked and peeked in, but she wasn't there. Max headed straight for the kitchen. Max and Cleary seemed to be the only people up. Linc was up too. Cleary had walked him.

"Good morning, Cleary."

"Good morning, Max. I made coffee," Cleary said, proud of the accomplishment. "She went for a run," he added while reading the newspaper.

"Who?" Max said.

Cleary looked up at Max with a look that said,

Do I look like a moron to you? I'm a Secret Service agent… I get paid to know what's going on around here.

Dana came in as Max was walking out with Linc. She walked right past them, breathing heavily. She looked at her Fitbit and said, "Sweaty… four miles… lots of hills." She could not help rubbing her hand across his cheek as she breezed by him. That stopped Max in his tracks.

Eva did that all the time.

He smiled and shrugged it off.

Max took Linc for a shorter walk than usual since Cleary had walked him earlier. Max didn't know how much time he had left to be around Dana. He scooted back to the house and went into the kitchen to get some breakfast going for the remainder of the crew.

"Everyone like Mexican? I make a helluva *huevos rancheros*," Max blurted out, amusing himself.

Dana shouted from upstairs, "Yes, I love Mexican!"

Cleary said, "I'm in."

Ed and Amy were still sleeping. Max ran upstairs to get the spices and some other supplies out of his bag. As he started to head back downstairs, Amy and Ed came out of the master bedroom together.

Max just said, "Good morning."

"Yes, it is. A very good morning, Max. How is your day going so far?" Amy asked with an all-knowing female smile.

"As good as it gets, Amy. *Huevos rancheros* okay with you two? It's my specialty."

Amy said, "Been a while… for *huevos rancheros*, too."

Ed laughed and said, "What the hell did you put in that turkey?" He pulled Amy close and kissed her.

"Love potion number one. Wait till you get to numbers two, three, and four." Max chuckled to himself.

"Well, I'm glad I don't have a heart condition. I don't need to pull a Rockefeller and die in the sack, hahaha. Mexican is fine," Curlander said.

The entire household sat down at the kitchen table like any American family after a holiday. There was nothing fancy; paper napkins, coffee in whatever you wanted it in, *huevos rancheros* from the frying pan to the plate. Of course, all the ingredients and spices were fresh, except for the M#1.

Breakfast was a big hit. Max had made enough for seconds, thirds in Cleary's case.

Cleary looked up and said to Max, "Okay, okay, you can have two of my Redskins tickets for one game only, except the Ravens game, on one condition: you gotta take the job." Everyone laughed, even Max. They all knew what "the job" meant.

Curlander said, "Listen, I have an idea: Dana, you still want to do that Christmas interview with me and Amy, right?"

"I sure do," Dana said.

"Can you do that interview at our town house in Georgetown instead of a soundstage?"

"Sure… Even better—real Americana," Dana said.

"Max, would you mind a repeat performance at Curlanders' South for Christmas dinner?"

Max had nowhere to go. He shot a quick look at Dana. She was staring at him, as though the correct answer would be the stamp of approval for the previous night.

Looking directly at Dana, Max said, "Sure, I'd love a repeat performance. Invite as many people as you like too, as long as our original crew is in attendance. I'm in."

For another night with Dana, I'd cook for the entire Congress and Senate… if you could get them to show up.

Max detected a smile on Dana's lips as she sipped her coffee, looking at Max over the top of her cup. Max did something he'd never done with Eva; he gave Dana a quick wink in reaction to her smile. He couldn't help it and didn't regret it. Her smile grew.

Dana said, while looking at her iPhone calendar, "How about we kill two birds with one stone? Max, would you and Lincoln be up for your interview as well at Christmas? Ed and Amy's interview will air on the twenty-third; we could air your interview then too. We need to film it on the twenty-second at the very latest. Christmas is on a Sunday this year. Is that a go?" Dana got professional awfully quick.

Max paused long enough to build some anticipation. "Sure. Why not? Do I need to buy a suit?"

Ed said, "All good on my end. Honey, are you okay with those dates?"

"I must follow my fearless leader wherever he goes."

"What's the best way to get Linc down there?" Max asked matter-of-factly.

"Hmmm… Do you think you can manage to get you and your dog over to the heliport on thirty fourth Street on the East River? It's right near the Water Club."

"Don't get crazy. I'll rent a car and drive down."

"Like hell you will! It's impossible to get out of Manhattan or into D.C. around Christmastime. I don't want any excuses for you not getting down here. Plan on staying for a week or more."

"I have to get moving. My shuttle to Reagan is at one," Dana said, looking at her watch.

"Ready when you guys are," Cleary said.

"Great! So it's settled: Christmas week at Curlander's South," Amy said.

Max said to Ed, "Let me give you back your clothes and…."

"Stop it! I can't get into them anymore anyway."

"I'll bring them back next trip."

Curlander just shook his head and smiled. Ed couldn't even give Max an old flannel shirt. Max Burns couldn't be bought. Dana thought it a rare trait as well. It was something she had never seen before in any political context, especially in Washington.

There is nothing political about Max Burns.

Dana found that refreshing. Both of them looked forward to the drive with each other.

It was nine forty-five by the time they left the driveway in an Escalade, Cleary driving with Dana and Max sitting in the back.

The Escalade was a tank. It had been armored up like the Humvees in Iraq and Afghanistan. Max figured it got about five miles to the gallon.

Dana looked adorable without any makeup. She was naturally beautiful. She had on a Washington Redskins baseball hat and a pair of sunglasses. She wore jeans and a tan leather jacket over a dark-brown cashmere turtleneck. She topped things off with cowboy boots that were worn down to that comfortable, impossible-to-throw-out stage. She knew Max would understand the cowboy boots. She noticed his long-overdue-for-the-dumpster loafers. She was a walking contradiction.

A beauty queen and a bronc rider? Max thought.

She didn't go out of her way to dazzle anyone… she didn't have to. He wasn't the type to be dazzled, or was he?

"Is that a Washington Redskins hat?" Max asked, to get things rolling.

"Why, yes it is. You know a Redskins game is a tough ticket, don't you?"

"Really? Doesn't seem that way. Every time I cook Cleary a meal, he doubles the offer for Redskins tickets. He's up to two now. Right, Cleary?" Max said.

"Well, next time you better take them if you know what's good for you!" Cleary said.

"You like football?" Max asked Dana.

"Of course! I love football. I thought you were from Pennsylvania." She turned her head and looked at Max. "You know, sometimes I think you're from another planet."

"Why is that?"

"Well, you… you have it all right in the palm of your hand. You have the president of the United States begging you to work for him and you blow him off like he's some headhunter at an employment agency. He's flying you and your dog to D.C. at Christmastime for a week at his house! Do you know how many people would kill for any part of that? And yes, I love football… the **Washington Redskins** to be precise!"

"Maybe I'd rather be his friend. That's difficult if you work for someone," Max said.

"Don't you see he needs you?" Dana whispered, so Cleary would not hear. Cleary took that as his cue to slid up the partition.

"They both need you, for Chrissake!"

Max liked the fact Dana was stepping up to bat for Ed and Amy.

"I did my service. I did everything Uncle Sam asked me to do. I stepped back into civilian life and completely screwed things up."

"**Stop feeling sorry for yourself!**"

Max gave her a double take. He looked out the window as though he were back in a New York City cab, only this time he spoke. "Is that what I'm doing? Feeling sorry for myself?"

"Big time!" Dana said, not quite as assertive as the first time. She wasn't sure whether she'd crossed any boundaries. It was all so new. "See what I mean? You are from another planet. Just tell me to shut up and mind my own goddamn business—that's what any red-blooded American chauvinist male would do right about now. Tell me to shut my big mouth… or…."

Max looked back at her and said, "Or **what**?"

She kissed him passionately on the lips and expertly unbuttoned his flannel shirt, the tempo of things quite different today. Max calculated that New York City was approximately twenty minutes away.

Max said, "Hey, this shirt belongs to…."

"Shut up!"

"You like saying that, don't you?" Max said, smiling.

Dana shimmied one leg out of her jeans and straddled Max, pulling today's thong to one side. Neither cared if Cleary could see or hear them through the closed partition. They both knew he would keep his mouth shut; until he published his memoirs. By that time, all three could laugh about it. It was during this ride that Max decided:

Bronc rider… definitely bronc rider!

By the time they arrived at Max's apartment building, the bronc-ride buzzer had long sounded, signaling a successful ride by the cowgirl from Harrisburg, Pennsylvania. Both rider and ridee had finished their event in time.

Max kissed her gently on the lips. Dana gave him her business card and also checked his cellphone for her correct number. Max stepped out and got Linc and his bag out of the back of the Escalade. He came back to the open door. **"Call me, or I'll kill you!"** Dana said as she slammed the door. She banged on the partition and never looked back.

CHAPTER 51

Max stretched as he looked around the neighborhood. It looked the same, albeit boring. The past few days seemed surreal.

"Quite a first Thanksgiving for ya, eh, Linc? They aren't all like that."

Max was encouraged, he could feel good again. He felt Eva would want him to be moving on with his life.

No guilt. That's good. Maybe I was feeling sorry for myself. I better cut that crap out.

Max checked the mailbox in the hallway before getting into the slowest elevator in Manhattan. In his apartment, the message light of his landline was blinking. Max thought, *Len and Margaret. Who else would be calling around Thanksgiving?* He felt bad he had not called them first.

He played the message: "Max Burns? This is Commander Nick Nicholson, or ex-Commander Nick Nicholson. Nick to my buddies. Anyway, hope I got the right sonuvabitchin' ranger, chef, badass, haha. Listen, I got a proposition for you in case you're bored. Call me back, West Coast time, when you get a chance. Don't make any longterm plans until we talk. My cell number is 252-258-6937. Those numbers spell Blacktower in case you lose your phone or the number. Don't give this number out. Talk soon. Nick."

What the hell is that all about?

Max put Nick's name and number into his cell phone. He saw Len and Margaret on the speed dial.

"I need to call Len and Margaret, Linc." Max dialed their number on the landline. It rang longer than usual. Finally, Len picked up.

"Hello," Len said.

"Hi, Len, it's Max. Happy Thanksgiving!"

"Who is this?" Len asked.

"Len, it's me, Max. How are you?"

"Who?" Len said.

"It's Max Burns in New York."

"Is this one of those robot calls?"

"No Len, It's Max Bu...." Max started to say before interrupted by Len.

"Who is this? Stop bothering me!" Len said.

Max started to worry at this point. "Is Margaret home?"

"Who?" Len said.

Just then Margaret took the phone from Len. "Hello!"

"Hello, Margaret? It's Max."

"Oh, Max, how are you?" Margaret asked nervously.

"I'm fine. Happy Thanksgiving."

"Oh yes, same to you, Max." Margaret was clearly not herself.

"Is everything okay there, Margaret? Is Len okay? He didn't know who I was. Maybe it was a bad connection, or a robocall. I get them all...."

Margaret interrupted Max. "It's the Alzheimer's disease causing his dementia. Sometimes he is okay, most times...not."

Max was in shock.

Len was always sharp.

"He seemed fine when he was up here. Quiet, but fine," Max said.

"He was medicated heavily for that trip, Max."

Max wondered whether Eva's death had something to do with the onset.

"Do you want me to come down there?"

"No, Max, don't worry about us. Don't make a special trip down here. Most of the time he is manageable."

"What do the doctors say?" Max asked.

"They say, it will take him."

"Do they know how long?"

"No idea. He forgets, then he remembers... mostly things we did when we were young. Sometimes I think he's the lucky one," Margaret said in a low tone, as if she were thinking out loud.

"Please, Margaret, I'd like to come down and spend some time with you two."

"No dear. Don't take this the wrong way, but you might scare him."

"Scare him?"

"Yes. His pal Alfie from next door came over and Len tried to hit him with a golf club. Len didn't recognize him."

"Jeez, Margaret, I feel helpless up here."

"Now you just sit tight. Call us every once in a while, and we will do the same. I promise," Margaret said.

"Sure. You bet. I love you two. Please call. I'll call as well," Max stammered into the phone.

"Goodbye, dear," Margaret said.

"Goodbye, Margaret."

Max stared at the phone. He was floored by the conversation. These two were as close to him as anyone since his parents had died. He couldn't help thinking that Len had retreated into the back roads of his mind because of Eva's death.

Margaret saying, "...sometimes I think he's the lucky one," was a killer for Max. They were devastated by Eva's death, no doubt.

Of course, you idiot!

Max went down to the basement. He needed a good workout to clear his mind. He recognized a lack of intensity as he hit the heavy bag. He tried to envision his own face on the bag. He only lasted twenty-two minutes. He attributed the lack of stamina to the Thanksgiving festivities and the ride home.

Some golf ball–size mushrooms had sprung up in his absence.

Children grow so quickly.

Max hung them out to dry. Then he took inventory of the various Mason jars. He had approximately six jars of each mushroom category. The M#10X, since it was finely powdered and the smallest part of the mushroom, took up two jars.

What the hell am I going to do with all this? Larger containers?

While he sat in the rocker and thought about it, he realized the contents of these Mason jars could very well incriminate him. If the police ever suspected him of wrongdoing in Louie's death, this storeroom could seal his fate. But the toxicology from the autopsy had come up with cocaine and heroin as the cause of death.

A chemistry lecture in high school came to mind. It had been a sidebar to an anti-drug forum, but it had been so interesting it had stuck in Max's brain: "Toxicity quotient can only be measured and ultimately determined by comparison to known toxins or their derivatives, in order to be specifically identified and quantified through established toxicological criteria." It was good to have a 147 IQ. *Long-term memory… me and Len.*

Max had taught himself to speed-read in grammar school from an old Evelyn Woods DVD course his mother had bought and never used. He'd mastered the methodology of the program while in bed with the mumps for three days in the seventh grade, practice made him a whiz at it. Max didn't like wasting time reading the prescribed, "silly grammar school books," when there was literature, science, and history to be consumed. He'd read all the literature assigned in the high school curriculum prior to entering the eighth grade. That had left time to read books on philosophy, quantum physics, history, cooking—any and all knowledge he could glean about the world he would eventually enter. When the internet came along, the entire game changed. Max liked the new technology but always maintained his love for books, although the internet was his go to method for research.

His thoughts turned to Len and Margaret.

Tough growing old.

Somehow Max didn't think that would be an issue for him. He thought of Eva — pleasant thoughts this time. He smiled. Was a peaceful happy life attainable for Max Burns?

Not likely.

He fell asleep in the rocking chair.

When he awoke, it was close to three in the afternoon. He went upstairs to find Linc asleep on the rug. "Tired, pal? Me too."

He looked at his cell phone and dialed Nicholson's number. Nicholson answered as though he had just been awakened. "Hey, Nick. It's Max Burns. How the hell are you?"

"What the fuck time is it?" Nick asked.

"It's noon out there—time to get outa your bunk and get your ass in gear, sister!"

"This ain't no navy-sub hammock I'm in, pal. And this broad ain't no *Penthouse* magazine either…" There was a pause, and Max could hear movement on the other end. "Run along, sweetie," Nick said, talking to a hooker. "The money is on the bureau… Leave your phone number… Don't take anything else or I'll snap your fucking neck!"

"Still a sweet talker, I see."

"Yeah, right. So things are looking up, Max. I mustered out six months ago," Nick said.

"I thought you were a lifer?"

"Me too… fuckin' brass and politicians put a halt to that dream."

"What happened?"

"Well, we got UBL or OBL or whatever the fuck they call him now. I guess you figured that was us… great fucking dinner by the way."

"Glad you liked it," Max said, chuckling to himself.

"Our operation was supposed to be hush-hush as much afterward as before, right? No names, no notoriety, just another job. None of my men were looking for anything but, 'job well done.' Well, these motherfuckers we have running this country started their red carpet tour with, Corning, and Neptune… Team Six guys… all around the fucking world, giving us up to everyone. Whispering out loud: These are the guys that got bin Laden… Shhh, don't tell anybody. Next thing you know, twenty-two Navy SEALs from Team Six get blown out of the sky in a CH-47 Chinook on a simple support mission in Arghandab.

"Motherfuckers! Nobody should have been told the bin Laden job was worked by SEALs! Next thing you know, it's on TV that Team Six SEALs did the job. We don't like that crap. We got families in the States that are vulnerable… All over the fucking television, Max!

"I am damn sure the firefight in Arghandab was an ambush. The whole fucking thing was a grudge hit on Team Six SEALs still in Kabul and J-Bad. The firefight angle was American bullshit. These dirt bags knew the team would respond immediately to a scrap so close to the capital. They waited till that Chinook came over a rise and hit it in the belly with two RPGs. Two troops, twenty-two of my guys… gone! Everyone you met at the dinner that night… gone! Everyone except me, Corning, and Neptune. We were under orders to be in Beverly fucking Hills as consultants on a fuckin' movie… and squired around like… like some carnival freaks. It's all bullshit! It's all politics, money, egos and bullshit!"

"Christ, Nick… I'm so sorry, man."

"I know. You get it. That's not the last of it. Then, Timmy Corning eats his gun under that stupid fucking Hollywood sign. Now, nothing in the papers—no mention the guy is a national treasure. 'Bad for morale,' they told us. Blows his fucking brains out all over the Hollywood sign… I still got his text: **'It's all bullshit! See ya.'**" There was a pause on both ends.

Then Nicholson said, "I'm goin' back!"

"Goin' back where?" Max asked.

"To Afghanistan, that's where! Where the fuck do you think?" Nick yelled. His nerves were obviously shot.

"I thought you mustered out?" Max said.

"I did. Listen to this: I got fifty-eight guys going back to do contract work for the Sam and the Afghan government. It's a sanctioned COIN operation. That's an acronym for counterinsurgency in case your mind got fried over some fuckin' stove. Sam is paying us a grand a day, no taxes, and a hundred-grand bonus if we catch big fish… plus anything you wanna take home… all pros, no rookies. You might even know a couple of these guys from ranger school. Army lost men in the chopper as well, in the thirty-eight KIAs: SEALs, rangers, contractors, and company ops. I'm trying hard not to take army mutts, but I am scraping the bottom of the barrel callin' you," he said, trying to make a joke.

"Why you mercenary bastard."

"That's right! Merc work, a grand a day plus expenses, put in the bank of your choice by your favorite uncle. Did I mention tax-fucking-free? What the bastards got for basically nothin' before, they are gonna pay for through the nose now!"

"Nice cake, but I don't know. How long in-country?" Max asked.

"One-year minimum contract. Listen, we deploy the twentieth of January. We land in Islamabad on the twenty-second. Op code name is Blacktower… same as my phone number."

"The twentieth! That's the day of the presidential inauguration!" Max exclaimed.

"Exactly. This is the last counterinsurgency black op under the current administration's watch. It won't get shut down or recalled for at least a year, unless the heads of both countries say so, and those Afghan thieves ain't goin' to say so. That's the contract, one year in-country. If you are home before a year, it'll be in a body bag. You can cook, kill, fuck, bird-watch, whatever the fuck you want to do over there. No rules except what I tell ya. We are taking fifty million bucks in cash with us. Do you know what for?"

"No, what for?"

"Roads. Roads for these goat-fucking bastards. After about every ten miles of road, you are in a different tribal area. We pay the different tribes to build a road through their territory. Imagine that! Then they can run dope and supplies to the fucking Taliban and al-Qaeda scumbags without any bumps. Brilliant, huh? You can't make this shit up, my friend … very fucked up.

"So, listen, you got my number. I need one more guy to fill the sixty-man roster, someone with balls, that can cook my eggs the way I like 'em. Only screwin' with ya, Maxy. We are shipping out on January 20, zero eight hundred hours, leaving from a closed airport: Floyd Bennett Field, near Rockaway Beach, Queens, New York. It's somewhere in your neck of the woods up there in New York City. You don't need a fuckin' thing. You got a favorite handgun, bring it. Beaucoup latest toys waiting for us in-country."

"I got a dog now!" Max said, as though that were a good answer why he couldn't make the trip.

"Bring the motherfucker with you. I got a guy bringing a macaw. Fuckin' thing flew into his convertible up in Harlem!

"Anyway, call me anytime before we take off, you prick. Last-minute decision? Just show up. No passport necessary. I got plenty extra. You can pick a new name and a favorite country. Oh yeah, make out a will. It's a million if you body-bag it home… on Sam. Take care, big guy! Happy Thanksgiving, fucko."

"Same here, Nick. Good luck. Rain, mud, shit, or blood, I'll see you soon," Max said, though he wasn't sure if that were true or not. His heart was pounding.

Max hung up the phone and paced his living room in a daze.

All those SEALs I fed that night in the Korengal… gone.

Max remembered their faces clearly and where each one sat at dinner.

Most of the guys that caught and capped the number one al-Qaeda honcho… gone. What a waste.

This country is in fucked-up shape. I hope Curlander can get a grip on it… Who the hell would want to be the president of the United States?

Max thought about what it would be like to go back to

Afghanistan. Somebody needed to keep an eye on Nicholson. Max had no ax to grind with the Afghan people. Nicholson, on the other hand, hated everyone in - country. Max thought about getting away from New York. He knew he had to do that. Then a strange thing happened. A face popped into his mind for a fleeting moment. It was Dante Liguori smiling back at him.

Max's phone rang again.

Nobody calls for weeks at a time and now…

It was Ed Curlander.

"How are you, Mr. President?"

"Pretty good, Max. Yourself?" Curlander sounded stressed to Max.

"I'm doing fine. Everything okay?" Max asked.

"Yeah, everything is good with us. I want to ask you something that is not to be repeated: What do you think about Dana Trudeau for my press secretary?"

"Oh man, Ed, you're asking me? Hell, you know her better than I do!"

"Tell me if you think she can handle the job! Do you think she is loyal? Is she a team player? Can she handle herself in front of the entire country and around jackals in the press corps? I need someone who has got some sand. Amy seems to think she has what it takes. Amy told me to ask you."

After a long pause, Max let an unedited stream of consciousness spew out. "She's bright. She knows when to talk, when to shut up. She is young. She has balls—"

Curlander interrupted. "Oh, you know that for a fact?"

"Very funny! I think she'd be an asset. You had a lot of young people that voted for you and they would relate to her. Plus… she's easy on the eyes. That might be a good distraction when needed. She has proved herself in front of large audiences. ***Yes!*** I think she's a good choice. She'd be a good point person. You don't want another starchy bastard searching for politically correct answers. You want someone that will answer a question… like you would. She's savvy enough to do that. Be ready to bail her out after an occasional, right-between-the-eyes shot, at times. If you can deal with that, she's spot on. Good choice!"

"Okay. **Done!** I'll announce it after the interview at Christmastime. Keep it under your hat," Curlander said.

Max Burns, an out-of-work chef, had put Dana Trudeau in the White House.

"What about a cabinet?" Max asked.

"Got an A-list crew in my mind, plus alternatives. We can talk more at Christmas."

"No former marines, I hope," Max quipped.

"Of course not, Max. Why would you say that?"

"One spot that **is** kicking my ass is the job none of them can handle: Director of Homeland Security. I can't seem to think of a good fit. That has got to be a hands-on guy, not a suit, three-star, or politician. I'm looking for a no-nonsense, street-savvy sonuvabitch that can think ahead of the curve. Know anybody?" Curlander asked, joking.

"Yeah," said Max without hesitation. "I got just the guy!"

"You do? And who might that be?" Ed asked, thinking Max would come back with a smart-ass answer.

"Deputy Inspector John Timoney of the NYPD. He's a streetwise cop—honest, brilliant, loyal, trustworthy, and a big fan of yours."

"Mayor Braunreuther would shit himself. Sure would solidify the police rank and file putting in one of their own right off the streets of New York. Hmmm, gotta think about that one. Good call."

"Keep me up to date on the cabinet. Remember what happened to Lincoln with all those bastards plotting against him while he was trying to keep the goddamn country together," Max said.

"I know. Especially being the American Bulldog Party leader. Hell, there's only one member!" Ed said, laughing.

"Don't forget Tubbs. Is that his real name?" Max asked again, in case Curlander had forgotten the original joke. Curlander laughed harder than the first time, maybe because he had forgotten.

"Glad you reminded me."

"Say hello to Amy."

"Oh, wait! Wear your uniform on the chopper. That way there's no bullshit about using Marine One for private purposes. You can still get into it, can't you?" Ed said.

"That's a big 10-4," Max said.

"Roger that!" Curlander said. "Here's Amy."

"Hello, my Max," Amy said.

"Hi, beautiful. Have you redone the White House yet?"

"Not yet. You can do the kitchen if you like. So, how did you like my friend?" Amy asked with a smile that came through the phone. Max decided to play with her a little bit.

"Your friend? And who might that be?"

"Don't you dare play that teenage crap with me!" Amy said, anxious for immediate feedback.

"And what game might that be, Madam First Lady?"

"Tell me what you think of Dana, you muscle head."

"She's okay."

"From what I overheard, you just got her appointed to be the press secretary to the president of the United States, and you say she's okay!" Amy said, losing the game to Max by way of anxiety. Max decided to let her off the hook.

"She is a doll. I had a very nice time with her. Thank you, by the way, for letting me do Thanksgiving. Great therapy," Max said.

"You made it wonderful," Amy said.

"When did you decide we would hit it off?"

"Right after my botched-up interview with her. That was when I had a good idea it was worth pursuing. She could have gotten her *Pulitzer*, showing me slobbering like a teenager on national television. That would have been the end of Ed's run for the presidency, maybe even my marriage. You and Dana are my two favorite people. And you both deserve to be happy. I… I think Eva would approve," Amy said, reluctant to mention Eva and Dana in the same breath.

Max took it better than either of them thought he would. Amy took a deep breath. That was the one hurdle she had trepidation over.

"You really think Eva would approve? I was under the impression that Eva didn't like her," Max said.

"That's because Eva saw how Dana looked at you. I remember sitting with Ed and Dana at Scirocco one evening. We all had a few cocktails in us. Dana was checking you out. Eva saw her. You know how Dana is. She said to Eva, '**Nice ass!**'"

"What did Eva say?"

"Eva said, 'Yeah, and you should see what's under the hood!' Then she walked over and pinched your behind."

"I remember that! I told her to wash her hands!" Max said.

"I told Dana, you and Eva were a great couple and she backed off immediately. Do you know what she said to me? 'That's what I've always wanted—a good, healthy relationship with a guy who isn't looking over my shoulder at some bimbo with store-bought tits! Good for her.'" Then Amy said, "So, I felt you two were looking for the same thing and…."

Max cut Amy off. "Whoa, Madam First Lady, you're getting a little ahead of yourself, aren't you?"

"Maybe, maybe not, but you wouldn't have recommended her to Ed if you didn't like her."

"Liking her had nothing to do with recommending her. It was about whether or not she could and would do a good job!" Max said.

"See! That is exactly why we love you and want you here. You and I are the only people that look out for him!"

"Okay, time to get off the phone," Max said. "I promise you I will think hard about it. I do know I have to get the hell out of New York City. I got a job offer this afternoon as a matter of fact. I need to weigh all my options." Max knew he shouldn't have said that, but he needed some slack in the rope that he felt tightening around his neck.

"A job offer? Where?"

Max paused and said, "It's not local."

There was silence on the phone.

"Not local. Is that all you're going to tell me? It's not local?"

"Please don't say anything, Amy. As soon as I digest everything, you and Ed will be the first to know. So keep this under your hat. It happened an hour ago, and I haven't had a chance to think about it yet. I need options. I hate feeling others are making decisions for me. I guess it's my ranger training with a bit of claustrophobia thrown in. I don't mean to hang you up with your invitation to be part of the team. You two are a big part of my life. I want you to know that. I love you guys. My decisions lately have… not been good ones."

There was silence on both ends of the phone. Amy thought she heard a little gulp on Max's end, a major emotional outburst for him. Amy paused and decided not to say anything else.

Max gathered himself. "I have to go. Goodbye, beautiful. See you in a few weeks for Christmas at Curlander's South." Max hung up and took a deep breath.

"Linc, let's go for a walk and let things soak in. How about we head up to Harlem to see how our old pal Rodrigo is coming along with his ark?" Linc barked in reply. They saddled up and started walking the thirty or so blocks to see the latest on Rodrigo.

It was a nice, brisk November afternoon, a good day for a walk. The streets were busy with people taking advantage of the long Thanksgiving weekend.

When Max and Linc got to the front of Rodrigo's Pet Shop, Max thought he had walked past the store. The windows were painted over, and there was a sign above the door that read, "Church of the Mystical Eyeball: All God's Creatures Welcome." Max looked through an unpainted spot on the window. All the cages and tanks were gone. Chairs were set up in rows with an aisle down the middle. There were makeshift curtains and a podium toward the back. Max saw a shadow go by. He knocked on the door. A man in a white robe and beard answered the door.

"*Sí, señor*? Oh, my friend Max, the chef. How are you? Come in. Services are not till seven, but come in and sit. Look at this beautiful dog with you. Could this be Lincoln: son of my champion?"

Max still didn't like Rodrigo, but he was getting a kick out of the whole scene.

"Rodrigo… what is going on? What happened to the pet shop? Where are the animals?" Max asked, looking around.

"Oh yes, the animals. A few are still with me; some others come and go. My people bring their animals here to pray, so I am still involved. And you, Linc, you are also welcome in my house of worship anytime," Rodrigo said in an exaggerated peaceful manner.

"Where did you get the name for your church: Mystical Eyeball?"

"From a dollar bill. There is an eyeball at the top of the pyramid on the dollar bill. This eyeball kept staring back at me. The message came through loud and clear: '**Start a church, Mahatma!**'" At this particular point in the conversation, a white rat ran right under Max's seat. Linc stood up and stared at the rat, as did Max. Rodrigo didn't move and only smiled as the rat ran by on his way to a hole in the wall. Max looked at Rodrigo for a reaction. There was none. Then a parakeet landed on Rodrigo's head. Linc was now at full attention. Rodrigo took some seeds out of his pocket. The parakeet flew into his hand and ate the seeds. Rodrigo didn't bat an eye. Then he said to Linc, "We are all God's creatures, aren't we Lincoln?" He was looking at Linc to concur. Linc stared back at him and then cocked his head to one side, as if to get a clearer perspective.

Max had to find out when the specific transition to ***Rodrigo of Assisi*** had actually occurred. Max needed to know whether this was a result of the mushroom dinner. After all, research must be followed up.

"So, Rodrigo…."

Rodrigo interrupted. "Please, call me… ***Mahatma***."

"***Mahatma***? You don't have an elephant here, do you?" Max asked, looking toward the back room.

"No. You have seen too many movies. ***Mahatma*** does not mean 'elephant,' boy. It means 'spiritual guardian.'"

"When did this sudden wave of love for ALL animals come over you? You never gave a damn about them… except to make a buck."

"Well, I think my enlightenment began with the death of Tango. He was the bravest of the brave. I remember the day he decided to sacrifice his life to show others ***The Way***. He gave his life for his beliefs," Rodrigo pontificated.

"Sounds familiar," Max said.

Rodrigo, a.k.a. ***Mahatma***, kept rambling. "I was too blind and greedy to see that all animals have souls. And you, my friend, you came and saw this dog, your Lincoln, ***the son of the prophet Tango: the Enlightened One.*** The spirit of the prophet needed a home in order to pursue his wondrous journey. You fed me your gracious food and did not chastise me. It was then I saw through the storm clouds of my past life. I went into deep meditation when a customer handed me a sacred message on a folded dollar bill. It all came together in my mind. And now… now I have my church, and my philosophy toward man and beast alike has changed." Rodrigo looked around at his church as he spoke.

A cockatoo flew by. It landed on the curtain rod and screeched loud enough to scare everything living or dead.

"It gets a little loud sometimes," Rodrigo said off character.

There was a bang on the radiator pipes and a muffled yell. "Shut that fucking thing up, you crazy bastard, or I'll come down there and beat you and that singing chicken of yours to death!"

"That's Mr. Cancellaro. He lives upstairs. He has yet to be converted," Mahatma said. "Will you be staying for the service? I'm sure my parishioners would love to meet Lincoln, the son of the prophet, Tango."

"Not this time. Perhaps in the future. Put me on your email list. Or send a homing pigeon with a schedule," Max said as he got up to leave with Linc. "C'mon, Linc. So long, Rod, er, ***Mahatma***. Good luck."

"And to you also, my friend. Peace and love to all God's creatures. Your visit will be mentioned in my latest version of the scriptures... as soon as my computer guy fixes my computer," ***Mahatma*** said. He was, indeed, the self-anointed and self-appointed Saint Francis of Harlem.

"Three weeks ago you were made the mascot for the American Bulldog Party, and now you are the son of the prophet," Max said to Linc. He shook his head as he waved goodbye to ***Mahatma***, who was snapping pictures of them.

Max hailed a cab. It was getting dark, and both he and Linc were beat. The cabdriver looked in the rearview mirror and said, "I know you!"

Max had to answer. "From where?"

"I picked you up once before coming out of that pet shop... church, whatever it is now. I live a block away and start my shift up here. Ever since that day, a macaw started living on my fire escape. I swear to God... a friggin' macaw. It scared the shit out of my wife the first time she opened the blinds. She fell back over an ottoman right on her ass, screamin' like a friggin' banshee. Now it lives with us. You'd think it was the Holy Ghost himself!"

"A macaw is a pretty big parrot." Max said.

"Yeah, it's a huge friggin' parrot! I had to look it up online at one of those Audubon Society sites. It's a blue-and-gold macaw, native to Central and South America. Thing eats better than I do now. Strange world. What are the odds?" the cabbie said.

"What do you mean?" Max asked.

"What are the odds I pick you up twice in this city of fourteen million people on a workday? Never happened to me before."

"Chances are it won't happen a third time," Max mumbled.

"Leavin' town?" the cabbie asked.

"Probably."

"Where you headin', if you don't mind me askin'?"

"Not sure yet."

"I'm Tom Ryder, last native New Yorker still hacking."

"Max Burns," Max said as they managed to shake hands. Then Ryder handed him a card with his cell phone number on it. It also had the Vietnam combat ribbon under the number.

"Nam vet, eh?"

"Two tours, twenty months in-country, First Air Cav.," Ryder said.

"Garyowen, eh? Special Forces myself. Two tours Iraq, one Afghanistan. Glad to meet you, Tom."

"Likewise, son," Ryder said. "I got a truck too. Me and my two boys have a little moving business on the side. You need me, call that number anytime, day or night. If you are moving anywhere stateside, we'll take care of you cheap for one of our own. Friggin' Sam ain't lookin' out for us!"

Max gave him a twenty for the eight-dollar cab ride downtown. Ryder thanked him and told him not to lose his card.

Off the cab went. Max was happy he hadn't stared out the window on this particular trip.

Ya gotta love a native New Yorker.

CHAPTER 52

Christmas was a week away. Max and Dana talked on the phone every evening before or after her last broadcast. Max was surprised at the ease of conversation. One call had lasted an hour and forty minutes. At the end of their last phone call, Dana had said she couldn't wait to see him at Christmastime. Max had told her he was looking forward to being with her as well. That was big for Max Burns. It felt good. He was surprised at how he was keeping his head above water. He didn't reflect back at all on Louie - the deed was not even in his rearview mirror.

Max was leaning toward the White House job. Dana was a big part of that inclination. He hadn't made his thoughts known to anyone. He never did until a decision was made.

"Most advice benefits the adviser."

Dana never once mentioned the White House chef job in their telephone conversations. She had made her point in the car ride home at Thanksgiving. She knew better than to push too hard. Dana never chased a man. She wasn't going to chase one now. But this was new territory for her. She had stopped dating after Thanksgiving, but it was too early to tell Max that. If Max wanted to know, he'd have to ask. Max and Dana both had their little secrets. Dana hoped she was a factor in his job decision. Amy advised Dana on where to tread and where not to venture. The two women had become very close. Ed held fast, not telling Dana about the forthcoming appointment.

Becoming press secretary was not even a long shot in Dana's eyes, although she did wonder who might be chosen. It was her line of work and she was curious. That took pressure away from Amy. One thing about Amy: she could keep her mouth shut. Ed knew that, and so did Max.

As far as Blacktower was concerned, the offer lingered but felt like another road that shouldn't be taken. Sure, there was part of him that craved the visceral adventures Afghanistan could provide. However, the killing lacked purpose for Max to a great extent. Nicholson took war personally. That was cool with Max. He killed for personal reasons too. But he had seen enough death, both in-country and stateside for now. As Max had said many times before, "I have no ax to grind with the Afghans."

He did with al-Qaeda, and that was a fact. He wasn't sure whether Nick gave a damn who wore a white *pakol* Afghan hat and who wore a black one. Nick would eventually cut his tether to Sam and go rogue. Point him in a direction and tell him to kill, and you had a killing machine on your hands… one difficult to stop. Max did not have to be in Afghanistan to know that. Max had seen it come forth in himself when his convoy was attacked.

That was reactive. Nick will be proactive. Big difference. He needs to be watched. The armed forces teaches you to kill. Once you're in their club… it gets easy.

Max thought about the cabbie, Tom Ryder.

He sounded an awful lot like Nick. All vets had residue

If Max were to go to Afghanistan, the odds were he would not be coming home alive. He knew Nick would not come home alive and probably had no plans to. Nick's original team was gone. It would not be Nick's job to get his men home … not this trip.

As much as Nick would rather shoot politicians, he had to take it all out on someone. He had to blame the people it was easy to blame. Max knew that was burning a hole in Nick's heart and his mind.

Timmy Corning's suicide made sure of that.

Max decided Corning's suicide was an act of bravery. The misery was over for Corning.

TC wasn't afraid to live. He just didn't want to!

There was no peaceful place for Corning's mind to go in this new life pattern. Max understood that as well. He understood Nick was not opposed to suicide either, or his variation on the theme. Max envisioned Nick going down in flames, running out of ammo and enough enemy to make the math impossible for survival.

A Hollywood ending as well.

Max considered the insanity of it all.

I should work this puzzle from the inside out. The friggin' president wants me! Why am I even thinking about this crazy bullshit?

But… there was something primal about going into the eye of the hurricane and looking death in the face. This, Max knew firsthand.

Why do I feel the latent need to feel that again? Let me break this down logically: work for a good friend who happens to be the president of the United States, be with one of the sharpest and most beautiful women in America, and become executive chef at the White House…. or go to Afghanistan and kill people, lose my dog, eat dirt, and most likely die: Door number one, please.

He was falling for Dana. It was time he admitted that was okay. Neither called it a relationship at this juncture, but the ship had sailed and they both knew it. There was a synergy and a trust between them that was growing… like a mushroom.

One evening around six o'clock, Max heard a knock on his door. Linc barked until Max pointed at him. Max opened the door. It was Mr. Woods.

"I am sorry to bother you, Mr. Burns, but my wife … she's … she's having a Tupperware party tonight, and she asked me to go around personally and ask all the tenants to come down and attend the festivities. I'm sorry to bother you. Jeez, a goddamn Tupperware party, for Chrissake. I am so fuckin' embarrassed asking you. I put a flyer in all the mailboxes. Nobody responded. So, here I am." Woods looked mortified.

Tupperware! Why not? They're airtight. I am outgrowing the supply of Mason jars.

"Sure. What time?" Max asked.

"Are you serious? In about an hour. Ah, don't eat… plenty of good eats to go 'round. Thank you, thank you." Woods was almost joyous. He couldn't believe that Max would come to a Tupperware party. Woods would miss the tenant in apartment 4A if he did leave New York.

Max whipped up some dinner for Linc and then took the elevator down to the basement. The apartment was not what you would have thought for a basement in New York City. It had about six rooms with many nooks and crannies. Woods had put the space to good use. Max liked Woods, and the feeling was now mutual.

Kindred spirits, army brothers, Tupperware.

Mrs. Woods had made ribs, fried chicken, corn bread, beans, collard greens, and all sorts of goodies, intended to loosen wallets. She was a good cook, and she and Max hit it off. Max apologized for disturbing her and her husband a few months back when he couldn't get into the building.

"Hush! And call me Mabel. I didn't know you were so cute. *Harold!* Why didn't you tell me he was so cute?" Mabel had a firm grip on Max's cheek as she yelled to Harold.

The party had begun.

Never piss off the superintendent of your New York City apartment building! Max thought. Evidently, the entire female contingency of the building had rallied to the call as well. At this juncture of the party, about twenty-five women, young and old, all colors, shapes, and sizes, were in attendance. Max had seen many of them in the elevator at one time or another.

Am I supposed to remember their names next elevator trip? I better start taking the stairs.

He tried to revive the old Evelyn Woods name-association

course, an addition to her speed-reading course, available for only a separate handling charge.

Max was the only man present except for Harold Woods. Woods confided in Max that his wife had ordered him to stay until the very end, under penalty of "no pussy." Max asked for the recipe for Mabel's fried chicken, which was the best Max had ever tasted. In exchange, he promised her some of his marinade for pork chops. "Me and Harold looooove pork chops," Mabel said.

Max bought over $400 worth of Tupperware, which was easier to do than he thought. He was, by far, the largest purchaser of Tupperware present. Harold Woods now insisted that henceforth he and his wife be called Harold and Mabel and Max would be Max. Harold asked Max, "What are you going to do with all those large containers?"

Max was prepared for the question. "I'll put my spices into larger containers to keep the air from spoiling them."

Max asked that Mabel call him when the Tupperware order arrived.

"You bet, Max, honey." Harold walked Max to the door when it was safe to leave. "Thanks, my brother. You saved my bacon tonight! She has a list of everyone that came, and that list is the list to be on, my man. You'd best believe what I am saying to your ass. That woman is a woman not to be fucked with," Harold whispered. Max did not have to be told.

"No problem, Harold. Let me know when it comes in, and I'll be down."

"You ain't movin' out, are you?" Harold asked.

"Not sure, Harold. Lots of things goin' on." Max walked a few steps and turned around. "Hey, Harold, ever think about doing **merc work**?"

"Every motherfuckin' day, my man… every motherfuckin' day." Harold shook his head as he backed into the apartment and slowly closed the door behind him.

Max laughed out loud in the elevator.

When he got back to his apartment, Max called Dana. She was in between shows at the studio. He told her about the Tupperware party. She said she wished the cameras had been rolling for it. Dana had no inkling about the forthcoming press secretary job offer. He wondered whether the dynamics of the two of them working together would be a good thing.

Dana said, "Remember, we're shooting the interview on the twenty-second, so we need to get to the Curlander house super early."

"What should I wear?" Max asked.

"Wear a dark suit. Blue or grayish. Not black—black isn't Christmassy."

"I don't own a suit," Max said. "I'll have my uniform on when I arrive that morning. Curlander wants it that way—protocol for the helo ride."

"I forgot, you don't own a suit. How can you not own a suit?"

"Or a tie, that isn't government issue," Max said. It was a fact.

"How about a Santa Claus outfit?" Dana asked.

"I have two of those, but I have trouble getting the pants on and off over my clown shoes."

"You won't need clown shoes when I get through with you. Santa better get his ass down here early on the twenty-second because Santa's little helper is going to be helping Santa get out of his outfit as soon as his sleigh bells stop ringing … clown shoes or not! Got it, Mr. Claus?"

Max chuckled. "Got it."

"Wear whatever you feel comfortable in. A sweater is fine. Just don't wear one of those wife-beater tanktops. Both interviews are being syndicated nationally, so put on your best face, lover boy. I have to run… Love ya, bye."

Max hung up and paused for a few seconds.

"Love ya, bye!"

He wondered whether it was spontaneous or planned. It sounded spur of the moment. Max wondered if Dana was thinking the same thing he was.

CHAPTER 53

At the TV studio in Georgetown that evening, Dana Trudeau sat staring at the mirror in her dressing room.

"OH SHIT! Did I just say that?"

Her makeup man, Marcel, asked, "What on earth are you babbling about, my dear?"

Marcel was one of the only people in the world Dana confided in with regard to her love life. He was very gay and very wise. He knew both sides of the love coin. Dana could talk to him about anything from afros to dildos. Marcel always had an answer.

"I said… 'Love ya' before I hung up with Max."

Marcel was thinking the same way Max was. "Well, my dear, had you plaaaaaaned on saying it?"

"Hell no, I hadn't plaaaaaaaned on saying it," she said as she stared at Marcel in the mirror.

"Then it must be true. How wonderful! It's about time you found someone that isn't a homophobic D.C. asshole that thinks he's a real man because he doesn't shave his balls! I am sooooo happy for you, my love. Ooooh, I said it too, and I didn't think about it… it must be true." Marcel tapped his cheek with a comb, making a popping sound.

They both laughed. Dana felt good about it but nervous. It was one of those things that you couldn't really feel comfortable with until you heard the same thing from the other side.

I wonder if he caught it. Of course he did! Nobody misses that. Not the first one.

Max had indeed caught it… right between the eyes.

CHAPTER 54

"I hope you don't get airsick, Linc, because this morning we are going for a helo ride. No puking allowed on Marine One. How do I look in uniform, pal? Fits like a glove, smells like mothballs. Fresh air oughta fix that."

It was six in the morning on December 22. Max had packed a bag for Linc and himself. The weather was clear in New York, and the forecast along the eastern seaboard called for more of the same. The soldier and his dog grabbed a cab and left for the heliport for their 7:00 a.m. pickup by: Marine Helicopter Squadron One (HMX-1) Nighthawk. The helo was a dressed-out Sea King, capable of doing four hundred knots. Curlander was very proud that the presidential helos was Marine Corps domain. He would be the first marine to take the oath of office as president of the United States. As far as the marines and former marines were concerned, it was about time.

Max was army. This became more evident as the marine crew checked Max and Linc out when they walked toward the chopper at the 34th street NewYork heliport. Max had mustered out as a master sergeant. He wore his medals and commendations proudly but not ostentatiously. Max knew who the true heroes were. It didn't matter to most combat veterans, what uniforms they had worn.

The helo attracted attention. The tarmac was cleared of all other aircraft. Two marines disembarked and stood on both sides of the stairway. Max covered Linc's eyes from the rotor-wash and carried him up the gangplank.

"Welcome aboard, sergeant." There were no salutes between noncommissioned officers but plenty of respect for the *Jell-O* displayed on Max's chest, especially the Silver Star with Valor and the Purple Heart. There were no remarks about a dog being on board. It was not for the marines to judge their cargo. It was their job simply to deliver it. Thirty seconds after getting on board, they took off for the nation's capital, making a bank to the starboard along the East River to catch a good northerly breeze, then continuing south past One World Trade Center. The pilot made sure everyone got a good look at One WTC and then the Statue of Liberty as they proceeded south across New York Harbor at the base of the Hudson River, then south.

Max introduced himself to the four marines on board. There were two gunny sergeants, as was protocol, and two officers, the pilot and copilot. Max had been in helicopters many times before: Apaches, Hueys, and Chinooks mostly. This tricked-out beauty was almost soundproof. Max asked the captain if it was okay to let Linc walk around.

"It's your bird for the trip, sergeant. You can do what you want for the next forty minutes. If that dog shits on the carpet, though, you'll have to answer to Sergeants Carruthers and Del Negra there ... 'cause they'll be cleaning it up!"

"He'll be okay, sir. **I** may be puking all over but Linc will be fine... I hope."

"So that's Lincoln Burns. He's the most famous dog in America, eh, sergeant?" the pilot said.

"It's him, all right," Max said.

"He's in every marine's locker and in every American consulate from here to Timbuk-fucking-tu. Ain't that right, Carruthers?"

"That is a fact, *mon capitaine*," Carruthers said, looking at Lincoln.

Gunny sergeant Del Negra asked, "Does he bite?"

"Only marines." There was a pause before they laughed. Max then said, "No. He is great with people, dogs… kids too. I let him run loose in Central Park. He's cool."

"Can we play with him? Maybe… take some pictures with him?" Caruthers asked.

"Roger that, gentlemen. He's all yours."

The two marine gunnies were like children playing with Linc and snapping cell phone pictures. Then the copilot left his station and came back to wrestle with Linc and get his picture taken. Eventually, the pilot handed the controls over to the copilot, and he came back for a tussle with Linc as well. Linc was loving it, and so were the marines.

Max liked being around military people again… even if they were marines.

The helo landed at the Langley C.I.A. heliport. Max had thought they would disembark at Dulles or Reagan Airport.

Not bad for an army chef.

Max disembarked and shook hands with the four marines. The captain asked if Max would take a picture of all four together with Linc in front of Marine One. Max obliged. Nobody asked Max to be in any of the pictures, which Max thought was pretty funny. He couldn't wait to tell Dana. He wouldn't have to wait long. Seeing that Max was a little disoriented as to where he and Linc should go, gunny sergeant Del Negra nodded toward the white BMW in the waiting-area parking lot. Max started walking toward the car, hoping the keys were in it along with a GPS.

How the hell am I supposed to find my way to Curlander's house?

When he and Linc were about thirty feet away from the BMW, the driver's door opened, and a beautiful set of legs swung outside the door. Dana stood up with a huge smile on her face as she hung on the door vamping.

"Hello, beautiful." He grabbed her around the waist and kissed her like nobody was lookin'… except the four marines, who were wondering at this point whether they had joined the wrong branch of the service.

"Hi, handsome," Dana said, and she kissed him back, the way every man oughta be kissed at least once in his life and, if he was really lucky, on a regular basis.

"Get in, soldier boy, and bring your dog with you," Dana said, with a pretty good Mae West imitation.

Max put Linc in the back seat and told him to lie down. Dana rubbed Linc's head and scratched behind his ears. Linc remembered her. Max and Dana kissed again, one for the road. Dana started the car and proceeded to the gate. She turned in her visitor's pass and signed out. Max signed out as well. The sergeant on duty nodded to Linc and asked Max, "Is that him, sergeant?"

"Yes, it is, sergeant… He can't write."

"Would you take a picture of me with him?"

Max rolled his eyes. "You bet." Max took the picture with the sergeant's cell phone and off they went.

"Are you sure you need me for this interview?" Max asked.

"What do you mean?" Dana asked.

"Well, this dog is ready for a monument down here, maybe something next to a fire hydrant, and in New York they want to canonize him. I'm wondering what you need me for."

"Now that you mention it…"

They both laughed.

"How about some breakfast?" Max said.

Dana shot him a look. "Breakfast! I've been waiting to jump your bones for a month and you want to go to IHOP?"

"Maybe lunch," Max said.

"How about a midnight snack?" Dana said.

"What about the interview shoot?" Max asked.

"I lied… It's tomorrow. You're all mine till noon tomorrow, soldier boy, and you better be at attention until then!"

"That's a **big** 10-4."

"It better be!"

He put his hand on top of hers as she rested it on the gear shift. She was beaming. Max hoped he had something to do with that.

"How's work?" Max thought he'd see whether anything was brewing on a corporate level.

"They're grooming me for something. I don't know what. This interview is a big help, going on a national platform. If that happens— you're a big part of it."

"You're a hard worker. Your future will open up like an oyster. Maybe I should call you Pearl," Max said, deflecting conversation about the future.

"You think so?"

"No doubt. Please keep your eyes on the road. How will you ever find an IHOP?"

"Sweet," Dana said.

"It's true," Max said as he looked out the window, watching the Virginia countryside roll past.

Far cry from Washington Heights.

"What's new with you?" Dana asked. "Anything in the works? Any opportunities knocking on your door?"

"Nothing positive… some bullshit craziness. Hey, why don't we go to the Scirocco for dinner one night?"

"Sure, if they're still open. The place has never been the same… since André left."

"You're a very funny lady. Seriously, is it doing poorly?"

"I hardly go there anymore but the place was empty a few nights back. And, Georgetown is still a late-night town."

They arrived at Dana's town house apartment. It was a duplex conveniently located right in the middle of Georgetown. Max felt strange being back in Georgetown. It wasn't New York City, but Georgetown had an upbeat atmosphere of its own. Dana scooted into the apartment while Max took Linc for a quick walk outside on the cobblestone street. The walk was not as long as Linc wanted, but it was plenty long enough for Dana and Max. Max grabbed his bag out of the car and got buzzed in by Dana.

"Nice digs. Where are you?" Max asked as he looked around the apartment.

"I'm in here."

Dana was standing by her bed in an old, faded blue Brooks Brothers button-down shirt with only one button done up. Max tossed his class - A jacket and beret on a chair, followed by his famous clip-on tie and dress shirt. She came over to him and started kissing his bare chest. He lifted her chin with both hands and began kissing her softly, until softly wouldn't do anymore. She unbuttoned his pants and took them off slowly. She was careful not to wrinkle them. The uniform might be called upon for the interview, if he hadn't brought acceptable civvies with him. Dana couldn't take any chances on his choice of clothing. She knew Max was not exactly a slave to fashion. She placed the slacks over chair. Dana turned around.

"Thanks for taking the socks off, Romeo."

"The cameras aren't rolling yet?"

The glib remarks ceased. There was no more to be said. They knelt on the bed and kissed and touched each other as they had the first time they'd made love. She felt wonderful to Max. Her skin was beautiful and bright, and her legs were strong.

She must have been a dancer at some point.

When she wrapped her legs around him, he felt the evidence of their fine-tuned strength.

Max and Dana were instantly in sync with each other. Not even the constant kissing could throw their rhythm off. Max was alive. He knew how lucky he was. The breath of life filled his lungs, on the way to his heart.

They made love again, longer this time, more physical. They both knew there was much more to explore.

They laughed in afterglow as they joked and chided each other.

When they next thought about the time and hunger began setting in, it was six o'clock. They had been dozing on and off when Max heard a scratching on the door. Linc was in need of a walk.

Max let Dana sleep. He slid out of bed and put on a pair of jeans and a flannel shirt from his bag. He had his old pair of loafers that most people would have thrown out a decade ago. Out they strolled. Linc was not used to cobblestone streets. A young couple passed by looking very Christmassy. Max overheard the young woman say to her boyfriend, "Honey, that looks like the mascot for the American Bulldog Party." They looked over at Max for affirmation.

Max nodded and smiled. "C'mon, Linc. I should've known it'd be worse down here. How about an ascot for the mascot? Some sunglasses and a beret, perhaps?" Max said to Linc.

Linc walked with his tongue half out, as if to laugh at Max.

Dana buzzed them in. Her blond hair was unkempt in a very sexy way. Max unleashed Linc and carried Dana back into the bedroom.

Dana lay on Max's chest as he twirled her hair and touched her soft, beautiful skin. He was glad she worked out and ran. They could run together and she would also understand when he needed a therapeutic run on his own.

"The Curlanders know you're here … I told Amy the Do Not Disturb sign is up until I call them. Imagine me, with the president and First Lady on hold!" She kissed him on the lips and jumped up.

"You've gotta be hungry." Max said. "I need to feed Linc first."

"Why don't we order in?" Dana said.

"Sure. What do you like?" Max asked.

"There is a great *Thai* place down the block, and they deliver. Have you ever had *Thai* food before? It's spicy. I like spicy," Dana said.

"Once or twice. Call them and put me on with them."

Dana called and was ready to order by her usual numbered selections. Max took the phone and spoke to the *Thai* gentleman… in Southern *Thai*. The only English spoken was Dana's name and the address. Max handed the phone back to Dana and went about putting his jeans back on. He looked over and saw the blank expression on Dana's face.

"What? I'm a chef, remember. I did my R & R in Bangkok."

Dana never ceased to be amazed by Max.

He is an enigma. He is simple yet complex, not impressed by things other men spend their lives trying to attain. He is an artist, a philosopher, a lover, a loyal friend, a protector, a hero. But… what else? What makes Max Burns tick? The reporter needed answers and the woman in love needed to know. *Scary he's so friggin' smart.*

What she saw was a different kind of man, a different species of man. She was falling in love with a puzzle with pieces yet to be found. The sense of ***good*** that permeated from him gave her solace. She would follow that trail, not caring if she ever understand him fully.

He was a cut above the rest.

Too good to be true, came to mind.

Dana also knew Max was still in recovery mode.

Hopefully not in rebound mode.

Dana didn't know whether Max was in love with her. Neither of them had gotten to the mutual proclamation stage, albeit, not counting her "Love ya" slip. It wasn't that important to Dana. If love was not possible for him at this juncture, at least she knew he was capable of love. She had seen it with her own eyes at the Scirocco, when Max had looked at Eva. She wanted him to love her with that intensity… and more.

Love is as different as the people involved. He's healing from many things. I will enjoy what I have in small pieces. If we can put those pieces together… great.

Max answered the door when the food was delivered. There were three deliverymen with the food. There was also two of everything Max had ordered, compliments of the House of *Thai*. Max invited the *Thai* gents into the kitchen and tipped each one after paying a very fair price for the food. It seemed the gents wanted to meet the *Thai*-speaking American that was with Dana Trudeau, the TV star. They were about to leave when they spotted Linc. The chatter from them was now out of control. **"Mascot, mascot, mascot!"** Proud of their English, they asked Max, "You take picture us with

Leencon, okay, boss?" The three bowed profusely as they left with their pictures and a hefty tip.

Max turned to a smiling Dana, who was standing akimbo with her shirt and some short shorts on.

"Is this the way it's going to be?" Dana asked.

"It sure looks like it," Max said.

"There is a guy in New York City that thinks Linc is the son of a prophet… whatever the hell that means. I was only trying to save this miserable mutt from getting euthanized, and now he is a deity and a political icon. ***Great country this!*"** Max said, recalling once again his family mantra. He poured Linc's food and water into cardboard dishes.

"It is that! Your pal Curlander is going to have his hands full manning the ship. I think the hardest part is knowing who are the guys with the white hats and who are the guys with the black hats," Dana said. "Chopsticks or forks?"

"Chopsticks." Max kissed her one more time.

Max turned out to be quite proficient with chopsticks.

Jeez, is there anything this guy can't do? Dana thought.

The *Thai* food was good, even by Max's standards.

"This is better than they ever made for me. What did you say to them?" Dana asked.

"I told them that I was the army ranger that knocked out Buakaw Bamru in a bar fight in Bangkok a few years back. My *Thai* is limited. I was showing off a bit. My Arabic and Farsi are better. Did you know that Arabic is the basis for—"

"Who?" Dana asked, stopping his rambling.

"Buakaw Bamru, the *Muay Thai* middleweight champion of Thailand. Not sure if he still is… I was pretty drunk."

"Spare me, Lord. Maybe you and Lincoln are both, sons of a prophet. I have never met anyone like you… or your friggin' dog, for that matter." They both laughed.

After dinner they put on some Leonard Cohen music and got comfortable on the couch. Dana fell asleep in his arms. Max was mesmerized by the beauty of the music and the strength in Cohen's lyrics. As Dana slept, Max could not help but assess his current situation.

Max knew they had a lot to learn about each other still. The process had only begun. So far, he liked what he saw in this no-nonsense woman. And he had no doubts about Dana becoming a great asset to Curlander's team.

Max wanted to spend more than vacation time with Dana. Curlander would need someone to watch his back here in Washington. Max wanted Curlander to do a good job as POTUS, not just for Ed and Amy Curlander's sake, but for the country's. America was in a political stalemate. There was no doubt about that in Max's mind, or others around the world. Washington kept coming up as the center of the universe for Max.

America buys her friends… and we're running out of money.

Max decided he would hold off until after New Year's to make any definitive decisions. He also wanted to see whom Ed would be surrounding himself with as far as a cabinet. For some reason that was bothersome to Max, not that he was well versed in presidential cabinet appointees, but the military gave him some perspective with regard to appointments. Many cabinet seekers didn't know their asses from their elbows, especially about the Middle East.

Max had little respect for politicians in general and only slightly more for many generals. He had seen firsthand as a young boy how his dad had to deal with politicians as mayor of Washington, Pennsylvania. His dad had talked about two things in particular: The glory of the U.S. military and the stench of US politics.

Tubbs came to mind. *The used car salesman turned vice president. He is perfect for the job. Curlander will need his guile. Who better to talk smack than a used car salesman?*

Banks robbing people… not the other way around. The foxes are in the henhouses across the nation. It's time for Curlander and Tubbs to clean out the henhouses by way of the big henhouse at 1600 Pennsylvania Avenue.

No, now was not the time for personal decisions, this was Christmastime, and he was with Dana. It was all good.

He took Linc out for his last walk of the night. When Max came back, he woke Dana, as she'd requested, to watch the evening newscast from the bedroom.

"Look at Felicity. Isn't she beautiful?" Dana said, looking at Max for a reaction.

Max didn't bite. "In a weather-girl sort of way."

Felicity was Dana's stand-in when Dana was on assignment or vacation. Max would have thought Dana would be a little jealous, perhaps even catty about Felicity. She was not. That impressed him.

Ed Curlander appeared on the news. It showed him cutting down a Christmas tree on a farm in Virginia.

Felicity asked Ed about his cabinet, reminding him how late it was getting. "Most presidents-elect reveal their cabinet members between Thanksgiving and Christmas," Felicity said as she put the microphone in Ed's face, hoping for a scoop.

Dana sat up. "Don't tell her anything, Ed. Dance around it."

Ed said, "I am well aware of what presidents have done in the past, Felicity. Remember one thing: I have the luxury of being able to choose the right people, for the right job, since I don't owe anybody anything. Most presidents promise positions to deep-pocket benefactors before they even get elected. I didn't promise anybody a thing, except to the American people, the best representatives for our country. That includes cabinet appointments. I have names right here in my head. I need to talk to them first. That's the proper thing to do. Maybe they won't want the jobs. Many are happily employed and don't want to be in politics. They all know I'll be a stern taskmaster. If they come on board, you can rest assured they aren't there for a cushy ride or a résumé boost. The men and women I ask to serve will be a reflection of the country, not just their president. Big jobs! Now I have a tree to cut down, young lady. You would be wise to leave the forest, my dear. God knows I don't want to start off on the wrong foot with the press." Ed waved to the camera. "Merry Christmas and happy holidays to all!" Curlander yelled, as he started his chainsaw.

"Phew. How'd you like that little two-step, Felicity?" Dana said, talking to the TV and smiling.

"What do you think?" Max asked.

"What's not to like? I hope nobody shoots him," Dana said, very matter of fact, as she watched Felicity continue the rest of her telecast.

"Jesus, Dana! What're you talking about?"

"C'mon, Max. Don't you worry about him being so forthright? This country is run by the rich. It was started by the rich. The laws are made by the rich… for the rich. In the past when a president would say, 'It's not about the money,' it was always about the money. This time, the rich that run this country are not in control. Ed Curlander came out of nowhere and is pissing off a lot of those big-money donors. Do you realize that 41 percent of all the money in the world is controlled by eighty-six people? Those people are the most powerful individuals in the world, and they are sitting in the weeds wide-eyed, waiting to see what Ed Curlander does, not what he says. It doesn't matter to them what he says. Make no mistake. He has a target on his back if he fucks with these people… every president does."

Dana went into the kitchen to tidy up. Max immediately thought of the enigmatic Zapruder film footage: frame-by-frame (minus the most important frame) black-and-white 8 mm film footage of the assassination of President John Fitzgerald Kennedy. Max was smelling the stench of politics for himself.

"Come here, you," Dana said.

CHAPTER 55

The alarm went off at 7:00 a.m. Max and Dana awoke together for the first time. Dana stretched and gave Max a good morning kiss. "Are you ready?" she asked

"Well, I just woke up but …."

"For a run, silly," Dana said as she whacked him gently on the arm.

Max was reminded of how Eva would punch him on the arm.

"We have a park down the block with a great jogging path. It loops around and comes back: five-point-two miles. Think you and your sidekick can handle it?"

"Linc, ole boy, we have a comedienne in our midst. Whaddya think, Lincoln? Five-point-two miles suit you today?"

Linc barked, and Max said to Dana, "Backward or forward?"

"Okay, fellas. Suit up."

Max got Linc some water. The weather was perfect for a run. Max walked him slowly to the park to empty him out. This would be Linc's longest run yet. Max hoped he would not fall short. Once they started running, there would be no stopping. By now Linc knew it. Max ran in shorts and a sweatshirt in most weather. Dana had on a pair of faded blue sweatpants, an old Penn State sweatshirt, and her Washington Redskins baseball hat. She draped a towel around her neck, and put on some nerdy glasses to further camouflage herself.

She was rated number one local newscaster for evening and late-night broadcasts: a local celebrity.

Max was happy she traveled incognito. He and Linc being stopped by fans was beginning to be a pain in the ass.

Nobody stops a run in progress.

As the three walked to the park, Dana said to Max, "Nice legs, soldier."

"Not as nice as yours," Max said, and he meant it. "You can take that from a die-hard leg man."

"You think so?"

"I know so," Max said as they got to the jogging path. "Let's see how well you can use them … now that you're vertical."

Dana punched him on the bicep and smiled as she sprinted down the path ahead of him. Max let her get around the bend while he hitched Linc around his waist. Max and Linc took off at their usual pace. They caught up to Dana seven minutes into the run.

"I've been waiting for you. Where've you been?" Dana asked, not breathing heavily.

"I'm here now. Linc's legs may be the same shape as yours, but they aren't as long," Max said as he and Linc took off at a six-minute-mile pace for the four remaining miles. Dana caught up and kept the pace. She was working hard but stayed close. At one point, through a break in the trees, they could see the Washington Monument and other D.C. landmarks. It was inspiring to Max. Dana watched Max as he stared at the Lincoln Memorial.

Max ran himself into his zone and flashed back on a time when, as a young boy in WashPa, he'd read the handwritten memoirs of his great-great-grandfather General William Tecumseh Sherman. The volumes had been tucked away in a glass case in his dad's library. Max noted how the general and others had been initially skeptical of Lincoln as leader of the Union. After three volumes of handwritten pages, Max witnessed the transformation and subsequent devotion that had evolved within General Sherman. Max took special note of a conversation that had taken place at Abraham Lincoln's second inauguration, between General Ulysses S. Grant, commander of all armies of the United States, and General Sherman, who would replace Grant as general of the army.

"You know, if the tall fella feels in his heart that something is right, he doesn't waiver, does he, Bill? Not that I recollect, General. I expect we won't see the likes of him for as long as this nation flies the colors," Grant said to Sherman.

"He's a good one all right. It's those bastards in his cabinet this country needs to keep an eye on!" Sherman had said to Grant. "Who the hell would want his job?"

Max always chuckled to himself at that last remark. Max wondered whether Grant, the next elected president after Lincoln's assassination, had ever answered Sherman's question.

Max thought about a comment his dad had made one evening as they discussed American history: "You will never hear a politician tell you bad news. And believe me, there's more bad news than good news to be told!" Those words had come from the eleven-term mayor of Washington, Pennsylvania.

"This is it! This is where we came in," Dana blurted. "See where that flagpole is down there? That makes this a full six-mile run. See you later!" She took off before he could answer. She had more gas left than Max thought. He couldn't let her win.

Max said to Linc, "Suck it up, big fella. Let's go!"

Both Max and Linc ran flat out, speeding to a five-minute-mile pace after running 5.2 miles. They passed Dana about fifty yards out and were drinking water at a fountain when she finished. She trotted over to them. Breathing heavily, she leaned on her thighs. Her skin gave off a healthy red-and-white glow. Max expected to hear some half-assed reason for losing.

"That was great!" she said as she hugged him tightly. Dana gave Linc a congratulatory scratch behind the ears for his valiant participation.

"What is he, a year old?" She'd expected Max to beat her, but not Linc. Dana had thought Linc would be her ticket to victory.

Max and Dana held hands as they cooled down on the walk home.

Max fed Linc. Dana walked toward the bathroom and said to Max, "C'mon, this hot-water tank was made for one person and we need to get to the Curlander house ASAP."

"I am all in for going green… Get started. I'll be right there," Max said.

Max got in behind Dana. Her eyes were closed as she prepared to wash her hair. Max took the shampoo and worked it into her hair, massaging her scalp. Dana cooed as Max slid up behind her. He gently rinsed the shampoo out and washed her from behind until he had to have her. He held her around the waist with his strong left arm as she arched her back to accommodate him. She reached back to touch his cheek as he kissed the back of her neck. They made slow, passionate love. As the water temperature ever so slightly began to cool, Max felt her body tremble, tighten, and release.

Dana turned around and, after a moment, kissed him gently on the lips. They both stepped slowly and carefully out of the shower. Max took a bath towel from the rack and gently patted Dana dry.

Who the hell is this guy? Dana thought, obligingly reciprocating with a towel of her own.

Dana's phone rang while she was drying her hair. It was her producer.

"I'll have all parties ready to go at two thirty," Dana said into the phone. "You can have access to the Curlander house after ten thirty, not before. I'll call you if that changes, and don't worry—this time we have everyone."

The last part of the conversation had to be in reference to Dana's aborted interview with Amy. Dana turned her back to Max. He was pleased to see her keep it to herself.

Fair enough, he thought.

They got dressed. Max put on a button-down shirt, a sweater, khaki pants, and his indomitable loafers.

Dana said, "Those loafers gotta go, pal."

"Not on your life, sweet lips. These are part of my physiology. I have had new soles and heels put on these babies six times," Max said, proud of the stamina and comfort they afforded.

"Only six? You fooled me," Dana said. "We'll shoot from the waist up."

Dana disappeared into her walk-in closet. She came out in a simple but elegant blue dress and high heels.

Kinda formal. God, what legs.

Max kissed her and told her how good she looked.

"Wait until Marcel works his magic. You are going to love Marcel… and vice versa."

Max and Dana were met outside the front door of the Curlanders' town house by the omnipresent Bob Cleary. As he held his hand out to Max, he stared at Dana walking up to him. She patted him on the cheek and said, "Don't forget our tickets for Sunday… **sweet lips**." It seemed she liked that little pet name. This was the first Max had heard about a football game. Max loved the way Dana handled Cleary. Cleary gave Linc a quick scratch, then simply knocked once on the door in a manner that no one else would use.

Amy came to the door. "Well, you made it." Amy hugged everyone, including Linc. "How are you, handsome?" she asked, holding Linc's face in her hands.

"Where's my kiss?" Max asked as he picked the future First Lady up in the air and gave her a spin along with a kiss you could hear around the block.

"Get inside," Amy said as she looked both ways. "Do you want to start a scandal before we even get into the White House?"

"Yes!" Max said as he kissed her again as though they were brother and sister. In certain ways, Max was closer to Amy than he was to Ed.

"Where's my hero?" Max asked Amy.

"He's on the phone with an old friend of yours, Max."

"An old friend of mine?" Max thought of Nick Nicholson for

some odd reason. Max was a little nervous at this point. "Who might that be?"

"Oh, I think I'll let him tell you," Amy said with a coy smile.

Curlander came down the stairs wearing a blue suit and red tie. Amy had made him promise to dress like a president for once. Actually, Max felt one of the reasons Curlander had been elected was his casual approach to people, including his wardrobe. But then again, who was Max to judge a First Lady's sartorial taste, wearing un-shined ten-year-old loafers?

"See, honey? Max isn't wearing a suit," Curlander blurted out like an eighth grader.

"Hey, I'm not the president, pal." They hugged and smacked each other on the back. Amy and Dana were all smiles.

"How the hell are you, Max?" Ed asked, looking deep into his eyes, hoping to find a true answer.

Max said, "I am doing good, Ed." That made Dana and Amy smile.

"How about a Bloody Mary for an eye-opener," Curlander said, rubbing his hands together.

Without missing a beat, Max said, "No can do, big fella. I promised Dana no cocktails until after both of the interviews. She told me that the camera picks up everything. So… we both gotta hold off on the sauce. What have you got for breakfast? I'll whip something up."

Max blew past Curlander and headed straight for the refuge of their kitchen. Curlander was staring at Dana, who looked back at him and said, "Those are my orders, Mr. Prez. This is national in scope tonight, not just D.C. locals." Then Dana grabbed Amy and Ed by the arms and off they went to see what Max was conjuring up.

Max was at the stove beating eggs with one hand and cracking more with the other. They all sat down around the kitchen table. Max got a kick out of the table. It was one of those metal tables with a silverware drawer in the middle. It was the same type of kitchen table he'd spent hours reading and studying at as a boy. As Max dished out perfect omelets for the four of them, Ed said to him, "Your pal said he would be honored to do it."

"My pal? Honored? Who are we talking about?" Max asked, holding his own omelet on the spatula in midair.

"Your pal John Timoney. He said he would be honored to head up the Department of Homeland Security," Ed said, digging into his omelet. "Mmm, this is good, Max."

"Holy shit! You're appointing John Timoney as the secretary for the Department of Homeland Security?"

"You said he would be good at it, didn't you? He vetted very well. Let me know right now if you don't think he is a good fit, so I can undo it!" Curlander said without a smile.

"No! No… he'll be great."

"Is this for public consumption?" Dana asked, a reporter's smile on her face.

Ed looked at Dana and said, "Did you see last night when I told your pal Felicity I'd announce 'in due time'?"

"You bet," Dana said.

"Well, I want you to be the one to break the story on my cabinet members and presidential staff at some point in the future… including yourself."

Dana sat there nodding. She did not fully digest what Ed had said. She'd gotten the part about breaking the story as each member was appointed but that was when her reporter's mind had stopped computing. "Thanks, Ed. Felicity will be pissed, but that's the way it goes in this town," Dana said as she ate her omelet.

Max kept his mouth shut. He was still absorbing the Timoney appointment. Dana had yet to comprehend her own appointment. Everyone slowed to a stop and looked at Dana.

"What?" Dana asked as she wiped her face, thinking there was egg on it. "What are y'all looking at?"

"Ed, you better tell her again," Amy said.

"Tell me what? I heard. Ed is going to let me break the cabinet appointments and staff positions on my show. Correct? I really do appreciate that, Ed. What? What am I missing?" Dana looked around quizzically at each person individually.

"Some reporter," Ed said, finishing off his omelet.

"Ed… once more, please," Amy said, leaning over and touching his arm.

"What?" Dana said, frustrated at missing something of importance that everyone else had caught.

"That you are my appointment for press secretary. That's what!"

"Ahhhhhhhh!" Dana jumped up. She stared at each of them with her mouth open, as though waiting for someone to laugh at the joke at her expense. When that didn't happen, she screamed, **"Oh my God! Oh my God! Is it true?"** She ran over and kissed Ed on the lips. Then she apologized to Amy for kissing Ed on the lips and proceeded to kiss her on the lips too. **"Oh my God!"** Then she kissed Max and asked, "**Did you know about this?"** Max said nothing. "**Oh my God!"** She went to kiss Linc, but he ran into the bathroom. She finally sat down and cried like a baby. **"My eyes… my makeup. Holy shit!"**

Max came up behind her and stroked her hair. "Congratulations," he said as she bawled her eyes out. She looked like a raccoon with her mascara and makeup destroyed.

"If you don't want to do it, I'm sure Felicity would appreciate the job," Ed said, breaking balls.

"Just try it, fella." She sat in his lap and kissed him again, this time on the forehead.

Max contemplated both new appointments. Lost in thought, he forgot about the omelet he'd started for Cleary. For the first time since he was twelve years old, he burnt an egg.

After Dana settled down somewhat, Curlander apologized for telling her right before the interviews. He then stated he wanted nothing said about Dana's appointment during the show. Max smiled over at Curlander. Max knew he was testing Dana.

If she can perform the interviews after hearing about her appointment, she's ready for the big time. If for some reason she blows her professionalism in the interviews, Curlander can still renege prior to a public announcement.

He said he would announce Dana's appointment in the near future, citing Dana's professionalism as a journalist, along with her skill at handling people. Dana agreed. She had to agree. However, Ed did say that if Dana pushed a little during his and Amy's interview today, he might tell the nation about his choice of N.Y.P.D. Deputy Inspector John Timoney as secretary for the Department of Homeland Security. He wanted the interview to continue his ongoing mantra: The right people for the right job. Timoney's cabinet appointment would emphasize this promise.

Ed had always been in the forefront of anti-lobbyist legislation. He found lobbying corrupt and dishonorable. He wanted Dana to head in that direction. Dana gathered herself and took notes. She got out her laptop and altered her questions accordingly. She did not consult with her producer. At this point, her orders came from the POTUS. She changed course to align with more of Ed and Amy's wishes and no surprise questions.

Max took the opportunity to take Linc for a walk. It was a cold day in Georgetown. Max stopped to talk to Cleary at the front door. Cleary was moving in place to keep warm.

Cleary and Max were very much alike in many ways. Cleary was single and a regular guy. He was devoted to his job and to the Curlanders. It wasn't a marine thing anymore. It was a: POTUS; country; Secret Service; friendship; **and** marine thing, along with a heavy dose of pride and admiration for his boss and his wife.

"What's up, Max?" Cleary said as they shook hands again. Max liked the familiarity of their relationship.

"Nothing much, Cleary."

"Thought about the job any further?" Cleary asked.

"Every fuckin' minute. Not sure about things as yet, but if you're a betting man, I would think I might wind up back here."

Cleary smiled.

"Have you been to the Scirocco lately?" Max asked Cleary.

"Not since One and Two stopped going. They tried it a few times after you were gone, but there was no heart left in the joint. The food was overpriced and not good."

"I'm going to take a quick look over there to check it out. Let me give you my cell number," Max said.

"I have it. I'll call if they need you. Don't stray too far. Oh, enjoy the game on Sunday. You're on the thirty-five-yard line, baby. You owe me big time, army."

"I'll get you an autographed picture with me and the dog," Max called as he started to walk off with Linc. Max and Cleary both laughed.

"Just the dog and you got a deal!" Cleary yelled back.

Max waved goodbye as he and Linc headed toward the old restaurant. Max was curious about the old place, but that was not his primary reason for taking this walk. Four doors down from the Scirocco was Mr. Klett's jewelry store. Mr. Klett had been a customer at the Scirocco, and he'd told Max, "When you and Eva are ready, come and see me." Max was hoping there would not be many questions about Eva. He wanted to get Dana something special for Christmas. He thought maybe a necklace—something he would be able to see her wearing on her news broadcasts.

The bell on the door to Mr. Klett's jewelry store jingled as Max stepped inside. The store had glass display cases running lengthwise down both sides and the back of the shop that formed a typical "U" shape. Max noticed the items got more expensive as he moved toward the back wall. The shop was a two-person operation. Klett spent most of his time in the back room, where he made his jewelry, and Mrs. Klett did the bargaining. Max was looking up at the cameras when Mr. Klett spotted him. Klett's jeweler's loupe dropped to his chest as he looked at Max coming toward him.

"Well, look what the cat—I mean the dog—dragged into my store. How are you, my young friend, the chef?" Klett asked as he came out to give Max a hug.

"I'm doing fine, Mr. Klett. And you and the missus?" Max asked.

"Ahhh, Mrs. Klett will be so upset she missed you today. She is having a… *procedure* done. She misses your apple strudel more than she misses me, that's for sure. Did you come back to rescue the restaurant? It's a good thing they gave Len and Margaret cash for the place or you'd be back there slinging eggs."

Max did not let that sink in too deeply.

"How are Len and Margaret doing in Florida?"

"Len and Margaret are doing okay." Max lied to keep things simple. "I'll call them Christmas Day and tell them you were asking for them."

"Please do that… good people. We heard about Eva. I want you to know, that I know. We were crushed when…ah, I'm sorry for your loss," Klett said, getting it out of the way.

"What brings you here, Max?" Klett asked, morphing into possible-sale mode. Klett was a fine jeweler and almost as good as his wife when it came to selling, though nobody could reach her level of persistence. Max knew that and felt lucky she was not available for consultation today. Mrs. Klett was famous for sending Max's dishes back to the kitchen for "proper attention."

"I'd like to look at a necklace for a young woman. I am not good at this, so you need to help me."

"How much do you want to spend, Max?"

"I'm not sure. I'll know when I see it."

"Someone special, eh? Good… I'm happy for you."

"Yes, someone special. This necklace is going to be on national television… many times. I want the person wearing it to be proud to show it off to the world," Max said as the volleying began.

"TV! Hmmm. Now we're talking. I have a prototype: a one-of-a-kind necklace I designed. I thought I could have it reproduced in time for Christmas, but I got caught up in making it. I think it is the most beautiful necklace I have ever made."

Klett went and locked the front door. "Come with me." Max

followed him around the counter to the back of the shop. Klett opened a huge safe on his workbench and took out a Moroccan leather box that was beautiful in and of itself. He opened the box and gently pinching the end of a gold chain, slowly lifted out the necklace. Klett held it up in front of Max at eye level and let it twist and turn as though it possessed hypnotic powers. It was beautiful. Max knew nothing about jewelry but he knew what he liked. This? This was art. There were diamonds in the middle of what looked like a Picassoesque design. The diamonds sparkled as the necklace twisted.

"It's 24 karat gold," Klett said.

"You're an artist," Max said.

"Thank you, Max. You are an artist too."

Max smiled at him and stared at the necklace in his hand.

"One of a kind," Klett said, grinning as he gently placed it in Max's hand. Klett looked at Max's face to see what price Max's enthusiasm might yield.

"How much… artist to artist?" Max asked, still looking at the piece.

Klett was a shrewd salesman but Max had spent time in souks all over the Middle East. Max had haggled with the best in the world for fresh fruits and vegetables four days a week for three years. He knew his way around *medinas* from Kabul to Baghdad.

"For you, Max, only two thousand dollars. For anyone else, four thousand, maybe more. One of a kind!"

"Huh… I knew it would be out of my league. It's beautiful all right, but I am out of work and …. What do you have out front here that is more affordable but still appropriate for television?"

"Max, this piece is worth at least three times that! It's one of a kind. I put months into this creation," Klett said.

"I guess it doesn't matter that it will be on national TV and local broadcasts tonight… before Christmas… and most every weeknight … actually, twice on weekday nights?" Max said.

"Who will be wearing it on TV?"

"Do you watch Dana Trudeau do the nightly news?" Max asked.

"Dana Trudeau? The Channel 4 News anchorwoman?"

"That's her," Max said.

"The most beautiful woman on television!" Klett said, with a nod of affirmation.

"I would make sure she told people that her favorite jeweler in Georgetown made it especially for her this Christmas," Max said.

Just then Max's phone rang. It was Ed Curlander. Max put the phone on speaker, hoping Klett would recognize the voice.

"Hey, Ed. What's up?"

"The TV crew is here, and they need all of us to get prepped right away. Get back ASAP."

"Is that? Is that… the president?"

"Yeah, I am getting interviewed today, and he and Amy are too. As a matter of fact, Dana is doing the interview. Sure would be nice if I gave her this Christmas present early so she could wear it on ***national*** television tonight. Oh well, maybe when I start a new job I can afford…."

Klett interrupted Max. "Could you do that? Could you have her wear it tonight?"

"Sure. But…."

Klett interrupted him again. "What can you afford?"

"I have five hundred dollars in my checking account, and that amount isn't going up anytime soon."

"Can you give me five hundred now and another five hundred when you get on your feet again?" Klett asked.

"I don't like being in debt, Mr. Klett. I really don't know where I will be in the near future. I tell you what. I see your Nikon over there. Why don't I take your picture with Lincoln here for your window? He's the…."

Klett interrupted Max once again. "That's Lincoln?" Klett said excitedly. "Okay, okay, take a picture. Give me five hundred and take a good picture of me and Lincoln the dog. The necklace is yours!"

"I need that box you had it in too," Max said.

"Are you sure we aren't related, Max?" Klett asked, and they both laughed.

Max took a dozen pictures of Linc and Mr. Klett and then wrote a check for $500 as Klett gift wrapped the necklace in the beautiful box. Max and Klett shook hands, and out Max and Linc went, mission accomplished. Max had to stop once for Linc to take a quick picture with a little girl.

When Max and Linc arrived back at the Curlanders', Cleary opened the door. "Good luck."

Max was blinded by the lighting necessary for the shoot. Linc growled, a low, long growl, which got everyone's attention. Dana was being made up in an adjoining room to the living room.

Dana said, "Don't worry about the dog, he hasn't eaten anyone today." Max laughed. No one else seemed to think the quip was humorous. Everyone went back to work piecing together the elements that went into a taped broadcast.

"Mr. Burns? I am Tim Wetherford, executive producer on this production. Would you be so kind as to sit here for a little makeup? Nothing fancy. It stops the glare."

Max sat as Marcel finished up with Dana. Dana was smiling as Marcel started working on Max.

"Hello! I am Marcel, makeup artist to the stars. Perhaps you have heard of me? I am also Dana Trudeau's makeup engineer and confidant extraordinaire." Max looked in the mirror at Marcel and then over at Dana. She was holding her face in her hands, trying not to ruin her makeup for the second time.

"I don't believe I've heard you mentioned, Marcel. Dana has been closemouthed about all her former lovers."

"Don't be foolish, darling... we were never lovers. But if you two ever need a third...." Marcel said suggestively as he pranced around Max.

"You'll be on the short list, Marcel. I am Max Burns. Pleased to meet you. I am anxious to see you ply your craft to this mug of mine."

"Your skin is clear if Marcel is here!" Marcel shouted as he glanced over at Dana to give her a silent *Ooh la la!*

When Marcel was finished, he said to Max, "There you go, lover boy. If you ever think of changing teams, here's my card." Marcel sauntered past Dana and said, "I'd do him in a second."

"Does the dog need anything?" Dana asked.

Marcel said from the other room, "Even I can't do anything with that kisser. He looks more like Eleanor Roosevelt than Lincoln."

"How are you doing?" Dana asked Max.

"Good. Piece of cake," Max said, trying to convince himself he wasn't nervous. "Should I be worried about anything?" He asked. "This is about Linc, correct?"

"Yes, it is. But there are some questions that may hurt, and I…."

"What d'ya mean?" Max asked.

"Max, you've been through hell, whether you think so or not. The average American viewer thinks you're a hero, and I need to ask you things that may be hard to answer."

"Don't worry about asking me things about my past. I have nothing to hide. But I hope you know me well enough to know where to tread and where not to. I leave my destiny in your hands … This can be edited, right?" Max said emphatically.

"By the way… Merry Christmas." Max reached into his pocket and took out the wrapped necklace. It caught Dana completely off guard. Max said, "I promised the man who made this that you'd wear it today!" Max watched her expression in the makeup mirror.

Dana opened the box. She looked at the necklace and held the sparkling beauty up in the air. She removed her pearls.

"It's… it's magnificent!"

She fastened the clasp and stared in the mirror. "Damn it! I'm going to cry again!"

"Never fear! Marcel is here!" Marcel yelled from the other room. He peeked his head in and looked appreciatively at the necklace. "Any more at home like you… like me, I mean?" he asked Max.

Dana hugged Max and planted a big kiss on his lips. This was all a shock to everyone in the room, especially to Tim Wetherford.

Ed Curlander said, "What are we shooting, a soap opera or an interview?" Everyone laughed as things started to pick up.

"So that's how she got this interview," an assistant producer whispered to Wetherford.

"I love **it**… and **you**… and that can't be edited," Dana said.

"I love you too," Max said. "And, Marcel, you've got the easiest job in America as far as I am concerned."

The preceding events gave a real and unexpected air of Christmas to the set and those involved, except Tim Wetherford.

"Places please. Five minutes," the director yelled. "Max Burns, Lincoln Burns, up first. Hit your marks, please. It's tight here."

"Do you want a chair for the dog, Mr. Burns?" an assistant asked.

"He brings his own chair," Max said as he gave Linc the command to sit.

"Are you ready?" Dana asked as she sat across from Max. She was radiant. Max smiled because, as the professional in the crowd, she was definitely showing more feelings than she should. Max wondered if she could turn that off for the rest of the world in the next five seconds.

The director said, "And…GO!"

Dana started her intro. "Good evening, ladies and gentlemen. I'm Dana Trudeau. We have a special holiday treat in store for you this evening. It is my pleasure to be interviewing four great Americans. The first two with us tonight are Maxwell Tecumseh Burns, better known as Max, and his dog, *the* dog, probably the most famous dog in America and perhaps the world these days. His name is Lincoln Burns… better known as Linc." Dana had regrouped like a pro and was 100 percent on her game. "Hello, Max… and hello there, Linc. Thank you so much for joining us tonight."

"Thank you, Dana," Max said.

"So, Max, the entire nation wants to know: What breed of dog is Lincoln Burns?"

"He's an Alapaha Blue Blood bulldog. Not many of them around," Max said. "The breed is a result of crossbreeding an American bulldog and a Louisiana Catahoula bulldog. He isn't a mutt, though, not that it matters. This breed has been recognized by the AKC since the early 1980s."

"How did your paths happen to cross?"

"I traded a meal for him up in New York City. It was a deal I made with a guy that specialized in dogfighting. Linc's father was killed in the pits. Don't worry. The pits were shut down right after I got Linc out of there."

"Did you have a hand in getting the place shut down?"

"I'd like to think so. Linc's father was a champion. I wanted his son to have a different kind of life."

"Sounds like you rescued him."

"In a way, yes… and in a way, he rescued me."

"How so, Max?"

"I was going through a tough period in my life. I moved to New York City from Georgetown after my service commitment was fulfilled. I… we… opened a restaurant up there. There was some gang violence in the neighborhood where the restaurant was located, and problems resulted in the death of someone special to me. Linc came along right after that. So you could say, we did rescue each other."

"You were responsible for putting one of New York's most violent criminals behind bars. Newspaper articles stated that you, and I quote, 'embarrassed and cajoled the gang leader into a street fight and… beat him… almost to death.'" Dana stumbled slightly.

"Correct."

Dana was hoping for a longer answer. She had to follow up with an improvised question. "Why would you do that? Why would you walk into a ghetto and challenge a killer to a fight… alone … no weapon… nobody on your side?" Dana asked, revealing personal interest.

"He was a bully. Bullies need public beatings. There's no sense beating a bully in private. A bully would never admit to a private beating. Those who are bullied are owed a certain amount of visual retribution. No… it has to be in a public forum."

"Can you elaborate on that for our audience, Max?"

After a pause, Max said, "The people that feared this particular bully needed to understand that he was never worthy of their fear. Me? I had a personal beef because he tried to extort money from me. That was what initially brought me to him. When I saw he had just raped a fourteen-year-old girl, I realized I had to pull back the curtain on this… local Wizard of Oz and give him the beating he deserved. That was my favorite part of the movie… revealing the wizard. *The Wizard of Oz* movie, I mean… I digress."

Max sat calmly as he waited for the next question from a stunned Dana.

"And subsequent to that, the entire Hispanic community stood behind you to convict one of their own to a seventy-five-year-to-life prison term. What made them stand behind a gringo from Pennsylvania against a fellow Latino?" Dana asked.

Ed and Amy were in the other room glued to a monitor for the interview. They wanted to hear the answers as much as Dana and the rest of America. Outside of a few relatives Max had in WashPa, Ed and Amy knew more about Max than anyone, but they, too, wanted to find out: What made Max Burns tick?

Max answered, "Simple really. His time was over. You see, the Latino community in Manhattan is made up of wonderful, hardworking people. They left their homelands to live the American dream. What they found… was another dictator. They must've thought, *It must be like this everywhere.* You could see it in their faces. They thought America was all lies. What they'd heard about America was too good to be true. It was sad to see. I couldn't let them think they were seeing the real America. Besides, this punk made it personal by threatening me and my loved ones. ***That*** did not help his cause." Max suddenly caught up to himself. "I thought you wanted to talk about my dog?"

"Yes… yes, we do. How… how did Linc become the mascot of the American Bulldog Party?" Dana asked.

"Actually, President-Elect Curlander and I are friends. When Ed, er, President-Elect Curlander heard I got a dog… an American dog, he decided to name his new independent party the American Bulldog Party. Good timing I guess."

"The party was named because of Linc and not the other way around?"

"Yes, that's correct. Lincoln came first, then the American Bulldog Party name."

"What's next for Max and Lincoln Burns?" Dana asked.

Max half smiled. "I'm a chef. I expect I'll be a chef somewhere in the world. I like to make people everywhere smile… like you do, Dana." He looked Dana right in the eyes when he said that and made her blush. "When I was a chef in the army, I enjoyed watching soldiers leave the mess hall smiling. The United States Army gets a bad rap for its food. The soldiers I fed had little enough to smile about in the places we were. I'll be cooking somewhere. You can bet on that."

"You were also an army ranger besides being a chef… and a decorated war hero and…."

Max interrupted her. "I'm **not** a hero. The heroes are still in-country — the rest are in VA hospitals and cemeteries all over the world. Many are trying to cope with their reentry issues: Mental, physical, financial, family, all of it. That needs to be thoroughly understood and addressed… **I am no hero**," Max said emphatically.

"You are to a lot of our viewers out there, Max. You are to Linc… and me too," Dana said as the camera panned over to Linc to give America a good look at him. Max was happy Linc didn't start licking his balls. Dana winked at Max and gave him a thumbs-up off camera. Then she said, "Forever more, there will be the elephant, the donkey, and now, the Alapaha blue blood bulldog… one named Lincoln Burns. Thank you both, Max and Lincoln. Stay tuned for our interview with President-Elect Edward Curlander and his First Lady, Amy Curlander."

Dana closed out the interview with a handshake and a paw shake. Linc was right on cue.

"That was great!" Dana said. "You're a natural… you too, Max." Dana chuckled and gave Max a careful kiss.

Tim Wetherford, the producer, came over. "Good job. Take my card. I'm thinking about doing a special. Give me your cell number!" Wetherford demanded, hoping Max would suck up to him in front of Dana.

"Dana's got it."

Dana smiled.

"Right." Wetherford was not smiling as he walked away to get ready for the next interview.

Max didn't stay for Ed and Amy's interview. Linc needed a walk. Besides, he would watch both interviews on TV tonight with Dana.

Cleary was by the door.

"Don't you ever sleep, Cleary?"

"Three, maybe four hours tops. It's one of the reasons I got the job."

Max didn't believe that at all. He walked Linc toward the Scirocco. It was getting close to dinnertime, and there should be some action.

It was about five thirty, a little early, but three people were dining when Max peered in through the window. He found himself in the exact spot where he had initially stared into the empty restaurant, soaked with rain and eager to start a new life. He envisioned Len, Margaret, and Eva buzzing about trying to avoid his presence. So much had transpired, and yet for a moment, it seemed like he was in that time and space again.

By the look of the place, the new owners had put big money into it. Max knew that was unnecessary.

People would rather have good food in a plain venue, more than bad food in a palace. He'd proved that twice in his civilian career.

It was now two days before Christmas. Max felt joy and sorrow.

Honey and salsa in my brain.

It was a strange mixture, with neither one overwhelming the other. Max knew he was dismissing decisions that needed to be on the front burner. The Curlanders needed him. Linc needed him, although Linc could write his own ticket about now.

Lincoln Burns, the first dog ever on a Wheaties box.

Dana? He wanted Dana to need him. Max knew he was blessed to have found two great women in one lifetime. Len and Margaret? They were going to need him. They were like parents and both were failing. He had an obligation there. He knew if Len went, Margaret would not be far behind. He decided to call Len and Margaret. He dialed them up to wish them a merry Christmas.

Len answered. "Hello! Hello!"

Max answered back, "Hello, Len. It's me, Max." For some odd reason, Max thought he should speak loudly into the phone to Len. He didn't know why. Then he remembered what Margaret had said about Len getting scared easily. He made an effort to calm himself and talk slowly and deliberately. "Is Margaret there, Len? Is Margaret home?"

"Who is this? Who is this?" Len kept shouting into the phone.

"It's Max, Len. Max. Is Margaret there?"

The phone disconnected.

Shit! I hope I didn't scare him. I gotta get down there. I gotta make sure nobody is screwing them over.

Max walked past the closed nightclub where the "**fightin' marine**" legend had been born. There was a campaign photo signed by Curlander in the window.

Max thought about Nicholson saddling up for his little adventure. There was something about that operation that Max couldn't shake. Part of him begged to go. If he hadn't met Dana, he might be on that plane to Islamabad with the other lunatics.

Hmmmm ... first time I said to myself I wouldn't go 'cause of Dana. How come it's not the White House opportunity that would keep me here? Most guys would kill for the White House "chef executive" job, as Ed likes to call it. Strange how my thoughts and values are different from most men's... Does that mean I'm crazy?

Max felt his instincts were still good, however. It was his ability to follow those instincts that got him out of trouble.

Of course, you have to be in trouble to get out of trouble.

He had lived on the edge. It was different now. He didn't mind getting his own ass in trouble. But now he had a dog, a girlfriend, and the president of the United States and the First Lady to mind. *That's all. Merry Christmas, Max!*

Back at the Curlander house, the show was a wrap. The crew had dismantled everything and begun packing the truck. Cleary was out front as usual, keeping an eye on the passersby. Outside of some Georgetown inhabitants, not many people actually knew this house belonged to the Curlanders. Cleary was amazed at the lack of attention this president was able to maintain. Of course, all this was pre-inaugural. By and large, it would be no big deal to Georgetown residents. For the most part, the neighborhood was comprised of the well-to-do. Cleary saw Max coming and waved him around the other side of the truck. Cleary didn't know how Linc might react to the equipment being loaded. Cleary had good instincts as well.

Max and Linc came in to find Wetherford talking to Dana. They stopped talking when Max showed his face.

"How do you think it went, Tim?" Max asked. He looked into Wetherford's eyes to see if he made the producer nervous. He did. Max liked to make certain people nervous. He was good at it and knew how to do it.

"Both went great. Talk to Dana. I've got some good ideas I'd like you to think about." Then he gave Dana a kiss on the cheek and shook Max's hand. Max's handshake let Wetherford know he should be careful. Wetherford left with his crew.

"How did the Curlanders' interview go?" Max asked Dana.

"Let's go home and watch it," Dana said. "We can order out again. Do you speak Mandarin?" she asked sarcastically.

"No… Cantonese and Szechuanese."

Dana wasn't sure whether he was kidding or not.

"I need to speak to Amy and Ed a second," Max said to Dana.

Ed was on the phone. Amy smiled and kissed Max on the cheek. "You were great! The dog was great! Dana was great! How were we?" Amy asked.

"I don't know. I went for a walk."

"You went for a walk? Are you teasing me again?"

"No, I want to watch it on TV with Dana. I want to see what the rest of the world sees," Max said, trying to redeem himself. It worked.

"Okay," Amy said.

"Amy, is Mrs. Prendergast still with you? Did she get the items I emailed you for the Christmas dinner?" Max asked.

"Max, she got everything you wanted except the perishables. Do you think for one minute she would let you down? 'Not that nice young man that made such a wonderful Thanksgiving dinner.'"

"By the way, thanks again for inviting Dana. She is one helluva lady."

"And you are one helluva guy, Max Burns. That's why I did it."

"I will be at your house at zero eight hundred hours on Christmas morning. Say good night to the king."

Max, Linc, and Dana walked home. Dana wanted some fresh air. She'd worn her running shoes during both interviews. Max thought that was pretty funny. He asked her about it.

"You should know what some of the anchors *don't* wear at their desks. On New Year's Eve, a famous anchor, whose name I will not mention, won a ten-grand bet for going on nude from the waist down. And it was his producer who lost the bet." She held fast to Max's arm. Max chuckled and kissed the top of her head as they walked.

CHAPTER 56

Linc headed for a throw-rug to sleep. Max quipped that Linc needed his beauty sleep if he was to pursue a career in television.

Dana had some fresh fruits and vegetables on hand. Max found an old juicer and went to work on smoothies. Dana was in bed with the TV on. Felicity was doing Dana's spot. The network considered the Curlander and Burns interviews an assignment for Dana; therefore, Felicity would be filling in for Christmas week. The more airtime the better—that was the credo by which a fill-in anchor lived. Not only could it start a fan base, but you also never knew what syndicated network, cable honcho, or sponsor bigwig might be on the lookout for an anchor. Dana would be off the air until January 2 and perhaps permanently, depending when Ed Curlander went public about her appointment.

Max put the fruit smoothies on the night table.

Dana had a Penn State sweatshirt on. Max threw on some old boxing trunks.

"This is delicious," Dana said. "Look at Felicity. She'll be fuming over me scooping her on the cop from New York getting the Homeland post." Dana sipped her drink. "Curlander told her he'd announce 'in due time.' I love her, but… she will be pissed. She'll have my job soon. She better behave herself, or it will cost her," Dana said, wallowing a bit.

Max asked Dana about the press corps.

"Good ole Abe Lincoln… it was his idea to establish a press corps. He wanted to make sure the plethora of newspapers in the country had an equal opportunity to hear what he had to say…and ask regional questions. Before that, presidents had a "pet newspaper, "they spoon fed selective information. But, even Lincoln's crafty plan backfired in D.C... These days the press secretary holds power over the press simply by playing favorites among the entire throng of reporters. Favorites are chosen based on a few factors: The periodical or network bias, an individual's party affiliation, the journalist's leaning or propensity, *i.e.*, neutral, friendly or adversarial. Adverse questions can definitely cost points with a press secretary. Crazy, huh! Press secretary is definitely a powerful position. Some times questions are planted. That can get you in the first row quicker than a Pulitzer," Dana said, staring at the TV.

"It's just like grammar school," she continued. "Watch the president take questions after a speech. It's all theater. The press is briefed on the speech, or they get a copy beforehand… depends. The president has his press secretary or an assistant collect most of the questions ahead of time. Each paper contains the correspondent's name, newspaper, network… whatever. The president reviews the questions, and the questioner, with the press secretary. They decide together who to call on and who to avoid: who has been friendly, who has been negative. Why do you think it gets unruly at times with reporters yelling out questions? They're frustrated and hope, number one: that it will be picked up as a sound bite; number two: they know everyone in the press room wants to know the answer to that same question, so maybe they'll shut up. They want to embarrass the secretary or the president into answering their pointed question. That is a no-no, but it happens. It's a chess game."

"How do you know all this already?" Max asked.

"I've lived it. I've been in that room, albeit in the back. I got moved up front once when short skirts were in vogue. I know what you are thinking, smart-ass. I wasn't around for the Clinton administration."

"You read my mind." Max smiled back at her and sipped his smoothie.

"Stay tuned for the Dana Trudeau interview at 8:00 p.m. You won't want to miss it," Felicity said as a sidebar comment.

"Bless her little heart. She didn't have to do that. I love that kid. She'll go far. She'll be sitting up front in the press room sooner rather than later. She needs work but I think she'll work with us."

"You go, girl. The wheels are spinning already."

"Adapt or die." Dana said.

She's a tough gal, this Dana Trudeau.

The world news came on. Dana turned the station to the BBC broadcast.

"What did you do that for?" Max asked.

"The BBC has no slant. They basically tell it like it is. If you want to know what is really going on in the world, listen to the Brits."

"Where are we in Russia or China?" Max asked.

"A little of each when it comes to the media. We can say what we want, which also means that the media can have a bias slant. It's a TV show, Max. At least in China they are honest about telling you what you won't see on state sponsored television. In America, you never know who pays for what or why certain spots even get televised. It's all about PR firms, money, image, bias…and taxes. It's agenda persuasion by sponsors and owners.

"For instance, Curlander scratched his way to the top in spite of big money trying to tear him down. Remember Alexander Blair? He was the original presidential candidate on the ticket, and Curlander was his VP candidate. Alexander Blair? Please, he didn't have a chance in hell of winning! If Blair doesn't win, his running mate, Ed Curlander, doesn't win. Ed loses along with Blair. Ed's a loser.

"Flash forward: The American Bulldog Party comes along; a coup that will go down in history as one of the greatest political moves ever made in a presidential election. Curlander caught both parties with their pants down. The country was sick of the pingpong game. Curlander won't follow the money, because — no big money came his way. Ironically, that's why the American people elected him. Americans aren't stupid... they're lazy. Lazy about politics and even voting. Not this time. This presidential election had more people voting than any other. That's why I worry about President Edward Pierce Curlander. That's also why Amy wants people like you and me around. If the money guys had gotten in, it would have been one more ventriloquist act... another dummy manipulated by big money. But Ed pulled an end run and got away with it... for now anyway."

Dana amazed herself by putting all that together unrehearsed. She'd never given that little speech to anyone before. It might not have been the best philosophy for career advancement at the network, but she certainly knew the score.

"So, where does the media stand with regard to this president?" Max asked.

"We'll know soon enough. They were quiet during the race for the most part. When he won, they shut up to regroup. We will know when the approval ratings start coming in. When the American people were eating well and working their forty-hour week, things were fine. Then all hell broke loose. The people finally started paying attention to whom they needed to elect. They were sick of getting screwed by the big boys and waiting for money to *trickle down*. The banks were on cruise control doing 90, while their elevator music lulled the nation to sleep. Big money was clamoring to let the fox in the henhouse. They were putting lipstick on pigs and sold them back and forth to each other at huge profits. Too big to fail, right? Then investment firms were allowed to become banks. *Voilà!*

The nouveau "banks" got free money from Uncle Sam after blowing up our economy and blamed it on the real estate market. All these fabricated products, like derivatives, were loosely based on mortgages that never should have been written. It all fell apart when mortgagors didn't get paid on the bad loans they provided. Banks imploded on the methane from their own garbage. Where do they run? Why... to their rich *uncle* of course. 'Bail us out, or the country will lapse into the greatest depression in history… on your watch, Mr. President.' The American people get screwed, and the big guys get paid for screwing John Q. Public with John Q. Public's own money!"

Ed has his work cut out for him, Max thought.

"It's on. Here we go," Dana said.

Max and Linc's interview aired first. They were the warmup band.

"I look like a thug," Max said.

"Shhh. You do not. Everybody thinks they look awful on TV."

"You don't!"

The interview turned out to be sixteen minutes long.

"Oh my God, they caught me blushing when you smiled at me," Dana said.

It was a candid TV moment that would result in thousands of emails and tweets to Dana saying things like, "What a great couple you two would make!"

"It shows you're human."

"Maybe you're right," she said.

"Most TV news anchors look like they were recruited from Madame Tussauds," Max said.

It was time for the Curlanders' interview.

Dana glowed as she interviewed her new boss and his First Lady.

"Good evening, Mr. President-Elect and Madam First Lady. Thank you for allowing us to come into your home this holiday season. Let me begin with you, Madam First Lady…."

Amy interrupted and said, "Please, call me Amy. It will make me less nervous." Both Amy and Ed smiled as he patted her hand. It was an unrehearsed moment that worked.

"Amy, you two were high school sweethearts. What were your thoughts when Ed joined the Marine Corps Officer Candidates School after graduating from Manhattan College in New York City?"

"I wasn't going to let him get away that easy. We got married right after he was commissioned... before he shipped out for the middle east."

"That must have been a worrisome time for you. How did you keep yourself busy?"

"I volunteered. I still do... VA hospitals. You'd think that would have made me more worried and nervous, but it didn't. I feel deeply for all our men and women that serve. I made Ed promise that if he got elected, he would do something about soldiers that come home all tattered and torn from war. They will not be forgotten, I promise you." Amy gave a thumbs-up to the camera. That caught everyone off guard, and it worked as well. The camera loved her.

It was a perfect segue to Curlander. "How about that, sir?" Dana asked.

"Amy didn't have to push me at all on that front. I've been in combat. I've lost many friends. The veterans of this country will not be forgotten on my watch."

Ed seemed a bit more starchy than Max hoped he'd be, as though he was trying to sound presidential. It pissed Max off. "What is he doing?"

"He gets better," Dana said, staring at the TV.

"What are some of your salient objectives that you will be targeting in your first year?" Dana asked.

"I'll be looking to fulfill the promises I made while campaigning. I don't have a timeline. The train leaves the station on January 20. That's when I will begin obeying the orders mandated by the American people at the polls last November. I carry a written list of those promises. I take them with me everywhere. I am buying—on my own dime I might add—a full page in both the *New York Times* and the *Washington Post,* listing all my campaign promises. I want the American people to stick that page on their refrigerators. I want them to check off my completed promises as we move along together. At the end of my four years as president, that will be my report card, just like what your children bring home from school. Tally it up. Refer to it often. I **want** the people to keep tabs on me."

"What about you being branded a 'stand-alone president'? What I mean is, no party backing. That can be troublesome for a president dealing with an adversarial Congress and Senate, don't you think?"

"Trouble for them, maybe! I'll keep the American people informed of every name in government blocking any critical measures. The American people have trusted me to implement changes and I will inform the American people of whom is blocking those changes. Complete transparency, no more pork, no more *quid pro quo.* No more special interest groups or bankers gouging this country. If representatives of the people ***say*** no, the American people will know ***why*** they said no. Let their representatives explain why they said no. If they have valid reasons let them explain it to their constituents who voted them into office. If they don't explain, the American people will know there is a separate agenda involved, because I'm going to tell them. Disgraceful… that I might need to do that. I hope I do not. I also want to double prison terms for public officials that get caught and convicted with their hands in the cookie jar. That cookie jar belongs to the people!"

"Sounds like scary days ahead for special interest groups," Dana said.

"Know this ***now***: Hidden agendas will be unveiled. I will have government agencies proactive in such endeavors. I am going to ask law school students and their professors to review the bills, laws, and regulations put forth by Congress. I will reduce college loans for savvy students that track down any connections to special interest groups, unsavory political activity, flagrant spending, and… well, you get my gist. The American people have had enough!" Curlander said as he sat back.

"Now he's Ed Curlander," Max said.

"You mentioned lobbyists being a subject that needed to be dealt with," Dana prompted.

Curlander leaned forward and looked into the camera. "Plain

and simple: it will be a crime to give undisclosed compensation or privileged information, American or foreign, to elected officials in any way, shape, or form. I will arrest both politicians and lobbyists alike. They can share the same cell if they wish to influence each other's lives. Anytime money is doing the talking and influencing an agenda, the American people are getting taken for a ride. If any elected member of the United States Congress votes against an anti-lobbying bill, I will consider them a hot target. Naysayers will arouse my curiosity and, as such, shall be scrutinized to the full length and breadth of the laws set forth in the Constitution of the United States of America. I know… it may sound like I will abuse the Constitution written by our nation's founding fathers. I will not do that! I am merely dusting it off and reading it aloud to the American people!"

"Sounds like either they're with you or against you," Dana said.

"Either they are for themselves or for the people of this country. I'll find out which."

"There's a new sheriff in town?" Dana blurted out.

"You might say that. But, that being said, this is not about big government. It's about efficient government—proper use of the people's money… all hands on deck, Dana. That is one reason why I am taking time to pick a cabinet. I am looking for the best of the best at federal, state, and local levels. Find me people that know how to do the job."

"Speaking of your cabinet, anything new on that front?" Dana asked.

"My short list is pretty much completed. I still have vetting and homework to do," Curlander said.

"This country is still reeling from 9/11. What are your thoughts, as a former military man, about our safety here at home?" Dana asked on cue.

"As far as the Department of Homeland Security, I searched high and low for the right man for that position. I found him. He is street savvy, not involved in politics, and dedicated to serve. There are diamonds in the rough like him all over this country, and I mean to seek them out—people that have made it their objective not to owe anybody any favors, like deputy inspector John Timoney of the New York City Police Department. He is my choice for the position of secretary of the Department of Homeland Security."

"Thank you for that exclusive, Mr. President-Elect," Dana said. "More about inspector John Timoney as soon as… we can find out more about inspector John Timoney." Dana turned toward the camera with a smile. She had scooped them all: major TV networks, cable news channels, newspapers, magazines and talk show hosts from New York to LA.

Dana thought it best to move away from Ed at this point. Her intuition was perfect, Ed had nothing more of that magnitude left to provide.

"Amy, any redecorating thoughts with regard to the White House?" Dana asked.

"Mary Todd Lincoln got herself in trouble for that, didn't she? I think Jackie Kennedy—all the previous First Ladies—did wonderful and tasteful treatments to an already beautiful home. My focus will be outside the White House. I hope to be busy working on some adjustments and additions to the Veterans Administration's hospital network. That's my promise. Am I allowed to promise too?"

"You are, Madam First Lady!" Dana stated with conviction.

Amy and Dana's little spontaneous addition at the end was a perfect ending. Dana wrapped it up with the usual thank you and kudos. She was on her game. It was a career changing interview that would solidify her competence as press secretary.

"Great job!" Max said and kissed her.

"Is that all you got, soldier?" she said as she rolled over on top of him. "I love my necklace, and I love you too! Is it okay to say that?"

"Only if you mean it."

They made love well into the night. They discovered that spooning was a favorite of both. Amy fell asleep first. Max nestled his nose into her hair, breathing deeply, enjoying her scent, before he dozed off as well.

The Channel 4 morning news drew 32,091 emails directed to Max and Linc… mostly Linc. People asked, "Does Linc have a Twitter account, Instagram, website, or Facebook? Is he on LinkedIn?" All the things Max ran from.

Dana laughed, saying, "Linc is ready for his own TV show!"

The Curlanders' score was 26,781 emails sent to the network and twice that to their own website/blog.

All in all, the interviews got rave reviews in the papers, on the news, across the internet, and at water coolers all over America. But the star of the show was none other than Lincoln Burns. The most popular question was, When will Linc be a daddy? It seemed everyone wanted a Lincoln Burns puppy.

Max received 126 marriage proposals; Dana, 256; and 2,279 people wanted to know why Dana had blushed. The rest could not be categorized.

Ed and Amy got high marks. Ed's decision to remind the people of his campaign promises was well received, giving him a 68 percent approval rating after all comments were tallied. The important number to Dana and the network was the market share number. The interviews received a 14.2 market share nationally. That was unheard of except for Super Bowls or World Series Game 7 telecasts. At this point, Dana could write her own ticket with or without Curlander, if she so desired. But, to the White House she would go.

Not bad for a twenty-five-year-old from Harrisburg, Pennsylvania, Max thought.

CHAPTER 57

It was Christmas Eve morning and also Sunday. Max asked Dana what she wanted to do.

"I'll tell you what we're going to do. The Redskins are playing the Steelers and we have seats on the thirty-five-yard line, thanks to Cleary. Let's go for a run and get back here in time to beat the traffic to JKC Stadium."

They had a good run on the same path as the previous day. They came back, showered together, and used up all the hot water again.

Dana had her press pass for parking, but that could never work for a seat at a 'skins game. There was not one vacant seat, and it was twenty-nine degrees at kickoff. Max hadn't been to a football game since high school. The Redskins fans were rabid. There were Steeler fans there as well, and they were no better or worse. It was football in D.C... The president himself would have had to sing the national anthem and play an entire quarter to get seats at this game. Dana was right there cheering and screaming with the rest of the Redskins junkies. Max found himself cheering for them as well. He'd walked in the stadium not caring one way or another about who won, but there he was, cheering like a madman for a team that was playing against the Pittsburgh Steelers - his dad's favorite team. A few people recognized Max and Dana, but their presence was worth nothing more than a quick glance. The Redskins were at home! Nobody cared who was attending, unless, of course, they were sitting in your seats. The beer flowed and flasks of liquor were passed around without words. The entire stadium was amped up.

The Steelers won 27–24 with a field goal in the last fourteen seconds. That totally bummed out Redskins fans, since Washington had been ahead 17–7 at halftime.

Dana grabbed Max by the hand. "Follow me. The Beltway will be bumper to bumper for two hours or so. We can go to the Hogs' Club until traffic thins out."

The Hogs' Club was a bar on the lowest level of the stadium… and of humanity. It wasn't a club at all. It was a basement filled with Redskins fanatics, otherwise known as Hogs—men dressed in women's clothing with pig masks. Max was not sure what pigs in women's clothing had to do with football or Native Americans.

I'll ask Dana later.

Some guys were shirtless. They hadn't even brought shirts. One of them was well on his way to the color blue.

"Is this a normal home game?" Max asked Dana.

"Pretty much. Maybe a touch more intense since the Steelers are in town. You have to see a Ravens or an Eagles game to appreciate the Hogs in all their glory. Uh-oh, there's Schmitty. I thought he was barred from here. Don't pay any attention to this moron," Dana said to Max as she and the rest of the crowd turned toward the bar, emitting mutual groans.

Schmitty stood six feet, six… and weighed about 325 pounds. Schmitty was the kind of guy who took advantage of his size. He was an intimidator. Max had been on guard since the doors swung open.

Schmitty was a buffoon-bully, in Max's self-styled taxonomy. He had outrun his welcome many times before at the Hogs' Club. He claimed, he'd gotten cut from the Redskins when his knee blew out during his tryout. The truth was Schmitty had never gotten closer to the field than section 189B, in the gray seats located in the north end zone… a section where the sun rarely shined. Hogs knew he was a liar, but nobody had the guts to relay that information back to Schmitty. When Schmitty showed up, the universal task of all Hogs became that of disengagement from conversation, accomplished by doing an about-face and attaching both elbows to the mahogany bar. Eye contact might be construed as an invitation for Schmitty to enter into conversation. Needless to say, he was even more obnoxious when the Redskins lost.

Dana turned to the bartender and said, "Harry, I thought you barred Schmitty?"

"I did!" Harry said, disgusted at the sight of him. "You throw him out." Harry headed down the bar to look for a conversation to hide in.

Max had spotted Schmitty's swagger as soon as he'd walked in the door. Nobody could size up trouble as well as Max Burns. Like a magnet, the asshole came over and started talking to Dana.

"Hey, cutie-pie." He reached out to touch Dana's face. Max took his arm and turned it in such a way as to put him flat on his back in an instant. He didn't hit the floor; Max more or less placed him on the floor. A hush came over the bar as soon as Schmitty went down. All eyes were on Max and Schmitty. Max still had pressure on his arm in case further attention was necessary. Schmitty started cursing and screaming. Max put his finger to Schmitty's lips and quietly said, "Shhhh." Then Max pulled him to a sitting position and whispered something in Schmitty's ear. Max let go of Schmitty's arm and stood up. He turned his back to Schmitty, like a bullfighter showing disdain for a confused and defeated bull. Max sipped his beer, all the while looking in the bar mirror. Schmitty scrambled to get up off the floor. He had a terrified look on his face as he ran toward the swinging doors at the Hogs' Club entrance. The entire bar stared incredulously at the doors until they swung to a standstill. It had taken about ten seconds from the time Schmitty had attempted to touch Dana until Schmitty was out of the Hogs' Club. Everyone waited for Schmitty to reenter but that was not to be. After all were assured of a Schmittyless postgame, the party commenced with a sense of freedom not seen in a long time at the Hogs' Club. Dana and Max were not permitted to buy a drink for the remainder of their stay. Everyone wanted to know what Max had said to Schmitty, especially Harry, the bartender. All Max said was "That's between me and Schmitty… He won't be back." Harry could have kissed Max on the lips, if Dana had not gotten there first.

"That moron has been the biggest pain in my ass since my mother-in-law moved in seventeen years ago!" Harry said.

Max and Dana received a rare but memorable goodbye from all the constituents of the Hogs' Club as they left. They got some fresh air and some fast food at the kiosks before they closed and walked off the beers in the cold evening air. It was around six thirty when they were greeted by Linc at the apartment door. It was past time for a good walk and his meal. Linc was behaving himself in Dana's apartment. He had his toys and seemed content there.

"How about having dinner at the Scirocco tonight?" Max asked Dana.

"Only if you tell me what you said to Schmitty."

"Sorry. Can't do that."

"C'mon."

"Will you go to the Scirocco with me?"

"If you tell me."

"Okay… I told him I was going to pull his pants off and show everybody his tiny dick. But if he left immediately and never came back, I wouldn't tell anyone that was his reason for leaving. So nobody will ever know why he left."

Dana stood there with her mouth open, not knowing whether to laugh or cry.

"How did you know he had a small dick?" Dana asked.

"In twenty-nine degrees, nobody has a big dick."

"I don't understand…"

"It's simple. If he thought I was going to show everyone in the Hogs' Club his little dick, he had a decision to make. He could stay, and I would put him on display. Or he could leave, and I wouldn't tell anyone what I said to him. When he chose to leave, he was admitting he had a small dick. The weather was definitely on my side."

Max excused himself and went to the bathroom.

Dana was totally confused and yelled after him, **"How do you think of these things?"**

Then she laughed hysterically as she jumped onto the bed.

CHAPTER 58

The Scirocco was about half-full. That made Max feel pretty good. He had met the new owners when Len and Margaret had sold. Neither was present. Absentee ownership for a restaurant was a recipe for disaster. Max and Dana were seated by a Moroccan gentleman that seemed pleasant. Max thought it fitting that he be a Moroccan, since *scirocco* was a Moorish word: a desert wind that came from nowhere. The word had Spanish and Arabic roots and had been adapted by the Tuareg, or "blue people," of the Western Sahara. But the menu was Italian cuisine.

Dana was going to order oysters. Max told her, "Not on Sunday… There are no seafood deliveries on Sunday or Saturday, much less on Christmas Eve. Have soup as a starter."

They both ordered *pasta e fagioli* and two veal dishes.

Dana started laughing and rubbed Max's cheek as she stared at him. Max ordered the same Chianti he had on his first visit… a lifetime ago.

"You know, I am going to have to tell my friends the Schmitty story."

"Up to you. But unless you want to have Schmitty as our personal pain in the ass forever, I suggest you keep it to yourself. You might want to consult with Harry, the bartender, with regard to the outcome of spilling the beans to anyone. He might have some input as to your final decision," Max said, sipping the wine. "But… I wouldn't tell Harry either." Max advised.

"Okay. I get it. Mum's the word." Dana understood that Max was a thinker as well as a protector. She thought, deep inside, Max must feel that he had failed Eva.

That's why he took Schmitty out immediately. He didn't hurt Schmitty. He very well could have… No banter… no posturing… no name calling. Put him down quickly and then get him out of the room. Amazing!

Dana understood him more each day.

Max and Dana had their first secret together. Dana said, "You're right! It will be our secret. We'll call it, a Schmitty—every time we want each other to shut up about something, we'll just mention good ole Schmitty." They toasted to it. Max was pleased she understood. He knew she could keep a secret.

The few people that were dining at the Scirocco recognized them, and Max raised his glass in recognition of their smiles. Then he devoted his time and thoughts to Dana.

Dana seems okay being here.

It started to snow—big flakes that spun their lazy way to the ground. The streetlight out front provided a Christmas card setting. The meal was fine according to Dana, palatable by Max's standards. It wasn't New York City Italian, but it was passable for anywhere else, except Chicago. Max critiqued it in his mind. He needed to Schmitty himself to keep this wonderful Christmas Eve in motion. Max and Dana walked home slowly, enjoying the snow. It would be a white Christmas. The end of a perfect Christmas for these two children of destiny.

CHAPTER 59

It had stopped snowing by the time Max and Dana rolled out of bed Christmas morning. No jog today. Max wanted to get to the Curlanders' early, though he had more than enough time to get the meal prepared. He had an ulterior motive for an early start: he didn't want Ed drinking too early. Max knew Ed felt it was okay to drink heavily around friends and relatives, especially in his own home, but Ed had to learn there was no safe harbor for the man, who was soon to be the most powerful man on the planet. Ed's deeply embedded philosophy of freedom to drink with friends needed to be drastically altered. Amy knew this as well. It was inevitable, at Ed's current pace, people outside his inner circle would find out about his drinking soon enough. The burning question: How to deal with the problem?

So it was with some trepidation that Max had consented to cook for the holidays. Dana was an incentive and worth the sacrifice ... Amy too. But Max knew he would have to be the one to stand up to Ed and take that drink out of the POTUS's hand like last holiday. That kind of policing had a statute of limitations when alcoholism was involved. Max knew there had to come a day when President Curlander would either refuse to put that drink down... or decide to put it down for good.

What then, Max Burns? What then?

Max had used his shaving kit to carry his spices. He'd brought M#1 to M#4 with him.

Why not?

Dana had a shopping bag filled with presents. She'd included Max's name on all the gifts.

Max, Dana, and Linc walked at a nice clip, saying "Merry Christmas," along the way to those who recognized them and many who did not. It was twelve blocks: one klic. They arrived at eight in the morning. Cleary greeted them at the door.

"Merry Christmas, Cleary," Dana said. She gave him a kiss on the cheek. That perked him up. Max thanked him for the Redskins tickets and leaned over to fake a kiss.

"That'll be enough of that," Cleary said.

Mrs. Prendergast was front and center at the kitchen door. She had everything laid out exactly as Max had specified. There would be ham as well as a turkey today. That bode well for the spices Max had in tow. Dana placed the gifts underneath the tree. There were already presents there with both their names on them. Even Linc had a present from Santa. Dana had gotten Cleary a Jerry Garcia tie. *Cleary needs a little pizzazz in his life.*

Max gave Mrs. Prendergast a kiss on the cheek and a "Merry Christmas.... great job, Mrs. P.," he said. She was a little embarrassed but proud. Max said hello to the two new waitresses that had been hired and wished them a merry Christmas. Max looked over at Cleary. Cleary gave him a nod with regard to their security clearance. Dana said her hellos and gave Mrs. Prendergast a hug.

Dana asked if the Curlanders were awake. "Not as yet," Mrs. Prendergast said. "I think it might be a while." Everyone knew what that meant.

Max asked, "Did they stay home last night?"

"Yes... **all** night," Mrs. Prendergast said, understanding the relevance of the question.

Mrs. Prendergast knew Ed Curlander was an alcoholic. She

had confided in Amy that her father and husband had both been alcoholics. Both had died from the disease in one way or another.

Amy had gotten Ed into a 12-step program back in New York City before running for the NY.S. a legislator. He had managed to remain somewhat anonymous back then. He had done well under a good sponsor and the threat of Amy leaving him. Amy stayed: The sponsor died. Ed had been sober for seven months and three days. Then he'd talked himself into a solution: drink management, i.e., switching to beer. The disease had won again. Forty pounds and five cases of beer a week later had proved Ed's theory wrong. He'd gone back to "sipping" twenty-year-old Scotch… for health purposes. He still managed to move up the political ladder. That had only strengthened his resolve that, he functioned better after a few drinks.

How cunning addiction is… Amy thought.

She had attended Al-Anon meetings to learn more about the disease. She found herself betwixt and between Ed's growing success and insatiable thirst. When he'd been elected to the United States Senate by a considerable margin, she had run out of ammunition, but not loyalty. She was fighting a losing battle.

"Let's hope he's too hungover to start over," Max said to Mrs. Prendergast.

"Good luck with that!" She'd had similar hopes many times before. Amy had stopped trying to hide Ed's alcoholism from Mrs. Prendergast after their conversation about the housekeeper's own experience. Amy knew Mrs. Prendergast was loyal, not only to the Curlanders, but also to her country. Mrs. Prendergast believed Ed was a good man. She believed he could accomplish great things. She also knew his drinking was the only thing that could stop him.

"The campaign trail did him in," Amy had said to Mrs. Prendergast after a particularly bad night. All those sleepless nights on the road in a tour bus, with nothing but a bottle and his driver to keep him company, had taken its toll. There were supporters starting the party over again at every stop, everyone feeling lucky to have "**a few pops**" with the next president. Always the hail-fellow-well-met.

Amy waited at home, waiting for a next-of-kin phone call. Ed called her every day. As soon as the phone call was out of the way, Ed could start his drinking. Rarely had Ed answered his cell phone after six in the evening on the campaign trail.

"Ed Curlander is a man's man… a regular guy… a former marine … one of us! Hell, he's what this country needs right now." That was the general consensus. The previous campaign manager had been on Blair's payroll, not Ed's. Ed had become a one-man show out of financial necessity. He liked it that way. There were fewer people telling him what to do, especially when it came to his drinking.

He used his singularity and no-frills campaign method as part of his grass-roots pitch against big pharma, oil interests, and the Wall Street mob. "I don't want any lobbyist money. I don't want to owe anyone… except the American people!" Ed would say, knowing his family money was all but gone. His bid for president was the last roll of the dice for him. If he'd lost the election, Amy would have gotten him back. That had been the agreement. Amy was no fool. She saw the momentum shift in her husband's favor. She'd always known that, if Ed got elected, he would need Max Burns, Dana Trudeau, Bob Cleary, Mrs. Prendergast, and others… a TEAM, to run interference for him and help him get things done as POTUS.

Max asked Dana if she was hungry. Dana said, "I could use some breakfast."

Mrs. Prendergast said, "I wouldn't say no."

Dana said, "I'll ask Cleary."

"No need. He's always hungry," Max said. It was true. Eating on the run was part of Cleary's MO. After Amy and Dana, nobody wanted Max to work for Curlander more than Cleary.

Max decided not to cook breakfast for Ed and Amy.

Let them sleep as long as needed.

Max made Eggs Benedict and french toast after he spotted a light-textured maple syrup in the pantry. They all feasted. Cleary had one of each.

Max had a trick with coffee. He sprinkled salt in the freshly pressed coffee, not much, just a pinch. Max got more satisfaction watching others enjoy his food than eating his own creations.

"Thanks again for the tickets, Cleary," Max said. "We had a great time."

"I heard."

Max and Dana looked over at him and then at each other.

"What did you hear, Cleary?" Dana asked, sipping her coffee nonchalantly.

"I heard your boy here took care of Schmitty in good fashion… that's what I heard. What did you say to him anyway?" Cleary asked, looking up from his cup of coffee.

"You'll have to ask Schmitty," Max said.

Dana almost spit her coffee out on the table.

"Max won't tell me either, Cleary," Dana said, taking herself out of the equation.

"Must've been somethin'. Nobody has seen him since."

"It might be a while. I don't think it will be at the Hogs' Club," Max said, picking up dishes.

Cleary looked at Max. Max did not flinch. That secret was going nowhere. It had been a long time since either Cleary or Dana had witnessed a well-kept secret within the confines of the Beltway.

"We got a **Deep Throat** scenario going on here, eh?" Cleary said.

Cleary was determined to make it his business to find out what Max had said to Schmitty. Cleary didn't like secrets he was not privy to. After all, he was in charge of all secrets. Cleary liked Max, but there was something about Max that Cleary couldn't quite put his finger on. He hoped it was nothing bad. It was just the cop in Cleary that made him cautious.

Nobody is this clean.

Max's phone rang. It was Timoney. "Merry Christmas, John… or are you in uniform, Inspector?" Max said, kidding with him.

"I am in a suit… is what I'm in, young man. I am in Malahide, a few klicks outside of Dublin, with Kieran and what remains of our family. It seems I have more relatives than when I left, especially when I enter a pub. I wanted to wish you a merry Christmas and thank you for your trust in me. I hope I can live up to America's expectations. I am honored, but nervous. I've become quite a hotshot overnight here on the old sod as well." Timoney seemed to have a tinge more brogue than when he'd left New York. There was a five-hour time difference between Ireland and New York. The new and improved Timoney family was already celebrating the appointment on the Emerald Isle.

Max said, "You better get stateside soon, or you'll be speaking Gaelic!"

"I heard you have a new lady. I'm happy for you. I want to meet her as soon as I get back for the inauguration. I am putting in my retirement papers for the nineteenth of January. I will see you at some point, either at the inauguration, or at one of the inaugural balls. Ya' know… I knew you were a suit the moment I met ye'. *Sláinte*, as we say in Gaelic. Merry Christmas to all!" Timoney hung up. If Max didn't know better, he would have thought Timoney was partaking of a pint or two at a local public house. Max hoped Timoney had the strength to keep fighting off his own demons.

Timoney would be an ideal person to help with Curlander's drinking problem… At least I'd have some help.

Max had a faraway look on his face. "What are you thinking?" Dana asked.

"Nothing really. That was inspector Timoney calling from Ireland. He's home visiting with family."

"He's from Ireland?"

"He is that!"

"Hmmmm, that will be a first."

"What will be a first?"

"A foreign-born naturalized citizen appointed as the secretary of Homeland Security."

Max had never mentioned that point when he'd suggested Timoney to Curlander.

Dana's on the ball.

"What better place to come from than Ireland when it comes to understanding terrorism?" Max said.

"Good point, soldier boy."

Everyone stayed to help clean up except Cleary. He conveniently had to go back outside to keep everyone safe. He asked Max if Linc could accompany him.

"Are you sure you are finished eating?" Max asked.

Cleary said, "Smart-ass. C'mon, Linc." Linc got up and went directly to Cleary. The dog had found another friend in D.C.

"He's all yours. If anybody asks you… your last detail was Lincoln. Hell, you oughta be ready for retirement right about now, Cleary."

There was no sign of Ed or Amy yet. It was getting a bit awkward not having them out and about in their own home… on Christmas.

Dana and Max had never had a conversation about Ed's drinking. However, Dana had had many conversations about it with Amy.

"Ed is **functional**," Amy had told Dana once early on in their friendship while waving the Senator Curlander banner.

Functional for a president and functional for an elevator operator are two distinct things, Dana had thought, but she hadn't shared that with Amy.

Amy was well aware of what one bad day could produce at home. She was loathe to think what one bad moment could bring from the leader of the free world. She prayed that the importance of the office would instill sobriety. Max was no expert but he knew it didn't work that way. He had seen enough drinking and drug use overseas to witness the results firsthand.

Generals to enlisted men… the disease takes no prisoners.

Ed's drinking was the big factor in why Max did not jump at the chance to be the presidential executive chef.

I'm not a babysitter! Who the hell is going to mind me?

Those thoughts popped up every time Max saw Ed with a drink in his hand. Even back in the Scirocco days, Max hated to have to cut Ed off. Each time presented an unexpected result and different situations. Cleary would not be able to deal with it …not from a person he not only took orders from, but swore an allegiance to obey.

Hell, that isn't part of his job description… a daunting task for Cleary. One wrong move, and it could cost him his career. Cleary's job is to keep the president and his family safe from harm. Does that mean if Curlander hurt himself drinking, Cleary would be responsible for ***letting*** *him drink to excess?*

Keeping an eye on the president would have to be a task for someone not in an official capacity, someone not afraid to lose their job. **A friend.**

At some point, Max needed to have an in-depth conversation with Timoney about all this, but Max did not want Timoney begging off his appointment before Curlander even took the oath of office.

Timoney probably has Ed pegged already. Not much gets past an Irishman when it comes to drink. Enough! It's Christmas.

Max started working his culinary magic. Once again, Mrs. Prendergast was all eyes and ears. She would have made a great chef herself. She asked the right questions at the right time. Max was a good teacher but always kept some secrets in the pantry.

Mushrooms anyone?

Dana was making a phone call to her parents in Harrisburg. Max overheard her talking to her mother "… More handsome than cute. You saw him on TV. What do **you** think?" There was a pause, then Dana said, **"Who the hell is the Marlboro Man?"**

Max thought about Len and Margaret. At a peaceful moment he would call again.

Dana had the BBC on the TV. The Curlanders were still not up. It was around eleven before there was any sign of them. Amy was up first. She came downstairs in her satin robe. She ran around and kissed everybody. "Where's Linc?"

"He is out with Cleary fighting crime," Max said, assessing her state of mind. "Where is King Edward?"

"Oh, he'll probably be a while. He took a little trip on the coffee table last night and banged up his knee," Amy said, trying not to look at anybody as she buzzed around. "My, my, look, there is still snow on the ground."

Max froze upon hearing about the coffee table incident. **Accidents** for alcoholics were on the bullshit side of the equation. Max could tell Dana knew alcohol had been involved. He would talk to Dana about all this back at her place… not here… not at Christmas.

"Oh God!" Dana exclaimed, looking at the BBC news broadcast. "Looks like an American soldier flipped out and fragged a house in Kabul: seven people killed, including three kids and two women."

Merry fuckin' Christmas.

The guests began to arrive. They were the usual suspects, the same people from Thanksgiving. Max wondered if this close circle of relatives had already proved their loyalty through discretion.

I'd love to be a fly on the wall when these folks get home.

The two nephews: Tweedledee and Tweedledum, immediately began their gawking at Dana. The niece stayed outside with Cleary and Linc until all three needed the warmth of the fireplace. Max whipped up some homemade hot chocolate. It was a big hit, especially with the little girl. Ed made his way gingerly down the stairs around noon. He looked pretty good, Max thought. He limped but nothing visible. Everyone let it slide, and so did Max.

Ed mustered up his "Merry Christmases" as cheerfully as he could. Then he walked over to the TV and watched as some troops came home from Afghanistan through JFK Airport.

Ed said, "Of all the '*stans* - Afghani*stan* is the biggest mess of all. We did our job, time to get the hell out! Once again, we have succeeded in having help turn into hate. Throwing money at them is not the answer either. Hell, they're using the U.S. Air Force planes to smuggle heroin, for Chrissake. Nobody better bitch about this marine taking soldiers out of harm's way because it interferes in the heroin trade!"

Well, he gets it!

"How 'bout an Irish coffee?" Ed asked.

Right on cue!

Max said, "How 'bout a hot chocolate? Great for a hangover."

"Oh, I forgot… my alter ego is here," Ed said as he put his hands up, feigning boxing.

"Better watch out. You look stiff from last night… your leg, that is," Max said sarcastically.

Amy smiled more inside than out. Dana had a smirk on her face.

How does he get away with his remarks?

Curlander took a hot chocolate from Mrs. Prendergast and sipped it. Then he said, "It could use a little Scotch." He had to let it slide when nobody agreed. He knew the odds were against him with so many teaming up to prevent his early start.

"We've got some presents for everyone. Come over by the tree and see what Santa brought you," Ed said. Everyone got the same box with the same present. It was a beautiful Christmas ornament with a White House inscription that said, "From the President of the United States of America and the First Lady: Edward Pierce Curlander and Amy Caroline Curlander." It was a beautiful keepsake to be cherished for generations. Then the Curlanders got to open their presents. It was quite a Christmas scene. Max and Dana felt privileged to be part of it. Dana was glowing, and Max's hors d'oeuvres were being devoured at a fast clip.

It was a Currier and Ives scene: a prelude to an American Christmas dinner. Everyone knew that Max had special talent since all present had partaken of his Thanksgiving prowess. What they didn't know was Max had taken things up a notch, providing the feast with his first-ever M#3 mushroom gravy!

The day went by quickly, and Amy soon announced, with seasonal sweetness in her voice, "Everyone, please be seated. Dinner is about to be served." She kept grace simple: "Lord, thank you for all your blessings and allowing us to all be here together on your birthday. Amen."

The lobster-salad appetizers came out and were short-lived. The pumpkin-ginger soup was next, followed by the fig-laced salad, all with proper intermezzo for palate cleansing and conversation. Then the main course: ham, glazed to perfection, followed by the turkey and all the trimmings. The different gravies arrived in four different boats, none of which lasted very long.

The actual meal was over within twenty-seven minutes from the time the appetizer came out until the last pat on the stomach by a satisfied president-elect.

"A little more wine for the ladies or perhaps a Napoleon brandy?" Ed said.

Max and Dana shot a quick look over at each other and smiled when the brandy made its appearance. This was the same bottle of Napoleon brandy they had partaken from the first night they made love. Dana was tickled that Max remembered.

Good soldier.

Ed did not currently have a brandy in his hand. Max knew the meal would absorb a good deal of alcohol. He brought a warmed snifter and the bottle of brandy over to Ed. Max wanted to show Ed he was not in charge of his abstinence.

Ed put his hand over the snifter and said, "No thank you, Max. I'm right where I want to be at this moment." He beckoned to Amy. She came over, and Ed put his arm around her as she sat on the arm of his chair. Amy put her hand on his forehead, thinking he might be ill. Amy sheepishly looked over at Dana and then at Max. She had never seen Ed turn down a drink, any drink… ever. Amy was beaming. Dana raised her glass ever so slightly toward Amy to acknowledge the victory.

Max raised his glass and said, "I'd like to propose a toast: To our POTUS and his beautiful First Lady. May you both be for our country the strength and backbone it so very much needs. May you be strong enough to keep on speaking the truth. And when you both leave this office, know in your hearts you have served the American people to the best of your ability … that you tried in earnest to leave our country in a better place than when you took office."

"Here, here!"

As they all sipped their wine and Napoleon brandy, Ed kissed Amy.

Is this my husband or some impostor? I'll take this guy!

He was her husband, and he did not imbibe the rest of the day or evening. Amy dared not ask why. But Max did go up to him at one point and asked why he wasn't drinking.

Ed said, "Oh, I don't know? I feel good right now. You know, once I am in office, I am going to have to cut way back on the booze… maybe get back in shape. Might as well start sooner than later. Come upstairs with me for a minute, Max." Max followed Ed upstairs to his bedroom. Ed handed Max a present the size of a cigar box. Max unwrapped the box. It was a pearl-handled, stainless steel Walther PPK, 7.65-millimeter semiautomatic pistol. The engraving on the barrel read, "To Max Burns, from his friend, President Edward Pierce Curlander."_The pearl grip had the presidential seal on both sides with the date below. It was magnificent.

"Is this Marine Corps standard issue for officers?" That was a little joke due to the caliber being smaller than the nine-millimeter or .45-caliber armed forces standard issue. The Walther PPK was the most reliable semiautomatic handgun ever made. Crafted in Germany, it was arguably the perfect concealed weapon.

"Mind if I teach Dana to use it?"

"She can use her own," Ed said as he showed Max another box. "Get her up here for a second."

"You bet. Thanks, pal. It's a beauty."

They hugged, and Ed patted Max on the cheek. "Ya know, I don't feel like drinking. Does that mean I'm finally a grownup?" They both laughed.

"Not sure," Max said.

When Max arrived downstairs, Dana shot him a look. He motioned for her to go upstairs. Dana was up there for a good twenty minutes or so. When she came down, you could see that she had been crying and had tried in vain to repair herself.

She walked over to Max. "Where's Marcel when I need him?

Do you think I'm going to need a gun?" Dana asked in a whimper.

Max smiled and hugged her. "Not the first few press conferences."

Dana punched him on the arm.

"I'll teach you how to use it. You'll need a federal carry permit for interstate travel… we both will. I only have a New York carry permit. I'll ask Cleary about it."

Everyone began singing Christmas carols. Ed had on all three of the scarves he had received and both pairs of fleece-lined slippers. Everyone seemed in great form. Amy was as happy as Max had ever seen her. Amy put on CDs of Christmas music, people started dancing. Mrs. Prendergast rolled up the shag rug in front of the fireplace while Cleary rolled up the one in the library. Ed and Amy, the brothers and sisters, and Max and Dana danced to Christmas standards.

Dana said, while dancing with Max, "I have your present at home."

"Too big to bring, eh?"

"I don't know whether it's this house or your cooking that gets me so horny," Dana said as she rubbed the back of his neck while grinding as close as possible.

"Are you ready for some death by chocolate?" Max whispered in her ear.

"I am ready for death by sex."

Max finished the dance and gently kissed her before heading to the kitchen to prepare the desserts: death by chocolate, apple strudel, and sundaes for the kids. As Max worked on the twenty-six desserts, he couldn't help but think that the M#3 might be responsible in some way for Ed's about-face on the brandy.

Wouldn't that be something? I'm feeling pretty good myself, come to think of it!

Dana peeked into the kitchen to watch Max at work. She was reminded of a movie she had seen about the life of abstract expressionist painter, Jackson Pollock. Pollock was a frenetic painter: Max was totally engrossed in his own studio… a kitchen.

Max was preparing lines of desserts simultaneously. There were thirteen strudels baking and thirteen plates of death by chocolate being prepared simultaneously. He knew Cleary was good for at least one of each. There was one more agent in the van. Max gave Cleary a full meal for him, albeit no gravy.

Mrs. Prendergast got everyone seated by announcing, "No dessert for anyone not seated immediately!"

The waitresses put out two desserts per place setting. It was time for the *coup de grâce*. There was silence except for the sound of mastication.

Amy proposed a toast: "To Max Burns: friend, confidant, and chef extraordinaire. May your talent be dedicated to the righteous and pure of heart. May your future endeavors be for the good of all mankind."

"Here, here!" sounded once again from one and all. Max raised his glass to the entire table and took a sip. He winked at Dana. She smiled proudly and went immediately back to her death by chocolate.

Things seemed different than Thanksgiving. Max observed smiles, rosy cheeks, snuggling by the fire, people relaxing on the floor, on couches and recliners, anywhere possible. Everyone, chilled out. There wasn't much conversation. Dancing flames in the fireplace became the main attraction. Occasionally, someone would put another log on the fire and everyone re-snuggled. The little girl had Linc in her lap as they both slept in a recliner. It could have been any home in America. Even Cleary remained transfixed on the fire in a rare unguarded moment.

Max took it all in. He made mental notes regarding M#3 amount and potency. The M#3 definitely possessed a calming effect. In Ed's case, maybe he found the elusive slice of well-being he searched for in alcohol. All Max knew for sure was; this was the best Christmas he'd ever had … at least as a grownup.

Everyone was asleep when Max nudged Dana.

Max and Dana were anxious to get home and celebrate the rest of Christmas alone. They gathered up Linc and their Christmas presents and left without disturbing anyone, except Cleary. Max woke Cleary because he didn't want the agent to feel compromised by falling asleep on the job. Cleary shook his head in approval and got up. He gave Max a thumbs-up, and they shook hands. Cleary straightened himself out and walked them to the door. Dana gave him a kiss on the cheek and a "Merry Christmas."

Cleary said, "Nice Christmas… I don't know, pal. Whatever you are packing into that turkey didn't come with the bird."

Max looked at him and said, "My mom's recipe. Merry Christmas, Cleary."

Max, Dana, and Linc walked home. They had Georgetown to themselves. The snow had melted. It was a pleasant fifty-six degrees according to a thermometer in the bank window. They were back at Dana's and into flannels and sweats within a few minutes.

Max hunkered down on the couch. Dana came out with a beautifully wrapped box with about the same dimensions as a deck of cards.

"Merry Christmas. I hope you like it," Dana said, snuggling on his arm as he opened the present. It was a wristwatch. It was quite unique. It had an empty, round, pitch-black face.

"You need to press this button to light up the face; click it again, and it's military time. I know how you always use military time. It also has a stopwatch for running *and* a GPS! It has this apartment already programmed into it. Click it here, and wherever you are anywhere in the world, you have directions back to me…Oh, and it's a phone. We have to set that up."

"Incredible," Max said.

"I got one for Ed too! That's why I was upstairs for so long. It's the same as yours, except for the back."

Max turned the watch over. It had an inscription that read, "To my soldier boy. Love always, Dana."

Max looked at it and kissed her. "This is great! You're great!"

"Only one more thing to unwrap, soldier boy…."

The morning sun found its way through a break in the curtains. Max watched the sun's sliver move gently across Dana's face before getting up and starting his day.

Dana awoke to the smell of fresh coffee. She sat up and stretched her arms as she took in the aroma of the coffee with a deep inhale.

Max and Linc had already gone for their morning walk. Steel-cut Irish oatmeal and some maple syrup were awaiting Dana. It was not unusual that she slept late. Her hours at the TV station did not get her home until well after midnight - no stops involved. Max, on the other hand, was an early riser from his WashPa days on the farm. Max brought Dana a tray with half a grapefruit, coffee, and the oatmeal with warmed maple syrup on the side. She sat up. "You're spoiling me, soldier boy."

"Precisely."

She had one dimple. It was on her right cheek. Whenever he saw that dimple, he knew things were okay. Max enjoyed seeing people smile where his cooking was concerned. When Dana smiled, it made his day.

Max sat on the bed with her as she ate.

"I need a workout," Max said.

"Did you run with Linc yet?" Dana asked.

"I had a good walk with him. I mean a real workout: heavy bag, speed bag, maybe some iron."

"Hmmmm. I just got a one-week guest pass to my gym. I think it's on the kitchen counter. I have girlie stuff to do today. I know you're up for a nail salon, right?" Dana said, smiling. "Why don't you walk over to the gym and introduce yourself to Sal? He owns the place. He was my personal trainer for six months. Good guy. Tell him you're my boyfriend."

"What kind of a gym is it?" Max asked.

"Don't worry, it's a real gym. Nothing namby-pamby about it, tough guy. It's right up your alley."

"Is it the place up the street with the windows greened out?"

"That's it: Sal's Gym. No frills. Do you have workout gear with you?" Dana asked.

"Always." Max jumped up, grabbed the guest pass, kissed her, scratched Linc, and off he went. The holidays were putting a crimp in Max's workouts. Running was not enough to stay sharp. It was good for the heart and lungs, but the heavy bag was for stamina and strength. Max knew that outlasting an opponent was the way to victory when all else failed.

Max walked into the gym and was greeted by Sal. Max introduced himself and explained his connection to Dana.

Sal put up his hand to stop further explanation and shook Max's hand. "No sweat, my man. I saw you on TV the other night with Dana. I knew sumpthin' was up between you two. She's a great doll!"

"Thanks. Okay to workout?" Max asked.

"The place is yours. Let me show you around: weights, machines, spin class, aerobics, steam room, showers, massage. Full service."

"What's in there?" Max asked, pointing to a door.

"In there? That's... *the gym*."

"Mind if I look?"

"Not at all," Sal said as he opened the door.

There it was, smell and all: two full-size rings, heavy bags, speed bags, reflex bags, trainers, fighters, and managers.

This is, ***the*** *gym, all right.*

"Is this part of the deal?"

"If you're up to it, sure. There are some heavy bags open. Three are water bags if your wrists are bad. Stay out of the way of the pros. I get a good buck from them, if they don't have to deal with wannabes cutting into their circuit training. Use any guest locker. You gotta lock?"

"Right here on my bag."

"It's all yours. Good to meet you. If you need anything shout," Sal said, walking back to the public side of his gym.

Max was in heaven with the buzz, the electricity, the sounds, and, most of all, the smell. It was a sensory flashback to his MMA days in the army. The night of his title fight at West Point against Nick Nicholson came immediately to mind.

Nicholson! I need to call him right after New Year's.

Max changed into his army MMA shorts with the ranger insignia on one side and the West Point coat of arms on the other. He had a torn T-shirt on under a cutoff sweatshirt and wore his running shoes.

A speed bag was first. His timing was off, but he got into sync. Max saw a jump rope hanging on a hook and decided to work up a sweat with a ten-minute jump session. His timing was off with the rope as well. He got it together and began skip-jumping.

A voice came from behind him. "Hey! That's my rope."

Max stopped jumping and took a breath. "Sorry," Max said, handing the guy the rope without an explanation. Max didn't appreciate the guy's lack of gym courtesy, but he was the "guest."

This guy looked like a pro with plenty of miles on him. His scars were a giveaway to his classification. The eyebrow cuts were wide, suggesting light or no gloves. The septum had been removed from his nose, which meant professional dedication.

Probably MMA.

This guy was a heavyweight, also the ugliest living thing Max had ever seen. The fact that his face looked like it had been in a rock fight did not indicate whether he was good at his craft or not. He had been on the receiving end but that did not mean he was poor on the dishing side. All true MMA fighters were eventually rough to look at. The true professionals stopped caring about their looks when substantial checks began to arise.

"You tryin' to steal my jump rope?"

"No, man. I saw it hanging there and…."

The guy interrupted Max. "You tryin' to steal it, huh?"

Max could feel the inevitable. His blood started to pump harder, as though filling him with fuel.

This is all I need… Dana's gym… a guest… Sal goes out of his way… the day after Christmas. Isn't today Boxing Day in England? Shut up, shit head. Stifle this situation before it gets out of control.

"Look, I apologize… Merry Christmas."

Max started to walk away, when the guy yelled, "Hey, ***jefe***. I like your shorts. Did you get them online? Maybe you wanna settle this in the ring?" Max stopped but did not turn around. He tried to suppress the chill - that watchtower chill, the chill he felt when he spotted enemy movement, the chill he appreciated for the warning it provided before engaging the enemy.

The ***jefe*** did it for him. Max didn't need a lot of time to justify what was next. ***Jefe!*** Another unfinished symphony Max needed to complete.

Maybe this moron is related to Louie and Paco? It sure sounded like it.

"You said all the right things, handsome. Get a ref; five minutes, ***jefe***," Max said as he went for his hand wraps and tape.

The speed bags waggled to a stop, there was no more jumping rope. Sparring ceased. All activity seemed to freeze except the hot blood pounding from Max Burns's heart, through his veins, and back again.

Fill 'er up!

The gym grew quiet. It was as though a death knell had sounded. The general consensus: This crazy rookie was going to die, or wish he had. They were obliged to watch, however. There was blood involved, and these guys were addicted to the sound, smell, and sight of a good beating. Good show or bad show, it really didn't matter.

This was a different challenge Max had gotten himself into. He knew there was a maliciousness involved when an MMA hopeful of any stature goaded a stranger into a fight. It was unheard of and so it garnered more curiosity than respect. Max knew that his opponent would be overconfident and probably show-off. Max knew nothing about this guy except he didn't like him. That was a good thing as far as Max was concerned. It helped with the justification he needed.

Jefe! *What's with the* ***jefe?*** *I must look like a* ***jefe****?*

Max went into his locker and got his cup. He looked at the hockey cup before sliding it into his jock and thought…

Good investment.

Max spotted some Vaseline. He dipped four fingers in and rubbed it into his hair, turning his mop of thick brown hair into a mass of shiny black grease.

If this prick grabs my hair, it might buy me a tenth of a second. Remember the clip-on tie in Thailand.

The rest went on Max's face to stave off dry cuts on bone close to the skin.

When Max came out of the locker room, Sal was waiting. "Look, Max, I can't be responsible for this kind of shit happening here. I got a license, and I am a responsible citizen now. I was doing you and Dana a favor. You can't get in there with this lunatic."

"Want me to sign something?" Max asked, looking at Sal's blank expression. **"No? Then wrap me."**

Sal wrapped and taped Max's hands professionally for MMA free-hand use.

"She's gonna kill me. Dana is gonna have me on the six o'clock news, coming out of here with a towel over my head and handcuffs," Sal whimpered.

Max was thinking that Sal might have to get in line.

Oh well, she sent me here for a workout!

"Sal, you the ref?" Max asked.

"Yeah. Who the hell else is gonna to stop this before he kills you? Listen to me. He's a natural southpaw, but he starts righty. He'll start with left jabs, then a quick right leg kick. Not sure where, but always a kick. Watch for his switch to southpaw. There's an opening there. He thinks it jams up opponents. If you know about it, you can get to him on the switch!" Sal whispered in Max's ear. "He's more street than Muay Thai, jujitsu, or boxer. Don't let him get a hold of you. Jesus! Have you ever been in an MMA fight before?"

"No... but I did stay at a Holiday Inn last night!"

"There goes my gym."

Sal got into the ring. "This is just sparring, right? I don't have a license for matches, so it's over when I say so. Agreed?" Both men nodded as they stared into each other's eyes.

"Any doctors or cut men in this gym right now?" Sal asked to the dozen or so onlookers. They'll shook their heads. "Jesus. If things get messy, we all help stopping this...**RIGHT**?" There was murmuring but no consensus.

As Max went to fist tap his opponent to start, the guy blew Max a kiss. Max asked him, "What did you call me before?"

"You mean, ***jefe***?"

"Yeah, that was it... ***jefe***."

Somebody rang the bell on Sal's signal.

Max stood in the middle of the ring while his opponent danced around talking to everyone as though he was Muhammad Ali. He was trying to distract Max. That would not happen. Max was locked in like the laser on a Barrett M82 sniper rifle. His concentration would not be the difficult part of this fight. He had not been in an actual ring since the service. He would have to conjure up all the cunning he could muster. Fighting was fifty percent mental. It was the other half that might be the problem today.

MMA and Muay Thai were about outguessing an opponent's

individual moves and countering with an effective one of your own. You hoped your countermoves were a surprise. Of course, Max had never seen this guy fight before.

If Sal is right, it will help.

The guy came in low at Max, trying to grab at his leg. Max backed off and slammed the guy's left kidney with a punch as the guy ran through. If it hurt him, he sure fooled Max. The guy jabbed with his left, just as Sal had said he would. Then he tried his initial kick. Max was ready but too slow to catch his leg.

Sal's right so far.

The guy was smiling and probably thinking about how he should take Max out. Max would stay in a defensive mode until he could figure out the predominant style. Max would not show him anything of his own.

Let him come get a taste if he wants to see something.

He finally came, like an enraged bull, trying to run Max down. Max slipped by him with a judo move that sent his opponent off the ropes. The guy switched to southpaw in boxing mode. Max jumped in and smacked him on his left temple before the kick could come.

Sal's right again!

Max's confidence was building. He decided to see if the guy could box. Max jabbed him twice in the nose.

Useless. His septum was probably removed in the fourth grade.

There was nothing left but sponge in the middle of his face. The guy leaped with a roundhouse right that caught Max on the back of his head. Max was lucky he took that punch so far back on the skull. If it had hit his jaw, the fight would have been over. Max jabbed him on the forehead twice and sideslipped a right hook from the southpaw stance. Frustration was starting to mount within the guy. His face distorted as he glanced at the smiling onlookers. That bode well for Max. Max faked a kick and threw a left hook to the liver and then a right cross to the jaw. The combination hurt and stunned the guy. It told him he couldn't outbox Max. If he kept boxing, it could be a source of embarrassment for him. Everyone watching perked up.

They were all professionals in some capacity. Even Sal was surprised the match was still in progress.

Max knew his opponent would try to come inside to grab him. He would try to wrestle Max to the mat and choke him to unconsciousness. Max could see the transition and made one of his own. He knew a fake kick and a charge would be coming. Max stayed in a boxer stance, looking the guy in the eye. Max did not want to give away the kick that he was about to throw. He caught the guy in the solar plexus with a knee. It knocked the wind out of him. Max moved in.

Big mistake.

The guy decoyed Max and smashed him with a right hand, high on Max's left cheek. Max could feel his left eye begin the closing process. He banged off the ropes and rolled to his right. Instinctively, Max knew he had about thirty seconds or so before the eye would be completely shut, leaving his left side vulnerable. The kicks would be coming from this guy's strong right leg, and once his right foot left the mat, Max would no longer be able to see it coming high or low. Max had to throw away his defensive method. Max had to wrestle him.

At least I'll know where he is.

He knew the guy would revert to his strength, which, if Sal was three for three, would be street mode. The blood was already blinding Max even before his eye fully closed. Sal walked in between the two of them to stop the fight. Max pushed him to the ropes. This fight would go until one of the two was no longer moving.

Max's eye was a mess. Now, he hoped his eye would close sooner rather than later. That way he could not instinctively try to look through the blood. The kick came. Max rolled his body into the guy and took the kick in the ribs. It was a thigh that landed on Max's ribs, too high up on the opponent's leg to have an effect. Max slammed his elbow into his opponent's larynx. He then grabbed the guy's head and flipped him onto the canvas in a judo move. He held the choke hold from behind and moved his leg instinctively around the guy's waist into a classic triangle choke hold. It was an illegal move in college wrestling, but a *coup de grâce* in MMA. Seconds before unconsciousness, the guy banged the canvas with his palm.

Max had to be pulled off the guy by Sal and two others. Max was in the netherworld world. All who watched the fight knew of that world. Some had been there themselves, never in defeat.

"There you go, ***jefe*!**" Max said with disdain as he got up.

One more bully down.

Max walked quickly out of the ring and straight to the locker-room sink to look in the mirror. He wanted to get out of the gym to avoid any of the commotion that was going on at ringside. Max's opponent had crawled to a bench to lie down.

Max's face wasn't pretty. It was more ugly than serious. Sal brought ice in a sandwich bag and put it on Max's eye.

Sal said, **"She's gonna fuckin' kill me!"**

"You!" Max said. "What do you think she's gonna do to **me**?"

"Come into my office," Sal said. "Lucky it's on the left brow. You've been cut there before, I see. Damn things never heal completely. People say scar tissue is tougher than skin… not if it's mush underneath. I don't know what spot this puts you in for the MMA heavyweight contender slot. Up until ten minutes ago, Tito Montalban out there was number one in line for the title shot. When word gets out that some gym rat kicked his ass in seven minutes, you're gonna think you're Richard fuckin' Kimball: The Fugitive! Every MMA freak in America will be hunting your ass down," Sal said as he worked on Max. "Where did you learn how to fight like that?"

Sal put pressure on the ice to get the swelling down as much as possible before closing the cut with stitches. Max had been stitched on the fly before, and this was as good a job as any clinic might have done. It was evident this wasn't Sal's first job as a cut man.

"Listen, Sal, you never saw me before, got it?"

"I wouldn't be lying there, would I?" Sal said. "Your eye is gonna be okay. It'll take a week or so, then you pull out the stitches or come back and… you pull them out. I'll probably be closed down by then. You gotta make yourself scarce around here, Max. Keep this iced all the way home. She's gonna kill me! You gotta tell Dana I wasn't here! No, that won't work. Tell her I didn't know you were back there. Tell her… tell her you got mugged!"

Max looked at Sal and said sarcastically, "That should work."

Max was packing up his bag one-handed when Sal said, "Listen, if you ever want to try this MMA thing for real… I mean, go pro. I am a good manager. No booze, no drugs, and I'm honest. We take all your winnings and put it into tax-free municipal bonds."

"I'll let you deal with Dana on that going forward, Sal," Max said with a wry smile. There was banging on the office door. "How do I get outa here without any bullshit?"

"Take this door to the alley on M Street. Here's my card. I'm serious about the MMA thing. I could get you into peak shape in three months. If we played up this Tito ass kickin', we could start near the top. There's getting to be some big cake in MMA… advertising… sponsors too."

Max thanked Sal and told him he'd have Dana call him.

"Don't you dare mention my name to that woman!"

CHAPTER 60

Max walked slowly back to Dana's apartment, hoping the ice would quell the swelling, but a fighter's face always looked worse before it looked better.

Hi! I'd like to introduce the president's press secretary, Ms. Dana Trudeau, and her boyfriend. In this corner, the street fighter, Max the Mauler Burns.

People were trying not to stare.

Good thing I don't have Linc with me.

Max got home to Dana's and looked in the bathroom mirror immediately. He examined his face with his functional eye. There had not been significant improvement during the walk home.

Sal knows what he is doing… Stitches are tight and symmetrical. He would be a good manager. Exactly what I need… another career choice.

He was on the couch when Dana came in and saw him. The scream wasn't a complete surprise to Max. He jumped to his feet to help pick up the groceries Dana threw into the air.

"It looks worse than it is!" Max said.

"The Forbidden Zone! You went into the back gym? I knew it! I thought about it later when I was getting my nails done. I couldn't call Sal, because my nails were wet. What happened in there? Who did this to you? I am going to kill Sal!" Dana said as she grabbed her cell phone with fully extended fingers. She pushed three wrong numbers, then threw the phone on the recliner. She came over to the couch and hugged Max.

"Oh my God! Are you okay?" she asked as she looked at his eye. Then she said, "I'm going to throw up." She ran into the bathroom. Max heard her scream again. He forgot he had left a blood-soaked towel in the sink.

"I guess it's time for me to go back to New York!" Max yelled through the bathroom door as Dana threw up again.

"This is why… I never became… a war correspondent… **the blood!**" Dana said in between heaves.

Max knew he'd screwed up big time. He wondered whether he was the type of guy that deserved a woman like Dana Trudeau. He always seemed to go off half-cocked.

Was I supposed to think about Dana and walk away from that mutt? Is that what a guy is supposed to do?

Max had never answered to anyone except his superior officers, and this was not the army.

Dana came out of the bathroom. She was as white as a sheet. As difficult as it was for her, she approached Max to examine his face.

"Is your eye still in there? Will you ever see again?" she asked just before she began to cry.

"It's okay. It'll be fine. I could see before it closed up."

"What happened?" Dana asked.

This is no time to start lying to her.

Max explained that he had been provoked… and that there had been no possible way to get out of the fight. He told her that the guy was a bully.

"Did you kick his ass?" Dana asked.

"I beat him… not sure you'd call it an ass kickin'."

"Why didn't the referee stop it when you got hurt? Don't they stop a fight when someone gets hurt?" Dana asked incredulously, as though MMA was regulated like badminton.

"There was only Sal. I couldn't blame…."

Dana cut him off. **"Fucking Sal!** I knew it. I am going to kill him. He was the referee?" Dana shouted.

"Not his fault, honey…"

Shit! There goes Sal.

"Look, maybe I oughta head back to New York and come back for New Year's Eve. What do you think?"

"What do I think? I think you better call your buddy, the POTUS, and tell him you'll be wearing a bag over your head for the president's New Year's Eve gala at the Kennedy Center. That's what I think!" Dana said as she tossed the invitation on the table in front of Max.

"When were you going to tell me about that?"

"I just found out about it myself. Amy told me they have permission to use the Kennedy Center."

"In a week this will hardly be noticeable," Max said.

"Five days. Today's the twenty-sixth," Dana said, holding back tears.

Max gave her a big hug. She melted in his arms. She didn't want to be some milksop girlie girl. She was, after all, a reporter. She had seen a few things in her time as a beat reporter. But she hated the sight of blood, anybody's blood, especially blood oozing from the head of the man she loved.

Dana kissed him on the cheek and asked, "Does it hurt?"

"Nah, a little bothersome not being able to see out of that eye. It'll be fine. This isn't my first black eye," Max said. "I'll put a steak on it."

"You call that a black eye! You could put a whole cow on that face and still not cover it."

"I gotta jump in the shower." Max said.

"No you're not! I am going to draw a nice hot bath, if I can conjure up enough hot water. You lie down on the couch for a few minutes. I'll take Linc out while you soak in Epsom salts for a good hour." Dana sprang into action.

Max didn't remember how long it usually took for his cuts and bruises to heal. It had never mattered before. It wouldn't matter now, except for: Dana; the New Year's Eve gala; the president and First Lady; the new cabinet member introductions; and the Kennedy Center gala in general.

How the hell is Curlander pulling this New Year's Eve gala off on such short notice? I guess it would be easier to give him something nonpolitical early on. The quid pro quo could be costly.

"Ten minutes or so and it should be ready," Dana shouted, as she tested the temperature from the waterspout.

"So, how does Curlander get everyone to his New Year's Eve party on such short notice?" Max asked.

"When a president-elect hasn't announced all his cabinet nominees, everyone comes. Don't worry about an empty room," Dana said as she put the leash on Linc. "I am going to take him for a short walk. Don't fall asleep, the water will overflow, we will both be living in the White House basement."

Max knew he was a lucky guy. He wasn't so sure about Sal.

Sal… Oh shit! That's where she's going!

Max called Sal and got his voice mail: "Yo, Sally here. Leave a message, and I'll be back at ya ASAP."

"Sal… It's Max! Dana's on her way down there as I speak. She knows everything. Get out of Dodge… Sorry!"

Max enjoyed being back in Georgetown, notwithstanding one functional eye, and it was all because of Dana. He did feel a slight tug to get back to New York. He felt he could make objective decisions up there. New Year's Eve in New York with Dana would have been nice, but he had nothing planned. He never thought about celebrating on New Year's Eve. He'd been in-country for three of them.

Holidays were a time for being well fed in the army. The troops always looked forward to, "the meal," on holidays.

When you work a kitchen, you relinquish holidays.

Max had looked forward to the holidays simply because the army provided him with the best food available. It was a time to shine and Max had always put on a great performance. He'd gotten a standing ovation at a Christmas dinner he prepared in Kabul. The C.O. made him come out and take a bow.

Did he really want to be executive chef to the president of the United States? It would be the most prestigious job in his field. No, he wasn't afraid of the position; it was his trepidations about how he might need to "handle" the president himself that caused concern. The thought of being a babysitter gnawed at him. Amy was already deferring to Max when Ed needed to be, "pulled up." He was no expert in the field of sobriety.

For God's sake, I was his drinking buddy. Max had his own issues with discipline, confirmed by the condition of his closed eye. Temper and lack of fear were Max's own crosses to bear.

How do all our wonderful qualities match up?

He thought about other presidents that had functioned as alcoholics in office. He remembered reading in General Sherman's memoirs that, upon being told that General Ulysses S. Grant was drinking too much, Abraham Lincoln said, "Let me know what he drinks, so I can order a case for each of my other generals!" Max loved that. It made him feel as if things could work out for Ed Curlander's presidency.

Max got up to check the tub. His timing was perfect. The water was high and hot. It felt good once he was able to slip all the way in. This tub was about half the size of his New York behemoth. It felt great nonetheless. The therapeutic salts seemed to extract the soreness from various parts of his aching body. Max rolled a towel to place behind his head. He slid his head under water to clear off some of the crud gathering around his eye. His head pounded from the sudden change in temperature—a small price to pay if it helped. He grabbed his shaving kit from the corner of the tub and took out the mirror he used for shaving on the road.

Sal's an artist.

The immediate application of ice had already reduced potential swelling considerably. He picked off some miscellaneous crap that made the eye look worse than it was.

I'm not made for this town! And what town are *you made for? Kabul?* he asked himself rhetorically.

As he put the mirror back, he grabbed the vial of M#4 from his shaving kit. *Why not?* he thought as he wet his pinky and took a taste of the unused portion. He slid back down in the tub.

Soon he was halfway between sleep and the netherworld. He was aware and yet beyond. There was no primary focus to his thoughts and no pain around his eye. He tried to dismiss the pounding as an amplification of the natural rhythm of his brain. With a concussive headache, there was usually pain and soreness with sudden movement.

This M#4 is better than those opioids I took after my I.E.D. explosion.

Max shook some into is mouth.

He began to drift. He saw an image of Eva dressed in a white burqa drifting through doorways, around the corners of a labyrinth… inaccessible and un-detained by his calling.

He saw Timoney dressed as a Latin American dictator, sporting a big hat and bedazzled uniform with sash and medals across his chest.

He saw Ghazi Haider dressed in a magnificent decorative robe. He had a black dot the size of a quarter on his forehead. There were rabbits playing all around him. Printed on his palm was one word: ***Honor.***

Len and Margaret appeared briefly. They were smiling and waving to him from the back of a train.

General Sherman appeared on his horse, Sam.

Max enjoyed how General Sherman described his horses in his memoir. The general had been particularly fond of Sam. Sam was a big horse in real life, and in Max's daydream, Sam was three times the size of a normal horse. Sam's eyes were wide with fire coming from his nostrils. The general reached down and pulled a young

Max Burns onto the back of his horse. They stood fast on a hill overlooking a burning city. The city was Atlanta.

General Sherman said to Max as he pointed, "This was not my idea. It was Mr. Lincoln's idea to burn the city. Mr. Lincoln said to me, 'You can always rebuild a city, Bill… a country may not be fixable. Sometimes you must do things for your country that you did not sign up to do. If burning a city saves one life, on either side in this most hideous of wars, I'd strike the match myself. Now go. Put an end to it all!'"

Max slid off the back of the horse and watched the general gallop toward the WashPa barn. Max's mom and dad were there to greet him and opened the barn doors to let him ride in. They waved goodbye to Max as they closed the doors behind them.

The front door of Dana's apartment slammed shut. Dana came walking into the bathroom. "How are you doing?" she asked.

"These salts are great."

"He wasn't there!" Dana said.

"Who?" Max asked, knowing full well Dana was on the hunt for Sal.

"Sal. I plan on killing him."

"Honey, this was not his fault. If he wasn't there, one of us might not have come out of that ring alive. You should thank him. He and I were both forced into it by some clown."

"You mean this clown?" Dana said as she displayed the cover of an issue of *Ring* magazine to Max. "I ran into my Zumba instructor, who informed me of the latest gym news… great timing."

The magazine was a year-end special issue on MMA. It had taken the magazine a long time to admit MMA as a permanent fixture in the fight game. Now it was the reason the magazine was still in business.

The full cover consisted of a close-up of Tito Montalban's face along with the caption "Can MMA heavyweight champ Bindi hold off Tito M. and retain the title? See page 12 for the tale of the tape."

Max knew that mug only too well.

He is one ugly sonuvabitch all right.

"Are you on your way to looking like this guy? Tell me now! Tell me right this minute. 'Cause I am… I mean you are… **out of here!** And out of my life, if you think I am going to be with this!" Dana said, poking Tito's face with her finger. Then she took the magazine over to Linc. Dana pointed to the cover again and shouted to the dog, "**You…** are better looking than he is!" Linc ran into the kitchen and hid under the table.

"Even your dog doesn't want to be with you. You'll need a steak in each pocket to get him to go for a walk." Dana sat down on the toilet bowl and began to cry. Max got out of the tub and wrapped a towel around his waist. She looked up at him and stopped crying. All at once he looked like a gladiator to her. His body was still pumped up. His hair was wet and not rid of the shine. His eye looked somewhat better. He put out his hand and walked her into the bedroom. There…the gladiator and the slave girl… made love.

CHAPTER 61

Max healed pretty well over the next five days. His eye was fully open. The eyeball was red where it should be white. Outside the eye socket was more yellow than blue. Other than that, his face looked almost normal. The more Dana got used to being with Max, the more she accepted who he was. He never complained about the pain or how he looked. His face was simply, a face that took a shot.

Max and Dana had a great week together being tourists.

Max insisted that they go to the Smithsonian Institute. While there, he recited tidbits of American history that fascinated Dana. The Civil War was his favorite subject. Volumes had been written about General William Tecumseh Sherman. There was a picture of Max's grandmother as a baby, in one of the display cabinets. The Lincoln exhibit held Max fast. He always thought of Abraham Lincoln as the greatest president in the nation's history. It was no accident Max had named his dog after him.

They walked all over the historic district four days in a row. They stopped at the White House on a clear afternoon. Max stared at it.

"I thought it was bigger."

"Everyone says that. It's big on the inside," Dana said, as she nudged him toward Ford's Theatre. Max found the scene of Abraham Lincoln's assassination discomforting. There was something surreal about it.

They walked across the street to the Petersen House, where Lincoln had passed away the next morning, Saturday, April 15, 1865, at 7:17 a.m.

"That's not the real bed. The real bed is in Chicago. The poor man had to lie diagonally because he was over six feet four inches tall," Max said. Secretary "Stanton had a cabinet meeting in that room back there. Early rumors were bandied about that cabinet members had taken part in the assassination conspiracy. John Wilkes Booth was engaged to a Northern senator's daughter at one point," Max said, rambling fact after fact of Lincoln trivia. Dana was amazed at the depth of his knowledge.

"Her name was Lucy Hale. She was the daughter of a New Hampshire senator, John Hale. It was a secret engagement. She broke it off. Booth's massive ego never let her forget it. Lucy Hale also dated Abraham Lincoln's son Robert Todd Lincoln for a time, prior to Booth. How's that for another little twist?" Max said as they walked out of the Petersen House. Max looked for the precise angle of the path that would have been taken from Ford's Theatre to the Petersen House. They walked in silence for a while. Dana held Max's arm and looked up at him from time to time. When he seemed deep in thought, Dana let him be. She had her own concerns with regard to the subject of presidential assassination.

Dana was tactful about not pushing Max toward a commitment to the White House staff appointment. She had her own issues. Without talking about it, Max understood Dana's trepidation with regard to her commitment as press secretary. It was not simply the magnitude of the position. No, it was Ed Curlander the person. Perhaps one of the reasons she never harped on Max to accept the White House offer was her own uneasiness with regard to Ed Curlander. Dana was in, and there would be no pulling out. If she didn't last long at the job for any reason, she was young enough to still write her own ticket.

While being on board, she knew that she would need some sage advice. She hoped Max would be the one to provide it… up-close. But she didn't push him.

CHAPTER 62

"It's a cummerbund," Dana said as she helped get Max dressed for the New Year's Eve gala. "Haven't you ever worn a tuxedo before?"

"The last time I wore one was for my senior prom in high school. I thought tuxedos only came in powder blue," Max said, only half joking.

"Powder blue, eh?" Dana said. "Did you wear white socks?"

"I don't remember. I did have a string tie."

"This one has a bow tie, my little prom king. Sit down in front of the mirror, and I'll tie it for you. I need to get dressed myself, you know," Dana said, in her bra and panties.

"Why? You look beautiful the way you are."

He turned around to hold her, but she interrupted him. **"No you don't… not now**. If you're a good boy and you don't punch anyone… maybe later."

"Will I ever hear the end of it?"

"Probably not!"

Dana got him squared away. She enjoyed every bit of taking care of her man. Max didn't mind either. Nobody ever spoiled Max Burns.

"There! You look very handsome. Your face is almost one color." She kissed him and went to the bedroom.

"Linc, mind the place. I am going to the Mad Hatter's ball,"

Max said as he scratched Linc. Linc was getting quite used to living in Georgetown.

"Will Cleary be at this shindig?" Max yelled through the door.

"I would think so. It's his detail. Why?"

"I wanted to check on our pistol permits. He put the papers in through the White House Police Force division of the Secret Service. That would give us peace officer status, not that you need a badge, but it could come in handy for armed interstate travel. You did send him your fingerprints, didn't you?" Max asked as he put a little vial of M#3 in his pocket. He didn't want to drink, but he wasn't going to be bored either.

"Yes, they scanned them from the Third Precinct, along with yours, on the twenty-seventh. Help me with this zipper, please," Dana said. She had on a beautiful black designer dress that clung to every curve. Those beautiful legs that Max loved were on full display. She was wearing the necklace Max had given her for Christmas. Dana looked better in person than on TV.

"How do I look?" she asked with a spin.

"You are the most beautiful woman in Washington," Max said and meant it.

"That's not saying much but thank you anyway. You look quite handsome yourself… in a Phantom of the Opera sort of way," Dana said as she kissed him gingerly to avoid a makeup disaster. They were early enough to get a cab.

The Kennedy Center was quite an edifice when dressed up. There were all kinds of rooms for every type of occasion. The festivities started out with cocktails and introductions in the concert hall: Ed Curlander and his First Lady, followed by Jeremy Tubbs and his wife, Chloe. A retired marine general who had been Ed's first appointment to the Joint Chiefs of Staff gave the introductions.

Friggin' marines.

Tubbs made a brief statement and thanked everyone for coming on such short notice. He said, "I was on short notice myself for the job." Everyone got a chuckle out of that.

Then it was Ed's turn to address the guests. "I want you all to have a wonderful time. This little soiree was paid for personally, by me and Vice President-Elect Jeremy Tubbs. No outside contributions were used. I want you all to know that. This is a thank-you to all of you from our families to yours for your support and friendship. Have fun. Serious business starts in three weeks." As they left the stage, the orchestra started playing "Hail to the Chief," which, by Washington protocol, was three weeks too early, but this was the Marine Corps band. It seemed everyone in America was anxious for these two gentlemen to start work.

Max guessed there were about 250 people in attendance, not a massive crowd as far as D.C. parties went. What was interesting to Max was the variety of guests: democrats, republicans, conservatives, liberals, protesters, #MeToo movement advocates, gun control advocates, this place and that place enthusiasts, and even Tea Party reps. It was an eclectic group. Festive traditional native garb appeared among the tuxes, with guests ranging from various African nations to indigenous Americans, from South Florida to the Alaska Peninsula, to rap artists.

Max asked Dana, "Where did Ed find this crew… central casting or lunchtime at the UN?"

"Each person here helped get Ed and Jeremy elected in some capacity, even some conservatives who had it with the stagnated government lent their support. They had the balls to support Ed, when their own parties blackballed them. There are some real Americans here, not the bankers and the oilmen who hide behind lobbyists. This is Ed's A-list and B-list. From within this coterie, you will find the future presidential cabinet members," Dana said while looking around.

There was military brass everywhere. That, was leather- ballsy. If you were stationed in D.C., you went where you were told to go. Nobody had been told to come here. They were all invited by their next commander in chief, US Marine colonel Edward Pierce Curlander, retired.

"That's another reason it took some time to announce this gala," Dana said. "Curlander and Tubbs were narrowing things down. Curlander, Tubbs, and Wiggins—wait till you meet Wiggins—wanted this to be a show of hands to publicly solidify support for their platform. They also wanted to look into the eyes of the men and women that had the guts to believe in them. If they show up tonight, they're all in play. It's Ed and Tubbs' job to separate the wheat from the chaff."

Max and Dana eventually found their way over to Ed and Amy's entourage. They all walked into the adjoining room for more cocktails and to meet and greet the Beltway mob.

Ed kissed Dana on the cheek. He hugged Max and whispered in his ear, "Let me know who you think are assholes."

"You look great in a tux, Max," Amy said.

"Thanks! They were all out of powder blue."

Max noted, the omnipresent Cleary was not far behind Ed. A waiter came by. Max took a glass of mineral water. Dana took a flute glass of champagne, as did Ed and Amy. The Curlanders made the rounds, as was protocol. Ed occasionally called Max and Dana over to introduce them to certain people. The last time Max had met a four-star general was when he'd graduated from Ranger School at Fort Benning. Tonight, he met two before dinner, along with an admiral and the commandant of the Marine Corps.

Off to the side, next to a two-story-high curtained window, Max noticed a solitary navy lieutenant commander observing the goings-on as though he had been forced to attend. He had the SEAL tridents and plenty of ribbons on his chest. He seemed uncomfortable. Max could relate. When Dana went to the powder room, Max went over to him and introduced himself.

"I know who you are," the SEAL said as they shook hands. He did not give Max his name. "You're Max Burns. We have a mutual friend, at least we used to." He said, looking around nervously.

Max was at a complete loss for words. Then he asked, "Who might that be?"

"Nick Nicholson. I worked with him. I was also his cornerman at the championship fight between you two. Best fight I ever saw. You scared us for a minute or two. By the looks of that left eye, you're still in the game."

Max chuckled. He noticed there was no name tag over the lieutenant commander's pocket. He was special ops to the bone.

"Thanks, Commander. He's the only man that ever beat me."

"He's a SEAL."

"Have you seen Nicholson lately?" Max asked, smiling inside at the comment. Max could tell this was no time for SEAL- Ranger banter.

"Not since he mustered out. I've been looking for him. I was with him in L.A. for a while, but he stopped taking my calls. Do you see or hear from him?" Before Max could answer, he handed Max a card with no name, only a phone number. "If you do, tell him Neptune needs to talk to him… before he leaves. He'll know who you're talking about."

"Copy that, commander. I plan on calling him within the next three weeks or so."

The commander looked hard at Max and asked, "You going?"

"No plans at this time."

"I need to talk to him… He's…he's in trouble. You get him to call me if you consider him a friend."

"Are you close to him?" Max asked.

"Abbottabad close."

Max heard Dana's voice. He turned toward her for a second.

"There you are," Dana said as she approached.

Max turned to introduce her to Neptune, but he was gone. Max looked around to no avail.

Spooks. Abbottabad close… I don't remember him at the Korengal dinner. Neptune… Neptune Spear! That was the name of the bin Laden operation. No wonder he's uncomfortable at this shindig. It's exactly what Nicholson was talking about... Corning, Nicholson, and Neptune, or whatever the hell his real name is... on the trophy soldier circuit.

Max excused himself and went to the men's room. He didn't take any M#3. He needed to stay sharp for now. Besides, Curlander was relying on his opinion of people.

These guests are not just the movers and shakers of America, but of the world. Dana thought.

Max got a kick out of Dana in action. She was very good. This was her baptism under fire, and both she and the president-elect knew it.

From time to time, Dana would tug on Max's arm to point out a movie star or some celebrity. Max couldn't care less. Dana liked the fact Max was not starstruck like most Beltway brown-noses.

Max is refreshing, in an outer space... alien sort of way.

Max and Dana moved from bureaucrat to politician to ambassador to soccer mom. Max spotted a couple dressed in northern Afghan ceremonial garb. They were off on their own as though they knew no one there. They were drinking water. Max surmised they were Muslim. The amount of alcohol being consumed might be making them uncomfortable. Max took Dana by the arm and walked her over to the couple. Max introduced himself and Dana in Dari. The couple was stunned. The gent introduced himself and his wife as Ahmed and Shana Karzai. The gent spoke in Dari for a few more sentences. When he realized Max could get well past an introduction stage in Dari, he noticed that Dana was completely lost. The gentleman changed to perfect English to include her. Max engaged the couple in conversation about his experience and admiration for the people of Afghanistan and the country itself. Max spoke about everything from the spices to the soil texture of various regions. Max felt obliged to mention Ahmad Shah Massoud, "Lion of Panjshir." They were both taken aback. No American had ever mentioned his name, not to mention a knowledge of his career as a freedom fighter with the C.I.A. against the Soviets. Max got up the nerve to ask Karzai if he knew a mullah known as Ghazi Haider. Max was curious as to the well-being of his friend. Max did not mention that he owed Haider his life, as did many other American soldiers, although no American other than Max knew it. Had Max cooked up a major dinner using the mushrooms of the Korengal, the entire camp would have been found dead in the mess hall. At this complicated stage of American withdrawal in Afghanistan, information like that could have negative consequences for Haider… and Max.

"Do you know this man you speak of?" Karzai asked Max.

"Yes. He is a friend."

"You should not say that too loudly around here, Mr. Burns. Ghazi Haider is not spoken of in good stead in America, much less at a presidential gala."

Max felt he was being tested. "Then he is misunderstood in this country. Is he alive and well?"

Max could see he was making the couple nervous by staying on this topic. Nevertheless, Karzai ventured an answer to Max. "I believe he is alive. And if Ghazi Haider is alive… then he is well. The man is a prophet… I am told," Karzai said, feeling that perhaps he had spoken too much about a person of interest in America.

"When you see him, please give him this for me. Tell him it is from his American friend Max, the American who knows he is… a man of honor." Max took off the ring that his father had given him on his sixteenth birthday. It was a family heirloom that had been originally handed down from General Sherman's widow, Max's maternal great-great-grandmother. "Tell him it belonged to a great general from our own American Civil War: General William Tecumseh Sherman, my great-great-grandfather. And also, if you would, tell him… I long for another walk in the Korengal and that I still pray for a time in the near future when Afghanistan will live in peace."

Dana stood there with her mouth open, staring first at Max,

then at the Karzais. The Karzais reacted the same as Dana. No one spoke a word for a few moments.

Then Ahmed said, "My brother will be meeting with him in the very near future. I will pass along your gift, your message, and your invocations, Mr. Burns."

"Is your brother Hamid Karzai, the former president of Afghanistan?" Max asked, putting the last name and the brother reference together.

"Yes, my brother is Hamid Karzai," Ahmed said.

Max said in Dari, "Then may Allah smile on the children of Afghanistan, and may the country be free of all invaders."

Ed and Amy were only steps away at this point. Max brought Ed and Amy over to meet the Karzais. Ed had been briefed on Hamid Karzai and knew his brother and sister-in-law would be attending. The Karzais were in D.C. to visit their embassy, Ed's assistants thought it prudent to invite them. Max got distracted by a phone call and excused himself for a moment. Ahmed and his wife were ecstatic to meet the Curlanders. They hadn't thought it possible with everyone vying for the attention of the president-elect and the future First Lady. But here was this young man, with a black eye and the beautiful press secretary, orchestrating the introduction with ease and aplomb. Nodding toward Max, Ahmed asked the president-elect, "Who is that young man?"

"Oh… I hope he's going to be my new chef."

"Your chef?" Karzai said quizzically.

"**If** he takes the job."

"**If** he takes the job?" Karzai said even more quizzically.

Max came back. Everyone stared at him, waiting for him to say something. Max thought the phone call needed an explanation, so he said, "My Tupperware is in." Max said with a satisfactory smile on his face.

Dana, having a little champagne buzz on, said, "**Really**? I am actually present for this scoop!"

"Tupperware?" Ahmed said, looking to his wife for an answer.

"Be careful using it in your microwave. Keep the tops unfastened," Shana said to Max, waving her finger at him. "They can explode if sealed!"

Max thanked her for the warning. The American contingent excused themselves and moved on. Max waved back at the Karzai couple. Ahmed held up the ring and waved.

"Why did you give a complete stranger a family heirloom?" Dana asked.

"It's on a journey. The person in Afghanistan that ring is intended for, must understand that Americans also hold honor in high regard."

Ahmed Karzai turned to his wife. "These Americans are very strange people… What is this … Tupperware he spoke of?" As they walked away, he examined the ring inscription: Wm. T. Sherman from A. Lincoln.

Next stop for Max and Dana was a little bald guy and his wife. He was one of those people who looked sloppy in everything. His tuxedo fit like he'd swam to the gala in it.

"Max Burns… Dana Trudeau, meet my chief of staff, Charlie Wiggins, and wife, Karen. Charlie has been with me since my New York days. He is the best at what he does and what he does is get things organized," Ed said.

"Pleased to meet you both. Dana, the sooner we sit and talk, the better," Wiggins said to Dana with a sense of urgency.

"Here's my card." Dana said.

"Call you tomorrow… I'll give you till noon to recover."

"Fine." Dana said, a little surprised at his abruptness.

Looking at Max, Wiggins asked, "And what about you? You on board or what?"

"I'll let you know very soon, Mr. Wiggins. Not tomorrow though."

"Make it quick! We're already late appointing staff and cabinet… If it's the pay you're holding out for - forget it. The number is the number." Wiggins said. He looked at Ed. "Call me tomorrow morning." Then Wiggins walked off with his wife in tow.

"He's a real charmer," Max said.

"Best in the business," Ed said.

Amy, smiling and waving at Karen, said, "he takes some getting used to. Ed is right, he's the best in the business."

"He oughta be the president," Ed said. "Are you guys having fun? Because you are not supposed to be having fun. Look upon yourselves as the human resources department - for the most powerful jobs on earth. I need you to keep a sharp eye out for good people and for assholes. Dana, you know the drill."

"I sure do. Assholes are easy to find. Got anybody in particular you want me to hone in on?"

"Anyone I introduce you to, is on a list for something. I am set on secretary of state, defense, interior, attorney general, and all the joint chiefs of staff. The rest… there's a short list. Keep your ears open," Ed said as he looked around, smiling and waving.

Max said to Dana, "I wouldn't know one from the other."

Dana said, "You know an asshole when you see one, don't you?"

Music began playing. It was a full orchestra that started with some classic Gershwin tunes.

Dana turned to Max. "I suppose you're too much of a tough guy to dance."

Max turned her around and, right on cue, dove into a waltz: perfect for the Gershwin rhapsody unfolding. Dana caught on quickly, as most women did. Once again, this big lug surprised her, this time with his dancing prowess. He was as light on his feet as anyone she had ever danced with before. When the tune ended, there was much attention being paid to the attractive couple.

"Where the hell did you learn to dance like that?" Dana asked as she straightened herself out.

"I had a boxing instructor in the army that made me take dance lessons. I also took ballet … and some Latin dance as well."

"Ballet?" Dana said with her eyes wide open.

"…More Latin really: *merengue*, *paso doble,* and some *Argentine tango*. Great for rhythm and foot work in the ring. All wonderful dances too… very sexy. Would you like me to request one?" Max asked as he started walking toward the orchestra.

"Me! Doing a tango!" Dana said as she grabbed him by the arm. "You're killing me, do you know that? We need to go on a long vacation together. I don't know anything about you. I feel like, like… Lois Lane, for God's sake! You come to Washington; you kick the crap out of some heavyweight caged gorilla; you give away an heirloom ring to a complete stranger… so he can give it to another stranger halfway around the world. Your dog is a national icon. You saved the president's ass in a fight…."

Max jumped in. "Ed told you about that?"

"No, Amy did. Don't interrupt. I'm on a roll!"

"How the hell did Amy find out about that?"

"When Ed got home that night he mumbled to Amy that you had knocked the crap out of a bunch of guys.

Please don't tell him I told you that. Amy would be in deep doo-doo." Dana kissed him on his good cheek and continued flashing her smile at the passersby.

"It was two." Max said.

"What was two?" Dana asked

"It was two guys… not a bunch of guys."

"I know it was two guys. I broke the story!"

Amy wandered over to Dana, off they went to the powder room again. Max had been looking for a break to call Nicholson and tell him about meeting Neptune.

Nicholson answered on the first ring. "Yo, my brother. How are ya? Made up your mind? I still got the spot."

"Not yet. Listen, I'm in D.C. at a presidential New Year's Eve party and…."

Nicholson interrupted Max. "Aren't **we** having fun!" he said. "Watch out, brother. You're in the tall weeds with the big dogs now."

"Yeah, right. I met someone who knows you. He has been trying to get in touch with you for a while. He calls himself Neptune. He's a…."

"I know who he is. Is he with you right now?"

"No! I wouldn't do that to you. He's been calling you. If you wanted to talk to him you would have called him back. I think he is in a bad way. I told him I'd ask you to call. Maybe I could find him again and…."

"No thanks, Max. He's going to try and talk me outta going back over. He thinks I am on a suicide mission. He wants me stateside in some fucking program he is connected with at Walter Reed. I've made up my mind. Don't get me wrong—he's a great guy and a helluva soldier. He was, feet on the ground, for us on Neptune Spears… without him, no OBL. Corning and I were his op leaders for the two ground teams. They still got him on the party circuit, I see. He's been on edge since Corning ate his gun. And now Neppy's worried about me. Love that bastard. There's a fuckin' SEAL! He was with Corning earlier on the night he blew his brains out under that fuckin' **Hollywood** sign… we both were. Huh, the last three guys alive to put holes in Osama bin Laden: me and Corning and Neptune."

And then there were two.

"He's afraid it'll be only him soon. Maybe he's right. Who the fuck knows? Who the fuck cares? I'll call him. Tell him I'll call him if you see him again. I got his number."

"Did I meet Neptune at the dinner?" Max asked.

"Nope…He was already in Abbottabad. "You still got the rendezvous point and ETD for the twentieth, right?"

"Roger that. It's a cab ride from my apartment."

"Show up, you army pussy! *Semper fi,* to the POTUS you brownnose motherfucker!" Max walked around hoping to spot Neptune.

This guy is a walking monument lost in a sea of bull shit.

Max finally spotted him across the room. Max gave him a thumbs-up with one hand and raised his cell phone with the other. Neptune got the message and smiled back. He banged a fist to his heart and then raised it toward Max. Neptune looked like he'd found his lost dog.

The champagne was beginning to work its magic on Dana. She wanted to dance with her hero. It was close to midnight. Max accommodated his beautiful princess to the dance floor. They danced fast and slow. It was actually a better evening than both had envisioned.

Midnight came along: balloons, confetti, horns, and, of course, "*Auld Lang Syne.*" Max and Dana kissed and paid little attention to anyone else for the next few minutes. This moment belonged to them.

Cleary came over and stuck an envelope in Max's inner pocket, saying, "Don't give this back with that rental tux… Happy New Year." He shook Max's hand. He turned to Dana and wished her a happy New Year as well. Dana gave him a big kiss and thanked him for a great year.

"I live to serve." Cleary smiled and went about his business.

Max took a quick look inside the envelope. In it were two federal carry permits for their pistols. Max tucked it away and said to Dana, "Don't let me forget this!"

Ed and Amy were making the rounds when Max and Dana caught up to them. They hugged and wished each other a happy New Year. Ed asked Max, "How long are you in town for?"

"I am heading back day after tomorrow," Max said.

"I'll have the chopper ready at Langley at zero nine hundred hours on the second," Ed said.

"Roger that, colonel. Thank you both for everything."

"I expect to hear a definitive answer from you by the inauguration on the twentieth. That's it! Yes or no. Got it?" Curlander said as he tapped Max gently on his still-tender cheek.

"I'll see you on or before January 20. We're going to head home now, unless you need us for something. Do I need a suit for the inauguration?" Max asked.

"Wear your uniform again. Anybody gives you shit about it, let me know. When they take pictures, you'll be able to tell your grandchildren you were the army guy kept safe by all those marines you'll be sitting with. I got everyone left that's alive from my unit coming in uniform… active duty or not," Curlander said.

Max and Dana went out the front door and walked to get a taxi before the limos started blocking the Kennedy Center access point. Max and Dana scurried off into the night.

"That was better than I expected," Dana said as she snuggled up to Max in the cab.

"I enjoyed it too! I haven't danced like that since my training days."

"Good thing the orchestra didn't play *The Nutcracker*," Dana said.

They were home in ten minutes. They threw on some sweats and took Linc for a walk around Georgetown. The weather was perfect for a walk. The streets were starting to fill up with the post–New Year's celebrants heading to their next stop. The horns and poppers were a little too much for Linc. All three were happy to get home. Max put on Dana's gas fireplace and snuggled on the couch. Max poured them both a glass of white wine. They made love on the couch, then spooned until the fire put them to sleep.

Max got up early to walk and feed Linc. When he got back to the apartment, Dana was in her running gear watching CNN. Dana knew CNN would have a more comprehensive domestic year-end summary than diluted international version by the BBC. They were scrolling a list of President-elect Curlander's cabinet appointments and nominees. Evidently Wiggins had pushed for the release. Max walked over and gave Dana a kiss on the cheek and watched along with her. She wrote down as many names as she could as they scrolled by.

"What do you think?" Max asked.

"Up to the Senate. These appointments are interim positions at this juncture. They sit in their appointed positions until they go before the Senate for approval. We'll see what kind of a reception Ed receives by his appointments that get approved. Now it gets political.

There are names here I've never heard of before. He sure dug deep. I'm proud of him for that. It doesn't look like any cushy jobs for retiring bank CEOs. Here's your man, John Timoney. He should raise some eyebrows. Usually an ex-C.I.A. or FBI insider gets DHS. Curlander finished the list. I wonder how many got finalized last night. He named advisers too. Staff is next!" Dana said. She was as nervous as Max had ever seen her.

"Look! There it is. And they spelled my name right," Dana said as she jumped up and down, pulling on Max. Linc started barking. She was babbling and crying at the same time. Max hugged her and told her, how proud he was.

Max said, "I don't recognize any of these people."

"Neither do I. It all depends on how good of a job they do," Dana said after calming down somewhat. "I need to call my parents."

After ten minutes of crying and laughter on the phone with her parents, Dana said, "How 'bout a run?"

"Sure. Let me get into my gear. You and I solo. Linc had his exercise," Max said.

The running path in the park was busy for New Year's Day. As they stretched, people walked or jogged by and congratulated Dana on her appointment. She thanked them and gave a sincere smile to all. She even signed some autographs for a few children.

"So… back to New York tomorrow, eh?" Dana said as they jogged.

"Yeah. And back to work for you or is that over with?"

"Oh, there'll be some hoopla back at the station. This is a big feather in their cap as well. I expect they'll milk it and try to keep me until the inauguration. It's really up to Wiggins," Dana said with trepidation.

"You'll be fine."

Then Dana said without looking over to him, "I hope you won't be too far away if I need you."

Max stopped and grabbed her arm, turning her around into his arms. He kissed her passionately on the lips and told her he loved her. He let her go and started jogging again. Dana caught up to him.

"I love you too," she said. "So… what the hell did that mean?"

"First of all, thank you for not beating me over the head about the White House situation. You have made my choices easier. I want to be near you. I don't intend to let you get away from me." Max had said more than he was prepared to say at this point. He couldn't help himself.

"**Choices?** What choices, if I may finally ask? The president of the United States has asked you to be on his staff. Do you think this is all about baking cookies for his milk? **He needs help**. He needs people he can trust that will help him make decisions for the country."

"Do you think I don't know that?"

"What other choices, Max? Please tell me. I feel the same way about you. I don't want to lose you either," Dana said as a few tears started to formulate.

"I have five options. In no order of importance they are: I could accept the chef position at the White House; take over the Scirocco; contract work in Afghanistan; be Linc's manager and do some advertising promotions; get into the MMA." Max said as they jogged.

"MMA?"

"Mixed martial arts. If that guy Tito is the number one contender and I was able to beat him, I can make money at it. It's an option, that's all," Max said as he continued running.

Dana stopped dead in her tracks. "Are you kidding me? Those are the options that've been milling around in your head?" Dana asked with her hands on her hips, watching Max jog ahead. Unbeknownst to Max, Dana then turned around and started jogging the other way. He was so occupied with his own agenda he did not realize Dana was no longer within earshot.

Damn it! I knew I should have left this morning.

Max was not sure what to do. He was no expert in the feelings and reactions of women.

She wanted to know what's going through my head. They're options, that's all. One more day and I fumble the ball on the one-yard line.

Max turned around and jogged back at a slow pace. He wasn't sure he wanted to catch Dana. He needed to think. He had always been a loner. Now he realized he toyed with being alone forever. For a man who enjoyed danger, he sure wasn't crazy about the terrible position he'd put his relationship into.

I have to let her know these are mere options. She is my top priority. No… that's no good. What a moron. I hate when my head spins like this.

He jogged back to the apartment. Dana was not there. Once again, only Linc was there to greet him. He was crushed and confused. He needed to explain. He looked on the kitchen table. His bag was packed with a note attached:

Dear Max,

I love you very much, but I have a life too. I hoped and prayed you would be a big part of that life. I guess I presumed too much. Good luck with your "options." Be safe, no matter what road you take.

Love, Dana
PS- You had it all!

"Jesus! I did it this time. C'mon, Lincoln."

Max Burns… Alone again.

He was sick at the thought of losing Dana. He had lost Eva tragically. This time there could be no doubt this was entirely his doing.

His phone rang. It was Amy Curlander.

"Max… it's Amy. Get over here immediately! Bring your bags. You can stay with us tonight."

"Thanks, Amy, but…."

Amy interrupted him. "No buts about it! Get over here now, you spoiled brat. We're a little busy ourselves, as you may have surmised," she said sarcastically before hanging up.

"Linc, what now? Another successful fuckup. We have to go and talk to Amy. Let's go take our - my - medicine. I need Amy to know how I feel. C'mon."

When they got to the Curlanders', there were reporters in front of the town house. Cleary was trying to keep them at bay with the help of another Secret Service agent and three uniformed White House cops. Cleary saw Max and waved him through. Nobody paid attention to Linc. There were serious matters and questions about the cabinet and staff picks to be discussed. The cute doggy picture days were over for the time being.

Max got a look from Cleary that seemed to say, *You did it this time, big fella.*

Curlander was on two phones at once.

Amy came down the stairs and said, "Library - two minutes!" Max walked into the library with Linc and waited at the bar for her. Amy pushed open the sliding doors. She hesitated for a moment before entering. Max was nervous. He never knew how to react when a woman was upset. He would rather be toe-to-toe with a heavyweight in a cage than have Amy pick him apart.

The tone had changed in everyone's demeanor from Cleary to Ed Curlander and beyond. Big things were in motion. Max knew there was no room for minutia and felt embarrassed as well as nervous.

This guy is going to be inaugurated as POTUS in three weeks, and I'm here with my doggy and girlfriend problems.

Amy closed the doors behind her. "How are you? Never mind. I don't care. Look, I want you to know something that may not have sunk into that thick head of yours: Ed and I think the world of you. We want you to come along with us for a ride into history. You have fought this opportunity, for what we feel, are very selfish reasons. And now your **reasons/options** have surfaced. Everyone is entitled to their own life… and choices. You, young man, have been thrust into the spotlight. You know what Winston Churchill said: 'Some are born to greatness, some achieve greatness, and some have greatness thrust upon them.'"

"Shakespeare," Max said.

"What?" Amy said.

"William Shakespeare wrote that in…."

Amy interrupted. "I don't give a damn who said it then… I'm saying it *now*! And you are right there in the biggest spotlight in the world. Do you think this job is about slinging hash for the First Family? **He needs you!** This country needs you! I need you! Dana needs you! What the hell is wrong with you?"

Amy strutted back and forth with her hands on her hips. She was frustrated. Max had never seen her like this before. She was upset, logical and functional.

"You have it all in the palm of your hand. But evidently you'd rather get shot or have your brains beaten to a bloody pulp or run another restaurant and get fat on strudel. You pain in the ass. I could strangle you. You are a spoiled brat!"

"Amy, I love Dana. I love you and Ed too… and I love my country. I… I'm afraid, Amy."

"We're all afraid! You think that man in the other room isn't afraid? You think I'm not afraid? Dana… poor Dana, you threw her a curveball right before her big day on national television. This is the biggest thing that can happen to a reporter—bigger than the Pulitzer! And she is out there somewhere crying like a baby right now. What are you thinking about, you selfish bastard?"

"I'm no babysitter, Amy. Ed's got a drinking problem and…." Amy turned slowly and walked up into Max's face. "I know he has a drinking problem. Anybody who really knows him, knows he has a drinking problem. Pretty soon, if we don't keep an eye on him, the whole goddamn world will know he has a drinking problem. He knows it too! Why do you think he's attempted to slow down his drinking? I told him he would be the first president divorced in the White House if he didn't get his ass into some kind of program. He is seeing counselors and trying to do a twelve-step program on his own. **Afraid?** Nobody is more afraid than that marine in the next room.

"Now let me tell you something else. I'm not sure how you put things to Dana... It's none of my goddamn business, except that I love you both and I think you love each other. When you two are together, nobody else exists. My heart sings when I see you two holding hands and giggling like teenagers. Do you think that happens often? Just because you're young, do you think that there is love around every corner? You're so lucky. Do you realize how lucky you are to have found two wonderful women like Eva and now Dana? Because if you don't, then you are a full-fledged idiot, and we're all wrong about you. Ed and I never had children, and by God, **we don't want any now**."

Amy took a deep breath and paced back and forth with her arms folded. Max saw clearly what a great First Lady she'd be. Max gave her a second to regroup from her comment about children. He needed a moment to digest it as well. Amy paced while Max thought.

Then Max asked, "What do I do now?"

Amy said, "I don't know! She is halfway between being brokenhearted and trying to figure out how to load the gun Ed gave her... to shoot YOU! Do you know she has more men after her than a Hollywood starlet? She gets embarrassed about it."

"I know... I love that trait in her. I saw it right away. Eva had that quality too..." Max said.

"**Eva is gone!**"

That producer guy, Wetherford, has been trying to get into Dana's pants for two years—offering her national network desks, anchor positions, everything else under the sun. She has a full-time job keeping him at arm's length, along with a dozen other heavyweights. And I don't mean MMA buffoons! You better wake up and smell the flowers.

"Oh yeah… one more item - you want to help your country? You won't be doing it over in Afghanistan with a bunch of drunken mercenaries banging whores and throwing dollars at goat herders. **You belong here! Right here!**

"If you lose that girl, you will be the saddest man on this earth. That, my friend, is a fact." Amy took a breather. Then she jumped right back into it.

"I loved Eva. I know you did too. But I see something different when I'm with you and Dana. It's big, and it's beautiful. I had that once." She turned away from Max in order to hide the tears that began to well up.

"Amy, I am in. Tell Ed. I will be back for the inauguration. What do I do about Dana? God, I hope I didn't blow it completely… They were just … options!"

"**Screw your goddamn options! You basically told Dana that she was an option!"**

"I'm not good at this stuff, Amy. I'm not! I don't want to lose her. I usually go with my gut, not my head… here I am in trouble again. I practically dragged Eva to New York City with me. It was my dream. It was my idea. She came because of me, and look what happened."

"It can't be all about you, Max, not with the gifts and talent you have. You were put here for more important reasons than being Max Burns, the hash slinger!"

"Can you talk to Dana? I'll be back for the inauguration… I won't let these other… things tug at me anymore. Should I see her before I go? Should I…."

Amy interrupted him again. "Get on that helicopter tomorrow and get your things in order up in New York. That will at least show some stability. I'm not sure what Dana's head is like right now. She called me hysterically crying, and I couldn't understand her very well. Give her some time to pull herself together. Wetherford has set up a syndicated interview tomorrow night for the six o'clock national news. They will be asking her questions regarding the cabinet and the staff. Wiggins will be prepping her beforehand on: Where she can and can't tread; what questions she needs to dance around, etcetera... She will be making her own decisions on the fly very soon, but for now she belongs to Charlie Wiggins. This is no time to continue this sophomoric teenage bullshit. This is the big time, sonny boy!"

Max had never seen Amy quite like this. She'd gotten an answer out of him.

She's quite a woman... and I'm quite a moron.

"How about flowers?" Max asked. "Should I send some flowers?"

"**You are such an asshole!** You are WAY past the flower stage. Any man that would tell a woman: They are not sure whether they would rather get killed in Afghanistan, fight in a boxing ring, or sling hash in some rundown restaurant than be with her—not to mention disregarding the oath you took in the army to support the president of the United States—is lightyears past the roses-and-chocolates stage." Amy said as she shook her head in disbelief. "You know where your room is. Stow your gear or whatever you macho bastards call putting your crap away is called. Cleary is here all night. He'll let you in and out and get you to Langley in the morning. I suggest you take a good long walk for yourself. Now get the hell out of here. I have work to do. And stay away from Ed, he is up to his ass in alligators and knows nothing about this silliness. Dinner at six. We are probably ordering out. You like Thai food?" Amy asked.

"Funny you should ask. Yes," Max said.

"Six o'clock! **Sharp**."

Max left the house from the side door with Linc. He didn't know where to go, but he needed to go someplace people wouldn't bother him. He needed to think.

I'm a spoiled bastard. I spoiled myself. I guess because I'm alone, I never had to consider anyone else in my decisions. When two people are together, that can't be the case. I should have realized that with Eva.

Her death should have made me realize, that being with someone you love is a two-way street. Eva shared ***my*** *dream. I never asked… if she had dreams of her own.*

Dana has her own dreams. Me? I need to run parallel for once… run alongside, not in front. Sorry… to both of you.

He walked aimlessly as his mind weaved half thoughts. He talked aloud to himself at times.

They think I'm on the phone.

Max didn't know whether people were looking at him because of his babbling or because they recognized Linc. Max was getting sick to his stomach. He stopped for some yogurt to quell the uneasiness in his stomach. A few pictures of Linc and a cup of yogurt later, his stomach settled. There was a part of him that couldn't wait to get back to New York. He could hide in New York. He wanted to sit in his rocker and stew like a vegetable.

If he had blown it with Dana, he would never forgive himself. He knew Tim Wetherford was trying to slither his way into Dana's life.

I didn't like that guy from the start. I should have recognized the pressure everyone is under—Dana, Amy, and Ed… ***Ed.*** *I thought I had things to work on. Ed has internal* ***and*** *external dragons to slay.*

Max thought about Amy.

Was she always this strong?

He thought about all she had said to him back at the house. She was right on the button.

She had me pegged.

He tried to look at himself from the outside. That was difficult because he'd never cared what anyone thought about him. He thought he handled himself honorably - albeit by his modified standards.

But no one had ever been as close to him as this crew… except in-country. It was all new to him.

What did I do, baby?

He realized it was Dana he was invoking for help, not Eva.

Already he was asking advice from Dana, as though she were standing in front of him.

Dana, don't give up on me.

He walked toward the park where they had run a few hours prior. He sat on a park bench and surveyed all his surroundings: Statues; monuments; memorials; all built to recognize men less selfish than he. He was amidst an unselfish world, one different than he had ever known.

He'd told Amy he was joining the team.

Can I jump back into the service of my country? The mushrooms... let's not forget the mushrooms... curse...blessing...both?

Max could not sit still. He inadvertently walked by the gym. Sal saw him and came out to greet him.

"Hey, Max." Sal said.

"Hello, Sal." Max was glad Sal hadn't seen him talking to himself like so many fighters that stayed in the game too long.

"Whoa... why the long face? I'd say you lost your dog, but he's right here." Sal said, smiling as he rubbed Linc behind his ears. "Your eye healed pretty good. Stitches out, I see. Dana's not with you, I hope." Sal looked both ways. "She sure gave me a ration of shit on the phone. Man, that gal is nuts about you, my friend. If I were you — don't get me wrong I'd manage you any day— don't lose that woman over the fight game. Not worth it." Sal said. "A woman like that is one of a kind... once in a lifetime."

Max was getting sick to his stomach again. "Yeah, I know," Max said. "Thanks, Sal. How is Tito's ego treating him?"

"Not too good. He's denying it ever happened and threatening everyone who was there. He oughta run for president, haha. He's not having too much success. He's an asshole anyway. You gave him what he deserved. There were enough people around that won't let your legend die. The beat reporters keep snooping around looking for a story. I don't need the aggravation, but gym membership is up 40%. You could come out of the woodwork and fight Tito in a grudge match and make yourself a bundle… with me as your manager of course.

Sounds great! YOU tell Dana your plan, okay?

"Not me! It should fizzle out in a few decades."

Then Sal asked about a picture. "Linc only, Sally. That's all we need… my face in your gym window." Max took their picture. He and Sal shook hands and wished each other luck. Max kept walking on his journey to nowhere. He went back to the park and sat on the same bench. He thought about how wonderful the past week with Dana had been.

About ten minutes or so went by. Linc stood up with his tail wagging. He was staring behind the bench. Max looked at Linc, then looked behind the bench. It was Dana, still in her running gear. She looked at Max. Max got up and slowly walked over to her, not knowing what to expect.

"I am so sorry!" he said to her. "I love you so much … I …."

"Shut up and kiss me," Dana said as she ran into his arms. "I'm sorry too. I didn't mean to push you. I promised myself I wouldn't push you."

Max interrupted her. "Listen to me. Whatever went on today was a good thing. It brought clarity. I love you, and I want to be with you. Sometimes things swirl around in my head. It's… it's complicated. The folks at Walter Reed they said things might get complicated at times."

Dana kissed him and said, "Come home."

Max held her in his arms so tightly, she couldn't breathe for a second. There were many things that needed to be discussed, not the least of which was how to handle what lay ahead. They were two strong-willed people that needed to figure out when, where and how to bend in order to make things work. The important thing - they both knew the future together was worthwhile. They held hands tightly and found themselves running, stopping, kissing, running again, laughing. The child in both of them returned. Back at the apartment, they left a trail of running gear from the front door to the bedroom. They couldn't stop kissing. They made love on top of the covers, then under the covers.

They held each other as though they would never see each other again. Max looked her in the eyes and asked, "Do you like Thai food?"

She laughed and said, "All depends on who orders it."

"How about for me, my dog, the POTUS, and his First Lady? I better call Amy and tell her you're coming."

"No need. I already talked to Amy after you left. Did you think I was going to take a chance on a handwritten note?"

"I'm such a rookie." Max said.

"Good! I don't need any players in my life."

They kissed and held each other. This would be their last day together for a while… they made love again in the shower—until the hot water ran out, of course.

Cleary let Max and Dana in the front door as usual and said, "You're not cooking tonight, Max?"

"Sorry. Presidential edict."

"Nice to see you… *both*."

Nothing got by Cleary. They smiled and walked in to find Amy, Ed, and Charlie Wiggins. Wiggins was leaving. As he walked past them on his way out, he told Max, "Welcome aboard." He said to Dana, "I'll meet you here at eight tomorrow morning." There was no getting out of a Wiggins mandate. Max would get picked up by one of Cleary's details at zero seven hundred hours at Dana's.

Amy was in First Lady mode as she hugged Dana, then Max. She looked Max right in the eye and winked at him.

He kissed her on the cheek and said, "Thank you."

Ed looked over at the both of them from the phone and waved with his hands to sit down. A young Secret Service agent brought the food in from the front door - delivered under Cleary's name. Max asked if he would be the *beefeater* for the president and First Lady. He had to explain what exactly a *beefeater* was: In the 1600s the monarchs of England had beefeaters test their meat, as oftentimes meat would be rancid due to the lack of refrigeration. It had also been a test for poison. It was the job of the *beefeater* to test all the food prepared for the king and queen.

Then a strange thought popped into Max's head.

Good thing Little Louie didn't have a beefeater.

It had been a long time since Max's thoughts had veered off in that direction.

***That** was random.*

He dismissed the thoughts from the streets of New York and came back to the president's dining room.

Ed finished his phone calls and looked over at Max and Dana. He was not privy to anything that had gone on between them, he was simply pleased they both had new jobs.

"Max, I am thrilled to have you with us. Amy told me earlier. I won't ask what convinced you. Dana, you know how happy I am about you being with us as well. You'll both do great jobs, no doubt. Understand, this is going to be on-the-job training for all of us. That's why we have Wiggins. I've spoken at great length with John Timoney. He's a good fit… Good call Max. Wiggins agrees. They're alike in many ways, those two. Wiggins is tough, but fair. Every once in a while I'll need to slap him around… and vice versa… for the most part he is usually right. He has been a sounding board for four presidents. I bet you guys never heard of him, have you? They all sweared by him, at him and about him. I had to beg him to come out of retirement. He helped me win my New York state senate seat and only agreed to come on board this trip, when I told him I was thinking about an independent third party. He thought the timing was perfect. By God… right again! This country owes him big time and nobody even knows who he is. That's the way he likes it too. A real American, that man." Ed took a deep breath and raised a glass of water. "So, here we are, the nucleus of our team!" Curlander said.

Amy cut him short. "I googled Wiggins: Bush 47 loved him, Reagan almost had a fistfight with him, George W. Bush didn't know what he was talking about and Clinton also said, 'He's the one that oughta be president!'"

"Good job, Madam First Lady. You need to pay attention, Dana, and listen carefully to what he says. There is no small talk with him. Take good notes. That's what I do," Ed said. "Max, the chopper will be ready at zero nine hundred hours. Great having you down here… like the old days, eh? I'll have the chopper back up there for you on the morning of January 20 for the inauguration… zero eight hundred hours… same place."

"You don't have to do that, Ed," Max said.

"Yes I do! I want the dog at the inauguration—invitation and all. That means no hang-ups with Amtrak or any bullshit with airlines. Be at the heliport early and prepare for takeoff at zero eight hundred hours." After a break in his mandates, Ed asked, "So…how was everybody's day today?"

Everyone laughed, and Max said, "You don't want to know, chief."

Ed looked at Amy, who said with a smile, "Eat your Thai food before it gets cold."

Ed looked over at Max. "Ever see any of those Muay Thai matches in Thailand, Max?"

Amy looked up and said, "Can we talk about something else, please?"

The three of them chuckled again as the president-elect remained oblivious.

"What the hell am I missing here? Fill me in… I'm the goddamn president of the United States!" Ed said as a dumpling dropped from between his chopsticks onto his pants.

"You have enough on your plate," Amy said, and they all laughed.

"Women!" Ed said.

Both ladies smiled their victory smile — a smile that said, *Fini.*

Max thought, *Amy is unerringly devoted to her husband becoming a great president… Nothing will get done without her imprimatur… a great First Lady. Can he be a great president?*

CHAPTER 63

On the walk home Dana asked Max what his plans were for the next three weeks. Max was glad that Dana felt comfortable enough to ask. It seemed to quell any tension that might have lingered.

"I think I might go to Florida to visit Len and Margaret. Len seems pretty sick, and Margaret is probably having a rough go of it. Those two have been together for fifty-something years. Len has that damn Alzheimer's disease now. He didn't even know me on the phone. He rambles. I think it's more advanced than Margaret is letting on."

"I remember them from the Scirocco. They were… are… adorable. Please keep me posted on things. Let me know if I can help. I'm going to miss you, soldier boy."

"I'll miss you too. You'll be busy as hell. We'll call and text each other. You're the one whose schedule will be chaotic. Don't worry about getting back to me right away if you are crazed. If I go down to Florida, I'll stop here on the way back."

Max then said, "Let me ask you something pretty dumb. Do I live at the White House? How the hell does that work? I don't think I want to be going in and out of the White House at all hours of the morning."

"They have quarters for certain staff members that are needed 24-7. I guess that means you. You'll be cooking for the Curlanders on a daily basis unless they let you off the hook. You will also be on call for state dinners and other functions. A senior staff member coordinates dates, special needs, suggested menu, all that, but the rest will be entirely up to Ed, Amy, and you. I would think, when the Curlanders are in residence, you might be staying there… I'm not sure… I'll check with Amy. They have suites and storage rooms for staff. Lots of history in those rooms too. I hope you will be staying with me when you don't have to be there." That was the invitation Max was looking for.

He kissed her gently and said, "Maybe you could come live with me in the White House? We could play Jack and Marilyn."

"The Lincoln bedroom will definitely be on our to-do list," Dana said.

It was about eight in the evening when they got to Dana's. They were both feeling flat about the almost perfect week coming to an end. Neither brought it up. They crawled into bed, more contemplative than enthusiastic. Max felt this was a good opportunity to talk about the future. Dana would have liked to talk about the past, specifically about the, "folks at Walter Reed" comment Max had made. She decided against it.

Bad timing.

Dana had also researched all she could about Max's amazing family history. Dana was from Pennsylvania, but she'd never heard anything about the Burns family, good or bad. No doubt they treasured their anonymity.

Fair enough. I couldn't be with a braggart.

Max's military mode of thinking kicked into high gear. *Logistics.* He said, "If they do have a place for me to stay in the White House and I'll be spending time here with you as well, wouldn't it be great if we had a place somewhere in the countryside? You know… a get away. I'm talking about a real fireplace, garden, backyard… a country place. We're both going to be frazzled. You will need to get away more than I… and I know I will. I'm not sure what I signed on for, but you will be swamped."

"It's going to be pretty intense. I can't remember a press secretary ever being unavailable because of something like a vacation… I know in the beginning it will be very consuming. Wiggins will be a stern taskmaster, and I am sure Curlander will be just as difficult in his own way. I don't know what I am in for either. Time will tell. A country getaway does sound great—that is, if we get to use it. Not a good time to be asking Wiggins about vacations, long weekends, and retreats to the countryside."

Max lay there projecting the future. "Be great if doable. I could grow my own herbs and spices. I'd love a place to do that down here. Maybe a small farm in Virginia somewhere."

"Where do you do that now?"

"In the basement of my apartment building." This was a conversation he did not want to delve into.

"In the basement?" Dana said.

"Yeah, a few exotic mushrooms in the dank areas of a storeroom… an urban garden thing. I like unusual ingredients."

"If you're looking for dark and humid, the bowels of the White House is the place for that. It's built on swampland. I did a documentary on the White House Christmas fire of 1929. It's like the catacombs down there. There are wine cellars, laboratories, bunkers, storage for food, a shooting range, bowling alleys… God knows what else. I think Eisenhower had bunkers put in. Grant probably had the wine cellar installed. Some people say it's haunted. Maybe you can grow your mushrooms right on the premises. You could can them and start a business. 'Made in the White House by Ghosts.'"

"Good thinking, farmer Dana," Max said, stroking her hair and thinking about the irony of hallucinogenic mushrooms being grown in the basement of the White House.

Maybe I could use JFK's rocking chair to mind the children.

Dana fell asleep on his chest listening to his heartbeat. She counted forty-six beats a minute before dozing off.

Max began prioritizing things with Len and Margaret at the top of the heap. They hadn't abandoned him after the Scirocco had been sold. He would never abandon them. He loved them as though they were his parents. He felt helpless. There was something in the back of his mind that bothered him. Did Len and Margaret not want to see him because of what had happened to Eva? It nagged at him. He would always remember them saying, "You take care of our (your) Eva."

Max needed to call Tom Ryder, the New York City cabdriver with the moving van. He would ask Ryder about moving his belongings to D.C.

If I need to put things in storage, I will. Then there are the mushrooms.

He would buy a vehicle eventually, one with four-wheel drive, when he got settled down here. He wondered where Timoney would live. Timoney had connections through the F.O.P., the Fraternal Order of Police.

Max imagined what living in the White House would be like.

There will be identification checks at every turn. Suppose I am out and about having a few drinks till three in the morning—what would it be like coming home, answering to the president? If Dana kicks my ass out at four in the morning in my pajamas, could I walk up to the White House cops at the gate and get my bloodshot retina scanned for ID?

He took off the wristwatch Dana had given him and set the alarm. He found it ironic that she'd bought him a watch with a pitch-black face that reminded him of a mushroom center. **"You have the watches; we have the time,"** Ghazi Haider had said to him. Sometimes he would stare at the watch until his eyes began to close. He didn't wake Dana. He would make love to her in the morning… at dawn.

The alarm rang at five in the morning. Dana was on Max's chest. She stirred and then snuggled tighter. She knew Max had to leave first. She touched him gently all over. She had made up her mind to show him he would never need any other woman. They made love as though they were going to the electric chair. It was a goodbye she wanted him to think about as soon as she was out of sight. He got up and showered. His bag was still conveniently packed from the day before. He put on his uniform.

He held Linc up to Dana for a goodbye scratch behind the ears and a kiss on his ugly mug. Then Max knelt on the floor next to her in bed. "Don't get up. Don't get out of bed." He held her hand and said, "Nobody will ever love you like I do." He kissed her gently on the lips. A tear rolled down her cheek. He drank it up before gravity took it. He blew her another kiss before closing the door. Off he went, feeling good that he had patched things up and bad that it was time to leave.

A Secret Service agent was waiting for him at the front door. He was a young black man who had drawn the short straw for the early-morning detail. He didn't seem to mind. He introduced himself and smiled when he saw Linc. He seemed to be thinking:

Now this is something to write home about: Lincoln Burns in my vehicle.

Max took the obligatory picture of Linc and the Secret Service agent, successfully hiding the apartment building. Then to Langley. The crew was the same bunch. Max guessed it was a permanent detail on Marine One. He was sure they were probably wondering who the hell he was at this point. They were more relaxed this time, knowing they didn't need to follow strict protocol with the likes of Max and their Marine One mascot; Lincoln Burns. The framed crew picture with Linc, taken on the initial trip, was posted proudly inside the cabin. "We got permission to keep the photo on the bulkhead wall… straight from number 1." Del Negra said proudly.

They were back in New York City in exactly forty-seven minutes, headwind notwithstanding. After a cab ride home, it was as though Max and Linc never left Manhattan.

Linc was more excited to be home than Max. Max's feelings about the past days in D.C. reinforced his resolve for a change of venue.

At least the weather will be better in D.C.

It was twenty-six degrees in New York, the wind brought the temperature into the teens. As the wind funneled through a side street, it reminded Max of a winter's day in Afghanistan. His mind drifted as the wind stung his face and made his eyes water.

Killing was seasonal in Afghanistan. In Max's experience, the bitter cold of winter had brought a welcome time-out to the fighting. Nick and his band of merry men would be getting there in the middle of winter but there would be no seasonal timeout for these hunters. Nick would be hell-bent on teaching some lessons asap to establish a **fear factor**. Max wondered what Nick's official assignment was, not that it mattered. His assignment was merely a kill permit… a ticket to ride.

Nick would be seeking out whoever had shot down the remaining members of his SEAL Team Six comrades. He already had a list of "*likelies*." Nick knew bragging would be going on among the enemy for such a huge accomplishment. A sack full of cash would help loosen tongues. There was no doubt in Max's mind: Nick would find out who was responsible for the ambush, right down to who pulled the RPG trigger. It would be ugly.

Max's decision to work for Curlander gave him solace; he was also optimistic about a future with Dana. Max was content. He'd committed to a plan. He felt secure.

Max and Linc went upstairs after a quick walk. There it was. The apartment looked small in comparison to Dana's place. It was definitely a New York City apartment. These prewar buildings had advantages: endless hot water, heat in the winter, cross-ventilation in summer, the best tap water in America, walls of plaster and wood laths to muffle sound. They were fortresses. You could scream, and nobody would hear you. The downside? Space cost money in NYC. Max's apartment was roughly one-quarter the size of Dana's.

You better love New York if you're going live in New York.

There wasn't much daylight pouring through the standardized windows that adorned these buildings. Max could feel himself mentally moving out. The process was in motion.

Max went down to the basement for a workout and to check on the mushrooms. There were a few good-size mushrooms. Max hung them by the furnace. Then he knocked on Mr. Woods's door to see about his Tupperware.

Mabel Woods answered. "Hello there, handsome." Mabel knew how to treat her best Tupperware customer.

"Hello, Mrs. Woods."

"Now, you hush with that Mrs. Woods dribble, honey. It's Mabel, remember?" She said with a pinch of his still-sore cheek. "I got your order right here." She pulled the box with his name on it out of a storage nook.

"Do I owe you anything additional, Mabel?"

"No sir! You already paid the freight. Do you need a hand bringing this over to the storage area?" Mabel asked.

"No thank you, Mabel… I can drag this down the hall and bring the extras up to the apartment." Max did just that. He pulled out the plastic Tupperware containers by size. He put them all on the floor and labeled them M#1 to M#10X, using duct tape and a Sharpie. There was a large amount of grated mushroom to be stowed, even in granular form. Max stared at the Mason jars.

In these plastic containers lies the potential to enhance a dish, alter a mood, or yield a last supper… and I'm bringing it to the White House. Literally, food for thought!

He labeled and poured. He was ever so careful in the process.

I'll throw it all out and start over if things get crazy.

He was surprised at how many Tupperware containers he filled. He ended up with two quart-size containers of the deadly M#10X. That shocked Max. He stacked the containers back into the box the Tupperware came in.

Then Max put in a half hour on the heavy bag. His hands were stiff and sore from the Tito episode. He thought of no one in particular as he banged away on the seventy-five pound monster.

Heavy bag… still the best workout mentally and physically.

After he finished he washed out the Mason jars and put them

in a separate box. Max took some mushroom samples upstairs in labeled film canisters. Max flashed back to what Dana had said about the White House being dank enough to grow mushrooms.

Wouldn't that be something? Deadlier plans have been hatched within the confines of the White House walls… but I doubt the weapons were manufactured on the premises.

His new address would be; 1600 Pennsylvania Avenue. Max chuckled to himself at the tack his life had taken. He could have just as easily had an address on Rikers Island for what he had done to Little Louie. In a few weeks some staff member would be sorting his mail along with the president's.

Max knew if the mushrooms were needed to help the president in any capacity, it would be his duty to respond. He didn't know how, why, or when he could be called upon but as Amy had reminded Max, "You took an oath to help your president and your country when called upon!" Max knew it would be good to have the means to help.

After all, isn't this why I am here in the first place?

Indeed, he would need a place to grow and nurture more mushrooms. He had enough stored away, but was he endangering the future reproduction process?

If the growing process is stymied, might it cease altogether? He could not rely on another freak accident of nature to rekindle the growing cycle. The mushrooms were a wonder of the Korengal Valley, a gift from Ghazi Haider.

Max thought about his ring and how its journey fared. Somehow, Max knew it would reach its destination. He only wished he could be there when it arrived. It was a gift. There was an obligation on Ahmed Karzai's part to deliver it, that was the Afghan way.

It's winter, for God's sake! Both men are probably playing Bujal Bazi on Friday nights at Hamid Karzai's compound.

Max thought, picturing them playing the Afghan game of marbles.

The ring will find its way.

Max called Dana. He had gotten used to daily communication with her over the past week. He missed her already. He wanted to wish her luck on her TV interview tomorrow.

Dana answered on the first ring. "Hello… Is this my soldier boy?"

"It is. Might this be the White House press secretary?"

"It is. How are you? I miss you terribly."

"Me too… I'll be back soon. I am getting spoiled with this Marine One pickup and delivery service."

"Don't get too used to it. Curlander could get jammed up if the wrong people got wind of it. I heard Wiggins telling him to cool it after the inauguration."

"That's okay. I'll be down there soon enough."

"You better be."

"So, you have plenty on your plate for now. Me? I am trying to get some things in order for the move. The furniture came with the apartment. I have my gear and some spices I might store until I get squared away down there."

"I have a garage you can use. I never park in it."

"Great… Am I allowed to use the White House gym?"

"I should think so… I'll ask Cleary."

"How is the rehearsal for the interview coming along?"

"Okay… Tim gave me the questions. I went over them this morning with Charlie Wiggins. He edited where necessary. Charlie knows what he's doing, Max. I think we're going to like him… once we get used to him. He's tough, but savvy."

"Who's doing the interview?"

"Tim is doing it himself… He said he wants it done right."

"I'll bet he does."

Dana laughed. "Don't worry. He knows to keep his hands off. The *#MeToo* movement has got everyone on good behavior."

"I don't like that guy. I definitely don't trust him."

"I think he knows you don't like him… He said you almost broke his hand at the Curlanders' house."

"Good. Then I won't have to show him anything later."

"He's harmless. I want you to keep me posted on what is going on with you up there. I am going to be swamped down here. If you don't hear from me, it's because I am crazed. I'll get back to you ASAP. You can always text me. When will you know about going to Florida?"

"I'll call them tomorrow night after your interview."

"All right… It's live. Call me about nine… twenty-one hundred hours to you, soldier boy. Get a good night's rest. I love you and miss you."

"I love you too. I'll see you soon… Sleep tight, baby."

Max reassured himself that his latest decisions fell onto the good side of his life ledger. Time would tell how well the ledger balanced. At least he would be starting out at the top of the heap. Max tried to look at the White House job from a soldier's perspective: Mysterious, somewhat dangerous, a challenge, demanding, intriguing. There would be action within and beyond the Doric columns of the White House.

And let's not forget the mushrooms… In the hands of a sane man, they can be a force for good.

Max decided to call Margaret immediately instead of waiting. He was nervous. He knew that Alzheimer's was a progressive disease.

The phone rang a few times before Len answered.

"Hello." Len said.

"Len, it's me, Max. How are you?"

"Oh, Max… how are you two? I was asking Margaret today how you and Eva were doing up there in New York," Len said, in a jovial mood.

Max was shaken and could not bring himself to get into a patronizing conversation with Len about Eva. "Is Margaret there?" Max asked instead.

"She is outside talking to… what's her name next door. The gardener lady. You know who I mean… How's the little guy? Growing like a weed, I bet… I can't wait to see him!"

"Yeah, Len… His name is Lincoln," Max said. "We want to come down and visit you two … if that's okay with you?"

"Sure! We can go fishin' and leave the girls to their gossip, heeheehee, but not tomorrow… tomorrow I get new meds."

"No, not tomorrow, Len… I promise. Will you please ask Margaret to call me?"

"Okay. Does she have your number?"

"Yes, she does. Tell her Max called."

"I'll tell her Max called today… And she has your number?"

"Yes, Len, she does. Goodbye, Len. I love you, and we will see you soon."

"Don't forget to bring the little guy," Len said.

"I won't. Goodbye now, Len."

Max wondered where Margaret was during the phone call.

He shouldn't be left alone. Margaret has her hands full. She probably needed a breath of fresh air.

Max walked Linc and went up to bed. As he lay there he wondered how Len had known about Linc.

A good sign. Len is sharp enough to remember seeing me and Linc in the newspapers or on TV. Maybe he isn't so bad after all. His meds might be working. I didn't need mine.

Max felt better about things. He would check in with Margaret tomorrow… if Len forgot to tell her about his call. He hoped Len would come through and deliver his message. That would prove hopeful. He thought about his own life and whether or not he would ever grow old. He'd always felt the odds were against that happening.

If I find myself losing my mind before my body, I think a strict mushroom diet will be on the menu.

This was Max's first night alone in a while. Perhaps making commitments had given him the peace that he craved. He slept through the night.

The next morning, Max fed Linc his breakfast and blended up a health food drink for himself. Linc seemed glad to be in familiar surroundings. They went out to the park to renew some old acquaintances. They walked to Dog Hill for a refresher course on socialization. Max noticed another Alapaha, along with a few similar-looking breeds roaming the hill.

That didn't take very long. Looks like you're the new dog du jour.

Few Americans had seen an Alapaha a few months ago; there were none living outside the U.S., as far as Max knew. Now people were scrambling to find breeders.

Where the hell are they getting them from?

The other Alapaha owners recognized Linc. Max was present simply in a custodial role. Max asked a few of the owners where they had gotten their pups from. It seemed there was a breeder in Louisiana who claimed to be breeding Linc's grandparents. The tariff: Ten grand a pup. Max made a mental note to check with Rodrigo.

While the dogs were at play, a beautiful redhead Max recognized as either a model or an actress walked up to Max and Linc. She had a four-month-old Alapaha female that was adorable.

Look at this pair of knockouts!

"She's a beauty!" Max said.

"Of course… so's he. Isn't he the one we owe this latest dog craze to?"

"This is Lincoln."

"Thought so… Bigger than I imagined!"

"Getting bigger every day too."

They began chatting about the breed. Max told her to keep her pup in contact with other dogs as much as possible. She would be thankful when the pup got older. Max gave her pointers; types of toys, proper diet, exercise. She was appreciative and seemed surprised that Max showed no interest in her.

She picked up her pup and started to leave. Max yelled over, "Let her walk. She needs to learn how to walk with you… and she needs to run."

The woman put the dog down, paused for a second, and walked

back to Max. She reached into her pocketbook and handed Max a business card. "Anytime you feel like breeding, give me a call!" She smiled and walked away, pulling her little pup behind her.

Max chuckled to himself.

Where were you when I needed you?

He watched her *runway-walk* down the path. She knew he would be looking.

They always know you're looking.

Max walked uptown to see Rodrigo. There was no time like the present to find out about Linc's A.K.C. papers.

Who knows? Maybe I can put ole Linc out for stud. I can picture him running around the White House lawn banging every female Alapaha blue blood bulldog in the country at ten grand a pop. A few eight-by-ten-inch glossy photos of Linc, president Curlander and the White House in the background. Maybe Curlander could sign a few… if a second term looked dim. That would sell some puppies. Haha.

They hoofed it up to the church. It looked as though Rodrigo was doing a booming business. He had taken over the stores on both sides of the original pet shop. Apparently pet-owners in the neighborhood not only accepted but welcomed Rodrigo's new vocation. Max knocked on the big wooden doors at the main entrance. A pretty Puerto Rican girl answered the door. She peeked out and asked what Max wanted. Then she looked down and saw Linc and said, "Oh, please come in." Inside, the pictures Rodrigo had taken of Max and Linc were displayed on one wall as a centerpiece, surrounded by hundreds of pictures of parishioners and their pets. There was seating for about 150 people. The pulpit looked like it hung from the ceiling. In fact, there was a stairway behind a curtain that went up to the pulpit. Rodrigo appeared from a door to the right of the stage.

Max said, "Hello, Rodrigo. It's…."

Rodrigo interrupted by putting his forefinger to his lips and whispered, "Mahatma, if you please."

"Yeah, I forgot. How are you? It looks like you are doing pretty well for yourself… Mahatma."

"Things are good, Max. My following is growing. I am thinking about my own cable show. And… how is Lincoln doing?"

"Take a look at him. He's over a year old and starting to feel his oats."

Mahatma said, "He is stronger than his father at one year."

"I have been meaning to ask you. What breeder did you get Tango from?" Max asked.

"The only breeder I could find was in Louisiana. Their family started breeding Alapahas back in the 1980s, when the A.K.C. first recognized the breed. I have their information in the back. They said I could keep Lincoln for free because the rest of the litter was still-born. I should have let him stay there and fuck his life away. They shipped Lincoln up for free to get rid of him… some Louisiana voodoo bullshit. Strange people. His mama was a blue-ribbon winner at many shows in Baton Rouge. Do you want his paperwork?"

Max was surprised. "You have Tango's and Linc's papers? I'd like both, please."

"Of course I have their papers. What do you take me for… a bad businessman? These papers are legit too!"

Mahatma went in the back. As the door shut, a canary flew overhead and landed on a curtain rod. The girl who had answered the door was petting Linc. She was very pleasant.

"Do you work here?"

"I am one of the Mahatma's wives… I help him, as we all do, with the church and with his work," she said as she smiled and stroked Linc.

"How many wives does he have… if you don't mind me asking?"

"Only three… He's allowed seven. That's his rule."

Mahatma returned with the papers. "Here you go, Lincoln. Now you and your father: Tango, are legitimate citizens. It's easier these days for a dog than a Latino!"

"Thanks, Mahatma. Can I give you anything toward your church?" Max asked, stumbling for words.

"Stick twenty dollars in the **Paw Box** by the door."

"You got it. Good luck, Mahatma."

"And to you, my friend. There is good karma for you and Lincoln in the future. But you must be aware of which path to travel in life. I see this... for you both, and for the many others that will rely on your work. Be careful, my friends. By the way, it's not all it's cracked up to be!" Mahatma said.

"What's not all that it's cracked up to be?"

"Three wives... a closing thought," Mahatma said as he shook Max's hand and scratched Linc. Max left Mahatma to tend his flock.

Max thought Mahatma's parting words about, "which path to travel in life," were rather strange but then again, there was nothing normal at the Church of the Mystical Eyeball. Oddly enough, Max always seemed in good spirits upon leaving the church.

As it should be when leaving such a sacred enclave.

Max liked Mahatma more than he ever liked Rodrigo. He was happy to have taken part in helping Mahatma find his true vocation.

Score a victory for the mushrooms.

There was very little Max, or anyone else in the Western world, knew about the Korengal mushrooms. Discretion would be important in his new capacity as the president's chef. There would have to be serious thought as far as number and dosage for usage on... special occasions.

Afghanistan is much like its mushroom; deadly and beautiful, depending on location. If I do come across the wrong kind of people in this job, they might do better eating somewhere other than the White House.

Max had time on his hands. He was mobile for now. That was one of the benefits of traveling light. He decided that, sooner or later, he had to go into Eva's closet. Eva had some beautiful clothes that Max had never gotten a chance to see her wear. They'd worked so hard to build a business they had almost forgotten to live their lives. Max would not let that happen with Dana. He thought about how alike Eva and Dana were in some cases and how different in others.

They are… were… both independent. Beautiful women can travel that road with ease. Probably another reason Eva was wary of Dana. Beautiful women don't seem to get along well with each other at least when they first meet.

Even a social klutz like Max knew he should not offer Dana Eva's clothes.

Here, honey, I want you to dress like my dead girlfriend.

He would give the clothes away. He remembered noticing a sign by the local Catholic church about a clothing drive for needy parishioners. Eva would like that. Max grabbed one of the unused boxes the Tupperware had come in and loaded it up with Eva's clothes and shoes. Some of the blouses still had dry cleaning plastic over them. He found himself burying his face in Eva's clothes as he packed them. He couldn't help himself. He was looking for a remnant; a last sensory perception. Some of the clothes were a reminder of specific times and events.

Not enough laughs… We should've had more fun.

Max left Linc at home and carried the box for the three blocks to the Church of Saint Paul the Apostle. He knocked on the rectory door. A bright-eyed, rotund priest in his mid-sixties answered the door. He must have been having pasta for lunch. He had a napkin tucked in his collar and a touch of marinara sauce on his upper lip.

"May I help you, my son?"

"Good afternoon, Padre. My name is Max Burns. I have some clothing that I want to donate…."

"Come in," the priest said, interrupting him. "Would you like some lunch?"

Max was always impressed by the craftsmanship of old churches. This rectory was no exception. He wondered whether the craftsmen had been more attentive to detail because of a better shot at redemption. The details of the marble, wood, and frescoes always seemed flawless.

"I am Father Peter Colapietro. Everyone calls me Father Pete. Come in, my boy. Eat with me. I'm going to fix you a small plate. My friends at Rayo's always think of me. God bless them… they need it." Father Pete said, chuckling as he put some pasta and a meatball on a plate for Max. "Where are you from, my boy?" he asked.

Max had to try the pasta that was put in front of him. It was quite good. He told Father Pete he was impressed. Evidently, Father Pete's friends had taken their time and used ripe plum tomatoes with a nice consistency of spices.

"I am originally from Saint Bonaventure Parish in Washington, Pennsylvania. I live a few blocks north on Ninety-Sixth Street now." Max purposely mentioned his parish in Pennsylvania to establish a connection, weak as it had become.

Father Pete nodded. He seemed to pay it little mind, with food remaining the important factor. Max had found a kindred spirit.

"Ahhh, you know your pasta and sauces. Are you Italian?"

"I'm a chef… Irish-American ancestry."

"Hmmm. God works in mysterious ways."

Max chuckled to himself.

"What are you doing with your culinary skills right now, may I ask?"

Max felt a trap coming. "I am starting a new job in three weeks in D.C.," Max said.

"Three weeks…huh… Do you believe in heaven, Mr. Burns?"

"I believe in hell, Padre," Max answered, not looking up.

"I see. What branch?"

"Army."

"Afghanistan? Iraq?"

"Both. Three tours."

"You have been to hell, my son. I thank you for your service."

Max abruptly changed the subject. "They do a great job at this Rayo's. I'd say six hours on the plum tomatoes at about two hundred twenty-five degrees in an old cast-iron twenty-gallon pot. Good to see a restaurant take such pains to do things right."

"Mr. Burns!"

Max interrupted him. "Call me Max, Father."

"Max… I run a soup kitchen here in the school auditorium but as of yesterday afternoon at two o'clock, my chef is now slinging hash on Rikers Island… and will be for some time if he can't meet bail. Would you be willing to give us a hand for a few weeks?"

Max was all set to wiggle his way out of this one. Then Max said, "let's see what you've got for a kitchen."

Father Pete reached into a cupboard and pulled out a nice bottle of Chianti. He held it up toward Max. "Here's to Rayo's," the Padre said as he poured wine into two water glasses.

"I have a dog, Padre," Max said, instinctively trying to establish an exit strategy if needed.

"You can leave him here with me while you cook," Father Pete said, determined not to let his fish off the hook.

Max felt the barb of the hook pierce his cheek… he was in. Good or bad decision, Max Burns was in.

"Do you have people I can train for you? I can't do this for very long."

"Sometimes a volunteer meanders in to help. I have one person I pay. She will be the only help you can rely on. You get what you pay for, Max, even doing God's work. 'Everyone knows the price of everything… and the value of nothing'—Oscar Wilde," Father Pete said.

Max liked the priest. He seemed a good person and sincere in his desire to help the homeless. Max welcomed the three weeks of penance. The obligation would keep him busy and clear some of the rust from the culinary portion of his brain.

"How many do you feed a day, Padre?"

"Depends…. It's winter and many of the homeless are in Florida. I would say it can range between one hundred twenty to one hundred sixty, four days a week. B'nai Brith over on the East Side does the other three nights."

"Where do you get the food?" Max asked.

"The New York State Restaurant Association sponsors a van that collects food from the member restaurants. The New York City branch of volunteers go around to those restaurants to pick up and drop off food: Cooked, semi-cooked, not cooked, that used to be thrown away. We never know what or how much to expect. We have a storeroom with pasta and other items with a long shelf life. We need to raid it once in a while to supplement donations. When the food runs out, we stop serving. It is strictly first come, first served. The homeless know that… believe me. They start lining up at five for the six o'clock evening meal. They know to behave or we don't serve them. Three problems from someone and we kick them out for good. There's no, *act of contrition,* for bad manners here at Saint Paul's."

"Let's have a look," Max said after Father Pete reached to pour some more wine for both of them.

They walked outside and into the school building next to the church.

"He doesn't bite, does he?" Father Pete asked.

"Who?"

"Your dog."

"No, Padre. He's a year old and housebroken."

"What kind of dog is he?"

"He is an Alapaha Blue Blood Bulldog—100% American."

"Really! As long as he doesn't bite and he's housebroken, we'll get along fine. I had a cockatoo land on my windowsill a while back… strangest thing," Father Pete said, pensively stroking his chin. "I thought it might have been the Holy Spirit for a moment… until he bit me." He let out a belly laugh.

The auditorium was typical, with folding metal chairs on a large tile floor, designed for meetings and late masses. It also served as a basketball court and gym for the grammar school. The adjoining room had a separate entrance. This was where the kitchen and dining area were situated. It functioned as the student lunchroom five days a week from noon to twelve forty-five. The kids were usually finished school by three. The homeless were not allowed to line up before four o'clock on school days. That was rule number one. Rule number two was any food from Rayo's passed through the rectory first.

Not unlike the military in that respect.

The pots and pans were spotless. Volunteers or not, someone was looking after the place. Max had decided, if the kitchen had been a mess, all bets were off.

"Let's see the storage facility, Padre," Max said, after inspecting the oven and stove. Everything was at least thirty years old, but it had been kept in excellent condition. The walk-in box refrigerator was more than adequate.

After looking over the storage facility, Max said, "okay, Padre, I'll give it a try. Which four days?"

"Tuesday through Friday, so you have a few days, since today is Saturday. I suggest you get here about three o'clock on Tuesday to see what you are in for. The kids are off for Christmas vacation for two more weeks. You can check out the restaurant wagon deliveries from the night before... Thank you, Max. I told you God works in mysterious ways, didn't I? If you've been to hell... and I know you have my son, then there must be a heaven as well... and you are well on your way there."

"Roger that, Padre. I'm not sure I'll know anybody when I get there, but - oh, Padre, the clothes I dropped off? Please see they go to good use. They belonged to someone special. Now that I think about it, she'd be the only one I'd know in heaven."

Max closed out the conversation with an exchange of phone numbers and a handshake.

"See you Tuesday, Padre," Max said, waving as he went down the rectory steps.

"Tuesday it is. God bless you, my son... and don't forget the dog!" Father Pete yelled, as he waved back at Max.

Max felt good about the commitment. He felt his life was moving in a positive direction.

All these religious people I'm hanging around with... mom'd be proud.

Max also needed to get back into a kitchen.

When he got home, he returned to Eva's closet again to look

through the other boxes on the floor. There was some jewelry in one box. He would take that down to Margaret when he went to visit.

Most of it probably came from Len and Margaret.

He wondered whether seeing the jewelry again would sadden Margaret or bring back fond memories.

Max thought about the standard operating procedure for K.I.A.'s in-country.

The army sends an officer to your bunk. He puts everything you had in your footlocker. They ship it to next of kin, after in-person K.I.A. notification is completed. Surviving relatives were entitled to a flag, perhaps a medal or two, and a burial service at the soldier's local family plot, or at Arlington National Cemetery if the K.I.A. had specified - eternity with brother warriors.

Max didn't dwell on the hereafter or interment. He couldn't remember whether he'd given a damn about getting killed when he was in-country. "If you are thinking about getting wasted, trust me, you **will** get wasted." Sergeant Nunez would say.

CHAPTER 64

It was almost time for Dana's interview. NBC, the parent company of Dana's affiliate station, was broadcasting her interview nationally.

My girlfriend is almost as famous as my dog.

Dana looked great. She came across poised, confident, and not at all starchy. Max could see Charlie Wiggins had done a good job prepping Dana. Wiggins had received the questions well in advance. The rest had been a matter of rehearsing the required answers and then making it sound as if they hadn't been rehearsed. Dana sounded more than competent… wise beyond her years.

There should not have been any surprises, but toward the end of the live interview, Wetherford jumped into scoop mode. He made a statement about how happy and content Dana seemed, which led to his unrehearsed question - "Is there someone special in your life right now, Dana?" It was totally inappropriate and furthermore, unprofessional and it could potentially throw Dana into a world of tabloid journalism. Dana stifled the look she really wanted to shoot back at Wetherford and, after a pause, said, "Just me… my man… and a dog." She ended the interview by embarrassing Wetherford. She stood up and simply shook his hand, turning away as he attempted to kiss her cheek. He nearly fell over her chair. It was hysterical. Dana handled him as though he was an awkward teenager.

When the cameras stopped, Dana turned to the NBC executive

producer and said, "Your boy just blew a first-row seat at press briefings. You can tell him that for me!"

The pupil had become the teacher.

"A man and his dog… hear that, Linc?" Max said as he roughed Linc up. Linc barked, as if answering his master. "She put that asshole in his place. That's our girl."

He had to call Dana and congratulate her.

She answered on the first ring. "I was just calling you," she said. "Do you believe that bastard, putting me on the spot like that?"

"You killed it! YOU made the whole thing seem unrehearsed. Don't worry about it."

"You're not upset, are you?" Dana asked.

"Why would I be upset? He almost fell over the chair."

"It didn't sound like you, me, and the dog are a threesome, did it?"

"That's okay—a threesome in this day and age is acceptable in many third world countries."

"You're not funny! I wish you were here. I miss you."

"Soon, honey, soon. I miss you too. I got a gig goin' on here at the local church. It should keep me busy four days a week and still give me time to go to Florida for a few days."

"You called Len and Margaret? How are they?"

"I got Len on the phone again. He sounded a little more coherent than the last phone call. He was rambling about Linc and going fishing with him. I'll definitely take Linc down there. I hadn't planned on it, but Len specifically asked me to bring him."

"Then you have to do it."

Max filled her in on the soup kitchen. She loved that. She said it would make a great human-interest story. Max said, "Forget it. It's only for a few weeks to kill time and help a local priest. I am going to call Len and Margaret again this evening. I hope she picks up. For some reason Len keeps answering the phone. I'll let you know. I probably won't be going down there until next Friday night or Saturday morning. I'll be at the church Tuesday through Friday from around three to eight. If you need me for anything, text me. You did great. I am very proud of you. I can't wait to get down there and get our lives started."

"I love you. Take care. Gotta run."

"Love you too."

The good phone call was out of the way. It was now time to call Len and Margaret.

Max dialed the number and prayed Margaret would answer.

"Hello," Margaret answered. Max was elated.

"Hello, Margaret. How are you?" he asked, waiting to hear some news he could rely on.

"Oh, Max, how are you, my dear? I think about you all the time. We hope you are doing well up there in New York," she said in a calm voice.

"Things are good here. How are you?"

"I'm doing fine... tired but fine." Margaret said. There was a long pause as she awaited the inevitable next question.

"And Len? How's he doing?"

"He is about the same. He has moments of clarity. Then... sometimes he doesn't even know me. He thinks I am someone else pretending to be me. Who'd pretend to be me? We go day to day."

"I spoke to him the other day, and he sounded pretty good. He knew about Lincoln and asked me to bring him down to visit. I'll do that if you think—"

Margaret interrupted him. "Wait! Hold on, Max. No... not your dog ... he doesn't mean bring your dog. He... he imagines things. He doesn't know you have a dog. He thinks you and Eva have... a son." Margaret's voice cracked.

"A son! Why would he think that? I thought he saw Lincoln on TV and ...." Max stopped himself.

"A son? Margaret, you need to get him into some professional care. You can't handle this on your own. It must be heartbreaking for you to have to listen to him about Eva and now this. Let me come down and maybe we can get him into some longterm care facility or a place that knows how to deal…."

Margaret interrupted Max again. "He's not too far off base, Max."

"Margaret! How can you say that? Eva and I… a son? Margaret, we need to do something. Let me help. Please let me come down and…."

"Max!" Margaret had to tell Max what had been eating away at both her and Len since Eva's death. "Max… Eva was pregnant when she died. It was a little boy." Margaret finally got the words out. "I was hoping you'd never find out but now you understand what I am going through down here and why you can't come and visit. It would break his heart to find out the truth. One heart broken in this house is enough. He'd be too confused. I'm sorry to have to tell you this, Max. You'd find out eventually if you came down. His doctors say, 'Let him be. Let him have his grandson,'" Margaret said, feeling both relief and sadness.

"Eva would have told me! She would have let me know. I would've been so happy. No, Margaret! You're wrong! Eva would've told me first! That's *crazy*! You make it sound like I wouldn't have been happy! This can't be true, Margaret. It can't be true!"

Margaret interrupted him. "Max, remember when Eva would go to work early without you? She'd stop by her obstetrician at Columbia-Presbyterian Hospital. She wanted to be sure before she told you. She'd just gotten her sonogram scanned to her computer the morning of… the accident. She emailed the ultrasound to us in Florida. She was going to surprise you when you came to pick her up at the restaurant. She wanted to show you his heartbeat on the computer… **A little boy!** Len is so confused. He doesn't even know Eva is gone much less understand that he has no grandson." Margaret paused. "I think Len may be better off than all of us. Please understand… we love you, but we can't see you. I'm sorry. Goodbye, Max." Margaret's trembling voice trailed off before the disconnect.

Max started shaking. He tried to continue the conversation before Margaret hung up, but he couldn't put a sentence together.

He lost his breath and fell onto his knees. Tears burst forth with a heave that emptied his stomach. He cried on and off for hours. He kept trying to process it all.

Did I hear Margaret correctly?

At one point he thought that Margaret might be punishing him for not protecting Eva, their most cherished gift. He retrieved Eva's IPad and fumbled away. They new each others passwords. He accessed Eva's emails.

There it was - an email from the hospital with an attachment. The subject line - "**Max Burns, Jr.**"

Max stood up dropping the IPad to the floor. He quickly picked it up. He had to see. He had to read anything that Eva might have said moments before her death.

He opened the attachment. It revealed an elliptical cocoon with a dark background with a form inside along with the haunting sound of a heartbeat. Then, as though he were candling an egg back on the farm, he reset and stared, reset and stared, over and over. He tried to decipher parts of his son's body. Nothing seemed clear enough for him… a head, legs, arms. He enlarged the ultrasound past clarity.

Is that Eva's heart…or my son's?

Max's finger hovered before he hit **delete**.

CHAPTER 65

My son! My family. Murdered.

Max wanted to either kill someone or die himself. He was not sure which would alleviate the gnawing pain. He cried for Eva. He cried for his son. He cried for Len and Margaret. He just cried.

It's not over… someone must pay.

Days and nights were spent the same way. He lay on the couch for long periods of time. He went down to the storeroom and sat in the rocker. He hated himself as he fought the intense memories and unwelcome events that fought their way into his muddled brain. Linc stared at Max and whimpered, knowing things were not right. Linc's walks became shorter. Max felt ashamed to be in public.

When Max's parents died, he rationalized that their suffering from cancer was over. They were finally at peace and Max dealt with it. However, the death of Max's high school pal, Tommy Hennelly had unleashed unforeseen forces within Max directed at the bully: Dante Liguori. THAT never bothered him. Max lost many brothers and sisters in combat. Even THAT beat a path to a logical conclusion.

THIS! Scratched at his brain searching for resolution.

Max had survived the I.E.D. that killed or maimed everyone around him, something Father Pete would call, an act of God. Max called it blind luck. He had been saved by two fifty-pound sacks of potatoes. His fortuitous survival brought with it an obligation for justice. And so, Sergeant Maxwell Burns, killed everyone who participated in the assault on his brothers and sisters that day. He'd never regretted his actions - the logic worked. Max never questioned why he was at peace with it all. He considered himself lucky not to deal with it. It was over…move on. Now, he wondered why he could not stop the tears and the intensity of a haunting, he had never felt before.

Something is incomplete.

A different kind of I.E.D. went off in his head—nobody left to fight; nobody left to kill. The distinct smell of the C-4 explosive returned to his nostrils. The fog in his mind only cleared to form the indelible vision of the sonogram: His unborn son and the sound of a beating heart.

Max remembered he had old photos down in the storeroom. He needed to see pictures of Eva. There were also old pictures of him as a child and all the way through his ranger training. He and Linc went downstairs to find them. When they got to the basement, he noticed some mushrooms he had forgotten to take down from behind the furnace. They had each shriveled to the size of a quarter. He tossed them on the crate next to the rocker.

The old suitcase that contained items from Washington, Pennsylvania, had not been opened in years. He wasn't sure what to expect. There were old photos of General Sherman posing in full dress uniform and photos of his grandparents. His eyes filled up. He wiped them on his shirtsleeve. He found photos of his mom and dad. Thankfully, they made him smile.

Am I to be the last Burns?

Max kept rummaging and found photos of himself, the only child, Maxwell Tecumseh Burns. The photos were tied up in a stack with a blue bow and arranged in chronological order. First, were the baby pictures. Max stared at them and wondered…

Is this what my son would have looked like?

Max was looking at a photographic time-line of his life on the farm. He remembered when and where many of the photos were taken. He remembered his parents' patience as they tried to make him be still for the old camera. There was the eighth-grade class photo. Thomas Hennelly was the only student in a shirt and tie. That photo saddened Max more than any other. The class photo had been taken only days before Hennelly's suicide. Max sat and rocked.

Would my son have been smart? An athlete? How much would he have looked like me and how much like Eva? Would he have had her piercing dark-brown eyes? Would he have had my temper?

Random thoughts whipped around his brain.

I feel like that, Wall of Death motorcycle rider at the county fair… round and round … faster and faster… climbing the wall at the edge of the barrel.

Max needed to move… a walk with Linc. He needed a different theater of thought.

The cold January air whipped through the cavernous apartment buildings of the Upper West Side.

It was near midnight. The streets were bare. Max and Linc walked south through Central Park, past the boathouse toward the carousel. The carousel lay eerily still. The eyes of the horses pierced the night. Max marveled at the intricacies of the carousel animals.

Craftsman from a forgotten era.

The glowing red eyes of one particular stallion seemed to stare back at Max as though it related to Max and the internal carousel swirling in his head. Max's mind slowed and eventually stopped. The mother of all carousels had pulled the plug. *No work tonight,* the horses seemed to say. *We are resting!*

The man and his dog sat on a bench before their walk home.

The two cops watching Max and Linc from their squad car turned the engine back on for heat when they saw Max had no bad intentions. They debated whether Max was Max… and Linc was Linc. It was too cold for pictures.

Max and Lin walked slowly back to the apartment. He almost wished that some kind of confrontation would take place. That would ease his tension - giving some dirtbag a good beating. Eva and his son would not vacate his thoughts. At the same time, he knew from military experience that he had to try and regroup to defend himself.

It was a man's job to protect his family... and his country at all costs.

He swore to the heavens that he would not let any harm come to Dana. He would do whatever necessary to keep Dana and Linc safe. He would also do his best to keep Ed and Amy safe. His promises went on from there. Len and Margaret also needed him. It dawned on him that he might never see Len and Margaret again. He hoped that would not be the case, but it was their call.

Max lay on the couch for, what he thought, a moment. His cell phone rang, jolting him.

Was I sleeping?

Eva? I mean, Dana!

"Hey, army... you okay?" It was Nicholson.

"Yeah... good," Max said, wishing he had not answered the call. But, Nicholson was a distraction, and any distraction was welcome.

"Well, you sound like shit. Anyway, I spoke to Neptune. Like I thought, he's trying to talk me out of our little vacation. By the end of our conversation, I think he got where I'm comin' from. Thanks for getting his message to me. And you're right: he's not in a good way. How's it going with you? Where the hell are you?"

"I'm back in New York City. Just got back from the Curlanders'. I think I'm going to take the chef's job at the White House," Max said, trying to finalize one option.

Simplify.

"Whatever's best for you, my brother. I'll leave the last spot on the manifest open in case you have a change of heart. It could happen. Everybody's world is upside fuckin' down right about now ... Every call I make has some shit in it."

"Anything's possible, Nick."

"You really do sound like shit," Nick said.

Max didn't answer.

"From a F.O.B. in the Korengal to the White House—not bad,

kid! We're on schedule for departure: Floyd Bennett Field, January 20, zero eight hundred hours."

"I got it! I'll keep it in mind," Max said.

"Adios, motherfucker," Nicholson said and hung up, not waiting for a goodbye.

Nicholson stared out his motel window in East Los Angeles and smiled.

Shit... the best fertilizer.

Max had his own thoughts:

Nick needs that visceral feeling of taking his troubles out on ANYone... And I get it to some extent. I guess the feds are happy he's not on the other side. They built him. Huh, they built me too... The Frankenstein Production Company... Jesus, that's why SAM wants Nicholson out of town: He's Alive!!! They're afraid of Frankenstein, so they "disappear" him. Make him somebody else's problem... Pay him if you have to.

The problem with Nick's mission? There was no problem with his mission. That was evident to Max.

The army was clear and unyielding with their rules of engagement.

IF you got caught.

Mercenaries had no rules. Max knew wars weren't won by following rules. The C.I.A. was supposed to be the oversight organization on mercenary contract work but in essence that meant the C.I.A. was the banker. C.I.A. field operatives were simply in charge of the money, doling it out where needed. That was basically all they did on contract jobs. Truth be told, most C.I.A. field officers were scared to death of mercenaries. Mercs were - more or less - free to do what they wanted, when they wanted, as long as they got results. There was little C.I.A. participation in the actual mission.

Simply put, the agencies only control was money. And, if money was not the prime motivator, as in this case, there was no control.

Am I considering Nick's vacation an option? OR…Am I to be the professional babysitter for the United States of America?

Max shook his head. Something familiar tugged at him… a visceral desire to be tossed into something where you must give your undivided attention with no room to think about anything else.

If Nicholson's plane was in front of me now, would I get on it? What the fuck!

He went down to the storeroom to look at more photos. He rocked back and forth and thought about what a great mother Eva would have been.

Max came back to a particular picture of himself and his dad. Max was on a horse. The year penciled in on the back would have made Max seven years old. His father was holding the bridle and standing in front of the horse. Max's legs were almost straight out to the sides. He had a big smile on his face, but it wasn't his smile that held his attention. It was his father's smile: the smile of a proud parent, a guardian, a man that held the bridle tightly for fear of the horse bolting. He was the mayor of WashPa, guarding his son like he guarded his constituents. Max began to cry, not knowing why, not understanding why the photo made him feel bad. He cursed as he rubbed his eyes clear.

He looked up at the fish tank and saw four mushrooms ready for harvest. He opened his ranger knife and, one at a time, methodically cut through the stems. He picked up the largest and played with it in his hand. He held it up and twirled it, as though it were a miniature umbrella from a fruit drink at some beach bar. He held it in front of his face and stared at the deadly black spot in the middle. Back and forth, he moved it to the focal point of his vision and beyond, until it became two separate black eyes staring back - the eyes of a killer. His mind went blank. The respite from thought was welcome only after moving it away.

Maybe I should wolf-down the whole goddamn thing?

It was a fleeting thought but a thought nonetheless. He laid the wrinkled mushrooms on the crate that served as his catchall. Max washed his hands in the sump sink and went upstairs to bed. He lay there for hours trying to avoid the nightly commencement of his cerebral merry-go-round.

He got up and went over to the box of mushroom-filled Tupperware containers. He rummaged around and found the M#6 container. He wet his finger, tapped it in the container, and then touched it to his tongue. He savored the strong, pungent taste of the M#6. Then he went to the couch and lay in the dark with Linc on the floor next to him. It took a few minutes, but his swirling head began to gear down.

What might have been euphoria to anyone else was merely relief to Max. Max closed his eyes.

A new stage had been set. The curtain was about to go up.

In color! Can't be a dream.

He stopped questioning where his mind would take him. He was away and thankful to be anywhere but from whence he came.

There I am, *right in the middle... the very middle. Whoa ... people from all parts of my life, including those I only heard about in stories. S that's what they look like. They're all circling around me... holding hands.* ***"Mother! Is that you?"***

Max's mother left the circle and came to him. She touched his cheek and said, "You must hold on and never let go!" She returned to her place... round and round... singing, laughing, happy.

"Are you all dead?"

Max asked, looking at faces as they whirled by.

Everyone laughed at him as they stopped circling. His father said, "What's the difference if we're dead or not? We're here, aren't we?"

They all laughed again. It was a healthy laugh, not condescending or veiled... a joyous laugh. Max looked older now. He was wearing the same clothes as in the horse picture.

Eva took her turn and walked slowly to Max and touched his cheek. "Don't worry about us. We are both with you," she said as she looked down and rubbed her pregnant stomach lovingly. She went back to her place.

It was General William Tecumseh Sherman's turn to break ranks and come forward in his full dress uniform. "Listen, son, we all have questions! I am still not sure I should have burned all those cities to the ground. It's done … and I can't do anything about it. Someone else will, though. Hell, someone else has!" He laughed and started walking back to his place in the circle. He stopped and turned to say to Max, "Your strengths are in your convictions. Find them … Never let go. That's an order!" Then he fell back into place with the others.

Len stepped forward. He was nattily attired in a suit and tie. "I'm a little daft lately … kinda fun! Not for Margaret, though. Oh well, Margaret will be here soon. I've been warned." Everyone laughed at that. "I get to do it all over again … a boy this time. I'll teach him how to fish someday soon!"

The doorbell rang. Max jumped up in a cold sweat not knowing where he was. He looked at the kitchen clock. It was 10:12 in the morning. Linc barked and sniffed at the door.

"Who is it?" Max called.

"Harold Woods."

"Just a second." Max gathered himself and tossed cold water on his face at the kitchen sink. He then opened the door, revealing Woods with a young couple.

"Sorry, Max. This here is Mrs. Palmieri's daughter - Lila Conti and her husband, Jim Conti. You know Mrs. Palmieri? She made the lasagna for the Tupperware party - the lady in 5G. Anyway, I mentioned that you might be leaving at the end of the month, and, well, Jim's just back from deployment in Afghanistan, and I thought, maybe we -"

Max didn't know why Woods was stammering. Certainly Woods had seen a prosthetic arm before. Max had a sense that something else might be on Woods' mind.

"Army?" Max asked.

"Marines!" the young man said proudly.

Max turned his right hand upside down to shake the young man's left hand. Max was still a little foggy, but having a brother soldier in the room made him concentrate. "Where'd you get the pross?" Max asked. Woods and Lila were both shocked at Max's lack of tact.

"Helmand Province is where I left it. I got fitted at the parts department in Landstuhl, Germany," Jim said, with a smile appreciated only by another who had been there. "How 'bout you?" Jim asked.

"Three tours in-country: one in Iraq, two in Afghanistan…up in the Korengal."

"Deep shit in the mountains." Jim said.

"Deep shit in Helmand. Deep shit all over," they said simultaneously, chuckling.

The young woman put out her hand and reintroduced herself as Lila Conti.

"Sorry, I'm Max Burns, and this is my dog, Linc." Linc had gone on guard when he saw the prosthetic arm, but he saw that Max was comfortable. Linc had been in a protective mode of late. Max was fine with it, as long as Linc knew his boundaries.

"Okay to show them around, Max?"

"Roger that."

"What you see is what you get. It's a one bedroom," Woods said, as he showed the couple around. "It's a sublet, so everything goes through me. Sixteen hundred bucks a month, with two months' rent as security deposit in advance."

Max saw Jim's head drop as he heard the rent amount. They had done the math, and apparently $4,800 up front was not in the cards.

"C'mon, honey," Jim said. "Nice meeting you, Max. Let's go."

"My mother pays four hundred sixty a month for the same apartment!" Lila blurted out, almost in tears.

"Ms. Conti, with all due respect to your mother and your grandmother before her, they've been in that same apartment since

World War II. She is protected under rent control laws," Woods said as gently as he could.

"I'm having a baby. What are we supposed to do, live on the street? He has no job… the benefits suck. What more do they want from us?" Lila started crying.

"C'mon, honey," Jim said again, a little more forcefully this time. They started to leave.

Max felt terrible for them.

What the hell are they supposed to do? This marine loses his arm and the government sends him six hundred bucks a month and the state lets him have a Purple Heart on his license plate!

"What can you do as far as rent goes?" Max asked.

"Why?" Jim asked.

"If you got past the initial nut on the downstroke, could you pay the monthly rent?"

"It'd be tight until I get a job. Lila doesn't go on maternity leave for another four months… Why?" Jim asked again.

"Harold, you still have my security deposit, right?" Max said.

"Yeah. So?" Woods said, a quizzical look on his face.

"Did you tell the people I sublet from that you're turning the apartment over?" Max asked.

"Not yet. You have until the end of the month, so I…."

Max interrupted Woods. "If you kept my security deposit and continued things the way they are, nobody would be the wiser, right?"

"I suppose."

"And the rent would stay at thirteen hundred dollars, plus fifty bucks for the storage room. Is that a possibility?" Max asked, knowing that continuance of the extra fifty dollars per month would make Woods think harder about making this happening.

"What about *your* money for the security deposit?" Woods asked.

"I don't need charity!" Jim interjected as he grabbed his wife's arm to leave.

"No charity… a loan. You can give me so much a month till you pay my security deposit back. By the way, it's twenty-seven hundred bucks. I'll give you four years to pay it back. That's the minimum amount of time I should be at my next address."

"Why would you do this?" Jim asked.

"Because I'm going to work for a former marine and if he found out I didn't do this, I'd be back in the Korengal before I could say jarhead… Hell, I might go back anyway!"

Jim was trying to digest what was going on. After the Korengal statement, he looked at Max as though he was committable.

"Harold, are we cool?" Max asked.

"We're cool," Woods said to Max. "The fifty dollars is in cash to me on the side, with the rent, on the first of the month," Woods said to Jim and Lila. They both nodded approval.

Max wrote his information on the back of a Gringo Smyth's business card he still kept in his wallet.

"The place is furnished, that should help…*PayPal* is fine." Max looked at Jim and asked, "Where are you from?"

"Columbus, Ohio," Jim said.

"You're in New York City now, my man. You better take it any way you can get it in this town!"

"We'll call you, Mr. Burns," Lila said.

"Call Mr. Woods. I'm leaving no matter what. You have my new address and phone number if you need me."

"Thank you so much. Is there anything we can do for you?" Lila asked as she pulled her husband down the hall.

"…Eva is a nice name for a girl. *Semper fi!*" Max said as he walked them to the door.

Curlander will get a kick out of this… friggin' marines!

Lila Conti was excited beyond words as she let herself in their 2004 Honda Civic. She hoped their luck was changing. Jim drove, as he had prior to his deployment.

"The guy's crazy, Lila. C'mon… three tours… and he said he

might go back. Half the guys in the psych ward at Landstuhl say the same thing!"

"I don't give a damn if he's nuts or not! I don't give a damn if *you're* nuts or not! All I know is, if you're going to find work you'll find it here. New York City is where the whole world fell apart and it will be people like Max Burns that understand our situation. **It's not charity!** It's payback, as far as I'm concerned. Don't you get it? We are having a baby, Jimmy! I'd name the baby Hitler if he asked me to!" Lila said, starting to whimper.

Jimmy looked out the driver-side window and then back at his wife. He touched her cheek. Lila saw something in his eyes that she had not seen since before he'd left to serve his country: she saw resolve. His eyes seemed different as he looked back at her. They shed some of the sadness that had laid over him like a shroud. Lila rubbed her tummy to convey the new message of hope to their baby. Jim smiled and continued driving north on Broadway.

"We're gonna pay him back… every damn cent. Where's he moving to?" Jim asked Lila.

Lila fumbled in her purse for the card with Max's new address. The card read, "Maxwell Burns, Chef Executive, 1600 Pennsylvania Avenue, Washington, D.C., 20500."

"Oh God! He is nuts," Lila said, covering her mouth and starting to cry over again.

"What's the matter?" Jim asked, trying to concentrate on driving.

"He thinks he's the president!" she cried loudly as she held out the card with the information.

"What are you talking about?" Jim said as he pulled the car over into a bus stop on Broadway. He grabbed the card and read it as Lila wept. "I told you he was a fuckin' nut!" Jim screamed and banged the wheel with his prosthesis. He stared back at the card for a few seconds.

"Wait a minute," he said. "I heard about this guy. He's a pal of president-elect Curlander. This could be legit! It's not ***chief*** executive; this says ***chef*** executive! Look, honey: c-h-e-f, not c-h-i-e-f."

Lila was looking at him and grabbed the card back.

"The guy **is** legit!" Jim said. "He is gonna work for a marine? That'd be Curlander!"

Lila burst out crying again as they hugged each other.

Jim knew how hard things had been on his wife. He seized control in a positive way for the first time since coming home from Afghanistan. He felt good about that too…they both did.

"Now your mom can help us with babysitting during the day. I'll find a job somewhere and maybe you can go back to work eventually. Things are going to be fine. Someone up there is finally looking out for the Conti family," Jim said, smiling for the first time in a very long time.

Had they read the front of the business card, they might have noticed that they were parked across the street from the building that once was the home of Gringo Smyth's restaurant. They might have also noticed the elderly Jewish landlord inspecting the renovation progress for his apartment building… on the corner of 168th Street and Broadway.

CHAPTER 66

Max felt a sense of relief about the Contis moving in. It added a sense of family to a place he and Eva would have started their own family. Somehow it filled a gap. He had to try and keep that ball rolling.

Lately, Linc had been eating better than Max. Max whipped up a quick health food drink for himself and some dry food for Linc before heading off to Central Park. They would both miss running around the park, their oasis in New York City.

Max knew some form of exercise was mandatory for clarity and a route back to logical thinking. He knew depression lurked, looking for a place to nest in his head. They started their run on the upper loop.

There seemed to be an abundance of jogging strollers out.

Looks like Mother's Day out here.

He tried not to pay it any mind.

After a mile or so, the mothers jogging with strollers seemed to be doing so in slow motion, smiling and nodding to Max as they passed. He could see their lips moving, as they greeted him. At first he attributed this to the notoriety of the TV interview, etc.... Only the women with strollers nodded in recognition - only women pushing babies moved slowly, while other runners maintained a normal pace. It turned surreal and discomforting the further Max jogged. He stopped at a water fountain and threw cold water on his face.

What the hell is going on?

Max and Linc continued running. Things got back to normal for a few minutes. Then, those same women that had passed by before, came by again.

They couldn't have run the four-mile loop!

Max decided to head for Dog Hill and let Linc run free. Max could lie in the grass there and gather his thoughts. There would be enough dogs to keep Linc busy.

Some of the regulars and a few new pups were romping around. This was alpha-dog time for Linc. He would play king of the hill until the next king showed up. Linc was puppy enough to play yet old enough at one year to feel his testosterone kicking in. Max checked frequently to make sure Linc was behaving.

It was not difficult to relate losing his unborn son and the baby's mother with the cartoon characters running around Central Park.

Better now than at night, Max thought as he stretched out on the cold, hard ground.

His mind drifted. He felt a foot nudge him. He looked up at a bright, shining orb with a blurred face in the middle. Max rolled to one side and shaded his eyes. It took Max a second to make sure she was actually of this world and not a mushroom configuration.

It was the young redhead he had met previously on Dog Hill.

"He's trying to hump my dog," she said nonchalantly as she nodded over toward Linc and her pup. Linc was sniffing around… more inspecting than humping.

"He has good taste," Max blurted out.

"It's okay, I guess. You can never start too young with these things." She put out her hand and helped pull Max up. "Karen Featherstone. We met a few weeks ago here. I gave you my card… **remember**?" She seemed pissed she hadn't gotten a call, which probably didn't happen often.

"Max Burns, nice to meet you… again."

"I told you to call about breeding? At least your dog got the message."

"I hope she takes his advances as the compliment it is. She's beautiful."

"She is, isn't she? I saw you guys on TV and fell in love with that mug on Lincoln...the entire country did. I call her Mugsy."

"Mugsy, huh. I knew a Mugsy, once... briefly." He was relaxed enough to drift a bit.

"Huh! My father had a friend called Mugsy. My dad said he got the name from the old black-and-white East Side Kids movies. The leader was a guy named Mugsy. What about your Mugsy? What was he like?" She asked, trying to pry a conversation out of Max.

"He was a hero... the Mugsy I met. I only knew him for a few hours... in Afghanistan. He was a Navy SEAL." He whistled for Linc. Linc regretfully obeyed and came to Max. Max put the lead on him.

"How is your Mugsy doing now?" She asked.

"He's dead... in a chopper that got shot down with twenty-two SEALs and sixteen others."

"Shit! I hate war. Nobody wins... lately anyway. At least somebody won the wars with numbers on them."

You're right! You had to kill everyone to do it... but you're right."

Max dusted himself off and hoped for an uneventful walk home with Linc.

"Which way are you going, Max?"

"I go north from here. Maybe finish our run and head out of the park at Ninety-Sixth. How about you?" Max asked.

"Oh, I am on the Upper East Side. Like my father's pal Mugsy, I'm an East Side kid."

"Maybe I'll see you around on Dog Hill before I leave," Max said, to make it clear he was not going to be in New York City much longer.

One woman was plenty for Max Burns. He was not a player. He had been lucky enough to find two great women at a young age. He was not about to complicate that gift.

"Where are you moving to?"

"Washington, D.C."

"Where in D.C.?" she asked. He'd been hoping that question wouldn't pop up.

"Right in the middle," he said, straightening Linc's collar.

"The middle is the White House."

"Yeah, my new job is at the White House. I'm the chef… Ed and Amy Curlander's chef, at least for the next four years or so."

"Now it makes sense: the TV interview. You and your dog are hot shit, Max Burns!"

Max wasn't the best reader of women. He wasn't sure if the redhead knew the facts or not. It didn't matter.

"No. You're the hot shit. Your photos are all over. I didn't know your name, but I recognized your face… among other things."

"You know what, Max Burns? You sound like you've got a girlfriend." Karen said, smiling.

"I do, as a matter of fact. She lives in D.C."

"She's a very lucky young lady. She paused to gather a thought - I wish you the best with her. It's refreshing to meet a man that's faithful to his woman… especially when she's out of town. You hold on to my card. Maybe sometime in the future we can get our puppies together. How does that sound?" Karen said.

"Our puppies were already together. Got your card right here in my wallet. Good luck in your career, Karen. See? You made a brand-new fan," Max said as hh started walking north.

"Fans? I have plenty of… ta-ta, Mister Max." They both laughed and went their separate ways.

I needed that Linc. Looks like you did too!

The walk home was uneventful.

Max picked up his mail and headed upstairs. A good hot shower helped. As the water beat on his head, thoughts of fatherhood and Eva popped up. Try as he might, Max could not inject Dana into a visual. Eva and his son dominated his every thought. The more he tried to dismiss the IMAX size presentations going on in his mind, the more vivid they became.

Max tried not to fall asleep as he lay on the couch. He needed to be exhausted at night. Sleep was needed then, not now, although sleep - any sleep - was an ally. Deep sleep was an unattainable luxury.

Let the demons take me… there will be no battle.

Surrender was a concept Max was not familiar with, but surrender to sleep was a tactic.

Max had scurried around the apartment packing haphazardly. There would be too much for a rented car or even a van for one trip. He would need Tom Ryder, the cabdriver/mover, to take the bulk of his things to Washington, D.C... Max was fine with some things being stored in Dana's garage. That solved one logistical problem. It all seemed permanent.

Can there ever be anything permanent in my life?

He thought about what kind of father he would have been. He recalled life lessons his father and grandfather had taught him. The old fishing hole on the farm came to mind. The fishing hole was where Max's grandfather and - years later - Max's dad had taken their sons to impart life lessons. He remembered how embarrassed he'd been when his father had gotten up the courage to talk about what he called, "the facts of life." The manner in which Max's father behaved prior to his attempt to educate his son, had Max racking his mind for what he might have done wrong. Instead, Max Burns Sr., while putting together his fishing pole, attempted to explain what an erection was and, subsequently, what to do with it. Max had stopped his dad mid-sentence to explain his understanding of the **other** use of a penis - outside of its urinating function - with pertinent biological and anatomical wording. His father thanked him, and they continued to fish in silence. They threw back all the small-mouth bass they caught - Max Sr. had been let off the hook as well.

The fishing hole was also where his dad told Max about his mother's breast cancer. She died two years later. His dad hadn't been able to bring himself to take Max to the fishing hole to tell him how serious his own pancreatic cancer had become. He was gone soon after. Max lost both parents in his senior year of high school.

Graduation from high school was the springboard that propelled Max out of WashPa. There had been enough insurance money and savings for Max to pay for his tuition at the Culinary Institute of America. Most everyone understood why he wanted to leave. Everyone hoped he would return someday.

But, Max had not been back to WashPa since then. He wasn't even sure whether his uncle Dick had sold the farm. He didn't care. Life in WashPa was over for him. He wasn't bitter: He was finished. Sure … there were uncles, aunts, and cousins, all good people—simple folk not out to screw anybody. If they'd all divided up the farm, that would be okay by Max. They had all lived in WashPa for generations. The one thing Max did insist upon was having his parents buried next to each other in the family cemetery, back by the edge of the fields, not far from the old fishing hole. That was something his dad had promised his mom. It had gone without saying that his dad would spend eternity there with her.

There were no photos of Max's high school graduation. There were no immediate family left to take pictures. Max said his goodbyes to his friends at the graduation parties after the commencement ceremony. Max had been class president and winner of seventeen academic scholarships, plus a dozen more for wrestling. But Max was most proud of being chosen, by his fellow students, to give the commencement address. The honor served him well, allowing him a final farewell to Thomas Hennelly. Max had graduated high school on a hot Saturday afternoon in late June, the number one academic student for his graduating class. He left WashPa the next day on his fully restored 650 cc 1964 Triumph Bonneville motorcycle, headed for Hyde Park, New York, to begin his tenure at the Culinary Institute of America.

Penn State offered him a four-year scholarship for wrestling - "a full boat"- the recruiter said. Max asked the recruiter, "Is there a culinary school at Penn State?"

The recruiter said, "Son, I don't rightly know what a culinary school is. But if it's a school, we got one at Penn State!" There was not.Max remembered telling Eva, "It was the first time I realized I was in charge of my own destiny."

CHAPTER 67

Night comes as though it can't wait to get here!

Max looked at some newly sprouted mushrooms. He was in his sweats. He started the ceremony of wrapping his hands, as he always did before hitting the heavy bag. The bag had duct tape around its middle. It had been hit so often and hard that one side had caved in and bulged out the back. Every once in a while Max unhooked it and turned it a quarter turn to give it new life. Hand wrapping was a time for thought. Max had to be methodical with his wraps. He hit the bag so hard that a loose wrap could cause a wrist to fracture or fingers to snap.

The session always became more intense when an unsolicited face appeared on the bag: It provided purpose, intensity and a reason to continue to exhaustion. Some worked better than others.

No guest appearance today?

Then it came: the mirror image of himself.

What are you smilin' about? Fair enough. I understand. I guess I deserve a good beating!

He hit hard and fast. Tears began to well up in his eyes. He tried not to lose rhythm as he wiped the tears with the top of his wraps.

Max beat the bag for an hour and seventeen minutes. Calloused skin had torn from his knuckles. Blood dripped through the holes of his gloves onto the floor and his face turned a pinkish hue from blood and tears.

Max didn't clean it up.

Let the rats have it.

He fell into the rocker. Linc jumped in Max's lap and licked his master's blood. The violent striking of the bag had become second nature to Linc - blood was new to him.

Max took off the wraps and dropped them into the sink. He let the cold water run on his hands and washed the wraps and his hands with a bar of brown soap. He put his hands into a towel and twisted the towel to produce pressure on the seeping cracks. The bleeding stopped.

Max buried his head in a towel and rocked slowly in his chair. Eventually he surfaced. He picked up the photos on the top of the suitcase in search of a happy moment in his life... that's when the carousel in his head opened for business.

Where are the controls for this carousel?

He looked at the crate next to him. The dried-out mushrooms from the night before were still there. He picked one up and stared at the black hole. There was a tiny light where the hanger had pierced the core. He had a strong impulse to bite the entire top off and laugh his way into eternity.

Max looked at Linc. "I wouldn't do that to you, pal. Who'd take care of you, huh? The POTUS... that's who. Don't worry. Rangers never leave anyone behind."

He stared again at the black center of the mushroom. He played his little game, bringing the crumpled black center past his focal point and watching it divide in two. He could not bring himself to call the mushrooms, "the children" anymore. He pulled the mushroom back to his focal point and then put it down. The carousel slowed to a halt on its own.

"Ahhhh, some peace.

Tomorrow we feed the homeless. You'll meet a new friend. He's a bit strange, as are all men of the cloth, but I think you'll like him. Let's go upstairs."

Upstairs, Max showered and got ready for bed. He realized he had not called Dana today. It was 10:40 p.m.

Max held his phone and prepared himself for the call.

"Hi, baby. How was your day?" Max asked, hoping for her to takeover.

"Hey, there you are. I'm good. How are you? You sound exhausted."

"I am. It's great," he said.

"What's great?" she asked.

"It's great to be exhausted."

"Hmmm...Things are okay here too. Charlie Wiggins is a bastard... but I'm learning. He should've coached at Green Bay."

"You're sharp enough to realize he's a teacher. Socrates was tough on his students too."

"Socrates? Why God saw fit to put that brain of yours into the body of a Clydesdale, I'll never know."

"Maybe it was the devil," Max said, only half kidding at this point in time.

"I want parts of that body inside parts of this body. That's what I want." Dana said.

"My sentiments exactly. Are you up for a little phone sex?" he asked with a smile.

"Why don't you wait till I'm on the air in ten minutes. I'll tell the audience, excuse me America, I have to answer this call... then I can start moaning and writhing in my chair. You can watch it on TV with everyone else."

Max was only half listening. "So, do you think you'll work right up until the inauguration?" he asked.

"Ratings are up since the announcement and the interviews. The mucky-mucks here are begging me to hold on as long as possible. I told them I'll accommodate them as best I can, as long as Wetherford is not in the picture and Wiggins is okay with it. But it's not easy with Wiggins on my ass every single day. Thank God he has the rest of the staff to contend with. He's also prepping cabinet members for their Senate grilling. The guy's unbelievable," Dana said. "Okay, I am on in six minutes… I love you. Talk tomorrow… Say hello to Lincoln for me."

"Break a leg, baby."

The phone call had a soothing effect on him. The merry-go-round was not running this evening. Physical exercise was a big part of his mental restoration. He was annoyed he had disregarded the peace afforded by exhaustion.

CHAPTER 68

At two o'clock the next afternoon, Max rang the rectory doorbell. Father Pete answered the door and said, "Good afternoon, my son. I see you brought Washington with you."

"Lincoln, Padre… His name is Lincoln," Max said, smiling.

"Of course… Lincoln. Does he like meatballs? Sure he does," Father Pete said, answering his own question.

Linc looked up at Max as if to say, "**Is this guy in the black dress for real?"** Max stayed around until Linc got acclimated to the rectory and Father Pete. It didn't take long… he smelled like food.

Father Pete gave Max the key to the auditorium door and told him, "Maisy will be there within an hour or so. She is the paid helper and the reason things are spotless. You'll like Maisy. She's a worker - she cares. There was a delivery from the restaurant wagon last night. Check the walk-in box. Good luck. Call me if you need me."

Maisy arrived at 3:00 p.m. sharp. She was a big black woman in her fifties. Max could tell immediately that this was her show. She reminded Max of Esperanza from the bodega.

Maybe God is a woman!

"You must be Max. Where's the dog? I brought my camera to get a picture with the dog!"

"And you're Maisy. Lincoln is in the rectory with Father Pete."

"I hope he doesn't eat him," Maisy said, shaking her head.

"No way… he's a good dog. He wouldn't bite anyone."

"I mean the priest! I hope he doesn't eat the dog." She said, laughing out loud as she headed for the walk-in box. "That man WILL eat! We could feed twice the people if he went on a mission to Africa."

Max laughed.

We'll get along fine.

Maisy checked on the delivery. "This is what's left after **Father Piranha** gets through with the Rayo's delivery," she said. "What I usually do is heat up the soups and mix them together... no choices. You can't let these people help themselves. Poor bastards will line their pockets with aluminum foil and fill 'em up with whatever they can get their hands on. Makes a mess too. Never again!" Maisy rolled up her sleeves. "You want to watch and see how I do it? You got anything to add, jump right on in, Mr. Max."

Maisy had it down to a science. It was not so much cooking as reheating and portion control. Max watched her swing into action. She had the top burners, microwave, and oven going all at once. The food got hot every way possible in Maisy's kitchen. Then the food was put into chafing dishes to be scooped out onto cardboard plates. It was an efficient operation.

"You can't rely on anyone else showin' up," Maisy said, as she worked the kitchen with both hands. "These poor folk need this meal. It is all they get to eat all day. We give 'em seconds, after everyone eats... if we got 'em. They'll keep gettin' in line until it's all gone, and that's okay." There wasn't much for Max to do until the doors opened. When they did open, it looked like a scene out of a documentary on the Great Depression. Max helped dole out the food.

Was it one horrendous decision, a series of bad decisions or plain bad luck... that put these people in the netherworld?

"Not too much!" Maisy snapped, watching the amount of food Max was apportioning. "We need to feed them all or we'll have a riot on our hands," she said. "Worst that can happen... a second wave comes through the door and no food left. That's when you come into play, my large friend. Lucky it's winter. Most of 'em are in Florida."

"Florida? How do they get down there?" Max asked as they worked together.

"Any way they can. Some still hoppin' freight trains... some hitchhike... others walk 'til it gets warm. But most get bused down by the City of New York. Politicians don't talk about that much. You notice that there ain't too many of 'em sleeping on the street no more. The city don't provide no more shelters neither. When Giuliani was mayor, the rich folk couldn't take the panhandlers and windshield washer people. They told the mayor to do something about it. He started busing them off with a one-way ticket to Florida. Let the rich folk down there take care of 'em. Nobody's supposed to know about it."

Max watched the faces of these people light up when the food hit their plates. He made a mental snapshot of these faces.

Maybe, as executive chef, I could start a national program with Amy as chairperson. It would be a great project for Amy to get involved with... lots of vets on this food line.

Max was surprised at the number of people in their thirties and forties lined up for a meal. Some still had field jackets from their various branches of service.

Most still have legible names on the left breast pocket. Not surplus and definitely not donated. Nobody gets rid of their field jacket. A field jacket is like an old friend. Maybe a wife or girlfriend wants to dump it but, by God, not the owner. A field jacket is to a vet what a security blanket is to a child.

Max was mesmerized by their faces.

"This was an easy one." Maisy said to Max, when they were done. "Tomorrow will be different. Tomorrow you should get some pasta going before I get here at three. I counted sixty-three today ... Tomorrow it'll be twice that. Most restaurants in New York City are closed on Mondays, so not much help with any restaurant surplus. Get prepped for about a hundred twenty plus. It gets nasty too ...

I hate Tuesdays. Tuesdays will be your day, Mr. Max. You cook it, and I'll hand it out."

As soon as the last scraps of food were off the plates, Maisy started cleaning up. She walked out into the dining area and reminded the diners to pick up their trays and dump the paper plates and plastic spoons in the proper recycling bins. Nobody messed with Maisy. "Y'all know I never forget a face. So get your asses in gear and clean up after yourselves. I ain't your maid, and if I see you make a mess, I ain't gonna be your cook neither."

Max helped clean up. Maisy was efficient. She made the soup kitchen a three-hour job from start to finish. Max had the feeling that anyone who interrupted Maisy's schedule would be dealt with accordingly.

I better get here early tomorrow for the prep work.

They finished cleaning up at five forty-five and were out by six.

"Where's Lincoln? Lincoln has to free this here slave and let her go home," Maisy bellowed with a laugh.

"I think some photos are definitely in order. Let's head for the rectory."

They knocked on the door. Father Pete came out to answer with his napkin in hand and a mouth full of half-chewed something.

"Well, how was your baptism under fire, Max?"

"Okay. I hear tomorrow is the real test. You got yourself a real professional here." Max said, patting Maisy on the back. Maisy appreciated it. Linc was at the door, blocked by Father Pete from escaping to the street.

"There he is!" Maisy said, looking down at Linc's head peeking out from underneath Father Pete's black cassock. Linc came out with his leash dragging behind his wagging tail. He went to Maisy, the newcomer. She loved it. She took her phone out and handed it to Max for the requisite picture. Father Pete started to get into the picture but Maisy said, "Uh-uh… not in this one… just me and the dawg!" She bent down and knelt next to Linc. Linc was getting used to the picture taking. It looked like he held his breath and slammed his tongue back in his mouth waiting for a picture to be snapped. Father Pete grabbed his phone for a picture as well. Linc was licking Father Pete's face profusely as Max took their picture. Maisy held out her hand, and Father Pete put an envelope in it. It was her pay.

Whatever the amount… it's not enough.

Father Pete told Max to hold on to the key for now.

Max felt good being around people. The soup kitchen was great therapy. As he and Linc walked away from the rectory, Linc kept turning around and looking back. It was as though he already missed his new friend. When they got home, Max put out some food for Linc. He sniffed it, looked up at Max, and walked away from his dish. That had never happened before. Linc's pal must have fed him like a king.

Great! Just what I need…you getting spoiled rotten by the clergy. Maybe Rodrigo… excuse me … Mahatma and Father Pete should both apply for sainthood status for you.

Max said his goodbyes and walked his dog home.

He wasn't hungry. He had nibbled away in the kitchen. The quality of the food depended on the which restaurants the donations came from. Today had an ample amount from some four star eateries. Max kicked back on the couch. He glanced over at the Tupperware containers he'd brought upstairs and thought about taking some M#7 tomorrow to spice things up - or calm things down. He thought about using a full film canister in the soup. The ratio should pose no problem as far as dosage. There were two sixteen-gallon soup pots used. That was enough for sufficient dilution.

Let's see what effect it has on the taste of soup.

Max put the M#7 in one of the old film canisters — approximately 2 ounces. He left it next to his keys.

Max changed into his sweats to hit the heavy bag. When he and Linc got into the elevator, a woman was in there. Max smiled but didn't know who she was. However, she knew very well who he was.

"Mr. Burns."

Max turned around and said, "Yes, ma'am."

"I'm Teresa Palmieri. I want to thank you for what you did for my daughter and her husband. That was above and beyond the call of duty, young man. May God bless you and keep you safe," she said as she touched his shoulder.

"Ma'am, it wasn't even close to above and beyond the call of duty. What your son-in-law and daughter have sacrificed for their country is above and beyond the call of duty. It was my pleasure to be around at the right time."

She smiled as she exited.

"That's a nice lady, Linc. I heard you growl when she touched my shoulder. You need to mind your manners."

No face on the bag at wrap time. He fought to keep his mind blank to see if it were possible to control the outcome. He used every military psych trick he could muster up. He had a good day - he needed a good night.

Max quickly got into rhythm. His punches were weak. Still no face… twenty minutes… and no face. Max stopped at twenty-three minutes. He was breathing heavier than he should've been for a short workout.

I guess I need motivation.

He started in again. Paco's face lit up the bag, and Max got up on his toes to pummel away. He went for an additional thirty-five minutes.

Max had a good sweat going, his mind was quiet. He wanted to keepit that way. Max picked a fresh mushroom and, once again, played his little visual game, bringing it close enough to tease his focal point. Max was mesmerized by the black spotted eye looming large as it came to get him before splitting off in two pieces.

Why not? Let's see what happens.

He bit a small piece out of the side. He was careful not to overstep into the dangerous area. It had more of a bitter taste than he'd expected. *Probably due to not being dried out.*

He sat back to enjoy any oncoming moments of peace. The sweat had drained him. He went to the sump sink and turned on the cold water. He cupped his hands to splash his face and quench his thirst. Max was amazed that nobody bottled New York City tap water for commercial purposes. It was great-tasting water. He washed the back of his neck to stop a light-headed feeling that came upon him. Max dropped into the rocker. All of a sudden he felt sick to his stomach and weak.

Uh-oh, am I going down?

The feeling did not originate in his brain. It was gastro-intestinally born - the feeling you get from food poisoning. He knew it well from the back alley souks and marketplaces he'd frequented. He felt the contents of his stomach come north. He got to the sink and heaved violently for a minute. He knew he was lucky to have emptied the contents of his stomach.

Way too much!

He managed to walk with Linc to the elevator. It seemed like an eternity getting to the fourth floor.

Max stood in a cold shower for about twenty minutes. He'd had this feeling once before, while bleeding out while firing a Ma Deuce .50-caliber machine gun until the barrel almost melted. That was the day his vehicle had been hit by the I.E.D... He had fought to stay conscious to make sure the enemy was dead before he passed out or bled out. Max hadn't known how bad he was hit at the time.

Nobody ever does.

He had passed out in the chopper that morning and woke up at the Battalion Aid Station. After a few blood transfusions and some hydrating liquids, he was weak but fully cognizant of his surroundings.

That O.J. at the B.A.S. center is still the best-tasting drink I ever had.

Max came out of the bathroom half-dried, a towel wrapped around his waist. He opened the refrigerator door to find a half-filled container of two-week-old orange juice. He needed to hydrate - it would have to do. He gulped it out of the container. It wasn't the same as Middle Eastern O.J., but it was liquid and not sour. He plopped down on the couch for a few minutes. He called Dana before dozing off. There was no answer.

She should be in between shows.

He really didn't have the energy to talk to her, but he didn't want her calling him if he did fall asleep. He decided to get into bed in case he slept all night. He grabbed a wastepaper basket in case of an emergency heave during the night. Linc moved gingerly around Max. He sensed all was not well with his master. Max lay on top of the covers in case a bathroom visit became necessary. He woke up underneath the covers six hours later. Max knew he was very lucky that his body had recognized the mushroom was too toxic.

Good thing tomorrow's M#7 is finely ground. Chunks? Not a good idea.

CHAPTER 69

Snow stuck to the sidewalks in the morning - rain dissolved it by noon. Max got to the kitchen at two o'clock to make sure he had a jump on things. He hadn't brought Linc this time, so he didn't stop at the rectory. The Padre would have to eat alone today. Max was sure, that wouldn't bother Fr. Pete much.

Max thought about serving pasta. He'd seen stacks of minestrone soup in two-gallon cans. Max figured about twelve gallons of soup and twenty-four pounds of pasta should be sufficient. There were refrigerated salad greens that were two days old but still fairly crisp. Max started boiling water in the ten-gallon pots for pasta. The sauce would have to come straight from the shelf supply.

Max split the M#7 film canister equally into the two soup pots and stirred as each heated up.

That should be okay for a hundred twenty people. This crew deserves the Max Burns soup du jour.

Max intended to leave them with a delicious meal along with smiles on their faces.

Maisy got there at three o'clock. There was no smile on her face with her anticipation of Tuesday's drudgery. Max asked, "What's wrong?"

"You'll find out, my man. You'll find out." Maisy said as she rolled up her sleeves. "That soup smells gooooood. I may have some of that myself."

"I added some ingredients to doll it up some." The pasta water bubbled. He added some olive oil so the pasta would not stick together. "What do you think, Maisy? What have I forgotten?"

"Lookin' good to me. They haven't had pasta in a while. I see some bread got delivered. I'll put it out on the tables. Let's hope they'll act civilized and not fight over it. I'll put out the pitchers of water and plastic cups… You watch the food."

Maisy came back and scooped some soup into a plastic cup and sipped away. "Mmmmm. That's some good minestrone soup. I've made this soup here for five years, it ain't never tasted like this before. You're not a chef… you're a witchdoctor!"

Maisy opened the doors at four o'clock. A hard rain was pouring down. The poor homeless gang had been getting soaked for who knows how long. Their unruly appearance was magnified from being soaked to the bone. It reminded Max of his first night at the Scirocco.

The soup will warm their innards.

Ironically, nobody took off their wet gear. Max was told by Maisy, "They're afraid someone will steal their only means of keeping warm."

Lack of a warm coat and shoes was a ticket to potter's field for the men and women of the street. Max counted four times as many men as women. They all bellied up to the serving station without a word. They were here for the food and nothing more. The fact that they were out of the rain was an added bonus. Max truly hoped they would enjoy the meal. They were not unruly at all as Maisy had led Max to believe they would be. They got their food, never looking up at the new face in town. Max looked over at Maisy and gave his - raised eye-brow look. She flashed back her - wait-and-see look. Max handled the pasta and sauce while Maisy doled out the soup, two ladles to a bowl. Max noticed that nobody said thank you.

There was an occasional nod of the head. One lady said "Bless you," to both Max and Maisy.

Maisy knew her and said, "Patricia, you look beautiful today." Maisy slid over to Max and said, "Patricia was a dancer in the original cast of *West Side Story* on Broadway. I know that for a fact. She was a really good dancer. Her son took her off the streets a few years ago… she ran away from him. She came back to be in New York City… all the way from Minnesota."

There was a low hum in the dining room. People began to talk to each other. Maisy looked out at the crowd with a great big smile.

She said to Max, "Ya know, I love these people. 'There… but for the grace of God, go I.' They seem extra cordial to each other today. Maybe 'cause your big pale ass is sittin' here behind the counter cookin' different vittles." Maisy laughed and slapped Max on his ass.

One of the old-timers stood up with his water cup in hand and tried to propose a toast to Maisy and her new friend. The guy looked at Max, fishing for a name.

"Max!" Maisy yelled.

"A toast to Maisy and Max for an outstanding meal!" he shouted out. Then the guy next to him threw water in his face. The toastmaster sat down as though it never happened.

The men and women had finished their meals in about ten minutes. Patricia got up and began dancing around the tables. She was probably close to eighty but still light on her feet. At the other end of the tables, an elderly gentleman in a field jacket began reciting Rudyard Kipling's poem, "Gunga Din," word for word. Not a soul gave a damn except Max, who happened to like Kipling. As though in slow motion, another old-timer with a full beard and plenty of street time under his belt started collecting the cardboard soup bowls and proceeded to stack them up. He balanced the six foot stack on his head and walked around the tables as Patricia danced around avoiding him at the turn. The place was coming alive. It was like the advent of spring - flowers blooming one at a time. Each person obliged to participate in the nascent ritual.

Maisy came over to Max in disbelief. "This is amazing. There are usually a few fistfights by this time. It must be you, Max." Then Maisy went out to Patricia. Patricia curtsied, and they proceeded to waltz around the floor together.

The mushrooms? At least the dosage was on the button. It was one whole film canister for 127 people - the party dosage.

Maisy was quite the hostess. Max was impressed that she knew most of them by name.

"Usually I kick their asses out when the trouble starts. Tonight? Tonight is a special night.... I can feel it. Thank you, Max. You were just what this place needed. Let's let them stay and dry out while we clean up. I usually have my baseball bat goin' on 'bout this time," Maisy said, nodding over to the bat in the corner of the cooking area. "I am so glad you volunteered to help. You make some ass-kickin' soup, baby. You best leave me **that** recipe." Max had to admit, it was damn good soup... coming from a can.

One gent put some salt down on the floor and started doing a soft-shoe dance routine that was amazing.

Maisy said, "Ya know, the last time he dumped salt on the floor, I hit him in the ass so hard with my bat, the Yankees were lookin' to sign me up. I thought he was messin' up the place... heeeeheeee."

Max watched bits and pieces of the show as he cleaned up. He found out something important: he could still smile. He had one more week of kitchen duty before January 20th rolled around.

Someone caught the corner of his eye. At first, he thought it might be a midget staring at him. Then he realized it was a young boy. He had on an oversize field jacket, a couple of beat-up high-top sneakers, and a vintage Pittsburgh Pirates baseball cap. He never moved a muscle. He stood there and stared at Max. Max hadn't served the kid any food. He would have remembered serving a child. Max noticed something else strange - the kid was dry. He waved him over but the boy didn't move. He just stared at Max. Max decided to bring him some soup and pasta. He put the tray down on the table nearest the boy. The boy still didn't move. His eyes were transfixed on Max. If he were a grown-up, Max would have been in his face looking for some answers. Evidently, this boy of eight or nine years of age, had issues. Max left the food on the table and walked away. Max thought he might've made the boy self-conscious or nervous. The boy sat down and ate everything. He got up, took his tray over to the garbage, and dumped it. He walked back to the same place he'd stood before and continued to stare at Max.

Max went over to Maisy and asked, "Who does that kid belong to?"

Maisy looked all around.

"Over there by the end table." Max said.

"What kid?" she asked.

"That - " Max stopped. There was no child. Max came out from behind the counter and searched the room. There was only one way in and out: the double doors which had not been reopened.

Max went back over to Maisy, who was singing a medley of *West Side Story* tunes with Patricia and her newly formed chorus.

"Maisy, you didn't see a kid in here with a baseball hat and a field jacket?"

"Max, there ain't no children ever come to this soup kitchen in the five years I been workin' here. I'd call the police if I saw a kid." She looked at Max strangely and resumed singing. Max shook his head. He looked all around the place to see if the kid could be hiding or maybe living in the building. It was a parish school but the students were on Christmas vacation.

No! He's one of the street people. He's no student… not looking like that.

Max did most of the cleanup, since Maisy was on her third attempt at singing, "Officer Krupke." Max was enjoying the party from afar. He looked over his shoulder every once in a while. The hair on the back of his neck never failed him.

Ghazi Haider is the only person ever to come up behind me undetected.

Max was back in the apartment by seven. He took Linc out after feeding him. Linc was eating his food a little more slowly these days. Max had the Padre to thank for that. It was close to eight thirty when he called Dana while he and Linc walked home. She had finished her early telecast.

"Hey," Max said. "How was the show?"

"Hi! The show went well. Ratings are better than ever. I miss you."

"I miss you too. The soup kitchen is a blast. It was a good move … I am enjoying it. They got some real characters there. It's sad yet happy in some ways. There was a little kid that showed up today. That threw me for a loop. I didn't expect to see a child in a soup kitchen." Max was sorry he'd brought it up.

"Really? Did you call child welfare services?"

"No. He… he disappeared. He must've run off or something. I turned around, and he was gone." Max wanted to change the subject. "The people were dancing around after the meal. I guess I haven't lost my touch in the kitchen." Max said, snickering to himself.

"You better not lose it… You owe me *beaucoup* death by chocolate, baby. And it's not only your desserts I'm ready to woof down. I'm not sure I can hold out for some lovin' without going electric."

"Only a week or so. Do you think I'm having an easy time sleeping alone?" Max said.

If she only knew about my sleep habits of late!

Max did miss her. She kept him sane and happy.

"Linc says hello. He has been getting more than I have. He was up on Dog Hill humping puppies. He likes 'em young," Max said. "How is Wiggins treating you?"

"Oh God, he has me studying foreign affairs going back to the Revolutionary War. He is brilliant, though. After I memorize the general state of affairs, I get his slant on what's factual. I am in for much more than I bargained for." Dana said.

"Don't worry; you'll be fine. I can help. I am anxious to hear his spin on current affairs in the Middle East and Southern Asia," Max said.

"Oh, I almost forgot... Wiggins gave me a little box to give to you. Ahmed Karzai, the brother of the ex-president of Afghanistan, gave it to him for you... and a letter. I have them at home on the bureau. I might let you get out of bed and check them out... if I happen to fall asleep."

"You've got a deal. Gotta be from Ghazi Haider."

"Who?" Dana asked.

"He's an old friend. I hope you meet him one day. He is a great man: a teacher, a man of God, an honorable man." Max said.

"I am gonna work out. Call me later."

"Miss you and love you, soldier boy. Be safe."

"Good night, baby. Love you too."

Max hung up and changed into sweats.

He and Linc went downstairs to the storeroom. More mushrooms had popped through the soil. He plucked them and hung them by the furnace. He carefully licked some green residue from his fingers and began to wrap his hands. Max stopped after wrapping his left hand. He thought about the WashPa suitcase. He hastily searched through the photos once again. He didn't know what had compelled him to do so in the middle of his wrapping ritual until he stopped on one particular picture of himself. He glanced at the date on the back of the photo which placed him at ten years old at the time. He was wearing a Pittsburgh Pirates baseball hat and some high-top Converse All Star sneakers. The hat was an older model—the same type the little boy in the soup kitchen had been wearing. It looked to be identical, although there were no other telltale signs, and no fatigue jacket.

Huh! Maybe the kid is from Pittsburgh?

He put the picture on the box so he wouldn't forget to bring it with him. He wanted to show the picture to Maisy and Father Pete. He wrapped his right hand and began his workout.

Tito, the fighter, popped up. It was Tito's lucky day to get his ass kicked… again. Max had incorporated kicks into his heavy bag routine. That added lower body to his workout. He put in a good hour and felt better for it. He grabbed the picture, then went upstairs for a shower.

Max had not thought about his unborn son - he'd been active enough not to dwell on it. Max liked this photo of himself standing in front of the basketball backboard attached to the barn. He remembered the first time he wore his dad's Chuck Taylor Converse All Stars. Max had still been a size and a half away from filling them at the time. No matter… he put on three pairs of sweat socks.

Jeez…mom used to get pissed off at that!

He put the picture on the night table and stretched out on the bed. He remembered the day his dad took the photo. Max had been looking into the sun. He'd tried not to blink before the shutter snapped. He'd held his eyelids open for a seemingly impossible length of time. It had only been a few seconds, but it had seemed like an eternity for the photo to be taken. That was one of his first lessons in self-discipline. Max had imposed a test - a small personal challenge - he could not pass up.

There would be many more tests to come. He had a scar on his wrist from when a friend in high school had bet him that he could not hold still long enough for a cigarette to burn a hole through a dollar bill. Then the boy had proceeded to wrap the dollar bill tightly around Max's wrist. Another boy had held the cigarette there for seven seconds. Naturally, it had not been able to burn through the bill, because of the insulation from Max's flesh. It had, however, caused a third-degree burn on Max's wrist. He would come to know the smell of burning flesh again… in Afghanistan and Iraq. There was also the time during ranger training when an instructor asked for a volunteer to demonstrate waterboarding. Max had been enthusiastic about trying it. He had a simple explanation for volunteering, "I'll know what to expect." He'd lasted twice as long as anyone the instructor had ever worked on for demonstration purposes… or at Abu Ghraib prison.

Max had the sand all right. But, his strong point was physical tolerance, not mental. The mental side was a different game. The mental game could truly be a combat soldier's nightmare and a wounded soldier's curse. Max was both.

Max's thoughts drifted toward making love to Dana on the soft hay of the first day of harvest, with the smell of earth and barn wood in the air, followed by the softened daylight of dusk. He thought of the golden rods of sun that found their way, like an ancient clock, through the separated planks on the west side of the barn wall. He remembered how the light eventually made its way across the dirt floor then disappeared in the darkness. He had never made love to a woman in the barn. It was now on his, "To do list."

Maybe Dana will take a trip back to WashPa with me someday.

Max didn't know which relatives lived on the old farm now. He didn't care. He knew he should care, but his life unfolded in stages and that stage was over. Max was not big on looking back and money had never been a motivating force in his life. It probably should have been. Max knew the farm was still in the family. That was a good thing. His only instructions had been: **Do not sell the farm**. He only hoped it was being put to good use by the remaining members of his family.

I hope they'll let me use the barn for an evening or two.

Max was getting sleepy. He welcomed the feeling and dozed off. He dreamed about his father and his grandfather. They were dressed in the clothes Max remembered from the Sunday family dinners: wide ties, pants, double-breasted jackets, and laced shoes. He could see the hair in their ears and the moles on their faces.

So vivid!

Max could tell by their hands, who they were… especially his father's. He saw his father carving a turkey. His uncle Andy was doing magic tricks. Uncle Dick was still writing notes to himself and others. General Sherman's ring was missing from his father's hand!

The scene changed when Max noticed the ring was not on his father's hand. In a flash Max saw Ghazi Haider presiding over a campfire meeting in the Korengal. He was talking to members of his tribe: "There is an American who understands that honor is the most important trait a man can have. Maybe there is hope for our two countries."

None of the tribal leaders agreed with him. Haider knew that would be the outcome. He sipped his mint tea and stared up at the crescent moon surrounded by diamond pinholes that peeked through the black sky. A shooting star catapulted across the galaxy as though on assignment to deliver a message. Max could smell the pure Afghan night air and could hear the crackle of burning conifers.

Max recalled the Afghan summer evenings, temperatures dropping as much as forty degrees in minutes after the sun disappeared behind the mountains to begin the night.

Dusk is the most beautiful time of day during the Afghanistan harvest, with farmers leaving their fields, anticipating a bountiful dinner with family… not so different in WashPa.

A young Max saw his father and grandfather walking toward him. Without saying a word, each took him by a hand and continued their walk. They were walking in a field and came face-to-face with a little boy. Max was sure this was the same little boy from the soup kitchen. He was wearing the Pirates hat, the oversize field jacket, the irrepressible Converse All Star sneakers, so tattered they barely stayed together. Max put his hand to introduce himself. As his father had taught him. The boy put out his hand, but there was nothing… no hand, no boy, no father or grandfather. Max's hand remained outstretched with no one to accept his introduction. Max turned around. The two men and the boy were hand in hand walking back.

"Wait! Wait for me!" Max yelled. The boy looked back over his shoulder at Max as dusk spent its final moment of light. Max ran after them. Max had to get to them before the night left him alone. He ran back toward the barn as the darkness descended. The little boy was standing by the barn doors under the basketball hoop. Max walked slowly up to the boy. The boy's face was dirty with eyes piercingly clear. The Pittsburgh Pirates hat covered a mop of blond hair that stuck out like the barn straw stacked inside.

The boy pointed to the sky. "**Look!**" he said as a shooting star streamed across the Milky Way under the crescent moon. Max was in awe of the clarity of the heavenly white streak. When he looked back toward the boy to acknowledge the celestial event, the boy was nowhere to be found.

"Come out and tell me your secrets. Tell me who you are. No more teasing! Do I know you? Do you know me? Where are you from?" Max used a soft tone so as not to scare the boy.

But the boy had ideas and powers of his own. He could disappear at will.

"Such magic you possess! What gifts you have. Show me. I will not tell your secrets to anyone. Be my friend."

But there was no young boy to be found. There was only Max, now standing all alone on top of a small hill next to a tall tree.

It was daylight again. Max touched the smooth skin of the tree. There had been no such tree like this one back on the farm. He looked around for the boy. His hand began to stick to the smooth bark of the tree. He pulled it away. A sticky brownish-green substance coated his palm and fingers. He looked straight up. The canopy of a huge mushroom covered the sky. It grew higher and higher until it pierced the clouds. Max walked down the hill toward the barn to gain perspective on the spectacle. He looked up into the bright sun. He had to move to the umbra of the mushroom to see. A tiny speck atop the stem slowly descended. It was the boy. He came into sight as he slid further down the stem splattering green residue. He was covered with the green residue, his piercing eyes staring through the slime. He stood about twenty feet in front of Max. As he stared silently at Max, he licked his fingers, as though covered in chocolate.

"I think I'll call you Jack… 'Jack and the Beanstalk,'" Max said, smiling. The boy put his hand over his heart and stared back at Max.

"Are you saying, the Pledge of Allegiance?" Max asked as he

moved forward one step. But the boy backed up a step to maintain the distance. Max felt a conversation was the way to gain the boy's confidence. The boy held his right hand over his heart and continued to lick the fingers of his left hand.

"Do I know you? Is that your dad's field jacket? It's awfully big on you." The boy nodded slowly and smiled. Max looked at the left pocket covered by the boy's right hand. He wasn't saying the Pledge of Allegiance - he was covering the surname and initials stenciled on all U.S. Army-issue field jackets. Max struggled to see between the boy's fingers to get the name. The boy would have none of it. He slowly backed away, outside the cover of the mushroom's umbra... and disappeared into the blinding sunlight.

CHAPTER 70

Max awoke from a sudden shock provided by Linc's cold nose on his arm. Max looked at his watch. It was 8:12 a.m... He had slept for seven hours straight and he felt okay. He remembered the dreams. He never used to remember them - now he couldn't forget them - more vivid and colorful than ever. Max didn't mind the high-def versions. He got himself organized and into his running gear. Then it was out for a run in the park. Linc was ready for it.

It was cold and would take a few minutes for both of them to warm up. They always ran to the park and walked back to cool down. The sun was out but didn't help much in the way of warmth.

Maisy had never mentioned what Wednesdays were like at the soup kitchen. Max figured if Wednesday was anything like Tuesday, he would have no trouble at all. He would bring a mushroom treat once again for the merry men and women of the soup kitchen. After all, they seemed to enjoy yesterday's meal.

It may be a slightly different menu today, but the soup du jour, once again, should be the highlight.

Max finished two lower loops of the park with Linc. Linc's body was becoming tight and muscular like that of his master. They stopped for water at the fountain. Max was amazed how the fountains in Central Park stayed open and didn't freeze. The city had thought of everything. Even the bathrooms stayed open year round, thanks to heated pipes.

"What a town, eh, Linc? There'll be many things I'll miss about New York... you will too, buddy. I think you'll like the White House. It has a big lawn." He walked out from the shadow of the trees to get some sun. He was reminded of his dream. He looked up to the sky at the cumulus clouds churning like the steam from an old Erie-Lackawanna locomotive passing through WashPa, at 7:14 a.m. and back again at 10:54p.m... When Max was very young, he'd wondered how they avoided colliding.

There were few runners today. It was late enough in the morning so that people were already heading to work. Max thought about Gringo Smyth's former staff. He had not seen any of them, with the exception of Carlos, in quite some time. Tony Easter came to mind. Tony had gone up to the projects to strangle Little Louie the morning Eva was killed. Max knew he would have done it too. There was some of Max in Easter...or vice versa. Easter was a New York City kid who was lucky he became a cop. If he hadn't become a cop, he'd be doing some hard time up in Attica. Tony Easter reminded Max of himself in many ways. Max thought it would have been a good fight—him and Tony.

Tony's a good guy... so is Ammo... good men to have in our foxhole. I hope Timoney still thinks so.

Max hoped some of the New York City boys would wind up on Timoney's Department of Homeland Security team. He'd ask at an appropriate time.

Max spotted his mailman a block away from the apartment building. He would have to leave a forwarding address.

I'll leave him fifty bucks to make sure all the mail gets forwarded to 1600 Pennsylvania Avenue.

Max chuckled every time the address came up. He was starting to rest a whole lot easier with the security of the Washington job. He was ready to be with Dana. But in the back of his mind, he could not stop the options from lingering.

Max couldn't be sure that the restaurant wagon had stopped by with a delivery, so he decided to go to the soup kitchen early. He would tell Father Pete this would be his last day. Max had planned to work ithe kitchen an extra week, but that would be cutting things too close. There were loose ends to be dealt with. He had phone calls to make and a few visits here and there. Max wanted to check in on Mahatma one more time. He wanted to take Linc to his first home for his last visit.

Max got to the soup kitchen at two o'clock. The restaurant wagon had made a drop. If there had been something from Rayo's, no doubt it was now sitting on a plate in front of Father Pete, at least for a short while.

I'll drop off the key after serving the last supper.

Max decided on New England clam chowder as the soup du jour. There was always a method to Max's madness; he wanted to see if the M#7 would change the cream color of the chowder in any way. It did not. He added the same amount as yesterday. This would be Max's swan song - a parting gift to his fan club. He hoped, once again, to leave a bunch of happy campers in his wake. They would remember the president's chef for a long time to come.

There was plenty of food: day-old salad, turkey, ham, pork chops, a potpourri of different vegetables. Max counted 139 people dining this evening. The word had spread - anybody who was anybody should be at the Saint Paul the Apostle soup kitchen this evening.

Maisy had her soup before anyone got there. "I love your soups! You can't tell it's out of a can, not the way you doctor it up… mmmm delicious."

She had two bowls before Max could say, "Save some for the po' folk, Maisy."

Max had a bowl himself. He thought the M#7 was an excellent addition. They seemed to have enough food to go around. Father Pete showed up. "Where is my friend Linc?" he asked, in a voice usually saved for the Sunday sermon.

"You were spoiling him, Padre. Had to leave him home for his own good. He wasn't eating his dog food. I wonder why?"

"Well, my son, he did have a steak bone and a meatball or two in your absence. I hope I see him next week."

"Padre, I don't think you will. This is my last day cooking for you. I need to get some things in order and be down in D.C. for the inauguration on the twentieth."

"Ahhh… too bad. I'll miss you both. And from the looks of these happy faces, I am not the only one. I'll have my picture with Lincoln on the rectory wall next to Saint Paul himself. And you, my son… you will be in my prayers and the prayers of all my parishioners." Father Pete shook Max's hand and turned to leave. Max called him back to give him the key to the auditorium. As Father Pete started back, Max remembered he had brought the picture of himself as a boy.

"Padre, have you ever seen a young boy hanging around here that looks somewhat like this young fellow?" Max asked with a smile.

"No… not that I recall. Does he attend school here?" Father Pete asked as he handed back the picture.

"I believe he's homeless. This is a picture of me as a boy. The boy wears the same Pirates hat and a field jacket that probably belonged to his father."

"I'll keep an eye out. If I can do anything for him, I will. The Franciscans have a home for runaways over in Hell's Kitchen. I'll see that he gets some attention if our paths cross." Father Pete walked away waving his arm. When he was halfway across the auditorium, he turned around and said, "Say goodbye to my four-legged friend, Lincoln." He continued waving at Max. Max noticed the boy walking next to Father Pete, waving as well.

Max looked at both of them and yelled, "**There he is, Padre. That's him!** Maisy, there he is next to Father Pete!"

"Where? I don't see nobody." Maisy said, confused. Father Pete was looking around as well. The boy stood there staring at Max.

Max walked gingerly toward Father Pete and the boy. Father Pete looked at Max oddly.

When Max got to them, the boy jumped behind Father Pete. Max grabbed Father Pete by the shoulders and moved him to one side, startling the priest. But the boy was nowhere to be found.

"What the fuck is going on here?" Max yelled.

"Max! What is the problem?" Father Pete asked, a bit leery of the sudden change in Max's demeanor.

"Didn't you see him? Didn't you see the boy standing next to you?" Max was exasperated. "He was just here. Maisy, Maisy. Did you?"

Maisy was over dancing with Patricia by this time and didn't answer.

"Jesus Christ! The whole world is nuts," Max said, running his fingers through his hair to tug on his brain.

"Maybe you should sit down, my boy," Father Pete said cautiously.

"Padre… I'm sorry. I dream about this boy, Jack. Then I see him in real life. At least I think I see him in real life. It doesn't seem like anybody else sees him though… just me." Max said as he sat down on one of the benches. Max knew the Padre wouldn't lie to him. Max would have to take his word on the subject. "If you didn't see the boy: The boy is not real. I am going to deal with it on that level and abandon the search."

"He has a name?" Father Pete said.

"I gave it to him. I don't know what his real name is… I don't even know if he exists."

"You know, Max, I was a navy chaplain for four years. I've seen many a combat vet coming home with varying degrees of P.T.S.D... I'm sure you have been interviewed upon your discharge… or separation from the army… perhaps you should see someone at Walter Reed National Military Medical Center when you get settled in D.C... It can't hurt. It's the best hospital in the world for Post Traumatic Stress Disorder and similar conditions."

Max looked at him without saying anything. He had never heard anyone use the full-proper name of Walter Reed hospital before.

Huh, P.T.S.D... Maybe he'd understand me better after a mushroom omelet.

"Good idea, Padre." Max said, to appease him. Max didn't want to leave him thinking that some nut job was heading for the White House.

"I'm going to leave the cleanup to Maisy tonight, Padre. It's her turn anyway. I'm going to head home, if that's okay."

Max hugged the Padre as they thanked each other for the mutual assistance. Max waved to Maisy, but she didn't see him. She was too busy staring at the light streaming through the stained glass window, oblivious to Patricia dancing impishly around her.

Max stepped out into the cold night air and took some deep breaths.

Jesus… if the Padre thinks I'm nuts, I really need to get things under control. I could be living in the White House for God's sake! That kid… I don't know why I feel so bad for a kid that may not even exist. He seems so real … maybe in another dimension. Listen to me, I am nuts!

Linc met Max at the door. While they walked, Max called Ryder to make arrangements to move his things down south. He told Ryder that Woods would give him a hand. Max mentioned the fish tank with the dirt in it. Max would clip the mushrooms down prior to leaving. He decided to take the heavy bag. He couldn't bear to throw out his old sparring partner. Besides, he hadn't totally beaten the stuffings out of it yet. There were five days left until the inauguration. Max felt as though he were on the five yard line and moving toward the goal line. He usually didn't drop the ball until the one-yard line, so he had a few days… and yards to go.

Walter Reed hospital, eh?

"Linc, what do you think? Am I nuts? Don't look at me like that." Max smiled at Linc, who was more than ready for a meal.

On their way back, Max stopped off to see Harold and Mabel

Woods. He told Woods he would leave the key for the storeroom and the alley door in Woods's mailbox. Max told Woods about Ryder coming by to pick up his things in both the apartment and in the storeroom. Woods said he would help. Max tried to give him fifty dollars, but Woods said, "No thanks. I saw what you did for a brother soldier last week. Been a pleasure to have served in the same army with you, Max. We'll be watching for you and Linc on TV. If President Curlander needs an ambassador to Jamaica, you tell him you got the right man for the job! You two gonna do fine. Do you mind if we get a picture with y'all and Linc?" Woods asked, as Mabel came out from behind the door.

"You mean you want me in the picture? Nobody ever wants me in the picture."

"We'll take one with you, Mabel, and Linc. Then you take one with Linc, me, and Mabel… how 'bout that?" They got all the photos out of the way and hugged each other, for the first and the last time.

Max had a few more things to do in New York City before leaving town. He'd read in the papers that Timoney would be back from Ireland to receive the Distinguished Service Medal from the NYPD on January 19. That was in a couple of days. He couldn't wait to see Mayor Braunreuther and Police Commissioner Radcliffe sucking up to Timoney. That would be worth the price of admission… as long as the ceremony didn't take place at the Audubon Ballroom. Max also felt a need to go back to the site of Gringo Smyth's. It would be a difficult goodbye but a necessary one. Yeah, he had things to do and people and places to say goodbye to. A new life was around the corner - all he had to do was make the turn.

Max left Linc upstairs. He had to put some duct tape on his belongings to make sure they got to D.C... Ryder had suggested it for the storeroom things Max wanted to take. Max did that and then plopped down into the rocker. He put two pieces of tape on the chair. He sat and rocked back and forth slowly. He thought about where he would go tomorrow. No need to call Timoney for an invite. Most of the boys from the NYPD knew Max on sight. He would miss the company and comfort of the best cops in the world. Nobody understood what made another New Yorker tick better than a New York City cop.

How the hell can anyone go to Ireland and not drink?

Timoney's will was ironclad. He knew his way around the Alcoholics Anonymous program and had been a sponsor for many a cop. He would be good for Curlander and, therefore, good for the country. Max would make sure Timoney gained Curlander's trust and vice versa. A good team was in the making.

It'll be fun watching Timoney and Wiggins square off.

As far as the rest of the staff and cabinet, Max didn't know anything about them. He had seen a list of potential names and had met a few on New Year's Eve at the Kennedy Center. There would be a certain amount of assholes. After all, they were politicians, bureaucrats and suck ups.

Who'd want these jobs?

Max looked over at the remnants of the mushroom he had nibbled on. He walked out to the furnace and threw it in. He watched it burn. He had never seen nor smelled one actually burning.

The odor was pungent and similar to that of burning flesh. Max didn't like that. On the other hand, the colors emitted as it burned were vivid and beautiful.

Complex things these mushrooms... not plant ... not animal... bullies beware, there's a new game in town.

Max jumped in the shower.

No water-saver contraptions inside this shower head. It pounds you like nails. I'll miss this sucker.

Max stayed in the shower for a long time. The pounding water reminded him of the first time he'd seen Eva through the restaurant window at the Scirocco. Max closed his eyes, tilted his head back, and opened his mouth to conjure up more of that rainy night in Georgetown.

He knew at some point his thoughts might turn to the boy, Jack.

He had a feeling the boy would perform be performing his theatrics. Max hoped to be sleeping when if curtain did go up. Max's ideal dream would be Dana taking him by the hand into the barn at WashPa. He smiled to himself, knowing he couldn't order a dream as though Chinese takeout.

Max managed to fall asleep but his dreams did not steer him toward his preferred scenario at the barn in WashPa. Instead, he was transported to unfamiliar territory. The boy, Jack would be his host for the evening. It started with Jack running through a forest of very tall trees. Max followed him. Max noticed that if he slowed down, Jack slowed as well. The boy wanted Max to follow him. Max did not trust Jack at the onset. This would be a long night. Jack's clothes seemed to become more tattered with each visit. Max attempted to decipher the name on the pocket, to no avail. Max knew many soldiers who had never made it home from Afghanistan and Iraq. Their sons and daughters treasured anything belonging to their loved ones.

Maybe I know the owner of this jacket… the original owner.

Just a glimpse and a few letters of the name would give Max something to go on. But Jack was a cunning fellow - another loner who had figured out how to survive - albeit in between dimensions. Max didn't care where the boy took him. There seemed to be no bad intention.

Such vivid colors… high-def dreams.

Max was enjoying the show and the sleep that came with it.

Jack stopped in the middle of a small clearing. There was a rabbit caught in a snare. Jack picked up the rabbit and showed it to Max. Max nodded to him in recognition. Then Jack picked a mushroom and fed part of it to the rabbit, as Ghazi Haider had that day in the Korengal. This time the rabbit transformed itself into a majestic peregrine falcon. The boy threw the falcon skyward, and both watched the fastest bird in the world circle high above the clearing. Then the bird stooped at a tremendous speed and landed on the boy's shoulder. The sharp talons did not seem to penetrate Jack's shoulder.

It was, after all, his dream to direct. Then Jack started spinning around as the bird hovered above him, like the Holy Ghost above Jesus in a stained glass church window. Jack spun like a dervish - faster and faster. He began slowing down and eventually came to a stop. He was no longer the boy Jack, but Ghazi Haider dressed in a flowing white robe. His arms folded across his chest. He looked to be seven feet tall. Max looked at Ghazi's left hand and saw the ring he had given to him. Ghazi gestured with his hand toward a path.

Ghazi said to Max, "I see your friends are coming back to Afghanistan. Will you come too?"

"No!" Max said.

"And why not?"

"They will kill you. They are soldiers without purpose… outlaws. Afghanistan belongs to you. If I did come with them, you must kill me." Max said.

"I am afraid it would be so. I am on his list. I have seen it. It is a bad list. It is deceitful - designed by traitors to both our countries. No matter. My people will fight… forever, if need be. You would too, my friend." They walked in silence for a few moments.

"I can see into your heart, Maxwell Burns. Afghanistan is home to you as well." Ghazi pointed at Jack, who was trying to stand tall on a tree stump. "And to him… and his mother."

"Who is he, Ghazi? Who is that boy? He will not let me close to him." Max said, looking for answers from the man who possessed all the answers.

Ghazi laughed and looked over at Max. "You have not officially met?" Ghazi asked, laughing again. He waved to the boy to come over. Jack jumped from the stump and ran obediently to Ghazi. The boy had his right hand over his left pocket as usual. The boy stood in front of both men. Ghazi put his arm on the boy's left shoulder. Ghazi looked at Max and asked, "What is it you call him?"

Max stared at the boy. He looked much like Max in the old photo, with slightly darker skin and piercing dark eyes.

"I call him Jack… not sure why. I don't know his name," Max said, staring at the boy, who was now staring back into Max's eyes.

I know those eyes.

"Then Jack shall be his name!" Ghazi said.

Max put out his hand to shake hands with him. Jack slowly dropped his hand away. Max looked at the name in stenciled print on the pocket: BURNS, M. T.

Max lost his breath as he stared at his own field jacket. Max stared at Jack's face with a questioning look. Jack turned around and ran to a woman bathed in a glowing light as she stood on the knoll Jack had ran from. Her outstretched arms welcomed the boy. She lovingly held him in her arms. Then… hand in hand, they slowly walked into the Korengal forest.

"I know that walk! That's Eva's walk… **Eva**… ***Wait!***"

Max's yelling went unheeded. He stood frozen as they disappeared into the verdant forest. Max turned around to ask Ghazi Haider, if Jack was his son. But Ghazi had played his role and had exited stage left.

Max gasped for air as he sat up in bed. He struggled to keep the pieces of his dream, message, family request…whatever it may be… available in his mind to decipher. He jumped up and went to his closet to find his field jacket.

It's not here! Where the hell …?

He knew he hadn't worn it for some time but didn't think it was lost.

It must be downstairs in the storeroom. No… it's not downstairs. I would have seen it when I packed everything. Did I take it to Dana's? I better call her.

Max looked over at the clock. It was 3:16 in the morning.

Shit, I can't call her now. She'll think I am completely out of my mind. Jesus! Did I leave it at Gringo Smyth's? I wore it going out for liquor and shopping. It was on the coatrack in the back office! It must have been right next to Eva when… Oh, Jesus… Eva and my son!

Why would they be in Afghanistan? I am so fucking crazy! I gotta go to the restaurant. My jacket is here. It's here in New York... ***NOT*** *Afghanistan!*

Max put on his hoody, sweatpants and running shoes. He leashed up Linc to accompany him. It was a bitterly cold January night but Max didn't feel anything as he and Linc ran northward. They soared - long gliding strides - more leaping than running.

When they arrived at the old site, it looked like renovations had begun on the apartments but not the restaurant.or where the restaurant once was. Plywood covered the front windows, that looked like the extent of the changes. The back door was buckled but locked. Max was shaking. He did not want to go in, but knew he must. The key to the back door was still on his key ring. He tried it. The key worked on the lock. Max pulled on the knob until enough of the door was opened. He grabbed at the door and pulled it open.

It was pitch black inside. The full moon helped visibility somewhat.

What the fuck am I doing here? How could a jacket survive such an explosion...and then the fire? Impossible... I know that. Maybe there's some remnant... a piece of something.

The office was completely charred. It was so black it seemed blue in the moonlight. Max went in with Linc. They moved slowly through the room. Max tested the floor with his feet, gingerly stepping forward. He didn't want to fall through to the basement. He was looking down at the floor when he bumped into, what he thought, was someone standing there. He instinctively jumped into a defensive posture, ready to kill any inhabitant of the evil place. Max's eyes became more acclimated to the dark. He had bumped into the steel coatrack. He grabbed at it with both hands, his fingers finding a material all too familiar to him. He pulled the cloth from the coatrack. He walked outside with his field jacket, unmarred and intact. Max began breathing heavily once again. He threw the jacket on the ground and backed away. Linc grabbed hold of the jacket in his jaws and walked it toward Max.

"No! Leave it. It's cursed."

But Linc would not put it down, so Max tore it from him. He wrapped it in a ball and put it under his arm. He pushed the door shut as though blocking any possible escape from hell.

Max and Linc walked at a brisk pace back toward the apartment. Max was visibly shaken. He began to cry. He cried because there seemed to be no solution to the utter confusion he was living. He cried for the son he would never know and the boy's mother, whom he would never see again. Or would he?

Tears froze to his cheeks, much like on bitter cold Afghan nights.

I am lost. I don't know where I belong… Where are you, Eva? Where are you, Jack? Are you in Afghanistan? Will I find you both if I go there? See, I have your coat. You will be cold without it. I will take care of you. I will bring it to you, Jack. Take care of your mother until I find you both.

Max cursed as he shook the field jacket at the smiling crescent moon in the clear night sky.

An old homeless man walked by. He was looking for a place to bed down for the night, searching for the warm steam that came up through subway gratings. He looked at Max and said, "The ***soup*** makes the meal!" He faded into the night with his cardboard mattress under his arm.

Max and Linc ran the rest of the way home. When Max found that none of his keys opened his apartment door, he ran at the door to break it down.

He awoke the instant his shoulder made contact with the door.

A dream? I'm having a dream? You must let me know!

Max sat up. He was breathing hard for real. He looked for Linc and found him sleeping on the bare floor. Max went over to his closet. The left sleeve of his field jacket protruded between two shirts.

Daylight!

Mushrooms… I only licked the residue. Is there a cumulative effect? I'm not sure what's real and what isn't anymore. Jesus, Eva… Is he my son? He's got your eyes… your coloring. He must be my boy.

It was morning. Max held his head in his hands. He had a headache. At least the headache guaranteed he was awake… if guarantees existed anymore.

Max fed Linc and tried to get a health food drink down but couldn't handle it all. He needed some real fresh air. He got Linc ready and started walking uptown. He would walk past Mahatma's church for a last look at the holy man's progress. After that, he planned to go to the site of Gringo Smyth's, perhaps for the second time today. He was anxious to see what it looked like.

CHAPTER 71

Max didn't recognize the Harlem street where he had bartered a meal for the most famous dog… in the world. The Church of the Mystical Eyeball now consisted of the entire block of storefronts with a main entrance on the corner. Small fences protected the grass patches at the base of the two columns guarding the main entrance. One fence had a sign that read: **"Curb your Dog!"**

"Mahatma seems to be on to something, Linc." The main entrance was open. Max guessed there were about two hundred people seated inside. The human half of the parishioners were dressed almost as well as their pets. It was at this point Max realized it was Sunday, January 18th. Tomorrow, Monday, Timoney would be getting his medal; and the following day would be the presidential inauguration… and wheels up for Afghanistan.

Max was losing track of time, place and everything in between. He'd spoken to Dana on the way uptown. She had been on the run and unable to talk for more than a few seconds.

Good.

He wasn't sure he would have made sense. His conversations with Dana had become difficult to maintain the degree of normalcy required to keep his torment under wraps.

"**Welcome, my friends!**" Said the satin - robed Mahatma from the pulpit, high above the parishioners by the rented forklift behind the curtain. The entire congregation turned around to see who was receiving the personal greeting. When the animal lovers recognized who had graced their presence, they were ecstatic: Lincoln Burns - the president's mascot and Mahatma's prophet - participating in the service. It would truly be a Sunday to remember for the congregation. Mahatma signaled for his forklift to be lowered in order to greet Max and Linc. Mahatma escorted them up to the altar as though they had been expected.

"You're just in time for the baptism." Mahatma said, as he went behind the curtain to bring out the parents of a diapered baby chimpanzee. The couple asked if Lincoln Burns would be the godfather to the chimp.

Max said, "Certainly! In dog years he's mature enough, I think." As Linc joined in the proceedings, Max reminded himself that if he ever wanted to be the sanest person in the room, he could always come to the Church of the Mystical Eyeball.

"He won't be insulting the iguana or the cockatoo by stepping in, will he?" Max asked Mahatma, nodding to the two animals at the altar that were the original intended godparents.

"It's the cockatoo that Linc will be replacing… and he won't mind. The iguana - Madam Iggy - is the godmother." Mahatma said.

Mahatma went through the entire baptism as though he was The Archbishop of Canterbury and the chimp - Sir Malcolm Gladstone, IV - was the heir apparent to the throne of England. Pictures were taken, followed by cake and coffee for the parishioners.

Mahatma ran a pretty good show. At a lull in the action, Max whispered a question to Mahatma,

"What do you charge for a baptism?"

"All depends." Was Mahatma's answer.

"Depends on what?"

"It depends on the animal, the ceremony, and what you wish to include as far as… amenities. Here is my card; prices are on the back. Of course, you and Linc would get a discount."

Max took the card and put it in his wallet. "Thank you, Mahatma… very kind of you."

Not giving up, Max asked, "How much did this one cost?"

"This one? This one was fifteen hundred." Mahatma said smiling and shaking hands.

"Did you take a look at the wall behind you?"

Max turned around, and there was a five-by-eight-foot photo of Linc with a brass plaque underneath that said: **Lincoln Burns lived here.**

Max looked up at the picture and said to Linc, "Don't tell Father Pete about this… he'll have you excommunicated… no more meatballs!"

"It's going to be a mural… after a few more baptisms," Mahatma said proudly.

Max and Linc's departure was lengthy. Mahatma held his enthusiasm in check to ensure his nonchalance. Many photos of Linc were taken as Max and Linc eased their way back toward the doors. Max shook his hand and told Mahatma they were leaving town.

Mahatma became human for a moment and wished them well. "You've been through a lot of shit, my man. I hope you and Linc have a good life wherever you go. You two are being watched over, you know. That's a fact." Mahatma hugged Max and gave Linc a good rub behind both ears. The owners of Sir Malcolm Gladstone, IV, came over and stuck the chimp's face in front of Max to get a kiss goodbye, which Max did with some hesitancy. They put the chimp down by Linc. He growled and looked away. Right about then a white dove flew overhead onto the curtain rod. It was followed by another.

Mahatma looked at Max and said, "Doves mate for life, you know. I hope you find such love." Then Mahatma and the entire congregation waved goodbye.

"All dogs go to heaven!" Max said.

Stopping at the Church of the Mystical Eyeball always helped Max feel better about his sanity.

He had grown to like Mahatma… in a New York kind of way.

When Max and Linc got to the site of what was formerly Gringo Smyth's, Max was stunned. He realized New York City was a living organism that survived when pieces were lost - 9 / 11 had proved that. Max now understood - his field jacket dream - was pure fiction.

There was a mattress store where the restaurant had once stood. Max smiled as he walked around to the rear, where a new door and lock had been put in place. He felt sane for the moment. One more test was still in order: Max took out his key to the back door to put it in the lock. It didn't fit. He stepped back to the curb, took the key off the ring, and dropped it down a sewer drain.

It was as though no tragedy had ever occurred on this corner. The store was closed on Sundays, so Max couldn't go inside. He looked in through the window to let his mind take a snapshot for posterity. Maybe this final moment would take root and give him peace. He covered the sides of his eyes to see in.

There, in the back of the store, jumping up and down on one of the beds, was boy Jack. He was wearing Max's field jacket. He seemed oblivious to Max. He was just a boy home alone having fun. Max leaped back from the window. He did not look in again. He needed no verification either way. He started walking south. He moved rapidly with Linc in tow. He walked past a man sleeping on a flattened cardboard box. The man awoke as Max walked by and said, "**Soup** makes the meal!"

Max started sweating. It was thirty-degrees.

Screw this. I gotta get out of town. Even Afghanistan is saner than this place! At least those guys know what they're in for. Gotta be something to all this mystical stuff. I need to find out.

Max walked quickly and in silence. Linc kept looking up at his master. This gait was different: Not a run, not a walk. Linc felt his masters urgency.

"Two days from now, Linc, the boys are on their way to Kabul. What do you think? Would you like to go to Afghanistan? Why not? This is bullshit. Maybe we oughta live in the land of mushrooms.

Maybe we already do?" Max was talking loud enough that other people noticed.

Fuck 'em! They probably think I'm on a cell phone… or talking to you. I don't care.

Max started laughing and couldn't stop. Every time he tried to figure out why he was laughing, he laughed harder and held his head in his free hand.

Max ran the last 5 blocks to the apartment. He jumped into the shower and alternated hot and cold water for about thirty minutes. He dried himself off and stared in the mirror.

What is my mission?

He fell on the bed to rest for a minute. On the night table, next to his bed, lay a single key. It was the key to the back door of Gringo Smyth's.

CHAPTER 72

"You look like shit!" Timoney said before the medal ceremony began.

"You've been partying before the big day tomorrow, eh? I know how you feel. I never felt so much like taking a drink as I did in Ireland the last few days. The Guinness looked like mother's milk to me. Thank God for AA meetings everywhere." Timoney said, smiling and holding Max by the shoulders. Max knew Timoney was putting forth a life lesson. Timoney had never mentioned AA meetings before to Max. Timoney was a sly old dog. He had left a door ajar in case Max needed help one day. Max filed it away. Max did feel like shit. Now he knew he looked like it.

"I am anxious to meet this new lady of yours that president Curlander told me about," Timoney continued. "She has got big shoes to fill. I am happy for you, Max. How is that mutt of yours doing? My entire village in Ireland wants a picture of me with that dog. They drove me crazy. You'd think he won the lottery."

"He did better than that. I would have brought him today, but I didn't want him to steal your thunder. How are you getting to D.C. tomorrow?" Max asked.

"I am taking Amtrak down tonight. How about you?"

"I am on Marine One in the morning. Do you want a lift?"

"No thanks. I've got all my plans tethered," Timoney said. "You don't sound good, Max," knowing something was not right.

"That's why you're the cop and I'm the chef." Max tried a little joke that he thought might work.

"What's up?" Timoney asked in earnest.

"We'll talk after the ceremony." Max said, trying to blow him off.

"Screw the ceremony. What's going on?" Timoney insisted.

"I'm not sure... I want to do this, John," Max said, feeling Timoney was the best person to confide in. "Other things have come up."

"Other things? Listen to me: This is a once-in-a-lifetime chance for both of us. Let me tell you a little something, you spoiled bastard! I came to this great country with my kid brother and sixty Irish pounds sewn into my jacket pocket. I had choices too. Serving this city...and America was the best of the lot. Kieran was fourteen, and I was sixteen. I joined the NYPD cadet program three days after turning eighteen. They took me... **with no green card**. When I graduated - to *the job* - at twenty one, I studied my ass off to get my economics degree at Hunter College. Now, by the grace of God, I've been called upon to keep this great country safe from scumbags who want to see her destroyed. I was at Ground Zero! I saw those poor bastards jumping out of windows a hundred stories up, choosing to die instantly rather than burn to death. I still hear the thud of bodies hitting the ground, seeing them crack open like cantaloupes. You? You were lucky enough to be born here. **Yes**, you served your country well... **no doubt**. I'm damn proud of you for that. But it's never over for the likes of us. It's never over if you can make any difference at all... big or small. You and I are on the short list for making a big difference. Giving back is an ongoing process as long as you call America your home. Now, I'm going out on that stage and playing the game one last time. Do you think for a minute I wouldn't like to go up there and tell all these assholes what I really think of them? I'm doing this today to let every cop in the United States know - what happened to me can happen to them. Every lion, tin man, and scarecrow with a badge walks a little taller today because

Ed Curlander pulled back the curtain and let the world know: The Wizard of Oz has left town.

Fuck medals!"

Timoney leaned over to finish with a whisper, "You and I have serious work to do. They need street-wise people. That is what we are, and that is what it will take to stop these animals. The fight is in the streets, not in jungles. This is not a nuclear armament race. Nobody knows better than you and me that this is guerrilla warfare… festering in every country. They started the fight here… to drag us over there. Brilliant! They're a cunning lot. They have been doing this for over two thousand years. They want us to think they're ignorant.They are a cunning lot. They trapped us, didn't they? Now, they need to keep up the pressure here, to keep us fighting over there, so they can demonstrate how we can be manipulated. That's how they grow… the cowards. Now dig in! Get your shit together and get on that helo tomorrow morning and be an American!"

Right on cue, Kieran Timoney started his introduction on stage. John stopped and glanced up at his brother. He turned back around to Max and pointed his long crooked forefinger at him. "I'll see you tomorrow afternoon at the inauguration, or I will hunt you down and bring you back in handcuffs… I can do that now, ya know?" He walked onto the stage with his trademark scowl on his face. Nobody ever knew whether John Sean Timoney was happy, sad, or pissed off. It was an attribute that made him a great cop.

John Timoney gave his brother Kieran a hug AND a kiss. He gave a good speech, in keeping with his Irish heritage.

HE HAS THE GIFT.

Timoney reiterated much of what he'd said to Max. He had his eye on Max as he spoke. Max stood in the back of the auditorium as New York City mayor Michael Braunreuther and New York State governor, Carl Paharik, fawned over Timoney. Timoney insisted that no politicians be involved at the podium…only Kieran.…only cops. Max chuckled to himself as he watched the bevy of politicians try to suck up to the man who had leapfrogged over all of them. John

Timoney was now the most powerful law enforcement officer in the United States of America… maybe the world.

He made it!

Max thought. Kieran was thinking the same thing.

Timoney was concerned about Max's state of mind along with the possibility of losing him. Max was the one man Timoney needed inside the White House. Timoney knew the POTUS trusted Max beyond all others. Timoney needed to be part of that pipeline.

It was critical that there be no leaks in this administration, confidentiality would be invaluable to a POTUS surrounded by two political parties that wanted his third party to be an aberration… extinct after four years. Cabinet members and staff would have to earn their loyalty. Max, and to a large extent Timoney, were in on the ground floor. But Timoney would need Max to constantly reinforce that bond: Ed Curlander, Max Burns, John Timone in that order.

Max left city hall by the side entrance he had become familiar with. He could feel Timoney's eyes follow him out of the building.

Max wasn't sure whether he would ever see John Timoney again. The tug of Afghanistan was now pulling hard. In moments of clarity, he knew Timoney was right. It was all here for him: a wonderful woman, a job that was much more than a job, a life that any man would not hesitate to begin. But Max was tired of hearing, what should do and what he had to do. The plane that would leave tomorrow from an abandoned airport in Queens, New York, tugged at him… like a child pulling at his pant leg.

There were secrets in Afghanistan. Did Afghanistan hold the key to his sanity?

Can I live here without knowing the answer to this riddle? Is my family telling me to come and be with them forever?

He had left them alone in New York for less than an hour. Now they were both gone… or were they?

Once I get to Kabul, I can leave the Blacktower mercs to their own insanity. I could head straight to the Korengal… Ghazi Haider can help.

He knew Nicholson had his own agenda regarding what should be done in-country. Sam was paying the freight but had no influence on what direction the rogue professional killers would take. Life and death would be controlled by Nicholson. Nicholson: The fallen angel. Death would soon surround him. That was what Nicholson wanted.

All I need is a lift over there. Waddya think, Linc? We can survive anything together. What about Dana? I love Dana. But if my family is waiting for me in the Korengal, I must try to bring them home. Dana would understand. She would have to understand. It's the honorable thing to do. I failed once, but if there's a chance my family is salvageable, don't I have an obligation to find them? I saw my son, Jack, running to his mother's arms, for God's sake. I saw him, not here in New York, but in Afghanistan. What's the message they are trying to send me? What is the reality? In eighteen hours the Blacktower plane will be taking off from Floyd Bennett Field. In eighteen hours the presidential helicopter will be taking off from the Thirty-First Street heliport. They will go in diametrically opposed directions: one with lofty goals - the other on the devil's pilgrimage.

It was time for their last run in Central Park.

Max thought about roots. Everyone seemed to have them except him. His family roots went back to pre–American Revolution days. That was merely history to Max. He never missed places or people anymore…only his family.

It was three in the afternoon. He called Dana as he and Linc walked to the park. He needed to hear her voice, the voice of the woman who knew nothing about the things going on in his head. He wanted to absorb her uncomplicated love and hoped it could cleanse him.

Pull me in, Dana!

"Hi, how're you?" he started off.

"Well… haven't heard from you in a while. How're you doing?" Dana asked.

"I'm okay… been busy trying to clear up loose ends. I was at Timoney's ceremony today at city hall. It was great. He was great… The whole thing was great."

"Oh, that's good. I'm anxious to meet him. You talk so much about him. I think of him as part of your family."

"Huh, that's a stretch. I guess he is…maybe. What's up with you? You still looking for a roommate? Are you on Craigslist?" Max asked, struggling for a funny line. It bombed.

"Roommate! Is that what you think you are going to be… my roommate?" Dana asked, perturbed.

"Hey, go easy on me. It's no fun being up here with everything that's going on," Max said, in what he thought was a quick rebound.

"It's no fun here either. I hope things get easier together, because it sure as hell is no fun alone. I almost walked out twice on that friggin' Wiggins. He doesn't end a sentence with a period… he ends it with a scream. I wonder if anybody ever got the chance to actually say goodbye to the Nazi prick!" Dana said in a huff.

"Whoa… he's getting to you. Remember—he's a stage director, that's all. You're about to go on the biggest stage in the biggest production in the world. Once he pushes your beautiful butt out onto that stage, the show is in your hands. So digest everything you can. Consider his meetings as dress rehearsals. You've worked for all kinds of producers and directors your entire career. Let him teach you what he knows. Think of it as theater."

"Ya know, this is one of the reasons I love you. How the hell did you get so levelheaded?" Dana asked.

Max's laugh did not match Dana's question.

Levelheaded! If she only knew how whacked-out I am. What would she say if she had the vaguest notion that I am contemplating leaving for Afghanistan in the morning instead of being with her at the inauguration of the president of the United States?

"Yeah, that's me: Levelheaded Max."

"But you are! You always know the right path to take. It may take time, but you do make the right decision." Dana said.

God help me!

Max wanted to end the conversation or at least divert it. He'd spoken of theater to Dana. He realized he was now acting in, the theater of the absurd. He was not good enough to make his way through the part of levelheaded decision-making.

"I meant to ask you about the box and note that Ahmed Karzai left for me. Please keep it safe."

"Of course!"

"They had a dinner for my last day at the network. Usually it's a lunch, but the network needs to stay close to the new press secretary. All the big shots were there. People flew in from the station affiliates and the New York home office. It was great. I would've invited you had I known about it. Tim Wetherford kind of made it a surprise party."

"I'll bet he did." Max said, knowing why Wetherford had kept it a secret. "Did he give one last shot at getting into the press secretary's pantsuit?"

"Actually, it was when he wanted to drive me home. Never fear: Marcel was here! Marcel is a big fan of yours. Wetherford gets it… now. He knew I was pissed off about the interview. I'm a one-guy girl. And if you aren't the same way, let me know right now, big fella."

"Sure, yea…I'm the same way."

"That's exactly what I need to hear." Dana said.

"One woman, one man, one dog. That's how it must be… You said that on national TV," Max said.

"You bet I did. Oh! Remember to bring Linc's invitation with you to the inauguration… and all the inaugural balls in case of red tape."

"I got the invitations in the mail. I was hoping to drop Linc off at your place," Max said, disappointed at the prospect of having to stop every few minutes for pictures.

"Those are orders straight from the POTUS. Photo ops… all that stuff. So, I guess I will see you at the ceremony. By the way, you will enter at the west gate behind and to the right of the Capitol. You can stow your bag there. Have photo identification with you. The Secret Service will do an eye scan and archive it for the future… then you're in. The dog won't need an eye scan. Linc is more famous than Curlander right now. I will see you there. I'll initially be down in front with the cabinet appointees, Joint Chiefs, and your pal Timoney. He'll be a very busy man since nobody knows who the hell he is. Try to keep your uniform neat for the inaugural balls. As long as Ed and Amy hold up, we're with them. It's going to be a long day and night."

"It sure is. Maybe a quickie in the powder room of the Capitol?" Max said.

"Maybe my second week on the job, big guy. See you tomorrow. Love you."

"Yeah, see you…."

He was glad she hung up before he said… "tomorrow."

The call ended at the park entrance. When Max talked with Dana, it was a time-out for him. There were no ghosts or crazy thoughts. Everything stayed on track. He craved that peace.

Max had read somewhere that it took eight miles to turn an aircraft carrier around on the open sea. The president would need a team that could turn on a dime on the streets of America … and the *medinas* of Helmand Province. Curlander would need good information in order to make informed decisions. John Timoney knew this as a street cop - Max learned it in combat.

"Maybe I'm just plain scared, Linc," Max said as they started their run. He had never said that before, not even to himself.

He often thought about whether he should be afraid in dangerous situations. The fact that he had to ask himself, whether he should be afraid, brought him to a logical conclusion: He **wasn't** afraid. It made sense to him.

Forget it! I have no idea what I'm talking about. I do know one thing: I need a clear head no matter which aircraft we board tomorrow. I am not going anywhere with a muddled brain.

If he said that to himself enough times, maybe he could convince himself it was true. He needed to see what little tidbits the night had in store: logic or insanity; reality or fantasy; life or death; love or hate.

The right thing to do should be simple. It was the man who was complex.

Max and Linc ran until dark. Last supper in Manhattan: Two porterhouse steaks, some spinach, and a couple of Idaho potatoes.

"Nothing fancy tonight, Linc… a good ole steak dinner."

Max was tense. He flashed back to something his father had told him:

"Good decisions on solid information…"

You would think that would narrow it down, Dad. Why am I drawn to the absurd?

Death: the ultimate mystery. Max didn't fear death. There had been times in battle, when thoughts of his mortality -or immortality - had invigorated him. It had made his heart pump faster and raised acuity. Only another seasoned combat veteran could understand that. Invigoration or terror: F**ight or flight -** the original **storming** of the brain, as the neurologist, explained to him back at Landstuhl Regional Medical Center in Germany. They weren't choices - they were how you're wired. And what scared him now was this new variation on the theme: a fourth dimension deal with.

Should he not take a step toward that threshold? Was he afraid to find out how, when, and where Eva and Jack existed or whether they exist at all? Further, could he do what was necessary to join them? He didn't have answers. So many questions begging answers demanding room in his crowded head.

CHAPTER 73

The potatoes went into the oven first. Max examined the marbling of the steaks. "It's a shame to cook them, Linc. Let's try a little M#1 for taste." Max went into his duffel bag to find the M#1 Tupperware container. Max added a touch to his steak.

"Sorry, none for you, my friend." Max kneaded the M#1 into the meat with some virgin olive oil. When the potatoes were almost done, he put the steaks in the broiler.

"Just a slow walk through a hot kitchen. That's the way to cook a steak, Linc."

The two pals enjoyed the meal. Linc devoured his in about sixty seconds; Max, a tinge longer, although he did understand Linc's aggressiveness with regard to this particular porterhouse. The M#1 was the perfect touch to the meat and the spinach. Max was relaxed as he cleaned up, considering the circumstances.

A line from the Lewis Carroll poem, The Walrus and the Carpenter came to mind: "'*The time has come, the Walrus said, 'to talk of many things…'* "

Max had more than he thought for Ryder to take. He had to finish packing his duffel bag. He needed to put his two handguns—the Kimber, 1911 and the Walther PPK—in his rucksack amongst some clothes. He would carry the ruck with him. He popped the clips and put each into a pair of socks.

Ryder would be taking a van full of odds and ends, including the aquarium, to Dana's. If Dana had to put everything in a storage facility at some point, so be it.

I'll have to dump the mushroom spores if I leave.

The Tupperware was packed and ready to go. Max always traveled light but had accumulated more than he ever had before. His dress blues were laid out, sheathed in dry cleaner's plastic, ready for the morning. His fatigues were in his ruck.

Max decided to spit shine his dress shoes. It had been a long time since he had done that. It always a time to reflect. He wrapped his index finger tightly around the same stained cloth he had used since boot camp. He filled the top of the polish tin with water and proceeded to polish away. In short order he could see his face in the black tip of his shoe. He got lost in his reflection. He started on the second shoe. Prior efforts on the shoes made the job easy. Max stared into the black circles he made, his mind transfixed. They transported him back to the Korengal.

The scene was a beautiful summer evening: not hot, not cool—perfect. He was alone. That was good. Max was walking through a forest.

It was never this beautiful in real life.

Max knew this was a dream. That was okay. He let it be. This dream was somewhat different from the helter-skelter versions he had participated in so far. His senses were more acute. He could hear the distinct sound of grass bending underfoot as he walked. Everything moved slowly. Max walked toward a statue off in the distance. It was an odd place for a statue, but wasn't everything odd in Max's new world? It was a larger-than-life statue of Nick Nicholson. All his features were discernible. Directly behind that statue was another, not visible to Max due to the direct alignment behind the Nicholson statue. It was a beautiful woman looking straight ahead, facing the east. It was Eva dressed in a *burqa*. She wore no veil. Behind her was a statue of the boy, Jack. He was standing with his hand over his heart as he stared up at his mother.

Max had to stay in this moment. It was important to be there.

He moved around the likenesses of all three. The statues were carved from a beautiful pink-tinted marble that, even so, could not do justice to Eva's beauty.

Max was fascinated by the statue of Nicholson. He carried the latest armaments slung around his massive body. His was the only statue that was larger than life-size.

Why would these people build a statue to a man who would destroy them? Max walked slowly around and in between the statues to carefully observe all three likenesses. Max stumbled on an empty stone base behind the Nicholson statue and Eva's rendering. It had no statue on it. Grass had not covered the square base. The monument was… incomplete.

Are these for the dead or for the living?

Max looked down at the base of each statue. There was nothing written.

Max touched the cold, hard marble and snapped back to the reality of a perfect spit shine. He leaned back on the couch and took a deep breath. He wasn't upset. He wasn't angry. He was perplexed. He needed digest this latest puzzle.

One way or another, Max had to be up at five in the morning to begin a new life.

Max drew up a will: He would leave all cash left in the bank, or future money he might earn, to Len and Margaret. He went down to the basement and asked Harold and Mabel Woods to witness his last will and testimony. They both signed it. Max licked the envelope and asked the Woods if they would be so kind as to mail it. They wished him luck. Max thanked them, said goodbye, as he walked back toward the slowest elevator in Manhattan. Harold Woods was reminded of a similar occasion - the day before he left for Viet Nam.

Max had attached a note:

Dear Len and Margaret,

I love you both. Thank you for being both friend and parent. I hope there is sufficient money left to help you in some way. Thank you for your faith in me. I loved Eva more than I can say in a note.

Maxwell Tecumseh Burns

MapQuest did not show a Floyd Bennet Field, neither did Waze. He thought about calling Ryder.

Ryder was born and raised in New York City…he'll know.

He wanted to call Dana, but she would instinctively know something was wrong. Timoney already knew something was wrong. Nicholson? He hoped something was wrong. He would greet Max with open arms. The crew of Marine One would do the same. Actually, they would greet Linc with open arms.

"Hey, Linc, you're either going to the inauguration of the president of the United States, or a souk in Kabul!" Max laughed quizzically. "Al-Qaeda, ISIS, ISIL, The Caliphate, Taliban - whatever they call themselves - they'd love to get their hands on you for ransom. I won't let that happen, pal. I'd have to shoot you, then eat my forty-five."

A late walk would be their final sojourn in New York City. Max and Linc walked together through the streets of Manhattan. Max stopped to look up at the sky. The moon was barely visible. If it were not for the streetlights, it would be the darkest night Max had seen since coming to Manhattan. He was tempted to go to the park but decided against it. That would be tempting fate. It was a mugging that had caused his problems in New York City. If it happened again he would kill or be killed. That was a fact: Someone would die and if it wasn't Max, he would be back in the DA's office explaining how he had managed to kill a mugger on the night before he was to attend the inauguration of the president of the United States …the first embarrassment for president Edward Pierce Curlander.

After walking Linc, Max decided to go up on the roof of the apartment building to get a good look at the stars without the encumbrance of street lamps. He dropped Linc off at the apartment and walked up the remaining three flights to the roof. The access door to the roof was locked. Max tried the universal key Woods gave him. It worked.

He walked out on the roof toward the Ninety-Sixth Street side. It was a beautiful clear night from the tar-covered rooftop. Max could only imagine what the views were like from the penthouse apartments that dotted the Manhattan skyline. There was no wind. The constellations were distinguishable. Max needed to search for the moon. The thin crescent peeked out like a smile and finally gave up its hiding place. He thought about Ghazi Haider.

"There is no honor in that." Ghazi's words found their way into Max's head.

He could have killed every American soldier within a hundred miles, had I cooked up those mushrooms... hundreds of Americans... I must speak with him.

The moon-god of the night played second fiddle to the planets and stars this night. Max loved the mystery of it all. He closed his eyes and took long, deep breaths. He exhaled, and his eyes opened wide... he found himself ascending upward, slowly at first, into the still night air. Through no effort of his own, he soared over rooftops. There was no feeling of surprise. It was for Max, the reason he was summoned to the rooftop. The journey: Not why; nor how, he was given this gift no man before him had received from the moon-god. He was being treated for a reason. He placed his arms at his sides. Not a breath of wind teared his eyes as he flew above and in between the highest buildings of Manhattan,.

Nobody sees me ...haha.

Max had Manhattan all to himself on this, his last night. He soared around Central Park and flew along his jogging route. He glided to Ground Zero. The newest tower, now taller than the Empire State Building, awaited anointment. He landed gently on the pinnacle that pierced the night sky.

I will continue to do what I can.

He noticed Venus just off the tip of the crescent moon. She was as bright as on any Korengal night.

A mere thought sent him on his way - uptown for a last look

at the old neighborhood, soaring under, then over the George Washington Bridge in Washington Heights.

Ah ...the beautiful double-span bridge that brings people to and fro: George on top - Martha on the bottom. Goodbye to both of you.

Feeling more confident in his willful ability, he flew down Broadway for a lazy circle above the old restaurant. Max didn't stop, he merely looked down and blew a soft kiss. He hovered a while over the Church of the Mystical Eyeball. That brought a smile to his face and the *finale* for his adieu to New York City. It was time to go home.

Max suddenly snapped to attention as a police siren pierced the night. The siren was not fading away, which meant it was coming closer. It grew louder until the constant siren came from the street directly below Max. He looked down and found himself standing on the roof ledge. Max was not afraid of heights, but the fact that he didn't remember climbing up onto the ledge unnerved him. The siren was coming from a quite recently vacated N.Y.P.D. squad car. A small crowd had gathered and pointed up at him. He jumped straight back onto the roof and decided the stairs would be the fastest way to the apartment. He surmised that the two patrolmen from the squad car were in the elevator on their way up. There wasn't a cop in New York that would walk up stairs if there was a functional elevator at hand. Max ran down the stairs to the fourth floor. It took him exactly six seconds. He slid into his apartment without anybody noticing and leaned against the back of the door after locking it.

"My God, Linc! That was incredible. Next time I'll take you."

Max jumped into the shower and turned it on as hot as he could stand it. The water beat on him. He shaved in the shower. It was 0300 hours exactly. The alarm was set for 0500. Everything was packed, and his rucksack was ready to go. By the time Max was out of the shower, the siren had stopped. Max hoped the cops would not be knocking on doors. He doubted they would.

No leaper: No problem.

Max jumped in bed and slid his hands behind his head to ponder this latest variation on his mushroom endeavor.

Cumulative effect… no doubt.

He knew it was time to stop his self-indulgence. He had his results. It was time to cleanse himself. A clear head was mandatory going forward… for either direction taken. He would begin that cleansing process immediately.

What's real: What is not?

"Screw it, Linc. Tomorrow we flip Nunez's coin. How does that suit you?" Max was dead serious about the coin… dead serious.

He had relied on the coin flip before. It never failed him. Others might think it a foolhardy way to make a life-changing decision. That was not so for Max. He was a big boy.

I was just standing on a ledge seven stories above the street, and I don't know how I got there. Not to mention my little sightseeing adventure around Manhattan Island… gotta admit - it was unbelievable!

There was something liberating about going back to Afghanistan to search for his family. He was twenty-eight years of age and trained to protect and defend. He had failed on that promise once before and paid the ultimate price. Did he owe it to Eva to find out whether he was crazy or hearing her message? Could Eva and their son be beckoning him to rescue them from the Korengal? How could he know for sure? The question tugged. It was like an itch he couldn't scratch. He nodded off and napped, undisturbed with a spent mind and tired body, until the alarm went off at 0500 hours.

Linc did some morning stretches in the dark. He drank some water and walked over to the leash that hung across the doorknob. This would be his last morning here, and he looked like he knew it. Max threw on his sweats and took Linc out. They were back in a flash. Max took a look out the window. The moon was still a sliver but in a different section of the sky. He fixed some chow for Linc and drank the last of a smoothie.

"What a ride!" shaking his head and looking at the moon. He stripped the bed, rolled the sheets and blankets neatly, and packed them into a box. Linc's bowls were the last items into the ruck.

Max always took his time with his dress blues. He had enough medals and commendations to look like a banana republic dictator. Ordinarily he wouldn't wear his medals but today was different. This tie would have its very own knot. There was no need for a clip-on for either destination. The uniform still fit perfectly. The film canister in his right shirt pocket did not protrude enough to alter the neatness of the dress blues.

Flight entertainment without headphones.

Max was not permitted to wear the uniform as a civilian, but this was a Curlander mandate - the army guy in the middle of his marines, thus the medals. Max wanted to be ranger sharp. If he was on a plane with a bunch of Navy SEALs, he wanted them to know that he was *pure* army. If they didn't like it, they could always try to do something about it, during the flight or after, it made no difference to Max.

And so, with his rucksack over his shoulder and his dog walking behind him, Max Burns dropped his keys into Harold and Mabel Woods's mailbox. He proceeded to the curb in front of the apartment building to hail a cab. Max took out *abuelo* Nunez's silver dollar from the confines of his wallet. This flip of the coin could be its last. He looked at Linc and said:

"Heads = Washington: Tails = Kabul."

Max flipped the coin high in the air. Both he and Linc followed the coin as it turned over and over in the air until it fell back into Max's open right hand. He turned it over onto his left wrist and stared at the result. A wry smile came over his face.

"Sonuvabitch... It never fails! Let's go, Lincoln. We will make our apologies at some later date. I hope you're ready for this."

Max laughed out loud, as though insanity had prevailed.

"Taxi!"

It was a good day for flying eastward over the Atlantic to Paris for the first refueling of the unmarked 747 jet. First stop after Orly would be to Bagram Air Force Base before a transport hop to

Kabul. The plane was a former Air Force One aircraft that had been decommissioned after the Clinton administration. There were no markings visible anymore. It touched down easily at the antiquated and unmanned Floyd Bennett Field airstrip in the New York City borough of Queens. The last time a military plane had landed there had been during the Korean War.

The only people who knew this plane had landed at Floyd Bennett Field at 0400 hours were the air traffic controllers (ATC) at John F. Kennedy Airport and LaGuardia Airport.

When the Kennedy Airport ATC supervisors asked Department of Defense officials, "Why the abandoned Floyd Bennett Field?" Someone at the DOD told the inquisitive supervisor, "None of your fucking business." Then came the order to, "Freeze all air traffic for one hour at zero eight hundred or until we tell you it's okay to resume civilian flight traffic. Do you copy, ATC JFK and ATC LGA? If you have any problems with this order from the secretary of defense, perhaps we could dig up President Reagan and have him fire your ATC asses again!"

The immediate response from the Kennedy ATC tower was no response… followed by: "Copy that DOD. Roger that, Air Force 1-X.

<u>This is ATC northeast:</u>

"No air traffic in or out until post zero nine hundred hours or further notice.

Commencing: zero eight hundred hours - alert all domestic airports on the East Coast to this priority one DOD order for delay or diversion for all domestic and international incoming traffic to and from LGA and JFK. Ladies and gentlemen, stack it up, divert to Newark if fuel a question.

Repeat: Divert immediately where necessary. All tarmacs with wheels OTG on hold. Immediate stacking for incoming: Aer Lingus, flight 414, out of Shannon, ETA zero eight thirty-one hours, JFK; also Lufthansa, flight 98, out of Munich, ETA zero eight five four JFK. Check fuel status and send them to Newark, Logan…

anywhere supportable if light. Stay in contact: Canada to IATA-Philly: CANADA this is **US**DOD code red - copy? 10-4, copy that ATC. **Over**."

At Floyd Bennett Field men boarded in dribs and drabs. None were dropped off by family members, that rarely happened. Most families never knew the specifics of "a job." Wives, lovers and family knew - WORRY takes up head space.

What was emphasized was large, untaxed amounts of money accumulating in a designated bank account on the third day of every month for as long as a contract was viable. The merc mantra: Rain, mud, shit, or blood, keep the money going to my family.

The "employees" were greeted at the top of the gangplank by their boss, Nick Nicholson. He was sporting a tan and a handlebar mustache. His twenty-three-inch biceps looked like billboards for a tattoo parlor. He seemed happier as each additional man came onboard. Each man reassured he was doing the right thing. Nicholson's battle cry for the best in the business had not gone unheeded. The fact that his message had included a promise to avenge the deaths of the Navy SEALs from SEAL Team Six, blown out of the sky in Afghanistan on August 6, 2011, had not hurt the turnout. Most of these guys were not in this for the money. One by one, each received his hug and some personal attention before disappearing inside the fuselage. Nicholson checked his watch and looked out across the field at the lone police car parked across the rusted gate. The two cops had no idea what was going on. They were merely obeying orders from their CO at the 101st Precinct in Rockaway Beach, Queens, mandated from N.Y.P.D. Hq, at One Police Plaza in Manhattan.

"No vehicles past the gate… and mind your own business!" Were the orders of the day from the CO at the 101st. When the rookie patrolman called the precinct house earlier and asked, 'where are the keys to the gate?' The CO told him, "Cut the lock with the bolt cutters in the trunk of your patrol car. You know where your patrol car is don't you? And don't ever call me back with a stupid question like that again, unless you'd like a career keeping the garbage dumps safe on Staten Island!"

The gate was approximately a hundred yards from the plane. Nicholson could distinguish who most of the men were by the way their walk. He chuckled to himself how many he got right, as the remaining members of Gold Squadron kept coming.

There will be hell to pay in Afghanistan!

It was 0730 hours. The jet turbines of the unmarked jet began to churn. There were fifty-six passengers on board at this point. Two more showed up in the same cab and ran toward the plane with rucksacks bouncing. One had an eye on the verge of closing, and the other had some fresh homemade stitches in his forehead. When they got up the gangplank, Nicholson hugged them.

The guy with the stitches said, "We better get the fuck out of here double time, boss" as he looked back to see if anyone was following them before ducking into the plane. That made fifty-nine, counting Nicholson - one more warrior to go. He grabbed his binoculars at 0757 hours. He looked down toward a rise in the road where the Belt Parkway exit turned onto the service road. There was nothing. "Hey boss," the copilot yelled to Nicholson at 0758 hours. "We got two minutes to takeoff. They're holding everything for us!"

"I know what time it is!" Nicholson snapped. There was nothing on the horizon. He let the binoculars hang down from his neck. He turned and went inside. He ordered the gangplank up, sealing the hatch. The plane began to move, making a slow, cumbersome turn on the ground in order to face the takeoff route over Rockaway Beach and over the Atlantic Ocean to Orly.

"Hey, boss, someone's comin'!" one of the men in a back window seat yelled.

Nicholson looked out the window. A big grin came across his face as he yelled, "*Hooooooyaaaaahhhhhh!* Would you look at that pretty dress uniform."

"What the hell is he pulling behind him?" another man asked.

"**STOP the plane!"** Nicholson shouted as he ran to the cockpit to order the pilot to stop and drop the gangplank. There would be no arguing with Nicholson. This was not a commercial flight with some passenger refusing to shut off a cell phone. The pilot looked into Nicholson's eyes and without hesitation instructed the copilot to stop the plane, open the sealed door and lower the gangplank.

Nicholson stepped outside and stood majestically to welcome the last piece of the puzzle.

"We're now complete, my brother! I knew in my heart you'd be here," Nicholson said. The two hugged each other and disappeared inside. That made sixty.

The gangplank rose and squeezed airtight. It was 0803 hours when the 747 took the entire runway to gather lift - then slowly banked to the starboard side - heading east northeast over the Atlantic Ocean with no other planes in the sky.

Marine One was also delayed leaving New York City. It was manned by the usual crew. They were pissed off about having to wait on the New York City heliport tarmac. The entire crew was going to the inauguration and had not planned on waiting around New York City on one of the greatest days in marine corps history.

They decided to wait the one hour. "Fuck it! We aren't waiting a second longer for anything or anybody. We're outa here at 0900 hours! They can shoot us the fuck down!"

And that ***was*** the exact time Marine One departed. The flight took forty-one minutes. The helicopter landing on the round crosshairs of the heliport behind the Capitol Building, as per the flight plan. There would be no traffic jam for these marines. They double-timed it to their seats in section 10. This was their day, and nothing was going to ruin it for them.

The inauguration festivities were scheduled to begin at 1100 hours with the vice presidential oath of office. Most of the invited guests had arrived early to be part of history. To be invited by the president and partake in the inauguration ceremony as a guest of the First Family was more than special, it was only bestowed on those closest to the First Family. To not show up, short of being killed on the way, was the ultimate insult. Unused invitations were noted and absentees would be relayed back to the White House. It was the first job for the First Lady's secretary to reckon with on the twenty first day of January, every four years.

The weather was perfect. It was brisk and sunny with a seven-mile-an-hour wind out of the east. The temperature was forty-six degrees. Ed Curlander would wear a blue suit and a red tie with no overcoat. He had the Marine Corps emblem: eagle, globe, and anchor—pinned on his lapel.

There was a sea of marines in the section off to the left of the stage facing out toward the people who gathered on Pennsylvania Avenue and beyond. The crowd was waving American flags and cheering.

A sign on a vacant seat in section 10, row 17—read, "Reserved for Maxwell Tecumseh Burns."

As the vice presidential oath of office neared, joy turned to excitement, not only for the marines in section 10, but for everyone in attendance and for Americans throughout the world. "The best man finally got the job!" read one sign. The marines hugged and shook each other upon greeting each other. The closer you sat to the president, the more important you felt.

Friend, foe, Republican, Democrat, or newly anointed Bulldog Party member, all would point to a yellowed-out photo of this Inauguration Day in the years to come. Grandparents and grandchildren alike would point to their blurry photo with pride.

At 1130 hours, the grandstands were filled to capacity, save the one vacant seat. The ceremony began on schedule with the oath of office for Vice President Jeremy Tubbs.

Three hours into the flight across the Atlantic, Gary "Nick" Nicholson, former US Navy SEAL commander, now private contractor employed by the U.S. government, stood in the aisle at the front of the plane he commanded. He stretched his massive arms out and touched both sides of the bulkhead. He looked as though he was already crucified. He addressed his men… as he had done many times prior to a mission. One of the men whistled loudly to stop the chatter. The warriors gave Nicholson their undivided attention.

"Thank you, my brothers. I knew I could count on you. I had to turn down ninety-seven others that begged to come. I never thought I would say you ugly bastards are the pick of the litter." There was chuckling throughout the cabin.

"Seriously, we have unfinished business in-country. We lost twenty-two of our brothers along with sixteen other American soldiers, contractors, and civilians recently. You don't read about it in the papers, but the bastards that ambushed our men are heroes to al-Qaeda, the Talis… Afghanis. They hate us over there. You know it. I know it. And pretty soon we're gonna give them good reason for that."

"Hoooooyah!"

"I have a list of names… twelve motherfuckers who participated, planned, or most likely had some involvement with the ambush that took the CH-47—**a friggin' Chinook**—out. I have questions for them. I want all twelve kept alive until I get some answers. I don't know about you guys, but I relive the circumstances around that mission every night as I lie in bed… wherever that may be. I don't understand a few things: I don't get thirty-eight professional warriors, including twenty-two Navy SEALs, being loaded into one Chinook helicopter, the slowest piece of shit in the air, to run a support job for NATO troops so close to Kabul. Where was perimeter security? Who ordered them into a Chinook, as opposed to six Blackhawks that could get out of harm's way and be offensive? How did the insurgents know the Chinook would be coming in over that specific knoll from the southwest at thirty feet? It doesn't compute… not the way I was taught." There were grumblings and nods throughout the cabin. Nicholson waved the paper with the names.

"Make no mistake! We will kill everyone on this list and their families. But first, I want to have a little powwow with them." There was more grumbling from the men.

"So, gentlemen, we are off again on another little adventure. We will succeed. Some of us may die. We **will** be in the thick of it. We will initiate our operations from Helmand Province, per our former UNCLE, to make things look pretty. Then, we will proceed through any **country** necessary to accomplish our mission. We will NOT be confined by ANY borders in our quest. We will seek the enemy out no matter WHERE they hide. We have friends and troops in some areas where we will be active. They know we are coming. SAM has already established liaison. That probably means the enemy knows we're coming. We must be careful not to get pulled up for doing something stupid. If that happens, of course we will not leave. But use your heads… if you want the greenbacks to keep hitting your bank account! Our official mission is to assist special ops deployed in the area and stop the hemorrhaging that has commenced since the withdrawal of US combat troops. We will do that… when we have time. **You take orders from me and me alone.** Remember—we are no longer military."

That comment elicited a cheer from all the men that lasted a good ten seconds, backslaps and all. "If any military officer from any branch of the US forces, tries to get in your face, and orders you to do something that is against my orders… ***Shoot Him or Her!*** " There was dead silence. Then Nicholson said, "… in the leg."

Some laughed - aLL were relieved. Nicholson did not smile as he sat down. He knew he had to qualify that statement for fear of one of his men shooting some full-bird colonel in the brainpan. That was the way it was.

CHAPTER 74

Vice President Tubbs did a good job. The vice presidential oath of office was actually longer than the president's. The marine band played "Hail, Columbia" as the vice president finally got to sit down. VP Tubbs garnered the attention of the Marine Corps section until the newly appointed press secretary, Dana Trudeau, came down the aisle of section 10. She stopped at empty seat A on the aisle of row 17. She looked confused. She turned to the soldier in seat B and said, "I think you're in the wrong seat, soldier?"

"Why, yes I am. But, ma'am, aren't you supposed to be sitting with the presidential staff members?" The soldier asked politely. She smiled, sat down, and looked straight ahead. The soldier in seat B was the envy of the entire Marine Corps, especially those in section 10.

Ed Curlander stood up to take the oath of office. Everyone stood up and cheered. It went on for a good five minutes. It was exactly high noon and high time for a new president.

The flight was bumpy over the Atlantic Ocean by commercial standards. As far as the Navy SEALs were concerned, the up-and-down motion helped them sleep… along with ambien. Nicholson looked at the brother warrior seated next to him. He was staring silently out the window, mesmerized by the clouds. Nicholson grabbed his hand on the armrest and said, "You did the right thing coming. There is nothing back there for us anymore. At least we'll get some fucking answers."

The oath of office completed, President Edward Pierce Curlander took his right hand from the Lincoln Bible. "Hail to the Chief" rang forth. President Curlander shook the hand of Chief Justice Roberts, who administered the oath. He then turned and kissed his wife and held her tightly. The crowd was going crazy.

Dana Trudeau slid her fingers inside the hand of the soldier standing next to her. She turned him around to face her.

They kissed. They kissed as though all the pomp and circumstance belonged to them.

About this same time, Nicholson turned toward Neptune and said, "I will ***not*** leave you behind!"

"Likewise!" Neptune said as they shook hands to solidify their agreement. Then both Navy SEALS stared forward at the bulkhead wall.

"By the way," Nicholson said, "love the wheelie suitcase."

Neptune said, "I would have gotten you one had you showed up for the movie premier."

It was about that very same time Dana said to Max Burns, "Don't ever leave me again!"

"Likewise!" Max Burns said. They sealed their pact with a kiss.

Dana looked down at Linc and said, "Lincoln Burns, thank you for the use of your seat. I think you're the only animal to ever have a seat for a presidential inauguration." Linc looked up at the two of them and commenced to scratch behind his right ear.

Dana fumbled around in her pocketbook. "Oh, I almost forgot. Here is the box Ahmed Karzai asked to give to you. He said it was most important that I give it to you in person."

Max opened the box. It contained a hand-carved silver pendant worn almost smooth with age, attached to rawhide. Max looked closely at the pendant. It was approximately the size of the two-headed silver dollar that Sergeant Nunez had given him, the silver dollar Max always kept in the rear compartment of his wallet.

Max held Dana once again. She pulled back for a moment. An object in his right breast pocket had caused her a moment's discomfort. "What's that?"

"A little something to change the world, my dear."

"Always the chef," Dana said.

EPILOGUE: THE LETTER

Max Burns,

I have received your gift. It is truly an extraordinary symbol of friendship. It brought with it hope, a warm smile to my face and strength to my heart.

I have become a student of your country's history since last we met. Yes, my friend, we do have the internet in the Korengal.

We are forgotten by others, so we must not forget our own history... or the history of others. Without history we would never know how other nations think.

I see your ancestor, General William Tecumseh Sherman, was a great general. He had an honorable task: Free people from bondage. I too, have a similar quest: Enlightenment of the minds of my people. I find it a more difficult task to free a mind than the body. But, if I am able to free the mind, the body must follow, and, perhaps a nation... maybe even the world.

Your General Sherman was correct to destroy what could be rebuilt. I read where he was much maligned for this decision. Men have much to learn.

I have been told that you are a close friend of your new president. I wish him well in his endeavors. I pray to Allah that he is a man of good moral conviction, as was your president Abraham Lincoln. I would have liked to have met your president Lincoln. Perhaps I shall.

In my country, to accept a gift - a gift must be given in return. Forgive my ancestor's crude workmanship. It is said that this amulet was first worn by the one westerners call, the Great Alexander, the son of Philip the second of Macedon. The Great Alexander also endeavored to conquer my country. What can be of value in this land that entices men to such folly? I have worn this amulet since the death of my cousin Ahmad Shah Massoud - the "Lion of Panjshir." He was killed by Osama bin Laden, two days before 9/11/01. It is important that you and your people understand: Massoud would not have let that fateful day befall your people. He would not have permitted the faithful of Islam to be disgraced by such a dishonorable act of cowardice. And this is why Massoud was killed. He would have stopped such an egregious act from being committed in the name of Allah... All praise to Allah.

So, I give this amulet to you, knowing in my heart it remains within my family - one brother to another. Centuries have faded its face but if one looks closely... you will see a peregrine falcon that sits upon the mushroom of the Korengal. He guards it from those that would use it for ill-gotten gains.

And so, my friend, I bring you back to where we began our journey... together again as friends.

Let this amulet sit over your heart as it has mine, and the many warriors before me. May Allah... or by whatever name you invoke the one true God... keep you safe until we meet again.

And yes, we will meet again, my friend, with our loved ones, when we will ride on golden clouds, racing across the Afghan sky in the chariots of the Lion of Panjshir, borne on a scirocco wind - a swift desert wind that seems to come from nowhere.

Man bayad beravam. (I must go now.)

Ghazi Haider

The End.

CPSIA information can be obtained
at www.ICGtesting.com
Printed in the USA
LVHW091811011119
636075LV00001BA/2/P

9 781532 079535